THE EVIL ONE . . .

Somebody was up on a hill, looking down at the cabin. Waiting. Waiting for Margaret. Thinking about what he was going to do to her.

Now the evil one was pausing on the front porch. Now walking through the front door. Now standing over Margaret as she sat paralyzed in a chair. Now shouting at her as she tried to talk. Now slapping her hard across the face, coldly, snapping her head to the side.

He bent over her, his lips moving, saying, Why do you make me do these things?

His hands were on Margaret's arms. He raised them, rested them lightly on her throat. The fingers tightened. She screamed . . .

IN A PLACE DARK AND SECRET

PHILLIP FINCH

JOVE BOOKS, NEW YORK

IN A PLACE DARK AND SECRET

A Jove Book / published by arrangement with
Franklin Watts

PRINTING HISTORY
Franklin Watts edition published 1985
Jove edition / November 1987

ISBN: 0-515-09251-7

Jove Books are published by The Berkley Publishing Group,
200 Madison Avenue, New York, NY 10016.
The name ''JOVE'' and the ''J'' logo
are trademarks belonging to Jove Publications, Inc.

PRINTED IN THE UNITED STATES OF AMERICA

10 9 8 7 6 5 4 3 2 1

For Memere

—ONE—

WEDNESDAY
AUGUST 22

FROM the sharp spine of a hill, beneath an old bent ash, Sherk waited for Margaret. He watched the cabin below him, a four-room bungalow with yellow asbestos shingles and a rusty tin roof. Out the back door was a five-year-old Ford pickup truck, a vegetable patch, a shed, and a creek that ran black with coal dust from the mines upstream. The front porch nudged a gravel road that led from the mines to a paved highway. Cabin, creek, and road filled a six-acre hollow between two steep razorback ridges that rose up like prison walls and seemed to support the sky. Beyond these hills were more hills of the Appalachian range, aligned north to south, resembling a frothy green sea that lapped against the horizon.

While he waited, Sherk stripped the bark from a length of fallen branch, and he began to whittle it down. He sat with his long legs bent, slowly pushing a buck knife the length of the stick. A paper-thin strip rose up from the knife's edge, then curled and fell away. Sherk moved his eyes between the stick and the cabin and back. Once he heard the throaty rumble of a coal truck, and he stopped to watch it pass. Then the hollow was quiet once more, except for the leaves that fluttered on the hillsides. Sherk went back to the stick. He was a patient man who knew how to wait.

1

When he heard gravel crunch again, he came alert, and peered down at the road. This was not a coal truck. In a few seconds a car came into view beneath him, a blue Pontiac convertible with a loud exhaust. The top was down and the radio was playing music. Sherk could see three figures in the front seat, four more in the back, teenaged boys and girls wearing shirts over swimsuits. There was laughter as the Pontiac fishtailed to a stop in front of the cabin. Sherk's eyes sought out a girl who clambered out of the back seat and ran up on the porch: Margaret. Sherk's throat was dry. The car turned around and went back down the road, and Margaret went inside.

At first Sherk didn't move. He felt the fire rising. He called it that because it felt white hot, like a cleansing flame that roared within him until it had burned everything, and he was empty inside. Empty and pure and clean.

He had sensed it coming on when he climbed the hill to wait. The other vices that were supposed to capture men—lust, drink, sloth—had never seriously tempted him. But this was different, this rage, this delicious madness. It had begun to blossom in him about a year earlier, but he suspected that it had always been there, ready to claim him. He craved these moments when he could stop being Sherk and let what was inside take hold.

The fire. He let it smolder until it felt good and hot.

His pulse was quicker now, his breathing short. While he stared down at the cabin, the buck knife slashed heavily at the branch, and sliced out three chunks as big as his thumb. Sherk stood, dropped the stick, and carefully replaced the knife in the scabbard that he wore at his hip. There was a rawness about Sherk: knobby elbows and knuckles, hair like the nest of a careless bird, whiskers that darkened his cheeks within an hour after he had shaved. His face was narrow and gaunt, suggesting not so much hunger as desiccation. He could soften the face with a smile. But now it was drawn up, mouth tight, eyes narrow.

He began to scuttle down the hillside, finding a path among the trees and the boulders that clung to the slope, a gangly figure in blue bib overalls and red flannel shirt.

When he walked Sherk had about him the awkwardness of a heron, all legs, moving in arrhythmic starts. But he could cover ground. Now he was moving fast, stepping and skidding down the hillside, and every stride brought him closer to the cabin.

When she came home from swimming, Margaret called for her father. She got no answer. From the kitchen window she could see that his truck was parked out back, but there was no sign of him in the shed where he sometimes worked afternoons. She changed into jeans and a shirt, and went into the kitchen to start dinner. She knew that he would be home soon. He was on the night shift this month, and he would want to eat before he left for work.

First she lit a burner on the stove and started water for coffee. There was chicken in the refrigerator; she put on an apron and began to bread the pieces. Since she was ten years old she had done most of the cooking. Somewhere there was supposed to be a mother, but she had left the hills before Margaret was a year old, and was living now in Louisville. For as long as Margaret could remember, there had only been the two of them, father and daughter, alone in the cabin.

She was working at the kitchen counter, with her back to the entrance, when Sherk came through the front door. She knew the footsteps. She called, "Hi, Daddy."

Sherk stood in the doorway and said nothing.

Margaret tossed a piece of chicken into the frying pan, gave him a smile over her shoulder, and said again, "Hi, Daddy."

He stared at her without a word.

She looked at him more closely now. Something in his stance, his silence, disturbed her. Then she knew. Her shoulders sagged, and she whimpered, "Oh no, Daddy, not again."

He rocked on his feet, glared at her, then looked down at the floor and began to pace. He strode into the front room and turned on a heel and strode back, then into the front room and back again. As he walked, his fists clenched and opened, clenched and opened. Margaret had seen him this way twice in the last year: suddenly changed, angry, hard, not the father she knew. Both times it had been bad while it lasted. She had dreaded it happening again, had prayed that it would not.

She sat in an armchair in the front room, hands in her lap, head bowed. She bit her bottom lip and waited for the tempest.

He stopped in front of her. When he spoke, his voice was low and harsh.

"You was swimming," he said.

"At the pool."

There was a community pool in town, built with government money. She went there often in the summer.

"There was boys," Sherk said.

"A couple."

"I seen 'em."

"Three, four boys," she said, looking away.

"Sons a bitches."

The words jarred her; he never talked that way.

"They're just boys, Daddy."

"They's dead meat if I get my hands on 'em."

She bent her head, cringing under the violence of his words. Tears came to her eyes. Sherk turned away to pace a small circle, his hands working at his sides. After a few seconds he stopped again in front of her.

"I told you, no running off to go swimming," he said. His voice was louder. "You been a bad girl, sneaking off."

He had waved goodbye to her in the car that morning.

"Daddy, you knew. You said I could go."

"Sneaking off."

"You said."

He hit her with the open palm of his right hand, knocked her head against the back of the chair. When she looked up again he was still looming over her, his eyes narrowed down to two small flints.

There was a noise from the kitchen, the kettle whistling. He looked toward it, and at that instant she bolted from the chair. The front door was open. She had nearly reached it when one big hand clamped down on one shoulder and yanked her back. Her feet flew out from under her and she fell, her back slamming down on the floor with such force that it drove the breath from her.

She was gasping for air when he hauled her up and slung her into the chair. When she opened her eyes he was leaning down, his face close.

"Why do you make me do these things?" he said.

Margaret tasted blood-salt and tears. His hands grasped her arms so tightly that she wanted to cry out.

"You been a bad girl," he said, in a tone that was colorless, almost detached. His right hand loosened its grip. Suddenly it swung and cracked against her cheek, snapping her head sideways. Blood was flowing from her nose now in a warm, viscous stream.

"A bad bad girl." The open hand swung back. His knuckles smacked wetly against the side of her mouth, and again her head jerked to the side.

A bad girl, he kept saying, and his open hand flayed her face. Margaret closed her eyes and tried to shut out the words and the blood and the awful pain in her heart that hurt even deeper than the pain from his blows. It would end, she told herself. This would go away and he would be right again. Most times he was a good daddy. Generous and gentle, kind and loving. He was good to her, a good daddy, the best a girl could want.

Sherk knew that he must have done something wrong. But he didn't know what it was, for when the fire passed it took away the memory. It had done that before. He could remember climbing to the top of the ridge behind the cabin. Now he was here, at the kitchen table. The hollow was in evening shadow, and Margaret was sobbing, and he knew that he had done wrong.

He went to her. She was sitting crossed-legged on the floor of her room. It was a small room, about ten feet by twelve, simply furnished with a bed and a dresser and a hooked rug on the linoleum floor. She had slept here since she was an infant, and all around him Sherk could see the evidence of the childhood that she was just now outgrowing: a stuffed bear in one corner, cutout angels dangling from the strings of a pasteboard mobile, Little Bo Peep stitched into the old quilt that was now folded at the foot of the bed. She was just a kid, Sherk thought, still the child that he had always tried to love and protect, and he felt ashamed of what he had done, whatever it was.

He could see that it must have been bad. Her face was livid and swollen, and dried blood streaked across her face where she had tried to wipe it clean. Fear showed on her face when she saw him.

"Margaret, sweetness, I'm sorry," he said in the gentle voice she had always known. He held out a hand. In a moment she touched it, and she let him pull her up. Sherk wanted to put his arms around her, but he knew that she wasn't ready for that, and he didn't want her to flinch.

"Kneel down with me," he said. "Let's talk to Jesus."

They knelt together at the foot of the bed, as they had done when she was a young child.

"Dear God," he whispered. "We want to be good. It's hard to do, life makes it hard for us, tries to get in our way, but we want to do right. Give us your grace, Lord, let us be good."

"Amen," they said together. Her voice was small.

They stood. She was crying again, but softly and without urgency.

"I have to go," he said. "Shift'll be starting soon."

He waited for her to kiss him, as she always did when he left for work. But she looked away. He touched his lips briefly to her forehead and mumbled a goodbye at the front door.

Sherk was a mechanic at an all-night truck stop on the interstate highway that passed east of the hills. It was thirty miles away, forty-five minutes each direction on the mountain roads that twisted down into the flatland. But the trip didn't bother Sherk. He kept his Ford running smooth, he got a discount on gas, and he would have driven even farther for a job that kept him above ground; mine work paid too little for what it took out of a man.

Besides, Sherk had always been good with machines and tools, anything that required a clear head and a fine touch. He was good with his hands, and he knew how to make things run.

He started his shift that evening with a ring job that the afternoon mechanic had left. Sherk liked that, a long task that required some concentration. He had been at it for about an hour when the night manager interrupted him.

"Joseph," the night manager said, "I want you to knock off."

Sherk's first thought was that the night manager never called him by his given name. Then he noticed that the man's right hand trembled as he held a cigarette. Sherk hadn't noticed that before.

"You got to go home," the night manager said. "Now. The po-lice just called from Harben."

That was the closest town to Sherk's cabin in the hollow. Sherk put down the socket wrench that he had been holding.

"About what?" Sherk said.

"Your place."

"What about my place?"

"I don't know, Joseph, he didn't say."

Sherk knew that was a lie, but he didn't want to hear bad news this way. He turned aside without a word and went to his truck and gunned it up into the hills.

The cabin was three miles back off the pavement. Sherk had just turned onto gravel when a pair of headlights and a pulsing red light poked out of the darkness in front of him. Sherk thought they belonged to a police car, and he held close to the right shoulder, to make room. The car approached slowly, no siren. When it was closer Sherk saw that it was an ambulance. He could make out nothing in the back when it passed. He watched it in his mirror until it turned left on the pavement, headed for Harben. Then he spun his wheels as he hurried to the hollow.

A county cop and his patrol car were parked there, waiting for him. The night was dark, but in his high beams Sherk could see a charred jumble where the cabin was supposed to be. Sherk's heart thumped. He jumped out of the truck and ran toward the cabin. There were scraps of asbestos shingles and roofing tin in the grass. Sherk smelled the dankness of wet ashes. He yelled, "Margaret! Margaret!"

The cop was walking toward him. Sherk was sure that she must be in the car—he wondered why she hadn't rushed out to greet him—and he brushed past the cop to see her.

The car was empty. Sherk heard himself calling his daughter's name again. It came out as a wail. The cop was reaching to him.

"Propane . . . the stove," Sherk heard the cop saying. "Must have been a valve open. It blew. Bad fire. She never got out, mister, I'm sorry."

—TWO—

THURSDAY
AUGUST 23

WHEN the movers loaded the truck, they carted all the life
out of the house on Berry Road. It was a house outside a
town called Johnson, in Vermont. The rooms were empty
now and the walls were bare. With the draperies gone,
summer sunlight lay heavily in big white patches on the
living room floor.

Sarah Stannard stood in one of the bright splashes, her
eyes moving around the room. She had never before seen
it this way, stripped and desolate, with the look of an
abandoned automobile. Gray tufts of dust lay in neglected
corners, and the carpet showed impressions from the legs
of long-standing furniture.

Sarah was aware of her mother standing at the front
door, one hand fidgeting on the knob.

"Sarah, love, we have to be on the road," Elise
Stannard said. "We have a long way to go, and you know
I'm nervous about driving at night."

"A little while longer, okay?"

"Dragging this out can only make it worse," her
mother said.

"Please leave me alone. Just a minute or two. Is that so
much to ask?"

"I only want what's best for you," Elise said.

"I wonder when you'll let me decide what's best for myself."

Elise stiffened, and answered in a tone that was almost petulant: "Pardon me for being concerned. I don't want to see you hurt, that's all."

"It couldn't get much worse," Sarah said. Her voice softened, and she gave a small, helpless shrug. "This little bit more won't make a difference. Just a couple of minutes, I'll be ready to go. Please."

Elise left, and the door closed hard behind her.

Same old argument, Sarah thought. For as long as she could remember, they had been fighting this tug of war, a rivalry of pride and will. The crazy part was that they really loved each other. Strangers wouldn't have fought so passionately. Love, perversely, seemed to put a cutting edge on their harsh words. It was worse now that they were alone; without her father to hold tempers in check, their arguments were more frequent, more hurtful.

He had been dead for nine months, dead at forty-three of a heart attack, and he had left a great empty spot in their lives. They were just now beginning to fill it, and they still had a long way to go.

As she stood alone in the warm light, Sarah tried to empty her mind, to concentrate on the gaping room around her. She told herself that this was the last time she would see these walls, and she wanted to let the feelings come as they might.

She was fifteen years old. This was the only home she had ever known, and she was leaving it for the last time.

From the driver's seat, Elise Stannard watched her daughter in the house. Sarah was standing at a window, backlit in sunshine that blanched her long yellow hair. She was tall and thin, gawky, her body stalled awkwardly in adolescence. Only the eyes belied her age. Dark and expressive, they could have belonged to a woman of fifty who had lived fully and without regret; the effect was unsettling in one so young.

Otherwise, there were only undertones of the woman she would be. Her fingers were slender, cheekbones high-set, chin straight and definite. All suggested a delicate loveliness that would not mature for a few years. When it emerged, it would be an old-fashioned kind of beauty, out of vogue in an age that idealizes the athlete's sinewy robustness for man and woman alike. Sarah would never be robust.

Standing framed now in the window, she seemed aloof and remote as she stared out over the front lawn. Her eyes avoided the car, and Elise was reminded of a zoo animal, remote and melancholy behind plate glass. The girl sometimes seemed so distant, baffling, beyond reach. They were closest when they quarreled; at least it was a kind of contact, the surest way Elise knew of touching her.

Up at the window, Sarah finally glanced toward the parked car. In her mind Elise extended open arms, reaching out, beckoning. But she remained motionless behind the wheel. Sarah's eyes lifted, and she turned away from the window, out of sight.

Hey hey, buck up, her father would say. Sarah could hear him now, could feel his strong hands gripping her shoulders as he looked at her liquid eyes, her quivering upper lip. It could have been a skinned knee, a slight from a classmate, anything that would bring a little girl to the brink of bawling. *Chin up, that's a champ, hold it in. Don't let 'em see you cry.*

It was the kind of thing that a father would say to a son, maybe. Not to a girl. But Jack Stannard had no son, only Sarah, and she would do anything for him. She could be a tough little kid if he wanted.

Sarah wandered through the empty home, her footsteps sonorous, memories and associations crowding in on her. So far she had kept it together all right. There was one room left, a little nook beyond the laundry. That one she had saved for last. It would be the hardest of all to take, but there was no avoiding it if she was really going to say goodbye to a childhood that was gone and out of reach.

Get it together, champ, don't lose it now.

Her breathing came hard, and she stepped into the room and looked around.

It had been her father's study, nothing much, just a place to be alone with his books. He had taught history at the state college in Johnson, and there had always been books stacked on the floor and in corners, cases jammed, shelves bowed under the weight. Now the books were in crates, on a moving van headed south. The shelves were empty, and the room looked disemboweled.

A place to be alone with his books. With his books and with his little girl.

Jack Stannard could spend hours here, his feet resting on the desktop, tilting back in a cocked chair so that the book in his lap would catch full daylight from the window behind him. Sarah would match him, hour for hour, happy to be near him. She had a spot. The desk was an old oak rolltop, and she would curl up in the footwell. Plenty of room for a kid in there. Even when she started to grow up she could fold herself into the space. She would be there for hours, basking in his presence, sublimely pleased to be his daughter.

She would read, and sometimes she would draw, bracing the sketchpad against her knees. She had been taking lessons since she was ten, and her father thought she had promise. While he read she would work on a drawing, then tear out the page and pass it up for his inspection. He would study it, and usually pass it back to her. But when he found a good one, a really good one, he would rise without a word and go to the one empty wall, the only one that wasn't covered with shelves. There he would thumbtack the paper to the wall. And she would be proud. She would know that she had done well.

Now Sarah walked across the empty room. She put out a hand, and her fingertips touched the tiny holes in the wall that his tacks had left, a random speckling. It brought her close to tears, and she gulped air to level out her ragged breathing.

Keep it together, champ.

He had taught her to be strong, had given her the face that she should show the rest of the world. But here, alone with him, she hadn't needed the face. Here she could be just Sarah, scared and vulnerable. He understood what lay within her, knew things that not even Elise fully grasped.

It wasn't fair, she thought. The father she mourned was

the one person in all the world with whom she could have shared this terrible burden of grief. But he was gone, and she knew what he would expect of her.

Tighten up, be tough, that's a champ.

With doors and windows shut, the house had become stuffy, trapping the morning warmth. She felt uncomfortable, and she knew that she had finished what she wanted to do. She left the room and walked quickly to the front door. There she paused to look around one last time. It was just a house, she told herself, brick and wood, nothing more, a place where another family would make memories now without ever knowing the old ones that had accumulated there.

Get it together, champ.

She squared her shoulders and held her head up, and went outside. Down the front walk, around the car, into the front seat beside her mother.

"I'm sorry," Elise said. "I'd have done anything to keep us here."

"Let's just go."

"Please don't blame me. I tried, you know I did."

Sarah didn't want to fight for a while. She didn't have it in her. So she leaned across the seat and kissed her mother on the cheek, and that made Elise smile.

"It doesn't matter," Sarah said. "I was afraid to leave, because I thought I might start to forget him. But I won't let that happen." She pressed her back against the seat. "I'm ready to go, really I am. We don't live here anymore."

Elise started the engine. She turned the car into the road, and they pulled away. After about a quarter of a mile the asphalt curved and dipped, and then the house was out of sight.

They were going to start a new life. Jack Stannard's parents had money, and they had made a place for their son's wife and daughter. Sarah and Elise were going to live in Annapolis.

The country road unwound before them.

He was the best father, Sarah thought. The best ever. She still needed him, and she didn't know what she was going to do without him.

—THREE—

SATURDAY
AUGUST 25

JOHN Burwell paused when he reached the top of the stairs. Before him was the door to the spare bedroom of his home, a two-story house in Harben where he lived with his wife. Sherk was on the other side of the door, and Burwell had stopped to gather himself up before he went in. There was something wrong with Sherk. Burwell couldn't say what it was, but he felt it all the same, and he dreaded seeing Sherk again, talking to him.

Burwell was a storekeeper in Harben, a stoop-shouldered man with wispy hair that he combed straight across the thin spots. In his left hand now he carried a blue worsted suit Sherk was supposed to wear today to his daughter's funeral.

To his right at the top of the stairs was a window, and Burwell saw a yellow haze above the low rooftops of the town, nearly obliterating the ridgelines a couple of miles distant. The hills were usually cooler than the flatlands, the air more clear, but even up here you could count on a half-dozen cruel days every summer when the air turned stagnant and an overcast clamped down over the hollows, and the town would stew in its own sweat.

A clammy rivulet ran down Burwell's spine as he stood on the landing. He turned from the window. The door was open a crack. He reached forward with his right hand and rapped on it lightly with his knuckles.

"Joseph? Can I come in? Joseph?"

There was no answer. After a few seconds Burwell stepped forward and slowly pushed open the door. He looked inside.

Sherk was in a chair, hands folded in his lap, staring out across the room. He was expressionless, so still he reminded Burwell of a wax figure. Burwell could believe he had been sitting that way for hours, and might have sat for hours more if he had not been disturbed.

After a few seconds Sherk turned an empty face to him.

Burwell held out the suit and spoke quickly. "The missus, she found this in a closet last night," he said. "Anywhere it's too loose, she can take it in with pins. It'll do."

Sherk's face didn't move. He didn't seem to have heard or understood.

"You're going to be needing this today," Burwell said gently.

Sherk did not respond.

It had seemed the Christian thing to do, the neighborly thing, to take in Sherk the night Margaret died. He and the Burwells had belonged to the same church for more than ten years, and almost every Sunday during that time they had attended services in the meeting house outside town, a grim little place with unadorned plaster walls and bare wooden floors and a cast-iron stove in one corner.

So the night that Margaret died, Sherk called the pastor, and the pastor had called the Burwells, who had an empty room. Just for a few days, the pastor had said, and they brought him into their home around midnight.

The first few hours had been bad, Sherk moaning and shouting desperate prayers upstairs. There had been no sleep for any of them. Yet as awful as that grief had been, Burwell thought, it was no more than you would expect from a man who had lost his only child so suddenly.

Since that first night, though, Sherk had been subdued and distant. Burwell thought that such calm was unnatural.

He realized that he had never known Sherk, not really. He had certainly never seen anyone mourn this way.

He held out the suit and waited for Sherk to move. Sherk looked blankly at him without seeing him: disconnected. Do something, Burwell thought. Your daughter is dead. Kick, curse, cry. *Anything*.

"Joseph," he said gently. "Pastor's going to be here in about an hour. You should be getting ready."

A quiet smile came over Sherk.

"I'm going to be all right," he said, speaking slowly, as if the thought had traveled a great distance from an obscure part of his mind.

"That's right," Burwell said. "You've got people who care about you, people who'll see you through this."

Sherk looked serene. That was wrong, Burwell thought. This wasn't bereavement; this was emptiness.

Sherk nodded several times, with increasing conviction.

"Going to be all right," he said firmly.

Burwell wanted to be away from him. Quickly he hung the suit on a hook, and he stepped out into the hall.

"We'll need to leave by noon," he said. "Pastor Drew'll be coming over a few minutes early."

He shut the door on Sherk's placid face and hurried downstairs, glad to be away.

"Dad-dy," said a girl's voice, singsong. "Dad-dy, I'm here."

Sherk's head snapped up and he looked around the room. He was alone. The voice lilted in his head again.

"Dad-dy. Down here."

Sherk looked through the open window beside his chair. Margaret was in the Burwells' back yard, her face lifted up to him. Sherk saw that she wore a pink taffeta dress, the fanciest she owned, her favorite. She waved a welcome.

"Margaret, sweetness, it's you," Sherk shouted, feeling his heart trying to leap from his chest. He leaned from the window. "It's you, it's really you."

"I wanted to see you," she said. Her face seemed full

of light. She was so beautiful that Sherk almost could not bear to look at her. "I wanted to tell you I love you, my daddy, my perfect daddy."

"And I love you," he yelled. He put out a hand, but she was far below him, too far to reach. "Come to Daddy, let me give you a big kiss."

She shook her head.

"I can't."

"Then I'll be down. Just wait, I'll be right there."

She shook her head again.

"No, Daddy, you can't, not right now." Sherk started from the window, but his legs were rooted to the floor. For all his will and desperation, he could not move his feet. Again he turned back to the window and leaned out. Margaret was looking up at him with wistful understanding.

"I have to go," she said.

"No!" he howled.

"Do you love me? Do you love your little girl?"

"I love you," Sherk said. "My baby."

She began to move away, walking slowly to the back gate behind the Burwells' house. Sherk shouted for her to stay, but she ignored him, and she went through the gate. There she looked over her shoulder at him. She whispered, but even at the distance Sherk could hear her clearly.

"Come find me," she said. "I'm awful lonely. Come get your little girl."

Then she turned away and ran lightly down the alley, the pink dress dancing brightly, and Sherk's eyes didn't leave her until she was gone.

Burwell's wife was waiting for him when he got out of the shower. Her hair was in curlers, and she was wearing a peach-colored satin slip, and she looked troubled as she glanced up at the ceiling.

"He's talking to somebody," she said.

Burwell listened as he rubbed himself with a towel. He heard nothing.

"He just stopped," she said. "But he was talking to somebody up there. Yelling. I think he was yelling out the back window."

After a pause she added, "I don't think there was anybody out there."

"He wasn't talking much, last time I saw him," Burwell said.

"Poor man, I'm worried about him," she said. "He's been through so much. You'd better go up, see if he needs anything."

"In a minute," Burwell said. He finished drying himself, and was immediately damp with sweat again. He put on a pair of boxer shorts and slipped into some khaki trousers. A fresh starched shirt wilted on him before he had finished buttoning the cuffs.

In his bare feet he padded up the stairs. Again he hesitated at the threshold, catching his breath from the climb upstairs. He tried to swallow the heaviness in his throat. Nerves, he thought.

He addressed the closed door: "Joseph? Everything all right in there?"

"Just fine, John." Sherk's voice was muffled, but Burwell thought that it did not sound as leaden as before. He wondered what could have happened in the last half-hour.

"How's that suit? Passable?"

He waited for an answer. Sweat dripped down his forehead into his eyes. There was no sound from behind the door, so he tried again.

"There's still time to take it in. Edna won't need but a couple minutes to put a few pins in it."

Sherk's voice from the other side was low and ominous.

"I don't need the suit," he said.

Burwell knew that Sherk had no clothes but what he wore. Everything else had been burned. He imagined Sherk wearing coveralls and a red flannel shirt into church.

"Sure you do," Burwell said. It was like reasoning with a child. "Wouldn't be fitting otherwise. Got to have a dark suit for a funeral."

"No funeral," Sherk said loudly.

Patience, Burwell thought.

"What do you mean, Joseph? What are you trying to tell me?"

"I'm not going to no funeral today."

Burwell felt suddenly weary. He stepped up to the door and put the open palm of his right hand against it, rested his left hand on the knob, and spoke a silent prayer, *Oh Lord help me out, please, I'm not ready to go round and round with this poor fella,* before he turned the knob and pushed open the door.

Sherk stood in the middle of the room, facing him, hands at his sides. His face was alive again—that was an improvement anyway, Burwell thought—and he seemed poised on his feet, waiting.

"You're going to do what's proper," Burwell said. "A father doesn't skip out of his daughter's funeral. No way. You're getting dressed and going."

Sherk shook his head emphatically. "My little girl is alive."

Burwell took a couple of steps toward him, closing the distance until he could lay a hand on Sherk's shoulder. A firm but compassionate hand, he thought.

"Now, Joseph, that just ain't so. Your daughter is dead," he said. "Remember? You lost her three nights ago, God rest her."

"No." Sherk's eyes flamed.

"She's laying in a casket this minute. Waiting for us to give her a Christian burial."

"No!" Sherk shrugged off Burwell's hand. He grunted like an animal from deep in his chest, and one arm flew upward, striking Burwell's face, knocking him off balance.

"Hey," Burwell said.

Sherk stepped forward and grabbed the front of Burwell's shirt, and threw him against the wall. Burwell hit hard, jarring loose a picture frame—he was dimly aware of it falling, the glass smashing—and he slid down to the floor.

Sherk strode toward him, his features contorted. Burwell had never seen anything so frightening. Frantically he tried to move, but his legs were spongy and wouldn't respond. Sherk knelt over him, across his chest.

"She's alive," Sherk said fiercely.

Burwell wanted to say, Sure, sure, she's alive, my mistake. But his mouth wouldn't work, and it came out a babble.

"She's alive," Sherk said again, glaring. His eyes never left Burwell's as he reached back with one hand, fingers fumbling at his hip.

He came up with the buck knife. In a second he had it open.

"Don't hurt me," Burwell said. His lips were thick. The knife was at his face, inches away, and Burwell threw his head back to avoid it.

The movement exposed his throat. Sherk put the flat of the blade against the pale pink skin, lightly at first.

"Oh no Joseph," Burwell said. "Oh my God no."

Sherk began to push the flat blade against the flesh of the throat, the pressure coming at the flat tip, gradually increasing.

"Please no," Burwell said in a hoarse whisper. "Please please no, don't kill me."

Sherk's fingers were white, gripping the knife. His wrist bent slightly, still holding the blade flat, depressing the soft flesh beneath it. He was unhurried, deliberate. The fury in his face had given way to an expression of detached evil that horrified Burwell. It was a malevolence beyond appeal. Burwell felt the pain build at his throat, dull at first, then hotter and sharper. A tiny red corona of blood appeared at the edge of the blade.

Sherk stared evenly at the tip of the blade as it sank into the skin. His hooded eyes showed a reptilian thoughtfulness. Burwell knew that this was what a killer must look like, and he told himself that Sherk was the last of this world that he would ever see.

A scream shrilled in Burwell's ears. He was frozen where he lay, but Sherk's head jerked around. It was Burwell's wife, standing in the open doorway. She put her hands to her face and screamed again.

Sherk looked away from her, down at the knife, back at Burwell's wife. Without haste he rose and straightened. Burwell felt the lifting of an enormous weight. The blade made a snicking sound as Sherk folded it into the handle. He put it away and looked down at Burwell.

"I'll find her," Sherk said. "She's waiting, and I'll git 'er."

Sherk turned for the door; Burwell's wife moved aside and let him pass. His feet banged on the stairs, and in the hall downstairs, and then he was gone.

Sherk drove to the bank in Harben, keeping to the back streets so that he wouldn't be spotted. Better that way, he thought. No more trouble today; he had a job to do, and he wanted to get on with it. He parked a couple of blocks from the bank and walked the rest of the way, his steps quick and purposeful.

Inside, a couple of pedestal-mounted electric fans pushed around stale air. Sherk went to the end of a four-deep line at the teller's cage, and he let his mind retreat to a soothing memory that he had recalled two nights earlier, at a time when he was sure that sorrow would crush him. The remembrance had given him strength at that moment, and it had buoyed him constantly since then, a warm and comforting image that, though ten years old, was more real to him than the summer heat and the hum of the fans. He brought it back instantly now.

Margaret was lost. It was a cool May morning, and she had wandered away from the cabin while Sherk turned earth in the garden patch. She was four, almost five, old enough to cover plenty of ground before Sherk realized that she was missing. He shouted himself hoarse trying to call her back, feeling panic seize him as he scrambled wildly up and down the hills around the cabin, once scuffing an elbow as he slipped in a patch of scree.

After about an hour, Sherk realized that Margaret had somehow found a way past the curtain of high hills that surrounded the hollow. She could be anywhere. A few phone calls brought a sheriff's deputy and some searchers, who fanned out over the slopes as the sun reached its height and began to fall. Sherk and a man named James Vansil started down the far side of one hill. They pushed through the forest, Sherk thinking, She's gone, my baby's gone, wondering if he could survive the loss.

Nearly four miles from the cabin, they reached a little creek called Weam's Run that ran beneath a dense over-hang of trees and shrubs. In the mud beside the creek they found a set of tiny footprints, headed upstream. Sherk and Vansil ran along the creek, shouting the girl's name. Sherk was splashing through calf-high water when he saw Margaret, her perfect golden hair shining even in the forest's deepening shadows. She was perched on a rock, looking pleased with herself, watching her father approach. Sherk grabbed her and held her so hard that she squeaked a protest. He wanted to yelp and cry and leap; he had never known such joy. He was saved.

Sherk could feel Margaret pressed to his chest as the water swirled around his legs. Vansil watched them briefly and then looked away, an intruder in this private moment. Then someone tapped Sherk's back as he stood in the creek with his baby daughter.

He looked around. A fat woman in a baggy blue cotton shift had appeared behind him in the creek. She was looking crossly at him, the pudgy fingers of her right hand poised to rap him in the back again.

"Mister, you're next," said Vansil in a voice that was curiously high-pitched. When Sherk turned back to look at him, Vansil had become a bank teller. The forest and the creek and Margaret were gone. Sherk was standing in the bank, at the head of the line now. The memory drained away, leaving mild euphoria. As he walked to the window his face bore a smile that seemed to come from deep within.

"I want to cash out my savings," he said. "Same with checking. Comes to something like nine hundred dollars."

A few minutes later he was working the truck through the narrow side streets. At the edge of town he turned up the main road, heading east and out of the hills.

About a mile along the highway was the meeting house where he had worshipped for so many Sundays. Now Sherk slowed the truck as he approached, and he stopped

across the road from it. He paused with the engine idling.
Parked in front of the church were a hearse and mourners'
cars, empty and unattended. Inside, sorrowful voices bat-
tled a hymn in a minor key.

Somehow Sherk knew that the funeral was for a teenage
girl. He couldn't have said how he knew this, but he was
certain of it all the same. The thought made him sad. A
father was going to bury his daughter today, and would
never be the same. He wondered who the pitiable man
was.

Welling tears distorted Sherk's vision. He cleared his
eyes roughly with the back of a sleeve. This was a tragedy, but it had nothing to do with him. He blinked his eyes
and turned away, and gunned the truck down the road. The
sound of the dirge faded. There was work to do. He had a
daughter to find.

He drove quickly down from the hills, and didn't stop
again until he had reached the shoulder of the cloverleaf
on-ramp of the Interstate. The two-lane entrance ramp
parted in front of him, demanding a choice. The right lane
turned to join southbound traffic, while the left crossed an
overpass before bending to merge with the northbound.

Sherk reached around to a back pocket, and he took out
his billfold. From a plastic liner in the wallet he extracted
a photograph. He had put it there less than a month earlier:
a photo of Margaret standing outside the cabin as she
waited for the school bus on the last day of school that
June. The photo showed a slim, almost frail girl with
delicate skin that shone in the morning light. Her golden
hair was bound in a single braid that fell over one shoulder. She was squinting slightly, and she was smiling.
Smiling at the camera. Smiling at her daddy.

Something was happening in his head, a hazy confusion, a mingling of real and imagined. Part of the jumble
was a pain that would sear his soul if he looked at it
directly, so he turned aside from it. He knew that Margaret
was gone. Lost. Like the day ten years past when she had
wandered away. Exactly. Margaret was . . . *out there*,
somewhere, waiting for him. He had seen her.

The question was where to begin. He might have gone

to Weam's Run, but the creek did not exist any longer. It
had been diverted several years earlier by a new mine
upstream. Anyway, he sensed that Margaret had gone
farther, beyond immediate reach. It was going to take
some work this time, and patience.

He turned to a road atlas that he kept in the cab. Its front
two pages showed the entire country, with cities and free-
ways and principal highways. With a thick fingertip he
touched the spot on the map where he now sat, beside the
heavy green line of the Interstate. He traced the line
southward, to Knoxville, Chattanooga, Birmingham, beyond. Then to the north: up through Virginia, past Washington and Baltimore, crossing the borders of Virginia,
West Virginia, Maryland, and Pennsylvania in a single
half-inch of map space.

His eyes moved from the map to the ramp ahead, then
back to the map. It showed a welter of roads, a drunkard's
lacework: more ramps to be taken or passed by, hundreds
more decisions like this one, all to be made on nothing
more than a whim.

Sherk tossed the atlas aside. This journey was not a test
of direction, but of faith. As long as he believed, there
were no wrong turns for him.

He tucked the photograph into a corner of his visor so
that Margaret would be smiling down on him whenever he
looked up. Then he put the truck in gear and checked his
mirrors, and pulled out into the road.

He felt full of confidence, of brilliant rightness, as he
approached the ramp. Where the lanes diverged he glanced
to the right; southbound trafic was heavy, and three cars
were stopped, waiting to merge. Sherk didn't want to wait.
He moved to the left lane, and sped over the bridge that
spanned the Interstate. His tires screeched around the sweeping curve that launched him out onto the great highway,
part of the endless fluid mass of people and machines
moving north.

When Burwell wiped away the blood, he saw that Sherk's
blade had left a small, crescent-shaped mark where the
pressing tip of the blade broke flesh. To look at, it was

little more than a shaving cut; the police weren't likely to be impressed. A couple of Band-Aids covered the wound. Burwell told only the pastor about what had happened.

Anyway, he was sure that he had nothing more to fear. He would never see Sherk again. None of them would.

So while others at the funeral mourned the departed Margaret Sherk, Burwell prayed for her father, who had departed on a journey of his own, Burwell thought, with a destination that was much less certain.

—FOUR—

SUNDAY
AUGUST 26

"She oughta be up and around by now," said Harry Stannard. "It's, what . . . quarter after ten, f'cryin' out loud. She's had plenty time to get up, get dressed, have breakfast. Fix her hair. Whatever teenage girls do in the morning."

"Harry," said his wife, "she said maybe. I remember. You told her that today would be a good day to do something together, and she said maybe you could take her for a drive. She said maybe. And she didn't say when. I distinctly recall the conversation."

"Very helpful of you."

"They're living with us. You'll see her every day. Lord. You'll drive all of us nuts, the way you go on."

Harry held up his hands, stubby fingers spread wide, miming surrender. He was a small, stocky man, with a head that was sunburned from brow to the back of his skull. Knotty calves showed between his yellow socks and his Madras shorts. He wore Hush Puppy loafers and a pink golf shirt that stretched over a belly as round and solid as a medicine ball.

"What am I doing that's so bad?" he said. "Waiting for my granddaughter is all. Sure, I'm anxious to see her. It's a crime now, a man wants to see his granddaughter?

Then go ahead, convict me, throw away the key—I'm guilty.''

His vehemence might have startled someone else. But Joy Stannard had lived with her husband for forty-five years, and she knew that he did nothing mildly. Without a word, without a change of expression, she sipped from her teacup and returned to the glossy pages of a mail-order catalog; at one elbow she had a stack of them thicker than the metropolitan Yellow Pages.

Harry and Joy were seated at opposite ends of a butcher-block table in their breakfast room, a bright place with walls the color of egg yolk, situated at one corner of their home near Annapolis. It was a late-Georgian colonial, designed and built by Harry on a twenty-acre tract that fronted for three hundred feet along the Severn River, extending back into a woodlot.

Harry had carefully selected the land, and had supervised construction with a knowing eye. His business was property and development—Harry's thumbprint was prominent on the great smudge of suburban housing that lies beyond Washington's Capitol Beltway, on what used to be pasture land and tobacco lots. He had built Tudor townhouses in Upper Marlboro, split-level ramblers in Bowie, Dutch colonials in Waldorf.

None, however, even remotely approached the magnificence of his own home. It was precisely faithful to the classic Georgian style, with a hipped roof, elaborate interior moldings, a leaded glass fanlight over the front door, and salmon-tinted brickwork laid in what is called the ''Flemish bond'' pattern. Less traditional were the swimming pool, finished in terrazzo and Italian tile, and the lighted tennis court, which reposed side-by-side about fifty yards behind the house.

''I figured I'd see her after breakfast,'' Harry said. His wife didn't look up. ''I mean, how long can it take to eat breakfast, anyway? The kid's had time to put away a seven-course meal.''

Joy tossed aside a Horchow and took a Trifles from the top of the pile.

''I'm her grandfather, f'goodness sake. You'd think

that'd mean something. You'd think she'd be anxious, you know, to get out with the old man. But I guess not.''

"You'll see her," his wife said without a glance.

"You'll see her," Harry mimicked.

He took a doughnut from a plate in the center of the table, broke it in half, dipped one fragment in his cup of coffee and jammed it into his mouth, leaving a trail of powdered sugar across the table and up the front of his shirt. As he chewed he picked up a spoon and tapped it on the tabletop. Harry was never totally at rest. Even at his most composed, some part of him was moving: a toe dancing in the air, head bobbing, eyes darting in the manner of a predatory bird.

Joy looked up when he began to crack his knuckles. "The girl will *be* here," she said.

Harry sighed elaborately and got up from the table. He paced around the room a few times and finally stopped at a window. Outside, the gardener was kneeling in a rose bed, plucking clover sprouts out of the peat. Beyond, the lawn lay like green baize over rolling ground that dropped away from the house down to a bluff that hid the Severn below.

From here, Harry could see the opposite bank, raw clay too steep for growth, and above it a lumpy hill mottled with homes and lawns and forest. To his immediate left was the steel-and-concrete span of the New Severn Bridge, arching high above the water. Farther downstream was the pierlike old bridge, built flat and much closer to the water, a narrow strand that connected at its far end with the Naval Academy and Annapolis. At the extreme left of his vision, nearly obscured by a treeline, Harry could make out a dull gray sliver of horizon: the Chesapeake.

"Maybe she forgot," Harry said, speaking to the window. He pursed his lips thoughtfully and nodded. "Sure. Kids that age, nothing stays with 'em for long. She prob'ly just forgot. Can't blame her. That's how kids are.''

He left the window, walked out of the room. Joy called after him: "Harry. You promised."

"I'm not doing anything," he said from the hall.

"You promised those two you'd give them peace."

"Nobody disturbing the peace out here," he said.

He walked to the end of the hall and tried the door there. Locked.

Well, he thought. He had spent a lot of money to coax Elise out of Vermont, Sarah with her. Sarah, of course, being the real prize. Eighty-eight thousand for the construction of a new wing; he had mentioned the sum to Elise several times. It had also cost him a promise of privacy: separate entrances, separate lives. No interference. No pressure, no problems, was the way he had put it.

Now Harry couldn't remember why he had made all these concessions. The house and the twenty acres were his domain, and he was a generally benevolent despot. But a despot all the same. The locked door rankled already. This was his house. Hell, his granddaughter.

He was powerful, but simple. Not so hard to read. Joy had gotten up from the table. Now she stood behind him in the hall.

"This is the wrong way to start," she said, "barging in on them."

"Can't call, phone's not in yet." He stared at the door.

"Harry, no."

"Sure," he said. "Give you some time alone with Elise. You'll have a chance to talk with her about you-know-what."

"That's your idea, you do it," Elise said, but Harry ignored her. He rapped sharply on the door. Thinking, Eighty-eight thou ought to buy a few privileges.

Harry came and left, dragging Sarah away, bludgeoning the morning quiet. Now he was gone, and stillness surrounded Elise again. She shook a couple of aspirin out of a bottle. Something had given her a headache—maybe Harry's bluster, maybe the fumes of fresh paint that had filled her nostrils since she arrived.

Elise swallowed the pills. She looked around her new living room and told herself that she had traded her home for a life in an ice palace.

The new wing was cold and austere. Its walls were snowbank white, pristine. A hard gleam shone on the bathroom porcelain. Kitchen appliances glistened, and a transparent glaze covered the oak floors. She didn't know if she would ever feel comfortable in such relentless perfection.

At least Harry hadn't skimped, she thought. Give him that. The addition was two stories, nearly 1,600 square feet, conforming strictly to the architectural standards of the main house. It included two big bedrooms (each with its own bathroom), a kitchen and dining room, a sitting room, and a top-floor solarium that Sarah might use as an artist's studio. The new wing was, in effect, a separate residence with its own entrance.

Give him something else, she thought: he was the most willful and single-minded individual she had ever known. For a while she had resisted his pleas to leave Vermont, to live in the big house on the Severn. She wanted to remain independent, she had told him. She would support Sarah and keep the house. But Harry had been unfazed. He had continued the construction, while constantly sending Elise more plans, more photos.

Meanwhile she was trying to earn a living for the first time ever. Johnson had no jobs. There was work in Burlington, but that was an hour's drive each way. The bills collected. They arrived as regularly as the letters and calls from Harry, keeping her up on the progress of the new wing. Nudging her, reassuring her. They would buy off her problems. No more struggle. This way she would have plenty of time with Sarah. And wasn't that the point of having a home?

In the end, she thought, the difference had been Harry's tenacity, his absolute unswerving determination. He had wanted her here, with Sarah—Sarah most of all. And here they were.

There was movement beyond the living room. Elise looked up; Joy Stannard was standing hesitantly in the hall.

"The door was open," she said. "Maybe Harry forgot to close it. I didn't know. Maybe we could talk? If you're not too busy?"

"Please," Elise said, and she gestured to a chair beside her. She liked Joy, admired her resilience. She thought that Joy deserved a Medal of Honor for surviving four and a half decades of marriage to a human steamroller.

"You're settling in?" Joy said. "I know it's hard, uprooting yourself, transplanting your life. Anything I can do, I want you to let me know."

"It'll take some time to feel at home."

"About Harry," she said. "You know he means well. He can't help himself sometimes. I tried to tell him this morning that he was going to make a pest out of himself. But he has his ways.

"When he decides he wants something—I don't have to tell you—there's no stopping him. You have to make allowances. If you understand that what he does is out of love, that he really wants the best for all of us, then it's not so hard to live with. So I have found." Her voice trailed off for a moment before she went on.

"Actually," she said, "it can be a very endearing quality if you see it in that light."

"I'm trying," Elise said.

"He has this idea . . ." Joy said, looking away, and Elise realized that there was a point to this conversation, and it had to do with Harry wanting something. Again.

"Maybe you'd better tell me."

"Harry doesn't think public schools are right for Sarah," Joy said.

"They've been good enough so far."

"That was Vermont. But Harry doesn't think much of the schools here."

"I suppose he has a better idea."

"A girl's academy in Annapolis," Joy said. "A really good one. Nordbrook, it's called. Nordbrook School. I know that all the best families try to send their daughters there. It has college prep courses, the highest standards. And art courses, too. Harry checked on that. This is a terrific place, Elise, very much in demand. You won't find any better, not even if you sent her all the way to Washington. Harry thinks that Sarah ought to have all the best."

She stuck out her chin, and looked directly at Elise for the first time.

"And in this case," Joy said, "he may be right."

At first Elise didn't say anything. She happened to agree: Sarah ought to have all the best. In Johnson, public school had been the only choice. But if there was better here, she wanted that for her daughter. She could even forgive Harry Stannard for pushing it on her.

But there was a problem. Sarah didn't like to be forced into anything. She would resist any coercion. And the harder she was forced, the stiffer her resistance would be.

"Is this school the best?" Elise said.

"Harry wouldn't settle for anything else."

"A place like that, if it's so good, it must have a waiting list. It can't be easy to get into, especially so late."

"All taken care of. Just fill out an application. Harry says he's greased the skids. His words. I didn't ask how."

"Tuition must be high," Elise said. "I'll have some money from the house."

"Keep your money, dear. Harry's taken care of that, too. He's a terrible bully, I know, the way he pushes people around. But he's no piker."

Harry had a BMW sedan—a 733, big and fast and sleek—and he knew some roads through the countryside where he could open it up. Cold air blasted out of the air conditioner. Past the Bay Bridge, east of Kent Narrows, he turned south onto a two-lane that skirted the Eastern Shore. The countryside was low, totally flat, as it streamed past on the other side of the glass. Cornfields and drooping, dusty shrubbery occasionally gave way to distant glimpses of the Chesapeake.

To Sarah it was a bleak vista. In Vermont there were always hills, and they imparted a feeling of security, as if they protected the farms and homes that nestled down among them. And no Vermont day was ever hot enough to batter the crispness out of the evergreens.

They drove in silence. It was unusual for her grandfather, she thought. Harry seemed restive. Several times his eyes left the road and went to her, and he seemed about to speak. But instead he would look away and leave an uneasy quiet.

He had promised her lunch—the best crab cakes in Maryland, he had said—and soon he turned down a farm road, packed yellow dirt, that cut between tobacco fields. It ended beside the bay, at a gravel parking lot. There stood a low clapboard building, one end resting on a concrete mooring, the other extending out over the water, supported by pilings.

DOT'S
GOOD FOOD

read a faded sign on the roof.

They sat on a screened porch overlooking the bay. Sarah watched a speedboat pulling a skier across the water, about a hundred yards off shore. The air was hot and clammy and she felt bereft, far from what she knew and loved.

Harry reached across the red plastic tablecloth. He took her hands, and his face had a pitying look.

She thought: Oh no you don't.

"Poor kid," he said, "you're feeling low, I can tell. Something's got you down."

So that was it. Harry was trying to play father. She was the poor little girl without a daddy and he was going to step in. No thank you.

"I'm fine," she said. "Just a little sleepy. I stayed up and watched the Creature Features until two in the morning."

"I thought maybe it was something else. Maybe moving to a new place, you don't like it so much." He was wrestling with the words. "You could tell me, you know, if something was bothering you. I guess you're entitled to a few rough days, the troubles you've had. You can tell me about it."

"I'd tell you, Grandpa, if I had something to talk about."

"You're sure."

"Honest."

He nodded and looked relieved, as if he had discharged

some difficult duty and could now put it behind him. When he spoke to her next his tone was lighter.

"So, kid," he said, "what do you want to be when you grow up?"

"I don't know, Grandpa. I think maybe I'm a little young yet to make up my mind." She looked straight at him. "What do you want to be when you grow up?"

He thought for a moment.

"Young lady, my ambition has always been to end up a rich old pain-in-the-ass. And I think I may be getting close to it."

She patted his hands, resting on the table.

"You're not *that* old, Grandpa," she said. She smiled brightly. "But two out of three isn't bad."

Sarah was subdued when she returned. She gave Elise a quick hello and then disappeared upstairs, up into the solarium. Elise waited a few minutes, going over in her mind what she wanted to do. Maybe she could force Sarah into Nordbrook School. Maybe, if she pushed hard enough. But there would be weeks of friction between them if she did. There had to be another way.

She went upstairs. Sarah was seated in a corner, partly hidden by a sketchbook on an easel. A tray of watercolors sat on a table beside her. She dabbed a slim brush into one of the color wells and lightly touched it to the paper.

"Sarah, honey, did you have fun today?"

She spoke without looking away from the easel: "It wasn't so bad."

"Harry didn't talk to you about school? A place called Nordbrook School?"

Now Sarah turned to her, interested and wary.

"What about school?"

"Apparently he's got this idea that you should go to a private school." She tried to sound casual. "A private girl's school in Annapolis. Joy told me that he insists on it."

"Oh, great. That's just great," Sarah said. "Grandpa deciding where I go to school."

"But I told her, no. No way would I let Harry dictate to you. Besides, it sounded terrible to me, a snooty kind of place that just wouldn't be right for you. I don't think it's your kind of environment."

Sarah said nothing.

"Anyway," Elise said, "I want you to know that I took care of it. You don't have to give it a thought."

There was a silence of a few seconds as Elise waited, knowing that if it didn't happen now, it never would.

She turned to leave. Before she reached the door, Sarah's voice stopped her.

"Mom, you could have talked to me first," she said.

Bullseye, Elise thought. She turned to face her daughter again.

"I mean, you treat me like a child sometimes." Sarah's voice was rising. "I'm the one who'll be going to school. I should have a say in it."

"I did what I thought was best for you."

"I know what's best for me," Sarah said, defiant.

"Maybe you do," Elise said. "I'm sorry if I spoke too soon. Harry can tell you more about the school. Go over and speak to him, right now. If this school is what you really want, I won't keep you from it."

She had warned Harry not to press. If he could manage, they would swing this.

Sarah walked stiffly out of the room, carrying herself like a fighter, with shoulders thrust back, head high. She left Elise alone in the room.

With Sarah, Elise thought, it was always a battle. The girl surrendered nothing without a fight. Her father had been that way: reserved, combative, foolishly proud. The difference was that he had showed a tough face to the world, but shed his carapace at home. It was a matter of economy, he would say. Give away too much to strangers, and you have nothing left for those who matter.

But Sarah let up with nobody.

Elise crossed the room to look at the work that sat up on the easel. Usually Sarah worked with pencil, or pen-and-ink. Watercolors were new, and Elise was curious to see the result.

She reached for the sketchpad. When she saw the painting, she was so startled that she nearly dropped the book.

Jack Stannard looked out at her from the white rag paper. He was about thirty years old, grinning a go-to-hell smile that had always made her melt inside. Sarah had been working from an old photo. But she had caught things that the camera missed: the kindness, the intelligence, the love—Lord, most of all the love—that had set him apart from any other man Elise had known. It was all there, rendered in brushstrokes.

For a moment Elise had to look away. Then she studied the painting again. It wasn't finished, and it lacked a professional's polish. But it *was* Jack Stannard.

Sarah really is good, she thought. No, not just good. The girl had recalled her father's essence, and had managed to put it on paper for someone else to see. That was talent; that was a gift. Then Elise had to hold the sketchbook at arm's length, because she didn't want her tears to smear the work.

The next day Sarah filled out the application form, and quickly she was accepted as an incoming sophomore at Nordbrook School. Elise rejoiced. She knew how important the choice of schools could be to her daughter's future.

Another occurrence which took place that afternoon, several miles away, proved to be even more significant. Though it escaped their notice at the time, it would shortly affect the lives of all of them in the showpiece house above the Severn.

It came about when a seventeen-year-old boy, having consumed six cans of beer in less than an hour, climbed into his father's Chrysler-powered speedboat. He cast off the lines, started the inboard V-8, and, though he was in the middle of a crowded and confined harbor, shoved the throttle to the firewall. With prow raised, the craft bolted across the water.

Within a few seconds it struck an unoccupied dingy that was tied off at a dock. The wheel was wrenched out of the boy's hands, and the boat became an aimless missile, accelerating. Miraculously, the joyriding teenager managed to leap from the craft an instant before it destroyed itself against a bridge piling.

The incident took place in a confined body of water, one of the narrow tidal fingers that extend inland near Annapolis. This one, its banks bristling with private docks, is navigable for more than a mile of its length. It is called Weems Creek.

—FIVE—

MONDAY
AUGUST 27

FIFTY-six hours after he left Harben, Sherk's daughter ran across the highway, at the edge of the glow cast by his highbeam headlights.

He had been driving most of that time, frenzied, fueled by hope and belief. He drove up through Virginia, over to Pittsburgh, across to Toledo and Chicago, St. Louis and Louisville in an erratic circle that, without plan, brought him within two hundred miles of Harben again as he tracked south on I-65.

In the evening darkness, she ran across the highway about five miles north of Bowling Green. She was oblivious to traffic, laughing, her hair bouncing behind her. Sherk could see her face clearly. She crossed the road, leaped lightly over the steel barrier beyond the gravel shoulder, and disappeared down an embankment.

Sherk braked suddenly and jerked the wheel to the right. He cut across two lanes of traffic and nearly collided with a station wagon. When his pickup had skidded to a stop, Sherk scrambled out and ran around to the embankment where he had seen her last.

It was a grassy slope, empty. She was gone. Beyond the slope was a farmer's pasture, also empty. He could see for a mile, and she was nowhere visible.

Sherk felt his heart collapse. He stood at the shoulder of the road, staring down at the slope and the pasture. A tractor-trailer blasted past him, and buffeted him with the wake it made in the air. Something was happening, and Sherk groped for an answer in the murky recesses of his mind. He was astonished. Not because he had seen her—he expected that—but because she had disappeared so suddenly.

Then he knew. He was being tested. He had been foolish to hope that she would be delivered up to him so easily, so neatly. His faith was on trial, and before it was finally rewarded he might have to prove it against unimaginable setbacks and disappointments.

He returned to the truck. Suddenly he was weary, and incredibly hungry.

To Alma Nettles, he was Wildeyes.

Alma faced dozens of people every day. She didn't name them all. She was a truck stop waitress, and most of the customers who bellied up to the counter were as plain as rice pudding. She would look at them without really seeing them, and they would disappear from her consciousness the moment they slid off the stool.

But out of the dozens and the hundreds, sometimes one would demand her eye, a gem among the dross. Different. She would know that he had a story, that he had peeked around corners and broken into locked boxes, that he had stood at life's perilous edges and from that perch had seen sights denied to all but the crazy and the brave. One look and she would know.

Then she would watch him for the few minutes that he sat at her counter, and she would give him a name—a label, really—by which she could retrieve him later, long after he had slapped down a tip and walked out of her life.

She spotted Wildeyes while he was still outside, gassing up his pickup, bleached blue by the mercury lamps above the pumps at the service island. She hoped that he would come in. He did. He took a seat at her counter, and by the time she had poured his coffee she had him named.

Wildeyes. Sometimes it was so easy.

He asked for a Western omelet, white toast, grits. It was

a slow night, so after Alma put in the order she had a chance to study him. His cheeks were sunken, and he looked as if he had started a beard without intending it. He seemed oblivious to his surroundings—not a zombie, not unaware, but hostage to whatever was churning inside him. To Alma, he looked as if he had been through war, and part of him was still under ambush.

She knew that she would remember Wildeyes for a long time. Even before the thing with the newspaper.

The first couple of minutes he sipped his coffee and stared at the wall behind the counter, looking at it only because it was there. Then he looked around and saw the newspaper on the seat beside him. It had been left there by a trucker, gone through and set aside, and Alma hadn't bothered to pick it up.

Wildeyes did. He started casually paging through it, and Alma could see the top of his head move as he scanned the headlines from side to side, top of the page to bottom.

She was standing off to the side, watching his face, the moment his expression changed. She saw life come to his haggard face, suddenly animating him. He leaned in closer to the page with an intense expression. The paper wrinkled where he gripped it.

Just that suddenly, he put the paper down and got up. He left in a hurry, striding out through the door and heading for his pickup. The cook was flipping over his omelet, and Alma considered running out to tell him that his meal was ready. But she knew that there was no point in bothering. He had forgotten food. He had forgotten everything but what he had seen in the paper.

She went over to where he had sat, and she picked up the paper. He had been reading a morning edition of the *Baltimore Sun,* an inside page of statewide news. As far as Alma could tell, the stories on the page were a typical recounting of a summer weekend's disasters—mishaps and carnage in places that meant nothing to her.

She read the first paragraph of each article, wondering which one had gotten Wildeyes out the door so fast. Two boys in Aberdeen burned by fireworks. A four-year-old girl drowns in the Patuxent River. In LaPlata, four teenag-

ers are killed in a single-car accident. An overturned trac-
tor seriously injures a farmer near Chestertown. And in
Annapolis, a runaway speedboat is demolished at a place
called Weems Creek.

Sherk found Maryland in his atlas, sharing a page with
Delaware and Virginia. Annapolis completed a triangle that
had Washington and Baltimore at its other corners. Annapolis. He would find her there. Not immediately, maybe,
but he would persist. She had to be there. Any place that
had a Weems Creek would have his daughter, too. That
was not logic, but faith.

   All along, he had needed only a sign.

—SIX—

TUESDAY
AUGUST 28

SHERK reached Annapolis around midday. At the city limits he crossed over a bridge with a sign that identified Weems Creek below. He stopped beside the highway and got out to look. The creek was a curled finger of water, motionless, glaring under a high sun; much wider and more placid than the little stream in the hills had been. Below him, a sailboat slipped under the bridge. Sherk could hear the raspy puttering of the outboard engine that pushed it toward open water.

He looked at the creek with mild curiosity. Already he had decided that Margaret wasn't going to be perched there, waiting. Most likely the creek had been a sign. His search would have to be broader this time, and he realized that much work, much disappointment, lay before him.

Up the road he could see the low skyline of Annapolis, a steeple and some squat office buildings, and the massive gray form of a football stadium, like a gray whale.

She was there, somewhere.

In West Virginia he had stolen a few hours' sleep. Now he felt invigorated, ready to start his search immediately. But first he needed a place to stay.

A couple of blocks up the road was a gas station. There a pump jockey recommended a motel on the other side of

town, on Old Solomons Road. Nothing fancy, he told
Sherk, but clean and not too expensive. It had kitchens and
weekly rates. He drew a map that Sherk followed around
the north side of the city, then across the South River.

Sherk paid a week's rent. He stopped in the room long
enough to look around and splash some water on his face.
Then he was ready. He felt like a soldier marching into
battle, nervous and elated and desperate.

He drove. From the South River Bridge he could see
Annapolis across the water, full of promise, and he knew
that he would never leave until it had returned to him what
was his.

"It's nearly two," Elise said. "This shouldn't take more
than forty-five minutes. An hour, at most. So I'll meet you
between quarter to three and three o'clock at . . . where?
Some place close."

"The city dock," Sarah said. It wasn't far from the
salon where Elise had an appointment for a haircut. "Front
door of the fish store, at the market square."

"Please be there," Elise said. "You know I'll worry if
you're late."

"I'll be there, Mom."

"And Sarah. Careful. Don't let anybody give you a
problem, okay?"

"Come *on*. Really!"

"I can't help it," Elise said. "I'm a mother."

They stood on the sidewalk and hugged briefly.

"See you," Sarah said, leaving. She was in a high
mood. "Three o'clock."

"Quarter of," Elise called after her. Sarah was already
on her way down the sidewalk, stepping lightly. She had
always enjoyed Annapolis, on trips here with her parents.
This would be the first time she would walk these streets
alone.

Sarah was on Main Street, headed downhill, away from
Church Circle. Below, at the end of Main, she could see
the harbor, a narrow notch of water intruding two blocks
inland, trapped by a high concrete seawall and surrounded
by the heart of the city. It is an anchorage for pleasure

craft and a small commercial fishing fleet. It is also the
focus of the city's auto traffic; seven different streets
converge at the harbor's head.

In the eighteenth century, hogsheads of export tobacco
filled the wharves. Now the trade is principally tourist.
Every year, visitors make their way to Annapolis by the
hundreds of thousands; most manage to spend a good deal
of their time and money around the harbor, shopping in the
galleries and boutiques that proliferate near the dockside.
By a wide margin, it is the busiest and most crowded
district in Annapolis and Anne Arundel County.

Sarah reached the bottom of Main. The atmosphere
around the dock had the carefree informality of a carnival:
wandering couples and young families, lots of jeans and
shorts and T-shirts. Small children clutched candy bars and
dribbled trails of warm ice cream.

For a few minutes Sarah milled with all the rest of them,
feeling happily unfettered; she liked being on her own. But
soon she was bored, so she set off down one of the side
streets that lead away from the harbor.

The change was almost immediate. After walking two
blocks she had left behind most of the tourists, and all of
the carnival. She had found a stately old neighborhood of
dark, ancient brick. The street was cobbled, and huge oaks
leaned over the roadway, their roots rippling unmortared
stone sidewalks.

Sarah walked slowly, trying to catch the details. They
were everywhere. Ivy running up a chimneyside, following the channels in the masonry. Windows of rippled
glass. Walled back yards and boxwood gardens. Iron
bootscrapers at the front doors. A sparrow's nest in the
triangular top-piece of a window frame. The rough, pitted
surface of a brick foundation that had seen three centuries
of weather.

Sarah wished that she had brought her sketchbook. Narrow your vision or broaden it, no matter; everywhere the
eye fell it found a study. She wondered whether she could
catch the distinct feel of the neighborhood. It wasn't prim
like some old New England towns she had seen, but was
somehow wise and knowing and tolerant.

Suddenly she realized that she had lost track of time. She didn't have a watch, but she thought that three o'clock must be near, if not past. Reluctantly, she headed back toward the dock.

Annapolis wasn't such a big city, Sherk thought. He had been across town once already, passing by the State House and the Naval Academy, and he saw that while it was large by hill standards, it wasn't the behemoth that he had feared, with skyscrapers and subways and throngs on every corner. Instead, he realized, it was a small town that had grown outward without sprawling.

All this gave him hope that he might not have to search too long before he discovered his daughter.

He had passed a sign for the city harbor, pointing this direction. Now traffic was slow, clogging the street. Ahead was a small bridge, and beyond he saw the masts of sailboats. The harbor, he thought. It seemed a busy place; there must have been several hundred people gathered at the dock.

But all this was on the other side of the small bridge. Now traffic halted completely. A large white cabin cruiser was coming up an inlet, approaching the bridge. It gave a loud, sustained blast of a horn; signal lights over the bridge began to flash, and the bridge rose—a drawbridge, he realized—and with everyone else in the line of traffic, Sherk watched the cruiser pass slowly in front of them.

Elise's new hairdresser, true to expectation, was a tyrant, an insufferable little twerp. Naturally she was intimidated.

"This year the new look is short, dear," he told her for the third time.

"I know," Elise said. "But I only want a trim today, a little off the bottom." Also for the third time.

He went back to work with an unconcealed sigh. The snipping of his scissors sounded petulant and disapproving.

Once Elise had been told that a woman will inevitably revive the hair style that she wore during the happiest time of her life. In her case, the maxim had proved true. Elise had never been happier than in the first several years of her marriage, a period when she had met life with joyful enthusiasm. Then she had worn her hair in a youthful shoulder-length flip. Recently, after trying a series of shags and page-boy cuts, she had let her hair grow back long and straight, in the style that the infant Sarah used to tangle in her fingers, that Jack Stannard languidly stroked during the soft silences following their lovemaking.

"You ought to let me add some color," the hairdresser said. His subtle way of pointing out the streaks of gray in the chestnut brown.

"No time today, thanks," she said.

He bore this with the expression of a long-suffering victim. After a few more snips he tossed comb and scissors down on a tray beside the wall.

"Did my very best," he said, "under the circumstances." He gave Elise a hand mirror and stood back, prepared to disclaim his work at once.

She lifted the mirror. The face that looked back at her was angular and sharply defined. She shared her best features with her daughter: prominent cheekbones, large and expressive eyes, a long, slim nose that was slightly turned up at the tip.

Her forehead showed lines of care that had become increasingly obvious in the last year, and her eyes looked worn—more a matter of attitude, maybe, than any physical effect. In all, though, the face in the mirror was still attractive, the skin still taut and ruddy, a face that the years had treated gently.

Too bad, she thought, that the same wasn't true of her soul. Too frequently these days she felt like an old woman, weary, ground down by time and fate. She had always expected that her spirit would be the last to go, but the shock of her husband's death, the struggle to keep the home in Vermont, the friction with Sarah, all had ground away at her. She realized that at forty-one she might be past the midpoint of her life. And lately she had begun to fear that the best of that life, the richest and most vivid episodes, might be behind her as well. A chilling thought, but she knew that it might be so.

She shook her hair and studied the effect in the mirror.

Yes. It was a young woman's haircut, but she could still carry it off.

"Not so bad," she said, looking directly at the hairdresser, "under the circumstances." She tipped him a dollar, which he accepted as though it had been dragged through a barnyard. The clock in the shop showed 2:55 when she walked out the door, and she hurried downhill.

The fish store was at the foot of Main, beside the harbor, sharing a roof with a bakery, a delicatessen, a farm market. Sarah wasn't where she had promised to be. Elise looked for her inside, walking up and down the aisles. Sarah wasn't there, either, and still wasn't at the door when Elise returned.

Elise began to pace up and down the sidewalk. She watched the shifting crowd around her, looking for Sarah. Once she stopped a passerby and asked the time; about 3:15, he said. Again she ducked into the market and looked around the aisles.

Now she was sorry she had let Sarah roam. The child was just a country girl, she told herself, not at all city-wise.

A tap on her shoulder. Sarah stood there, beaming.

"Mom," she said, "I found the greatest old street, as good as Disneyland, but real."

"Sarah, you're late." The voice was tense, distraught.

"You didn't have to worry, Mom, I was just walking."

Elise swallowed the angry lecture that was ready in her throat. She wasn't going to be the nagging harridan. Not this time, anyway.

"You should have been more careful," she said. "But I'm glad you had a good time. This is a lovely city, isn't it?"

It was frightening, she thought, how much Sarah meant to her. Jack was gone and her home was gone; Sarah was all that remained. If she should ever be taken away . . .

Elise shrank from the thought.

Their car was nearby, on Compromise Street. As they were walking, an air horn split the afternoon. They looked up together and saw traffic halt as a section of the roadway tilted upward. It was the Eastport Bridge, a drawbridge,

rising to make way for a huge white motor cruiser that
seemed to fill up Spa Creek.

For a few seconds they watched the cruiser slide carefully between the bulkheads of the bridge. But before it
had cleared the channel, Elise and Sarah were in the car.
With the bridge closed behind her, there was no inbound
traffic on Compromise—a rare opportunity—and Elise took
advantage of the open street. She drove to the foot of Main
and then up the hill, north toward the big house above the
Severn.

The cabin cruiser left the channel and picked up speed as it
nosed into open water. The bridge came down, the signal
lights stopped blinking, and in a moment traffic moved
forward, carrying Sherk along with it.

When he got across the bridge, he had a better view of
the harbor. It was full of people, most of whom appeared
to be sightseers. That was good, he thought. If the city got
plenty of tourists, he wouldn't be conspicuous as he wandered the streets.

Annapolis. It was a friendly old city, not so imposing
after all. It would yield her up.

—SEVEN—

THURSDAY
AUGUST 30

SAINT Bartholomew's Church was almost always a cool, somber place. It had high granite walls and narrow stained-glass windows, so even on the brightest days the sunlight was low inside. Frank Herrity, who saw it at all hours, liked it best when it was quiet and empty, when a whisper would carry to the farthest corners. He was monsignor of the parish; with three other priests, he ministered to a congregation that numbered more than three thousand.

Catholics had been worshipping on this spot for more than three centuries. What served now as the vestibule had once been a small chapel of pre-Revolution vintage, though it had long since lost its original rustic character. A small plaque near the front door noted that Charles Carroll, one of the signers of the Declaration of Independence, had attended Mass there regularly.

The main church was built in the mid-19th century, when stone and labor were both cheap. The gray walls were more than forty feet high, and the roof pitched up steeply from there. The pews and the altar rail were of brown mahogany. It was an imposing and somber place. That was, he thought, exactly how a church ought to be.

Some he had seen, built in the past thirty years, resembled cabanas more than houses of worship.

Tonight he sat on a padded bench in a confessional box that was built into one wall in the church. On each side of him was a stall where the penitent would kneel for confession. It had been at least a quarter of an hour since he had heard the familar creak of the kneelers. He pressed a button on the side of his watch. The lighted digital display showed 8:11; Thursday night confessions ran from seven to eight.

After a few more minutes he let himself out of the box and walked slowly by a side aisle up to the sacristy. He was a short, lumpy figure in the shadows of the empty church, his loafers squeaking on the marble floor. At the head of the aisle a bank of votive candles winked and wavered in their red glass cups. He knew of churches that had replaced the candles with tiny colored electric lights; drop a quarter in the slot and get a few minutes of light, just like TV sets in an airport waiting room. The idea scandalized him.

He loved the church. While he knew that prayer ought to be in the heart, and that worship required no roof, the truth was that people often needed a special place to feel close to God. Most had no trouble believing that this was His house. Its walls were a fortress against the rancorous and profane. Saint Bartholomew's was a sanctuary where life eddied undisturbed.

It was a place apart.

Margaret was screaming. Her mouth was open, her face contorted in fear. Her eyes were looking straight at him, beseeching. And an awful shriek welled up out of her throat and tore at Sherk's heart.

Sherk sat up in bed, snapped awake by the nightmare. His hands were trembling. For a second he didn't know where he was. Then he remembered. Annapolis. The motel.

He slid back into bed. That wasn't Margaret, he told himself. It was just a bad dream from sleeping in a strange bed. But it felt real, not so much a dream as a dreamed memory.

Sherk lay awake in the dark. The silence in the room felt fragile. Even the room itself, the bed, the black of night, seemed insubstantial and unreal, more than the dream itself had been. He was still awake, tensed, when morning light bled through the curtains.

—EIGHT—

FRIDAY
AUGUST 31

THE green Pontiac was following him; Sherk was certain of it. He had noticed the car behind him as he crossed the South River Bridge, and again as he drove into the city. It was still there, trailing him by a couple of hundred yards, as he headed down Duke of Gloucester Street.

He spotted an open parking space at the curb and slid into it. The Pontiac was in his side mirror, cruising slowly. As it passed, Sherk leaned from the window to get a better look at the driver: a thirtyish woman with two kids in the back seat. She drove by without a glance at Sherk, and turned left on Newman Street.

Sherk had never seen the woman before, and he didn't know why she should be following him. No matter; he didn't want to be here if she should circle the block and come around again. He jumped from the truck, quickly locked the door, and hurried down to the city dock.

When he got there the sidewalks were dense with people. Tourists were perched on the seawall like magpies on a telephone wire. In the last couple of days Sherk had spent most of his time here and in the surrounding blocks of downtown. Sometimes he drove up and down the streets and sometimes he would park and walk, looking at the faces in the crowd. He would see more faces in an hour here than during a full day elsewhere in the city.

In the crowd he felt safe from prying eyes. He knew that he was being watched, being trailed. Like the green Pontiac; somehow the woman had picked him out. At different moments he would get that feeling of being stared at. If he turned around quickly enough he would catch some stranger furtively looking away. Surely it had to do with forces that were trying to keep him from Margaret.

Now he found an open spot on the wall and leaned against it to watch the people flow steadily past him. Soon he lost track of time as his eyes moved among them, sorting through them, discarding one after another.

Suddenly Sherk straightened. Through the crowd he saw a long blond braid. It belonged to a girl who was turned away from him, headed up Main Street. He watched, alert. Shifting bodies moved back and forth between them, briefly blocking his vision and then revealing her again. She was tall and slight, wearing jeans and red running shoes— Margaret often wore both.

He hadn't yet seen her face, but everything else fit. Everything else was exactly right. She was walking away from him, up the hill. Sherk pushed off from the wall and began to move toward her, keeping her in sight, avoiding those who got in his path or brushing them aside.

His stride lengthened and quickened, until he was almost running. He felt his heart surge, breath coming shorter and faster.

She stopped to look at a shop window. In turning she showed him her profile, and what he saw made Sherk pull up short about fifty feet away from her. She was not Margaret. Not even a girl, but a woman at least twenty-five years old.

Sherk looked at her with disgust. He hated her for being a grown woman, for having blond hair in a braid down her back. He hated her for not being Margaret. He felt the urge to go to her, grab her, thrash the life out of her. Simply because she was not Margaret. He couldn't do it here, but he knew what would have happened if they had been alone.

Though the sidewalk was crowded, she became aware of his presence. She turned her head toward him and saw the naked antipathy in his face. It startled her, but she was unable to pull her gaze away. Finally she turned her back to Sherk and walked away hastily, without looking back.

Sherk felt the fire subside. He turned and headed in the opposite direction, downhill toward the harbor. People were looking at him now. He was sure of it. He could feel their stares burning in his back, people all up and down the street, staring at him and trying to pry open the hidden chambers of his soul.

—NINE—

WEDNESDAY
SEPTEMBER 5

THE classroom building at Nordbrook School had the mien of a dowager empress, proud and aloof. It was a large, three-story brick structure that, at first appearance, might have been an exceptionally grand manor house. It was situated in the middle of a thirty-acre plot, surrounded by grass and trees. From the street it could be reached only by a long paved driveway that ended in a circle at the school's front steps.

To Sarah, approaching it for the first time, the place was imposing. As she sat beside Elise in the car, she nervously smoothed the pleats in a charcoal-gray skirt that would not have been her choice for the first day of class. But she had no choice; the skirt was part of a school uniform that included a white blouse and burgundy blazer with a Nordbrook crest on the breast pocket.

She had never attended a school that required a uniform, nor one that looked as if it belonged on the campus of Oxford University. This was the first time she had seen the place, and she was dismayed to think that she would have to make a niche for herself in these surroundings. She didn't belong here.

"Don't be nervous," Elise said as she drove.

"I'm not. I'm not nervous. I've got nothing to worry about."

"Just be yourself, everything will go fine."

"I know that. Can we hurry, please? I don't want to be late."

She saw that she had plenty of time. At least two dozen girls, in groups of three or four, still stood on the broad stone steps out front. But she wanted to get on with it. She had learned that waiting is the worst part of an ordeal, and that if unpleasantness cannot be avoided, the next best choice is to attack it as soon as possible.

To the left, the car passed a line of tennis courts. On the other side was a grassy athletic field, the boundaries marked in chalk, with field hockey goals at each end. Past the field was an ordered row of maple trees that bordered the school property on one side. The maples made Sarah think of Vermont, and she wished that she were there now, ready to walk into a school that she knew, about to see friends and familiar faces.

They reached the circular turnaround in front of the main building.

"I'll be here to pick you up at half past three," Elise said.

Sarah nodded. She was looking at the school building and the strangers who stood in front of it. The car slowed and stopped.

"Enjoy yourself," Elise was saying. "And for goodness sake, don't worry. You'll fit in just fine."

"I'm not worried," Sarah said. "Everything's going to be great, just great."

She got out of the car without kissing her mother, without even closing the door; Elise had to reach across the seat to shut it. Then the car pulled away. A couple of girls nearby broke off their conversation and looked at her, and Sarah, though she kept her eyes straight ahead, was acutely aware of their gaze.

Looking me over already.

She imagined that her father was watching, and that gave her strength. With shoulders back, eyes front, she marched up the steps.

* * *

Sherk drove slowly through the city. He idled down streets and through intersections, dividing his attention between the traffic and the sidewalks. He was tireless. She was here; he *knew,* and that kept him going. And as he drove, Margaret smiled down at him from the sun visor.

Sarah found her name on a seating chart taped to the door of home room 2-C, and she took her place among twenty-three other sophomore girls. There was no teacher yet.

She felt a tap at her shoulder and turned.

"You're new, right?" said the girl behind Sarah: plump-faced, freckled, with curly red hair. "Ever go to private school before?"

Sarah shook her head.

"Then you never had to wear glad rags like these." The girl gestured toward the uniform.

"Pretty weird," Sarah said.

"Just like permanent disfigurement—you get used to it after a while. Coming to a new school, I guess you feel strange, huh?"

Sarah nodded. At that moment a teacher walked into the room, took the seating chart off the door, asked for silence, and introduced herself.

"Then you'll fit right in," the girl whispered. "Everybody here is strange. There's no such thing as a normal Brookie."

The teacher was reading from the seating chart and then looking out at the class as she spoke the names of the girls. When she reached Sarah she hesitated; the eyes flicked down to the chart twice. She asked Sarah to stand.

"You're Sarah Stannard?" She sounded doubtful.

"Yes I am," Sarah said. She felt uncomfortable with the teacher looking her over. *Let me sit down. Please.*

"You're a new girl?"

"Well, I've been a girl all my life. But this is my first day at Nordbrook." There was a tittering around her. The teacher gave Sarah a narrow, level look, then allowed herself a smile.

"I don't suppose you've had a chance to meet Emily

Caldwell yet," the teacher said. "She's a sophomore, too. I taught her last year."

"I don't think I've seen her."

The teacher's laugh was surprisingly loud.

"You would know if you had," she said. "That's not something you're likely to forget. Oh yes, you've got a real surprise ahead of you."

As she sat at lunch that day in the cafeteria, Sarah got a start on an overnight reading assignment. She was on the third page of *Pride and Prejudice* when a husky voice from in front of her table said, "You must be Sarah."

A girl was standing directly in front of her, holding a tray of food. Sarah looked up from the book, up into a face that was a fair likeness of her own.

The girl put down her tray and stuck out her hand.

"Emily Caldwell," she said. "I heard about you this morning, and when I saw you sitting there, I knew you had to be the celebrated imposter."

She had a commanding, throaty voice, and a manner to match. Both reminded Sarah of Katharine Hepburn in an old movie. Sarah envied her effortless composure; she saw herself as a desperate stand-up comic.

"Come on, stand beside me, let's see how we measure up."

Sarah obeyed. They stood shoulder to shoulder. Emily was perhaps half an inch taller, maybe four or five pounds heavier. When Sarah studied her face, she could see some differences. Emily's cheeks were less prominent, her nose slightly broader at the base. Both girls had the same small-boned, loose-limbed build. Each had the kind of complexion that, rather than tanning, reddens and blisters in the sun. Both had pale, fine blond hair below the shoulders, pulled back over the ears and fastened with barrettes.

"What do you think, Stannard? Close enough to fool anybody in low light, I'd say."

There was one difference, Sarah thought. This girl believed unquestionably in herself. Sarah thought that it must be wonderful to pass through life unassailed by doubt, to exude confidence and not have to feign it.

"We could fool anybody but our mothers," Sarah said.

"That's it. We're not identical twins . . ." she looked Sarah up and down again ". . . but we sure could be sisters. We sure could be."

She clapped Sarah on an arm.

"Tell you what, Stannard," she said. "I'll make you a deal. You try your best not to do anything that'll make me look bad, and I'll do the same for you. And if you can't manage that, at least tell me what I'm going to get blamed for, so I can go out and do it myself. Is that fair enough?"

Sarah nodded and the girl thumped her on the shoulder again.

"That's fine," she said. "It'll be fun to have you here, Stannard. Between us, we'll keep 'em on their toes, won't we?"

While most of her classmates streamed out of school with the final bell that afternoon, Emily Caldwell went to a lavatory in the basement of the school auditorium and replaced the Nordbrook uniform with loose denims and a rumpled cotton shirt. She took a series of deep, deliberate breaths. This technique was supposed to slow her pulse and loosen the tightness in her stomach. Or so she had been taught. But when she was finished her heart still tripped over itself, and a leaden lump still remained in her belly.

In a few minutes she was going to read for the part of Millie in *Picnic*. The school's drama department was producing the play with a boy's boarding school nearby. Emily had done small parts last year, nothing like this. But she thought she was ready. She understood Millie, a girl with big dreams who concealed her insecurities with bluster and big talk.

She had studied the play for three weeks, had learned the entire part and most of the others. The denims and the shirt were clothes that Millie might wear. But something looked wrong. She examined herself in the mirror, and realized that she hadn't changed her hair. Her normal style was out of place on a country girl from Kansas.

Not much time—the auditions would begin in a couple of minutes. She took out the barrettes, quickly combed out the hair, and tied it back in a pony tail. No, she thought, much too Olivia Newton-John. Too cute. Millie wasn't pert.

She got an idea. Until she was twelve, she had worn her hair in a braid down the back. She had learned to do the braid without help then, and she thought she could do it now.

In about a minute and a half, it was finished. She tossed her head. It looked right. Not the neatest braid she had ever seen, maybe, but it wasn't so bad. She pictured Millie as slightly scruffy.

She couldn't look at herself in the mirror any longer. Anyway, it was time. The fist in her stomach tightened, and she went up the stairs.

Elise was parked and waiting when school let out. She spotted Sarah first, at the top of the stairs, near the back of a packed mass of girls who were waiting for school buses. Then Sarah saw her and made her way to the car.

She slammed the door behind her. Elise leaned across to kiss her. Sarah responded with a quick buss, and she slouched in the seat, as if to make herself less conspicuous.

"Mama, do you think we could kind of pull out of here?"

"Good afternoon," Elise said, "and I missed you, too."

"I'd find it a lot easier to talk if half the school wasn't standing here watching."

Elise pulled around the circle and started up the driveway. Sarah looked backward for a moment before she turned and straightened in the seat.

"Do you know how many other girls were getting picked up by their mothers today? About three. And I think they were freshmen. Mama, this sucks."

"Nice language. And here I was afraid you wouldn't learn anything at this fancy place."

'I'm sorry. But I feel out-of-it enough already. Now

everybody thinks that I can't get back and forth to school without my mother.''

Elise listened carefully to this. It wasn't much, she thought, but it was the first time in many months that her daughter had even come close to confessing weakness or insecurity.

"What would you rather do?" she said.

"I found out there's a bus that leaves at ten after three, that goes through the city and up the Ritchie Highway."

This was the state road that ran beside the Severn, behind the heavy grove of trees at the eastern side of Harry's property.

"Will it bring you all the way home?"

"Not all the way. But it'll pick me up and drop me off right at the lane, you know, and it's not a long walk from there."

Elise knew that the lane must run at least half a mile, some of it through dense woods, before it reached the back of Harry's lot. She thought of her daughter walking alone every day, alone through the forest. Twice a day, coming and going. The image made her nervous. But she also knew that Sarah ought to be rewarded for opening up— however narrowly and obliquely.

"I'll make a deal with you," Elise said. "The bus can't get you to school as fast as I can. So why don't you let me save you some sleep? In the mornings, let me bring you in. After school, if you want, you can try the bus. We'll try that, see how it works out. What do you think?"

Sarah pondered this for a few seconds before she turned to Elise.

"Deal," she said.

When they were out of the city, crossing the Old Severn Bridge, Sarah turned to her.

"Mama," she said, "maybe you ought to think about taking a class, something like that, in the afternoons. It would give you something to do during the day."

"I already have something to do," Elise said stiffly. "I'm your mother."

Sherk was near the city harbor when he saw three Brookies

get off a city bus and go into a record store on Main
Street. He had noticed the uniforms that morning on a
couple of teenage girls waiting at a bus stop. They were
schoolgirls, he thought. Their school must be around here
someplace. It was something else to remember about Annapolis.

Somehow she got the lines out. Her throat went dry the
moment she stepped front and center on the stage, but
Emily Caldwell got the lines out anyway.

The scene ended with Millie leaving the stage. Emily
returned from the curtains and the director asked her to
come down. He was a thin, serious young man with a
wispy moustache; she had wanted desperately to please
him since the first time they met.

"A good job," he said. "You were ready."

He called one of the two senior girls who were going to
read for the part of Millie's older sister. Without looking at
Emily he said, "Rehearsals start tomorrow. Count on two
hours an afternoon the first three weeks, then Lord knows
how long from there on in."

"I got the part?"

"It's yours, if you think you can handle it."

"I know I can," she said.

He looked toward the stage and said, "End of Act Two,
Hal is on the porch. I'll read Hal. Madge enters from stage
right. Any time."

As the girl walked offstage to make her entrance, the
director turned to Emily again.

"By the way, I liked the pigtail, whatever you call it.
Nice touch. I think we'll keep that."

She kept herself gathered up long enough to walk quietly up the center aisle and out the back of the auditorium.
But when the door closed behind her she whooped and
took the stairs three at a time down to where she had left
her uniform.

Quickly she put on her skirt and blouse, then the blazer.
She was about to comb out the braid when she stopped. It
had been good to her, she thought. She would wear it for a
few more hours before she combed it out tonight. She

crammed the clothes with her books into a canvas bag and went outside.

This late in the afternoon, the school shuttles were long gone, and today she had no patience for the city bus. Home was just a mile and a half away, and she felt as if she could do handstands for a mile and a half. She began to walk.

It was by the dock that he saw her first. The sight of her made Sherk draw in his breath. So beautiful, he wanted to cry.

She walked out of a shop along the market square, near the foot of Main Street. Sherk watched from the truck, and remembered the vision of her running across the highway near Bowling Green, how real she had looked then. This time he had to be certain.

He idled the truck closer, leaning from the window, studying her. She was wearing that coat, that skirt, the uniform he had seen on others. He wondered briefly how she had come into that. Not that it mattered. As he watched, he became convinced that it really was her this time—not some teasing apparition, but truly Margaret.

Yes. People made room for her on the sidewalk. She occupied space. A boy on a skateboard jostled her as he wheeled past. This time she was real.

She was crossing an intersection, turning up a one-way street, leaving the harbor. Sherk called to her. She didn't turn her head. Too far, he thought; she couldn't hear.

A Chrysler pulled out of a metered space at the end of the block. Sherk hurried the truck into it, jumped out, and followed her as quickly as his legs would carry him.

The Caldwells lived on Hanover Street in a 260-year-old townhouse, across the street from the masonry wall that cloisters the U.S. Naval Academy from the rest of the world. It is an old and stately quarter of the city, and it has in abundance the charm and history and (above all) the age, that Annapolis prizes in its dwellings. In the entire city—for that matter, in all the state of Maryland—few neighborhoods are more desirable or expensive. Houses on

Hanover seldom reach the Multiple Listings, and when they do they quickly fetch prices that would stagger their original owners.

If she had walked directly home, Emily's route would have taken her above Main Street, past the State House that crowns the hill. She would have skirted the north end of the downtown district, and would have avoided the harbor altogether.

But she rarely avoided the harbor. It was too good to miss, the way the stores and boutiques shouldered one another on the sidewalk. Some of it she could do without: the galleries with their bronze seagulls and turgid sea-scapes, the novelty stores that sold "I Got Crabs in Anna-polis" sweatshirts, were strictly for the weekend crowd. But Ralph Lauren had a store at the dockside, and there was a Benetton shop around the corner; that was worth a detour.

She browsed for about half an hour. When she finally started for home, it was not out of boredom, but hunger. She hadn't eaten since lunch, and she knew that the left-overs of last night's linguini marinara would be in the refrigerator.

The trip from the dockside shops to the Caldwells' townhouse on Hanover is about a ten-minute walk. The boundaries of the commercial area are abrupt in that part of town, and within a couple of minutes after she had left the harbor, Emily was on a residential street where a low wind rustled the black oaks and sycamores overhanging the street.

There, about four blocks from home, she noticed the shouts for the first time. At first she didn't pay attention. The man's voice was shouting, "Margaret," and she was sure that he wanted someone else. But his voice got louder as he came up behind her, and she could see nobody else on the sidewalk.

"Margaret, stop!"

She looked around and saw the gaunt-faced man who would lope through her nightmares for the next six months. He was walking purposefully, arms and legs jerking him forward, propelling him toward her. His eyes connected with hers, and a chill overcame her when she realized that he wanted *her*.

"Margaret!" he shouted, and he waved a hand to stop her. She turned away. As if caught in a storm, she put her head down and clutched the canvas book bag to her chest, and she began to walk faster, resolutely.

His footsteps came thumping up the sidewalk behind her. She heard his voice again, even more urgent than before. It had a pleading note in it now: "Margaret, sweetheart . . ."

His footsteps were louder, shoes slapping the brickwork. Both of them were nearly running now as she approached the end of the block, an intersection.

"Margaret . . . Margaret . . . turn around, sweetie, it's me, it's your daddy."

She thought: I can't believe this is happening to me.

She was a few steps from the corner, hurrying, her head low so that he wouldn't catch her eyes again.

Halfway home, almost there.

Emily stepped off the curb. A car slewed around the corner, directly across her path. She pulled up quickly, leaned backward, felt a rush of air as the car rocked past her, inches away.

His hand came down on her shoulder, turning her about to face him.

"It's me," he said fiercely. "Look!"

"I don't know you." She tried to keep her voice calm.

He looked stunned, and groped for words. She tried to slip away, but the hand held her where she stood. His mouth moved without making a sound, and finally he spoke the name again: Margaret. It came out tenderly, and the moment struck her as inexpressibly sad.

But she was still frightened.

"I'm sorry, you're mistaken," she said. Her eyes shifted from side to side, looking up and down the street. No traffic this time. "I'm not Margaret. Please, give me back my arm. Thank you. I'm very sorry, but I'm not the person you want."

This seemed to astonish him. His grip relaxed. She turned on a heel and crossed the street, putting distance between them, listening for his footsteps, hearing only her own.

It was her, Sherk thought. It *was*. He had touched her, seen her, looked into her eyes.

He had imagined this moment a hundred different ways, but never once had it come out like this, Margaret looking at him as if he were a stranger, being frightened—oh, he had seen it, had felt her fear—being frightened and bolting away.

He found the truck still running where he had left it.

She didn't dare look around. But there were no more shouts and no more footsteps behind her, and soon she slowed. She was breathless. He had left her, whoever he was. A crazy man.

She wondered whether to tell her parents. No, she decided. No point. Daddy would just get nervous about her staying late for rehearsals. The man had made a mistake, that's all. Scary, but no harm done.

Home was close now. She was on King George Street, one block from Hanover. Bisecting the block was a cobblestone alley that ran between walled backyard gardens. During the last year, Emily had grown tall enough to look over the brickwork at the trellis roses and peonies and the clipped boxwood that sheltered behind the walls.

She turned down the alley. At the end of it she could see Hanover Street. She had gotten about halfway through when a blue pickup truck stopped momentarily on Hanover, then turned into the entrance, moving slowly in her direction. It was a wide truck in a passage built for carriages, and she moved to one side so that it could pass.

Sunlight was glaring off the windshield. She couldn't see the driver. As the truck approached, it rolled into a spot of tree shade.

Then she saw.

Oh God it's him. He's got me.

She turned and ran. The truck accelerated. She heard it gunning, closer, closer, and she flattened against a wall so that she wouldn't be run over. The truck roared past and she could see her pursuer's face, thin and grizzled and haunted.

She fled back toward Hanover. Blue smoke rose from the tires as he braked and stopped. She could smell the burned rubber. Behind her the truck's door opened, and his feet thumped the stones as he pursued her.

He was too fast. Before she could get ten steps down the alley he threw out a hand. It swiped her in the back, knocked her forward, and she sprawled. Before she could recover, he caught her by an arm and held tight.

"Margaret!" he said. "Look at me, baby, don't run away."

"Please . . ." She tried to twist free. "You're wrong. I'm not the one you want."

He shouted: "Don't do this to your daddy. Don't hurt me this way."

He was pulling her by one arm, pulling her to the truck. She fought against him, but his grip was strong and he was determined. Her heels dragged on the cobblestones.

"Somebody help," she cried, but it came out weakly.

Again: "Help me, somebody, please."

"We're going," he said, muttering now, impatient. She writhed and twisted but his grip was solid. He seemed insanely determined, and she told herself that this was stupid, this was't real, it couldn't happen.

"You're crazy," she gasped.

The words seemed to jolt him. He jerked her by the arm and flung her against the brick wall.

"Bad girl," he shouted. He was transformed. Until now he had seemed, by turns, confused and irritated and hurt. But now he was seething.

"You're a *bad* girl," he said, and the back of his right hand flashed out and cracked against her mouth.

His strength seemed multiplied by fury. With his right arm around her waist, he swept her up and carried her to the truck, and threw her into the cab. She lay across the seat. He shoved her to make room for himself.

Then she noticed the boys. Two teenagers had entered the alley at the far end, off Hanover. They were blocky and muscular kids, both wearing the mesh cutoff jerseys that were a favorite of young jocks. At that moment they seemed to notice the struggle in the truck, and they stopped, uncertain of what was happening and what they ought to do.

Her captor saw. When his head turned to them, she moved fast, pulling up the lock button, yanking back the door handle. He reached across the seat. Emily pushed against the door, and as his hand grabbed for her she tumbled out into the alley.

The truck sat between her and the boys, who were now approaching the truck in a hesitant trot. The King George end of the alley was open, but she knew that if she ran that way the gaunt-faced man would scoop her up again.

And there was the wall, about five feet high on both sides of the alley.

The gaunt man was stretching across the seat, his fingers inches away, closer, clutching for her.

Emily got up. She couldn't climb the wall, but she could scramble up on the hood of the truck. She did. He looked startled to see her there. The boys were running toward her now, and she knew that they would help her if she only gave them a few more seconds.

From the hood she looked down into the garden on the other side. One step up and over, and she was standing on the wall. The gaunt man got out of the truck and moved forward to catch her.

She jumped. She fell away from him, into the garden, landing in a low bush of daisies. She hit off balance and tumbled forward onto a brick patio. When she rose to hands and knees, she could see the screen door at the rear entrance of the house, and the back door half-open behind that. She ran for it without looking back.

Sherk watched her run. The two boys were still coming on, but Sherk couldn't look away from her.

An overwhelming sadness replaced his rage. His own daughter had looked at him with fear and hatred. That wasn't at all what he wanted.

His instinct was to chase her again. But he couldn't bear

any more humiliation. That look of fear in her eyes had cut too deeply.

The two boys came near, approaching at a careful walk. Puppies, Sherk thought. He snarled silently, and shot them a stare of such utter loathing that they stopped short and let him return to his truck. He got in and retreated up the alley to King George Street.

Terence Dean, a seven-year patrolman with the Annapolis Police Department, answered the call on Hanover Street. As he listened to the story he got the feeling that what had happened to the girl was an incomprehensible small part of something bigger. It was like following a baseball game by watching only the second baseman.

"You're sure he called you his daughter?" he said.

"Yes. No. Not exactly." Emily Caldwell, seated on a couch between her parents in the living room of their home, held an ice pack against her swollen right cheek. Her eyes were swollen and red from weeping, and she stammered slightly when she spoke. Gone was the poise that had impressed Sarah Stannard a few hours earlier. "What he said was, he was my father."

"That was the word he used?"

"That was what he said." Her breath came noisily. "No, wait a minute. He said, 'Don't do this to your daddy.' "

Dean lined out the word "father?" he had written in his spiral-bound notebook, and changed it to "daddy." That made more sense.

Carl Caldwell interrupted sharply: "Does it matter what word he used?" He was a tanned, trim man with a thirty-dollar haircut. Tennis all summer, Dean thought, and plenty of squash at the club.

"It matters," Dean said. " 'Daddy' can be slang. Sweetheart, sugar daddy, that kind of thing."

"No," Emily said. Her voice was stronger now. "He was too . . . I don't know, too plain . . . too plain to talk that way. You understand? Besides, I saw the way he looked at me. He believed I was his daughter. I'm sure of it."

If that was so, Dean thought, he was some father. His one blow had raised a livid welt on Emily's face. Dean wondered what the man might have done if he hadn't been interrupted.

"Could be he just made a mistake," Dean said. He felt the need to explain it, to understand. "Maybe he saw you from a distance, really did think you were his daughter, and got surprised when he had a good look at you."

She was shaking her head before he got the thought out.

"He looked straight at me the first time from closer than you are to me right now. The second time he stared right at me and he still held on. He had this terrible look in his eyes."

That was one of the things that bothered Dean. The school uniform set the girl apart; even from a distance she couldn't be just anyone.

"You never saw him before?"

Emily shook her head, and ice rattled in the bag.

He tried once more: "It's possible that he has a daughter who looks like you and goes to your school, and he just assumed . . ."

Emily smiled for the first time.

"Officer, you have to believe me," she said. "This was not somebody who'd have a daughter at Nordbrook School."

Dean repeated the physical description she had given him: blue pickup truck of unknown make, model and license; suspect about forty-five, six-two or slightly taller, slender and bony—"with crazy eyes and cheeks that sunk in," she added—wearing a red plaid flannel shirt and bib overalls. Dean had nothing more; the teenage boys had vanished.

The leather of his cartridge belt squeaked as Dean got up to leave.

"Can you catch this maniac?" her father said.

"We'll get the description out. The best possibility is to look for him in the harbor area, since that's a popular place and it's apparently where he saw your girl. His appearance is somewhat unusual. That's a help."

The truth was that his description would be mentioned at roll call briefings the next day. But he would soon be forgotten unless he repeated his act. Whatever that had been, Dean thought. Mistake a girl for his daughter? How often was that likely to happen?

Dean and Carl Caldwell went outside together. They stood on the sidewalk.

"I don't think you've got a lot to worry about," Dean said. "You might want to see that she doesn't go out alone for the next couple of weeks. And keep her away from the harbor for the time being."

Dean was in the car when the father leaned down and spoke to him through the open passenger window.

"Officer," he said, "what the hell happened in that alley?"

Dean wished he hadn't heard the question. He hated to come up short.

"I can give you the simple answer," he said. "Which is that your daughter is wrong about what she heard. In that case, the guy is a creep who tried too hard to pick up an underage girl. That's rotten, but it's no mystery. It happens."

"I believe her," Carl Caldwell said. "If she says the man called her his daughter, I believe her."

Dean also believed her, but he didn't want to admit it.

"If she's right," he said, "then I can't explain it. I'd just be groping, sir, that's the truth."

Terry Dean drove away dissatisfied. He believed that there were no truly inexplicable occurrences, only obscure ones. And the occasional obscure event fascinated him. He knew that he would toss this one around for a few days, until he got tired of feeling stupid.

Sherk sat up past midnight trying to figure what had happened. His head could work that way. Part of his mind was a stew of fantasy and illusion, while another part lived by rules of logic in the here-and-now. But it was all one mind, and the two parts met so seamlessly that Sherk couldn't tell them apart, and he had stopped trying.

So that night he reasoned the unreasonable.

He had found Margaret. That much he knew, and never questioned. But something had happened to her. She didn't know him, and she was scared of him, and there would be trouble if he wasn't careful. It was a cruel turn, but he couldn't change it.

He could leave or he could stay. Leaving was unthinkable, but if he stayed he would have to be cautious. Watch and wait. Sherk didn't know what came after waiting, but he would see.

He lay back in bed and turned out the light on the nightstand. He thought of the skirt, blouse and the burgundy jacket.

Margaret, he thought. My baby. You don't know it yet, but your daddy has found you.

Every time she shut her eyes to sleep, Emily Caldwell saw the gaunt-faced man, and felt his grip on her wrist, his knuckles cracking against her cheek.

Like Terry Dean, she wanted to understand. She had been there. She had heard the man and seen him, yet she still couldn't explain what had happened.

At some point in her sleepless night she recalled what Dean had suggested.

A daughter who looks like you and goes to your school.

For the first time she remembered the new girl who resembled her so closely. Emily had envied her self-assurance; it was much more real than her own protective bluster. But that girl's name was Sarah. And Emily could still hear every inflection of the gaunt man crying for Margaret, Margaret.

Besides, it was inconceivable that the father of a Brookie would act that way. Never.

So she put away the thought that there could be any connection between her assailant and the new girl who, in the right light, could have been her double. It was weeks before anyone mentioned it again.

—TEN—

THURSDAY
SEPTEMBER 6

FIVE Brookies stood at a street corner and waited for the Nordbrook morning shuttle. That summer a TV station in Baltimore had played reruns of "The Beverly Hillbillies," so when one of the girls nudged another and whispered, "Hey, look, Jed Clampett," they all knew what she meant.

The unshaven man in flannel shirt and bib overalls was crossing the street in their direction. He stopped in front of them.

" 'Scuse me," he said. "I noticed you was all wearin' the same jackets—" one of the girls giggled, thinking that he even sounded like a hillbilly "—and I was wonderin', is that a school uniform?"

Any one of them, alone, would have been frightened of him. But in a group they felt safe.

"Uh-huh," said the boldest. "Nordbrook School."

"And where's that?"

She told him the street address and gave him general directions.

"And when does school let out in the afternoons?"

"We get out at three."

"Well, thank you," he said. "I was just wonderin'."

He left them. Before he was across the street, one of the

girls hummed the first bar of the bluegrass banjo theme from *Deliverance,* and they all giggled again.

> WANTED: maintenance engineer. Local institution seeks experienced, stable individual with full range of mechanical, plumbing, and carpentry skills. Some janitorial and groundskeeping required. $900/mo. Apply in person 9–5 M–F to J. Davis, 220 Ivy, Annapls. EOE.

Two-twenty Ivy turned out to be the rectory of Saint Bartholomew's Catholic church, and J. Davis was a crew-cut young priest in a short-sleeved black shirt. He looked like a Marine recruit with a Roman collar. Sherk told him why he had come.

"Call me Father Jim," the priest said, pumping Sherk's hand. They went into the rectory's front room. It was expensively, neutrally furnished, like a model suite in a furniture store. On an end table, there was a small statuette of the Virgin Mary in blue and white robes, with her arms spread before her. Sherk felt some apprehension; he had known few Catholics, and the religion had always seemed mysterious and walled-off, a little threatening. He wasn't sure he wanted to work for a Catholic church.

"We're looking for a handyman," the priest said. He spoke with the residue of a drawl, slightly dragging his vowels. "That's what the job is, really. There are four priests here, including the monsignor, but building maintenance isn't something they teach at the seminary."

Sherk saw that this was supposed to be a joke. He gave a low grunt.

"Not that we'd have the time," the priest said. "We need somebody who can keep this place together."

Sherk briefly took in the room.

"I don't mean just the rectory," Davis said. "There's a church hall, a parish elementary school, a convent for the sisters. And the church, of course. It's a full-time job. There's always something to do, and hiring outside contractors is awful expensive. Makes much more sense to have someone here full-time. The more that person can do, the better for us.''

"With the right tools I can do almost anything," Sherk said.

The priest looked doubtful.

"There's painting," he said, "inside walls and exterior trim. Some of the plumbing is at least thirty years old, so you can imagine the problems. The heating system for the church and the hall is oil-fired steam heat, a real antique. And generally a few times a year we'll have some minor wiring to do.''

He paused, waiting for Sherk to protest the litany. Sherk said nothing and the priest plunged on. "The parish has two cars and a van that need routine maintenance. There are odd carpentry jobs. Also we prefer to avoid the expense of outside landscapers and gardeners. How much of all that can you handle?''

"I've done it all at one time or another," Sherk said. "Where I come from, you learn to do for yourself. I've always been real good at makin' things work.''

"Where is it," the priest said, "that you come from? I'm from Atlanta, but I don't place the accent.''

"Southwest corner of Virginia," Sherk said. "Near Kentucky and Tennessee. In the Appalachians.''

"And what brings you to Annapolis?''

Sherk's gaze narrowed briefly before he spoke. "I come to be near my daughter.''

"She's living apart from you now?" the priest said. "I'm sorry to hear that. You must love her a great deal to move yourself out here just for her.''

"That I do," Sherk said.

"Maybe I should give you the grand tour," the priest said. "Show you what you'd be getting yourself into.''

The parish grounds occupied an entire city block about a mile west of downtown Annapolis. There were five main buildings, as well as a garage and a shed. Rectory, school, and convent all faced in a row on Ivy Street. Behind them was a huge paved parking lot that also served as a school playground. Across the lake of asphalt were the church building and the parish hall, which fronted in the opposite direction, on Bellflower Street.

The priest led Sherk out the back door of the rectory, through the first floor of the school building, then across the parking lot. It was lunch hour and the asphalt was full of children, running and laughing and squealing; the priest told Sherk that the school had nearly five hundred students in eight grades.

They went into the back of the parish hall, a low brick structure built in 1950. The bluff gray walls of the church made it appear squat and ordinary.

Downstairs, the basement of the hall was close and dark, the ceiling low. The pipes and ducts of the heating system cast long, reaching shadows from a couple of bare light bulbs. It was a secluded place with the look of neglect and the smell of machinery, and Sherk immediately felt at ease. Beside one wall was a tool cabinet, and Sherk examined it briefly. He found a flashlight and studied the boiler, looked at the pressure gauges and tried the valves and finally told the priest that it was not so hard to understand; he could keep it working.

The priest wanted to know whether Sherk had come alone to Annapolis. Sherk said that he had. Had he found a permanent place to live yet? No, Sherk said. He was going to look today.

Then the priest led him to a one-room apartment across the basement. It was clean and plain, furnished with a cot and a dresser, a table and a couple of chairs. There was a hot plate and a toaster oven, and a bathroom with a shower. A mustiness in the air mingled with an odor of fuel oil from the boiler across the basement. But Sherk thought that he had seen worse places.

"The apartment goes with the job," the priest said. "You wouldn't have to use it. The last man to have the job was married, lived with his family, so it hasn't been used for a few years. Obviously it's to our advantage, having someone close like this. But you can save yourself at least a couple of hundred a month in rent."

Sherk didn't say anything. He still wasn't sure about working for priests.

"We'll take a quick look at the church," the priest said. Sherk followed him up into the hall, then through a covered passageway that connected the hall and the church.

They came out in the church sacristy. It was a small room off the altar. Sherk's eye caught an open closet full of vestments, robes of green and white and purple silk, embroidered in gold thread. The preacher at his church in Harben wore a blue serge suit for services.

One door from the sacristy opened out onto the altar. The door was open as they passed by it, and Sherk got a glimpse of a huge, raised slab of marble with a gold tabernacle situated in the middle. The priest led him through another door. This one took them out to one side of the church, behind a communion rail. The priest pushed the rail, and a section of it swung out. They stepped through it and walked out along the front pews.

Sherk was enthralled. First he stared at the altar. Behind it, raised on a pedestal, was a larger-than-life crucifix, and on the wall behind the crucifix was a mural that showed the Holy Trinity elevated in the clouds, far above the earth.

His eyes moved upward from there and followed the peak of the roof, dim and distant from where he stood. The place reminded him of a cavern, with far corners that never felt a human touch.

The priest was walking down the wide center aisle. Sherk followed a few feet behind him, his eyes still taking in the walls and the roof and the high windows and the dark brown woodwork. When they walked past the last pew, they were in the vestibule. This was a much smaller, more intimate space. Sherk was reminded of his church in Harben.

"The wood behind the plaster," said the priest, "is at least three hundred years old. This was the first Catholic church in the city. I suppose it meant too much to tear down, so when the main church went up—that's about a hundred and twenty years ago, give or take a few—they put the two churches together, somehow."

What had been done was obvious to Sherk. The big church had been built exactly against the back of the

chapel. The back wall of the chapel had been torn out, and
the front door enlarged. They had turned the old chapel
into a good-sized vestibule.

Sherk went back into the church. Its silent vastness
fascinated him. He could imagine himself passing many
hours in this moody quiet. Besides, it was the perfect job.
The priests had other concerns; he would be left alone, and
as long as the work got done he would not have to account
for his hours.

"I want the job," Sherk said as the priest came up
behind him. "I'm what you need, and I want the job."

They went into the rectory again. The priest had an
application form, and Sherk filled it out in an awkward
handwriting, pressing the ball point pen deep into the
paper.

The corridors at Nordbrook filled instantly at three that
afternoon, as they did every school day.

At that moment, Emily Caldwell was camped in front
of the television in her parents' home on Hanover Street.
Her mother, seeing the purple bruise that had blossomed
overnight on her cheek, had declared her unfit to be seen
in class.

While Emily switched channels to catch the opening
scenes of "General Hospital," Sarah Stannard was joining
nearly one hundred other Brookies who waited to board
the school's shuttle buses.

There were three shuttles. The first wound through
Annapolis without ever leaving the city limits. The second
headed over the South River Bridge and then into the
western suburbs. The third followed a route east and around
the peninsula that is bounded by the Severn and the Ma-
gothy rivers. This was the bus that Sarah would ride, the
last of the three that pulled up in the circular drive.

Three lines formed as the buses parked. Sarah took a
place in line and filed on with the others. She was mildly
surprised—pleased, but still surprised—that Elise hadn't
driven down to meet her after all.

It was a start, she thought. She had to grow up some
time.

• • •

By a quarter to three, Sherk had found a parking place across the street from Nordbrook.

He saw that the school was set back some distance from the street. About two hundred yards, he guessed. Sherk knew that he must be cautious, or there would be more trouble.

When the first burgundy blazers appeared on the front steps, he got out of the truck and crossed the road. He stood on the sidewalk. The view was distant, but unobstructed. He could make out individual faces across the lawn, and he was sure that he would be able to find Margaret when she appeared.

Three school buses turned into the driveway. At that moment he saw her on the top step, in the mass of girls who had formed around the circle drive. There was something different, he thought. Her hair. The braid was gone. For a moment he was unsettled, and he questioned whether this was Margaret. He wanted to rush up to her and look at her as closely as he had seen her yesterday. But he knew that he shouldn't get closer, and the doubt passed quickly. Even at this distance there was no mistaking her slender form and fine features, her ethereal loveliness.

The girls were forming three lines along the front steps. Margaret came down the steps and into the crowd, but he got a flash of the blond hair again as the bodies shifted.

Now the buses had reached the end of the drive, and were pulling up in front of the school. Margaret was in a line to board the last one. Sherk ran across the street. He got into his truck, waited as the buses filled, and started his engine as they headed back up the drive.

The buses reached the street and paused. The first turned right and drove down the street, away from Sherk. The second did the same. Sherk watched the third. It turned left, and swung beside him. He knew he would have no trouble keeping it in sight, so he let a couple of cars pass before he pulled out into traffic.

He followed it toward downtown, then across the Old Severn Bridge and into a wooded residential area beside the river. It made several stops. Each time Sherk watched the girls who got off the bus.

They were two or three minutes beyond the bridge when the bus's red brake lights shone, and the yellow flashers along the roof began to blink. The bus stopped, and so did the car behind it, and so did Sherk. There was a chuff of compressed air. The bus's front door flipped open and Margaret got out. Traffic was stopped in both directions; she ran across the highway.

The bus pulled away. Sherk drove slowly past. In his rearview mirror he saw her enter a grove of woods across the road. Today he was just watching. Today, and until he decided what he must do to reclaim her.

He pulled over to the shoulder of the highway and got out. There was a grassy hummock beside the road, and when he climbed it he could see that Margaret had crossed into a shady lane that entered onto the highway. It disappeared into a heavy stand of trees as it ran down toward the river. She was walking nonchalantly now, unaware of him, arms swinging at her sides. It took all his strength to restrain himself from calling out her name. But he kept silent, and watched her from the hummock until she was gone.

Then he looked around for landmarks. He would want to find this place again.

Jim Davis found the monsignor in his rectory office, wolfing a slice of chocolate cake. On his desk was a tumbler of milk. Frank Herrity was a small, round man with a chipmunk's cheeks, a serene omnivore who was perpetually either beginning or breaking a diet.

"Come in, Father," the monsignor said around a mouthful of cake. He put down the plate. "Come in, and please close the door behind you. Yvonne will be merciless if she finds that I've been cheating."

Yvonne was the housekeeper, a French-Canadian grandmother who supervised his diets with the light touch of a Torquemada. Herrity sometimes said that he was indifferent to the archbishop, respectful of the Pontiff, and terrified of Yvonne Duranleau.

"Sit down," Herrity said. "What can I do for you, Father?"

"Monsignor, I think I've found a handyman," Davis said. "He answered the ad in the paper."

He held out Sherk's application. Herrity took the form and looked at it for a few seconds.

"Feel the air conditioning," Davis said. He put a hand under the duct opening that was above the monsignor's desk. "Feel how cold it is."

"It feels good."

"You mentioned a few days ago that it didn't seem to be keeping the house cool."

"It didn't."

"He noticed the same thing, and he told me he'd fix it. He found a tank of Freon gas in the basement of the hall, and brought the system up to pressure. And then he replaced the filter. He said it hadn't been changed in months, that somebody must have forgotten it."

"I didn't know it had a filter," the monsignor said.

"He knew," Davis said. "He says he can fix anything." He imitated Sherk's pronunciation of these last two words: *fee-yux ainuh-thun* was how he said it. "He's down from the hills, Virginia, and he looks it."

"Family?"

"A daughter living here. He says that he came here because of her. He'd use the apartment in the hall basement."

Herrity's brows lifted. "That would be a convenience, wouldn't it? We'd have to be careful that we didn't abuse it, Father. This place would occupy a man all day and night if we let it, and there are laws against indentured servitude."

Herrity looked down at the form again.

"He's a Baptist," Davis said.

"I noticed." Sherk had listed the pastor of his church among his references. "Father, it's an ecumenical age. Besides, if you were stuck on a ledge, who would you want to rescue you, a Baptist with a long rope, or a good Catholic with nothing but a prayer?"

"I told him it wouldn't matter. I also said that you'd

want to meet him, and that if you approved, the job was his.''

"Not necessary. He can start tomorrow, if you think he's a good man.''

He looked closer at the priest.

"You do think he's a good man, Father?''

Davis didn't answer at first. The truth was that for all his salesman's heartiness, people didn't open up to him quickly, and he was slow—too slow—to get a feel for others. It meant going through life at arm's length, which was not the best way to judge character.

He answered after a few seconds: "I believe so.''

"Then you should hire him.''

Down the hall a woman shouted. "Someone's been into the cake! Oh, no, Monsignor, not again.''

"The woman is astounding," Herrity said. "Clairvoyant. How does she do it?''

Davis watched him hide the plate of cake in a desk drawer. The glass of milk he put behind a potted *ficus*. They could hear her steps coming up the hall. The monsignor patted his pockets for a handkerchief, and when he found none he wiped his mouth with the sleeve of his cassock.

"Don't hide in there," she said from the other side of the door. "I know what you've been up to. I told you the cake was for those who can have it.''

"Yvonne, you don't have to stand out in the hall and shout," the monsignor said. "Come in—Father, open the door for her—come in and let me see your friendly face.''

Davis let himself out of the office. That evening he realized that he had left Sherk's application with the monsignor. He told himself that he should retrieve it in the morning. He wanted to call the Baptist minister to ask about Sherk. But he was busy the next day. He never saw the application again, and he never did call.

This time when she screamed Sherk didn't awaken immediately. It was the same as before, a dream that didn't feel like a dream, but when Margaret shrieked so horribly this time, he had to keep watching. He saw that she was terrified of something—no, of some *person*—he could not see. A horror was about to occur, and Margaret knew it, and there was nothing he could do to help her.

A hand gripped her throat, and she screamed again, and only then he woke, sick and shaken.

He wished he could have seen more. The dream was horrible, but somehow it was important. He wanted to see more, so that he could understand it.

Next time, he thought, he would try not to wake up. He didn't know if that was possible in a dream, but he would try. There was something inside him, hidden, trying to get out. And he had to see it.

—ELEVEN—

THURSDAY
NOVEMBER 1

HOWARD Warner was late for his best friend's retirement party. Half an hour before the end of his shift he answered a call on an armed robbery of a liquor store in Tyler Heights, and it ate up the time he had planned to spend taking a shower and changing clothes. By the time he was finished at the liquor store he was already an hour behind, so he drove straight to the VFW hall where Frank Gephardt was having his send-off.

He was disheveled and he knew that he was rank. But he also knew that Gephardt would understand. Gephardt had seen him in much worse shape.

The hall was a flat-roofed cinder-block building behind a cemetery. Perfect, Warner thought. When he pulled into the parking lot behind the hall, he noticed a panel truck belonging to a crab house. Also perfect. Warner couldn't remember the last retirement party for an Annapolis cop that hadn't been held in a cinder-block hall, catered by a crab house.

He got out of the car and walked toward the hall. Once he had been an athlete, and he still had an athlete's step: weight forward, arms swinging in measured arcs at the sides, head up. The suggestion of control and pent-up power was still there, though his body was far from lithe.

His chest, always broad, no longer tapered down to meet the hips, the way it once had. His neck was half a size thicker than it had been the year before, and his butt looked the way any forty-six-year-old butt will look when it spends most of its time in an office chair or the front seat of an automobile. At this point, he figured, he was fighting to hold the line, nothing more. Two things he would never be again: young and slim.

He stopped outside the front door of the hall and listened to the noise that came through an open window, laughter and garbled conversation that sounded like static on the radio. Only an effort of will kept him from going back to the car and driving away. Anybody else's party, he would have left.

Warner had dreaded this evening since Gephardt announced that he had decided to take early retirement at age fifty-five. He didn't want Gephardt to leave. He was nine years younger than Gephardt, and Warner had always seen in him a vision of what he himself would be in a few years. So the idea of Gephardt getting tired and kissing it all away—which he had been doing, by degrees, for the last few years—was unsettling for Warner, nothing to celebrate.

He went inside. The door opened on a reception room with a bar along one end. Most of the guests had left to pick out chairs in the dining room. At least half of the Annapolis police department was there, and some from the Anne Arundel County force—more than a hundred cops, plus friends and mates.

Warner found Gephardt at the bar, tossing back the dregs of a highball. Gephardt grinned when he saw him.

"Damn, boy, I didn't think you'd make it."

"Duty calls."

Gephardt made a derisive snort and raised the empty glass in a toast.

"The good old P.D.," he said. "Last refuge of the all-day sucker."

Gephardt was already a little drunk, a little loud. He lurched off the bar stool. Warner reached out and steadied him. The linoleum floor was slippery with beer.

"Son, shall we make our entrance?" Gephardt said. He curled an arm around Warner's neck and they walked into the dining room. On the walls were photographs of Gephardt, enlarged to poster size. They showed an American Legion baseball player, a Marine in Korea, a father balancing his four-year-old girl on the hood of a Studebaker. Warner had a hard time looking at the thin-waisted, dark-haired man in the pictures. He had an especially hard time with the one that showed a proud rookie patrolman wearing his badge the way a new mother carries her baby.

They reached the table where the chief of police was sitting with the captain of detectives. The chief motioned Warner toward an empty chair beside him.

"No way," Gephardt roared, and he locked his arm around Warner's neck. "I ain't letting you waste your time with the brass asses. This is my party. You're sitting with the good folks tonight."

Warner let himself be led to a chair at the head table. There sat Gephardt's wife, and his two married daughters with their husbands. Warner felt that he belonged with Gephardt's family. The two men had worked the last fourteen years as detective partners, and they had shared more, done more together, than most brothers. After he got divorced in 1978, Warner had found himself eating two or three dinners a week with the Gephardts. It was still a rare month when he did not spend at least one evening with Frank and Alice at their home. Now he kissed Alice, kissed each of the girls on the cheek, shook hands with their husbands. He sat down and made small talk and pretended that tonight was not the end of something that mattered.

Soon the waiters brought the first crabs, a half-bushel basket for each table. For about an hour they all cracked crabs with wooden mallets, and tore the meat out of the broken shells, and drank pitchers of beer. The waiters kept running into the kitchen carrying crab waste and empty pitchers and running out with the baskets and the pitchers full.

Dinner ended too soon for Warner. After the beer and the crabs came speeches, and he hated that part. Only dead

cops and going-away cops got speeches, and he wasn't
ready to think about Gephardt either way yet. It was awful:
beery detectives telling stories that they had all heard a
dozen times, wandering reminiscences full of used-to-be
and do-you-remember, and then, worst of all, the chief and
a city councilman telling Gephardt what a credit he had
been to the force and how much the city would miss him.

Even Warner had to take his turn; the chief had insisted
that he present Gephardt with his retirement gift. He started
by saying that Annapolis wasn't good enough for Frank
Gephardt now; he and Alice had sold their home and
bought a bungalow on the Eastern Shore, Talbot County,
and instead of chasing bad guys he was going to go after
the real big ones. Warner asked Gephardt if he was going
to read the Miranda to every rockfish that he hooked, and
then a couple of uniforms carried in the new Evinrude
outboard motor that they had all bought. That gave Warner
a chance to escape. He went out a side door of the hall to a
narrow deck that looked over the cemetery.

For a while he was alone, leaning his elbows against a
railing. He watched a half moon rise on the eastern horizon, coming up out of the weeds that grew along the
cemetery fence. Warner saw that it was not a well-kept
cemetery.

The door opened behind him.

"Hey," Gephardt said. "You like the company better
out here?"

Warner made a waving movement with one hand:
"You know, Frank, all the smoke . . ."

"And the hot air," Gephardt said.

"That too."

Gephardt held up two snifters with a deep amber liquid
inside. "I got just the cure."

Warner took one of the snifters and brought it to his
nose. It was cognac; the fumes warmed the back of his
throat. They tapped the glasses together, and Warner said,
"To your new life," and they sipped.

Warner swallowed and looked out at the moon and
said, "You lousy son of a bitch, why'd you have to go
quit on me?"

Gephardt looked amused. It was the first time Warner had been able to talk about this.

"It was time," he said. "Couldn't you tell? You never once noticed that Frank Gephardt wasn't quite the same bad-ass crook-chasing cop he used to be?"

"We all change," Warner said.

"I changed all right. I started thinking. A very dangerous practice. I started thinking that if I stayed here for the rest of my life playing good guys and bad guys, where would it get me? What difference would it make?"

"You're a cop," Warner said. "Cops are supposed to make a difference."

"And you," Gephardt said, "are old enough to recognize a lie like that one when it comes around."

Gephardt tasted the cognac before he spoke again.

"I worked like a bastard for thirty years," he said. He smiled and shrugged. "Okay, twenty-five. Maybe I have been skating by just a little, these last few. The old bones get tired. But I'll tell you. I earned this time and I'm gonna enjoy it. Sit in the sun, grow some tomatoes, kill some fish. I might even get a chance to talk with my wife once in a while."

"I know you. You're going to miss it. It's part of you, and you'll be sorry you ever left."

"Nope. I know the signs. When you stop caring, that's the time to give 'em back their damn badge and let another cowboy have a go at it."

His face took on a smile—a smirk, almost—that made Warner uncomfortable.

"B'sides," he said. "It's done. All washed and put out to dry. Who you trying to convince? Me? Or yourself?"

Warner took a long swallow so that he wouldn't have to answer. At that moment he decided to get drunk. For Warner, getting drunk was like buying a new sportcoat. He didn't do it often, and never without good reason and some deliberation. He had been thinking about it for an hour.

He drained the glass and held it out again.

"Frank," he said, "I believe that I'd like to get the top of my head ripped off tonight."

"Howard, I believe I'm going to do the same. Let's hope the movers don't come too early in the morning."

"Movers?" Warner couldn't believe it. "Already?"

"We didn't buy that place to let it sit empty."

"You're on two days next week."

"Didn't I tell you? They found twenty hours of annual leave somewhere. I come in Saturday morning, clean out my desk, that's it."

It was all happening so fast, Warner thought.

"You're going to be gone," he said, as if this were some revelation.

"That, buddy-boy, is the whole idea."

Their cognac was almost gone. Gephardt went in for some more, and returned with a bottle of ouzo. It wasn't so bad, he said. After the first couple of drinks you barely taste it.

The rest of the night passed in a series of brief blackout skits. There was Gephardt clamping the Evinrude to a table so that he could try it, getting himself sweaty and red in the face pulling the starter cord until somebody convinced him that it needed gas and oil to run. There was Warner trying to talk the captain of detectives into an arm-wrestling match, and getting only a thin sober smile. There was Gephardt with his arms around Alice, singing "Let Me Call You Sweetheart," and Warner joining in with his arms around both of them. There was Warner finding the lavatory full, going outside, pissing into the weeds around the unkempt cemetery. And looking up at the moon that was now high over head, yelling hoarsely up at it, cursing the way it kept moving across the sky. Cursing time, shouting about the way it puts the screws to you, it never lets up, what a ballbuster it is.

—TWELVE—

FRIDAY
NOVEMBER 2

THERE he was again. Seven minutes before three in the afternoon, and there was Sherk leaving.

From his office in the rectory, the monsignor could see the parking lot between the church and the rectory. For the fourth time in as many days he had watched Sherk walk out of the church hall and go to his pickup truck, which was parked on a small patch of asphalt between the hall and an entrance to the church parking lot.

Each day it had happened at the same time, just before three in the afternoon. Each day Sherk had driven across the parking lot to the same exit, and had turned left. He remembered having seen Sherk leave like this, at about the same time, several times in the last few weeks. But it had never struck him until this week.

The monsignor liked to think that not much around him went unnoticed and unexamined, and Sherk was by far the most intriguing new figure to have entered his world in some while. They had spoken several times. He reminded the monsignor of an iceberg, hard and stolid.

Now here he was, once again driving off. The monsignor wondered what duty might move him so regularly, so punctually. What did the church need every day at three? Nothing, as far as he knew. What happened every day at three? A plane arriving? A TV show? Didn't make sense.

90

He turned away from the window as Sherk's truck disappeared in traffic. He could easily, happily, have lost an hour in such mental recreation. But there was work on his desk, and he reminded himself that a monsignor of the church—of all people—should be willing to abide some of life's mysteries, great and small.

"Sarah! Hey, Stannard!"

Sarah stopped in the main corridor and turned toward the sound. She was in the middle of the corridor, and was jostled by the torrent of girls seeking the exits.

"Stannard!"

Sarah saw her then: a girl named Stephanie, who sat beside her in home room. They talked and studied together every day. And a popular girl, with plenty of friends. She was standing in a classroom door; Sarah went over to her.

"Want to come bum around?" the girl said. "My older sister, the one that's a junior, she got to drive in today 'cause she had to go to the dentist at lunch hour. So we've got it the rest of the afternoon."

"The three of us?"

"And a couple others. We're just gonna go up to the shopping center and hang out with all the other mall rats."

It didn't matter what they did, Sarah thought. It just sounded good, the freedom.

"I don't think I can," Sarah said. "My mother . . . you know how mothers are."

"Call her."

But it would be such trouble, Sarah thought. Explaining who she would be with and what they were going to do. Elise didn't like spur-of-the-moment decisions.

"She'll just hassle me," Sarah said.

"Then don't tell her. We won't be gone long. We'll get you home by four-thirty, quarter of five at the latest. She can't complain about that."

"You have to be kidding," Sarah said. The idea was laughable. "She'd go crazy if I tried that."

"You can't come?"

"If I knew a day ahead of time, I could clear it with her. It wouldn't be a problem."

"But it doesn't always work out that way," Stephanie said. "That's the breaks, huh? Maybe another time."

She went out through the crowd, across the corridor to the rear exit that opened out to the student parking area. Sarah watched her leave, then stepped out into the hall and got pushed along to the front door.

Sherk parked his truck beside the Ritchie Highway, about three hundred yards south of the spot where the school bus stopped every afternoon. On the other side of the road was a stand of forest. Sherk crossed over, straight to a narrow trail that ran in among the trees, virtually invisible.

Sherk took the trail into the woods. He found his spot, behind a berry bush. There he crouched and waited.

To Sarah, the best part of her new home was a path of packed gravel called Whittier Lane, a half-mile strip of private road that ran among the trees between her grandparents' home and Ritchie Highway. It was quiet and shaded, and the few minutes she spent alone on it every afternoon were often the most pleasant of her day.

It was 3:20 when (as she did every weekday) she got off the school shuttle, crossed the highway, and entered the lane. Surrounding it, in some places blocking out the sky, were maples and pin oaks, and some evergreens as well. Among the trees it was easy to pretend that she was in Vermont, walking through one of the green forests that she loved.

This afternoon, as always, the road was empty. She took off her blazer; the day was warm and still. As she walked, gray squirrels chittered urgently across the gravel in front of her, hurrying into the cover of the brush.

Her grandparents' home was the southernmost of six twenty-acre lots arrayed side-by-side along the east bank of the Severn. Each tract fronted the river and extended back to Ritchie Highway. Sprawling across the rear of the properties was a wooded grove, half a mile long and more than two hundred feet deep in places, preserved as a buffer between the highway and the six big homes along the river. It smothered noise from the road and obliterated all sight of traffic.

Whittier Lane cut through the grove, across the back of each lot. It was a common right-of-way, and every few hundred feet a bluestone driveway joined the lane and ran west to one of the homes owned by families named Burke and Marquardt, Allison, Henry, and Harrison.

The lane was built around the contours of the property, and by now she knew every twist in it. She knew the woods were thinnest near the Marquardts' home, where the lane approached the west end of the grove. Past that point, as she walked south, the lane swung left and into the heart of the woods, tunneling through the foliage. It was a still, secluded spot, deeply shaded by a growth that was almost tropical. Here even the birds were subdued.

Now she approached that tunnel through the trees and the bush. She shivered inwardly. A tune worked its way into her head. She hummed it at first, then quietly sang. That seemed to dispel the gloom. Her pace picked up, and she hurried forward through the forest.

Sullen and disconsolate, Sherk crouched in the brush and waited. Berry bushes and tall grass grew thick along the edge of the lane, and Sherk knew that he was perfectly concealed. He had tried several spots, but this one was best. It had heavy cover and a good view for nearly thirty yards in both directions, and it was easily reached from the highway, where he parked his truck.

It reminded Sherk of deer hunting in the woods. You didn't just go out and get a deer. First you had to watch the deer, learn where they fed and watered. You had to know their habits. Then you found a place along their path where you could stay hidden, where you knew they would pass close by. He was good at that. Sherk always had his buck picked out a month before hunting season. On opening day, he would be back home in time for lunch, with the deer hung out back, bled and gutted.

He was on one knee in the brush, hunched over. Cautiously he lifted a berry leaf so that he could see the lane more clearly. He knew that she ought to be along any time now. This was like deer hunting in another way: the anticipation, the barely contained excitement that grew in him as the moment approached.

There was something else, too. He felt the fire. Not as big as before, but a tiny candle-flame that licked at him, too hot to ignore. It had come upon him these last few days as he hid to watch his daughter. He knew why it had returned. It was from wanting Margaret so fiercely.

He heard footsteps; his daughter appeared from around a bend in the lane. Sherk did not question that this was Margaret. The girl who now came toward him, kicking a pebble in front of her and singing to herself, had become the Margaret of his memory and his imagination.

She was closer now. Sometimes she passed him on the far side of the lane, but today he could see that her path was going to bring her within an arm's length of where he hid. Her singing was louder now, and then she was in front of him, so close he could see only the gray of her skirt as she went by. It took all his effort to remain still.

He watched her stride away. Sherk's vision blurred moistly. She stopped to watch a squirrel dart across the lane, and she went on. The lane curved away and the foliage swallowed her up. She was gone.

Sherk didn't move at first. He let his eyes clear and he waited to be sure she wouldn't return.

At first these moments in the woods had been only joyful. He was seeing Margaret again, and that was enough. But now he needed more. The past few days, he had barely restrained himself from rushing out of the bushes and taking her. Still fresh in his mind was the shock and shame he had felt when she ran from him in Annapolis. He couldn't bear such humiliation again.

And yet he was tempted. The little red flicker was in him, reminding him of its presence. He knew by now that it was never far from the surface, ready to test his restraint.

It wasn't fair, he thought. He had found his daughter, but he couldn't have her.

She wasn't coming back today, Sherk knew. She never did. He got up and picked his way through the underbrush, back to the trail and the highway.

• • •

When it bent toward the Stannard home, the lane broke out of the denseness, and the forest opened up slightly and let in some more light. Sarah felt better as she hurried out of the shade. That short stretch in the depth of the woods—it couldn't have been more than a hundred yards—was the only part of the walk that she didn't truly enjoy. She got a creepy feeling there, and she couldn't help it.

Now the lane turned toward the river. The forest fell away on both sides, and presented Harry Stannard's showpiece colonial, his tennis court and his swimming pool, all arrayed on the putting-green lawn. Sarah was hungry; the walk always seemed to put a fine edge on her afternoon appetite. She hurried up to the house and ran into the kitchen entrance of the new wing.

Sherk returned to work forlorn and angry. He was installing doors on classroom cabinets in the school, a rote job that let his mind return to the lane. She had come so close this time, unaware; if he had only extended an arm he would have touched her. His effort to remain still had been excruciating.

The job went quickly in the empty classroom, and in a few minutes Sherk was tightening the hinge screws with a thin, sharp-bladed screwdriver. He thought about having a daughter who didn't know him, who feared him and would scream at the sight of him, the unfairness of it. It made his hands sweat as he turned in the last screw. He stared vacantly into the cabinet, and all the tension of hiding in the woods, all his maddening frustration, seemed to flow up through his right arm and into his hand.

He shifted his grip on the screwdriver, holding it as if it were an ice pick. Slowly he raised it shoulder-high, and he drove it down hard into the oak veneer of the new door. It made a deep gash. The blade came up once more, and once more slashed deep into the wood. Sherk felt as if he were watching this from a distance, the arm and the hand beyond his control as they raised up and flashed down. Again. Again. Again.

He stopped. The door was broken and splintered. Sherk

let his breathing subside. Then he removed the hinge that held the broken door. He gathered all the scraps and pieces, and he carried them to a waste bin outside. Then he walked across the parking lot to the church. He knew a place that would ease his mind, a soothing place, and he needed to be there now.

"He's strange," Yvonne Duranleau said. "I'm telling you, he's a queer one."

"The man's sexual tastes are between him and the Lord," the monsignor told her.

"The things you say! I don't mean that, and you know it. I'm talking about that face of his. It looks like he's hiding something. You can see right through an honest man. But not that one, not him."

They were in Herrity's office, watching Sherk leave the school with his tool box. The monsignor was at his desk, the housekeeper ostensibly dusting bookshelves behind him. But her eyes never left Sherk.

"He's reserved," the monsignor said. "No harm in that."

"He looks like he's dried up inside. And to talk to him—half the·time it's like he's not there. I don't like him, that's all. I'm sorry he ever came here."

"He's a good worker, Yvonne."

"I still wish he had never showed up." Sherk was walking out of sight around the church. "I'm telling you. He's trouble, that one."

There were two steps up to the door of the vestibule. Sherk wriggled into the tight space beneath them. He pushed aside several loose boards that lay across the stone foundation, revealing in the masonry a rectangular opening that was barely wide enough for his hips and shoulders. He slid his legs in first, and then pulled his upper body through, head and shoulders disappearing into the maw.

His feet dropped and then touched solid ground. He straightened.

He was standing in a cellar beneath the vestibule, the old chapel. The floor was packed dirt, the walls identical to the mortared stone of the foundation. Above him were the vestibule's exposed floor joists, where cobwebs hung so thick they seemed a solid fabric. The cellar was crypt-like, the air cool and undisturbed.

Sherk sat cross-legged on the floor, comfortable in the darkness and the emptiness. He could be alone here. Really alone. It was unlikely that anyone else knew of this spot. When he had opened it the first time—expecting to find a crawl space where he might store some tools—the boards across the entrance had been fastened with square-cut nails, old-fashioned nails. At least fifty years old, was his guess. It meant that whoever had sealed up the entrance was probably dead, the cellar long forgotten. Certainly none of the priests suspected its existence; since his first day, he had been astonished by how little they knew about the building where they worked and prayed. No, this was his alone.

He let his mind drift, let the quiet overtake him. He must have dozed, he told himself later. Because as he sat there in the darkness, his dream returned.

It started differently this time, but he recognized the peculiar feel of it, the strange texture that was unlike any other dream he had ever known.

Somebody was up on a hill, looking down at the cabin. Waiting. Waiting for Margaret. Thinking about what he was going to do to her.

Sherk couldn't see the face, but somehow he felt the malevolence inside this evil man up on the hill.

There was Margaret, getting out of a car, laughing, skipping up into the cabin. Up on the hill, the evil one was thinking, Bad girl. Bad bad girl, then starting down toward the cabin.

Sherk tried to shout, Run! to the dream-Margaret in the cabin. But he knew that she couldn't hear, that he was powerless to interfere in what was taking place.

Now the evil one was pausing on the front porch. Now walking through the front door. Now standing over Margaret as she sat paralyzed in a chair. Now shouting at her as she tried to talk. Now slapping her hard across the face, coldly snapping her head to the side.

*He bent over her, his lips moving, saying, Why do you
make me do these things?*

*His hands were on Margaret's arms. He raised them,
rested them lightly on her throat. The fingers tightened.
She screamed. The fingers got tighter and she screamed
again.*

Sherk writhed in the dirt and somehow escaped from the
dream. He felt sick, wanted to retch.

He had seen much more this time, but he knew that
there was still more to see. It was inside his head somehow, behind a door, pounding to get out, awful stuff.

Sherk wanted to tell himself that it was just a dream.
But from the start it had never felt like any other dream.

And this time he could not remember having fallen
asleep.

—THIRTEEN—

FRIDAY
NOVEMBER 2

THE captain of detectives—his name was Blatchford—peeled back his upper lip in a mirthless parody of a smile, exposing a row of perfect teeth. Warner found it a frightening display.

"So, Howard, you survived. Last night I'd have made it eight-to-five, against."

Supposedly this was said in jest. Warner tried to return a grin.

"I guess things got a little loose," Warner said, wondering whether Blatchford remembered the arm-wrestling episode. Then he thought: sure he remembers. *He* was sober.

"Well. Nothing wrong with some occasional comradely horseplay," the captain said, "within limits."

The smile vanished, and Warner understood that this was his way of moving past preliminaries, of getting serious. They were in the captain's office, seated at opposite sides of a desk. The captain leaned forward in his swivel chair, hands clasped in front of him. He was a small, trim man, a couple of years younger than Warner, unbelievably dapper. He wore three-piece suits that fit him close to the body, double-vented in the back, never a wrinkle. He looked like a little French banker.

"I thought we ought to have a talk," the captain said. "With Frank gone, there'll have to be some changes. Adjustments, you might say. Obviously you'll be the most immediately affected."

Warner tried to concentrate on the words, not easy to do this morning. But this sounded ominous.

"It may be a while before we fill the position, at least full time. That means we'll all have to pull a little harder to take up the slack. I'd go so far as to say you might have a little farther to pull than others."

"Wait a minute. I work hard." Warner sounded more defensive than he wanted.

The captain sat back in his chair and looked directly at him for several seconds.

"I don't want to be harsh," the captain said. "But I think we'd both agree that Frank Gephardt has not exactly been . . . how do I put this? . . . a dynamo. A whirlwind of enthusiasm. After a while that has to reflect on his partner." Again he exposed his teeth without a sound. Warner remembered what Gephardt used to say whenever anyone complained about the captain: Don't speak ill of the deadly.

The captain shifted forward again, and spread his palms up on the table.

"Don't get me wrong, Howard. I'm not accusing you. But bad habits are contagious. I can understand how difficult it might be to keep playing hard when your partner really isn't in the game. I can appreciate that."

"You're talking about my friend," Warner said.

The captain shook his head.

"Not at all. Frank Gephardt's gone. And the point is, the people who are left will have to do that much more if we're going to keep up to standards. I'm sure that you'll do your part." Saying this as if he was sure of no such thing.

He looked away, picked a piece of lint off a blue flannel sleeve, and flicked it into the air before he returned to Warner.

"I give Frank full marks in one respect," he said. "He knew that when you lose the fire in your belly, it's time to get out.'' He looked directly at Warner. "Otherwise you're cheating everybody. The force, the city, yourself.''

Warner's shift ended at six. He was typing reports at six-fifteen when the captain went home, giving him a curt nod and that arid, passionless smile as he marched out.

Warner was a two-finger typist, sloppy but fast. His big forefingers jumped at the board of a Royal manual, pouncing on the keys. As he typed he heard the captain talking about fire in the belly. The captain wanted to hang him because he was no longer a crusader. And it was true. Nobody could keep that up.

Fire in the belly. A fine phrase. But you couldn't let the job eat at you. You didn't see doctors constantly agonizing. Or lawyers losing sleep. Was a cop any different, wanting to do the job and then leave it alone? It didn't mean you were a jerk. Just realistic.

His fingers pounded the keys harder, perforating the page. Fire in the belly. Some nerve.

He finished the report, filed it, and left for home. He was still thinking about the captain's lecture, the part about cheating the city. That didn't anger him as much as it hurt. He cared about the city. He didn't like to throw the word around, but he would go so far as to say that he loved Annapolis, the feeling was that strong. And it wasn't some superficial infatuation. Cops know their cities better than anyone—they see it all—and after twenty-one years as a cop there Warner knew Annapolis without illusion.

On one level there was the Annapolis of the weekend tourist, the cobbled streets, store windows full of antiques and nautical brass, classic colonial architecture, light opera midshipmen, sailboats rocking at their berths, all as perfectly composed as a stage set. Warner wasn't immune to the charm. He could remember dawns of unreal perfection—the streets empty, the air clear and the early light pure—when the city seemed to await the lifting of a curtain.

But for Warner that was a rare delight, not because he didn't enjoy the beauty, but because he had seen too much besides.

Such as the woman who had lived in the magnificent

colonial near Maryland Avenue, a spectacular place that appears in all the guidebooks. Tourists collect at its iron fence, snapping pictures and exclaiming at the flawless hedges, the fluted doorposts, the intricate cornice at the roofline. Warner had been in the house once, his second year as a patrolman, and he had cut down the body of a woman who had hung herself from a bannister. She had worn a purple bathrobe. While suffocating she had grabbed handfuls of the terrycloth fabric, and the terrible desperation of that gesture had shocked Warner. He drove past the house at least three or four times a week, but even now when he looked at it he couldn't see the gardens or the fluted columns without also seeing the woman's dead fingers clutching her bathrobe.

Dozens of associations tinged his view of the colonial houses and the old brick and the cobblestones. So in a way it had been spoiled for him. He had been denied that unsullied ignorance which is the first necessity of a happy sightseer.

But for all that he had seen and learned, he still cared about the city, not with a weekend infatuation but with the deep and knowing appreciation of an old lover. He knew that it was not a gingerbread village that would molder when the tourists departed. Annapolis had foundations which no seasonal squall of visitors would ever shake.

Cheating the force and the city. Boy, that hurt. He wanted to tell the captain that only three things were really important in his life. Two of them were the force and the city. The third was *Amaranth*. For a couple of days, anyway, he was setting aside the first two. Now he was going to see *Amaranth*.

He pulled into the parking lot of a marina on the South River. This was always one of the best moments of his existence, stepping out of an imperfect world into one where he had never been disappointed, never left empty. Here *Amaranth* waited.

She was at the end of the dock: a 38-foot aft cockpit sloop, trimmed in deep brown teak. Warner stepped aboard, placing his feet carefully so that the heels of his street shoes wouldn't leave a mark on the white fiberglass. As always, he looked around anxiously to be sure all was well with her; nothing was amiss. He unlocked the cabin and went in.

The air was stale. Warner slid open the two slit port-holes and cracked the ventilation hatch overhead. A power boat droned by in the harbor and in a few seconds its wake was slapping against the hull as Warner undressed and hung his clothes out of sight. He quickly put on corduroys and a cotton pullover, and he came up into the sunlight.

On a cop's salary, a 38-foot sailboat is a remarkable extravagance. Warner had swung the deal six years earlier, when he sold his house to settle accounts with his ex-wife. His share of the profts had made a good down payment on the boat, and he eked out the monthly installments. Except for the boat, he lived frugally. He had a studio apartment, and when he wasn't driving the city's car, he got by with a nine-year-old Toyota. For *Amaranth* he would have sacri-ficed a great deal more.

In four years his loan on the boat would be paid. At the same time he would have twenty-five years in. He would be fifty. Warner had never taken *Amaranth* out of the bay, but she was built for blue-water sailing. She could be sailed around the world single-handed, if the one hand was up to the job.

For now he had the weekend. The forecast was fair weather, warmer than seasonable, maybe the last weekend of the year when sailing would be a pleasure and not an act of devotion. Warner knew an anchorage on the other side of Kent Island that he could make before sunset.

There was a fresh southwesterly breeze when he cast off the lines. He got out of the marina on the diesel, and then he set the mainsail. It billowed and filled. A ridge of green water climbed halfway up the bow, and Warner's heart lifted. Off the bow Warner watched an old sloop-rigged ketch plowing up furrows of vermillion. Ahead, to the port side, was the low treed outline of Marshy Point. Beyond was the bay, shimmering in the low sun. And to hell with all the rest, he thought.

—FOURTEEN—

SATURDAY
NOVEMBER 3

SHERK heard a scratching behind the wall. He was making slow work of painting the vestibule, rolling on a fresh coat of ecru, when he heard the sound of an animal's claws brushing the other side of the plaster, moving up the space between the inside and outside walls.

He put down the roller and listened. The scratching moved slowly upward, stopping at the ceiling.

Too big for a rat, he thought. A possum, maybe, or a coon. He had known coons to get into some tight places. Beneath the floor was his hidden cellar, which was surely where the animal had come from. But he wondered where it could have gone when it got to the ceiling.

The job had to be finished. Sherk worked quickly now. He rolled paint onto the walls with long, smooth strokes, thinking all the while about the vestibule and how it had changed over the centuries, what it had looked like originally and what had been done to it to make it look the way it did now. Thinking about old buildings, and the secrets that their walls conceal.

First he set a couple of live-traps in the cellar, baited with scraps of food. These were rigid wire cages with doors that would snap shut behind any animal that entered. Coon, possum, whatever the animal was, he ought to get it out of the building.

Then he went up into the church with a flashlight. He climbed up into the choir loft—a balcony extending over the last ten rows of pews—that was reached by an enclosed staircase in a back corner of the church.

He began by tapping the wall at the top of the stairs. It was plaster over brick or stone. Solid. More of the same along the passage that led out into the loft. Then he was out in the loft itself, moving along the back wall where the smooth gray granite was exposed. A pipe organ sat against the wall. Sherk was sure there could only be more stone behind it.

When he had worked his way across the back of the loft, he came to a walk-in closet where the choir members hung their robes. It was built into the wall, near the far corner of the loft. In the church's symmetrical design, this recess in the wall corresponded to the stairwell passage on the other side.

Sherk walked in. He pushed the robes aside. The sides of the closet were wainscotted from belt level down to the floor, and in the corners were stacks of hymnals and boxes of candles.

He closed the door behind him. The church was empty, and nobody noticed that Sherk was in the closet for more than an hour before he emerged. Marveling again at the secrets that old buildings hold.

—FIFTEEN—

SUNDAY
NOVEMBER 4

SARAH was laughing. Elise didn't know the last time she had heard the sound. The girl was playing tennis with her grandfather, bantering with him, really enjoying herself. She actually seemed whole.

And today, Elise thought, of all days.

"Grandpa, it was out by a foot!" Sarah yelled.

"Nicked the line," said Harry Stannard. "Don't argue, just play the game."

"The ball hit right here," she said, tapping her racquet at a spot beyond the end line. "Mama, Grandma, you tell him."

"Out," said Elise, sitting in a lawn chair near the court.

"Out," said Joy, sitting beside Elise.

"That makes it three to one," Sarah said.

"So what? Only my vote counts. Forty-all, serve the ball, stop complaining."

"Don't you feel ashamed," Sarah said, "cheating that way?"

"Not the least little bit. I'm sixty-seven, I'll take anything I can get any way I can get it."

"You're terrible," she said, but laughing as she said it.

Was it possible, Elise wondered, that she had forgotten? That she would not notice this day pass? Elise herself had

remembered only when she saw the date on the morning
paper, and then it came back to her. She had had a good
cry before she came outside with the others.

She glanced at Joy's eyes, red-rimmed and slightly puffed,
and guessed that she, too, had remembered. Exactly one
year ago they had all lost Jack Stannard: son, husband, and
father.

Sarah slammed a shot down the middle of the court.

"Try and steal that one." She was grinning as she said
it.

"It was close. I'll give it to you this once."

"You're horrible," she said. "The most disagreeable
person I ever knew."

"Sweet talk will get you nowhere," Harry said. "Serve
the ball, and this time try to keep it in the court."

Sarah tossed the ball and hit a hard serve that Harry
grounded into the net. Sarah whooped and tossed her
racquet and caught it.

"All right, my game!" she yelled.

"The sun," Harry said. "The sun was in my eyes."

Maybe she had put it behind her, Elise thought. The
young are resilient. Let it be so, she told herself. The girl
has suffered enough.

Usually Sherk didn't go near the church on Sunday. Too
many people for his taste. There were five Masses through
the day, and the church would be nearly full for each one.

But this morning he had his cages to check. There was a
nine o'clock Mass, and at 8:40 he clambered down into the
cellar and turned the flashlight on the cages.

A pair of iridescent green eyes shone back at him from
one cage; the other was empty. Sherk went over to the
animal and squatted beside it: a raccoon, fat and healthy.

The floorboards rumbled overhead. People walking across,
arriving for Mass. Sherk didn't want them looking when he
carried the coon and the cage out from under the steps. He
didn't want to be stared at and he didn't want to give away
his secret, so he decided to wait for a few minutes, until
Mass was underway and they would all be in church, and
he could climb out unseen.

He turned off the flashlight and sat motionless in the dark, footsteps and low voices filtering down to him. In the cage, the coon shifted nervously. Without even trying, Sherk summoned a sudden hatred for the people passing overhead. On other Sundays, he had watched the worshippers as they arrived. Happy families, most of them. Carefree. Together. He imagined the people above him now, smug and satisfied. *Together.* They had no idea of misery.

Sherk sat in the dark, listening to the noises overhead. Heard murmuring and shuffled feet, a wailing infant. These were the sounds of life going past him, oblivious to him. He thought about home, about all the days and nights he had known with Margaret in the little cabin there, the two of them hidden away and untouchable, life passing them by. The coon's sharp claws clicked on the bare wire of the cage. And at that moment Sherk knew what he was going to do. He could see it all. He knew.

"She's tough," Harry said. "You'd think she might give an old man a break, you know, out of respect. But no. I couldn't get a single close call."

"Spare me," Sarah said. They were sitting with Joy and Elise, drinking lemonade. Sarah was doing her best to stay focused, not let her mind drift away, but it was hard.

"That's a wicked forehand she's got. You see the way she hits the ball?" Sarah was listening to Harry, but she was telling herself that the four of them together seemed incomplete. *Like somebody else ought to be here.*

"How does a skinny kid like you hit so hard?" Harry was saying.

"I guess you bring out the best in me, Grandpa."

Harry went on and on. He had them all smiling, and Sarah even heard herself giggling at one of his jokes.

She got up. She had done her best, she thought.

"I think I'll go in," she said.

"How 'bout another set?" Harry said. "No cheating this time, I promise."

"No way, Grandpa. You're too much for me."

She felt tremendous relief when she was finally able to

leave them and head for the house, where she wouldn't have to show her face to anyone for a while.

A year ago today, she told herself. It was a terrible anniversary, but really no worse than any of the 365 days that had preceded it.

Up in her room, she stretched out on the bed, face buried in a pillow. There was nothing harder than keeping in grief, feeling it weigh her down. But she told herself that she had done pretty well today. Nobody would have guessed.

Then she felt it come spilling out, and she sobbed into her pillow, sobbed *Daddy, Daddy I need you,* feeling very small and very helpless.

—SIXTEEN—

MONDAY
NOVEMBER 5

SHERK was at the hardware store in Parole Plaza when it opened in the morning. He needed plenty: duct tape, a canvas tarpaulin, screw eyes, webbed rope. A strong hammock, some kind of buckles or fasteners, a kerosene lamp. At an Army-Navy surplus store he picked out a mummy-style sleeping bag and some camping equipment, including a camp toilet, that cost him more than two weeks' salary in all. He had to go to Bladensburg to find a leather goods store that had a supple piece of deerskin in stock; it was expensive, but softer than most leather, and Sherk wanted it soft.

That night he went to work. If something could be made with hands and tools, Sherk would find a way. He had never worked with leather before, but he turned the deerskin into what he needed. And though he had never used heavy thread and needle, he made what he wanted out of the buckles and the canvas.

After four nights' work, he was ready.

—SEVENTEEN—

THURSDAY
NOVEMBER 8

FOR nearly a week, Joy Stannard had been trying to talk Elise into an all-day trip to D.C. They would go on a White House tour, have lunch at a downtown restaurant, spend the afternoon at the National Gallery. Maybe even squeeze in some shopping.

Elise, without knowing why, put her off at first. But Joy's arguments were convincing. They both spent too much time in the house, she said. It was a shame to live within fifty miles of Washington and not visit the city as often as possible. And what obligations did they have, anyway, that should keep them from doing what they wanted, when they pleased?

Finally Elise agreed. She told Sarah about it that evening.

"There won't be anyone here when you get home," she said. "I suppose we'll be out until at least four. And with rush hour, who knows? Harry might be the first to get back."

"Take all the time you want," Sarah said.

"You don't have to sound so happy about getting rid of me."

"I'm happy you're getting out, that's all. You ought to do it more often."

"You realize that you might be alone for a couple of hours?"

"I think I'll survive."

"Don't be flip, Sarah."

"Mom, I know plenty of girls who're alone every afternoon. I'll be fine. I promise not to burn the place down, and if I have a party I won't use up more than a gallon of Grandpa's bourbon."

Elise glared at her.

"Hey, just kidding," Sarah said. "But you're making too big a deal out of this. Are you going tomorrow?"

"If the weather's good for driving. We'll drop you at school first."

"You'll have a great time."

There was still a trace of doubt in Elise's face.

"I'll be fine. Really. *Go*. And I'll see you when you get back."

—EIGHTEEN—

FRIDAY
NOVEMBER 9

THEY took Harry's BMW for the day. Joy wore a red Galanos suit and a mink; she lent Elise a silver fox jacket, and as they pulled out of Whittier Lane and drove south down Ritchie Highway, Elise told herself that maybe Harry and Joy were ostentatious, maybe they did tend to overdo, but sometimes there was no harm in that. Sometimes it was fun to pretend that money was the answer, whatever the question.

As Elise drove, Sarah rode in the back seat, wearing the Nordbrook uniform. Elise had briefly talked herself into keeping Sarah out of class today so that she could go along. It would be an adventure for them both, something to share. But mid-terms were near, and she knew that afterward she would feel guilty about slighting the girl's education for what, after all, was just a lark.

The BMW rolled down the school's long driveway and stopped in the turnaround. Sarah leaned over the front seat and kissed Joy and her mother.

"You've got your key?" Elise said.

"Got it."

"There's plenty of food in the refrigerator, and I'll get dinner as soon as we get back."

"I don't think I'll starve."

"And don't worry if we're a little late," Elise said. "Traffic in Washington can get pretty bad."

"If you don't get going, you'll never get back," Sarah said. She climbed out of the car, closed the door, and gave them a wave before she went up the steps.

And Elise, though she knew that Joy was impatient to be going, didn't pull away until she had watched her daughter disappear through the front door.

Howard Warner was slow to awaken. He tossed in the covers, hid his head under a pillow, fought the onset of consciousness, and finally surrendered. He opened his eyes and looked at the clock on the night stand. Twelve-twenty.

By one he had showered and shaved, and was boiling water for instant coffee in the kitchen of his efficiency apartment. Half an hour later he was heating a can of spaghetti that was going to be his first nourishment of the day.

All week he had been on the late shift, subbing for a detective who had court duty, never asleep before three in the morning. Brushing his teeth and reading the sports pages at an hour when everyone else was on lunch break made him feel vaguely estranged from society. Which he found not at all an undesirable way to feel.

He looked outside. When he woke there had been plenty of light through the blinds, but now a low, tweedy layer of rolling clouds covered the sky as far as he could see. Snow, he thought—the clouds have that look about them. He remembered finding a heavy layer of rime ice on his windshield when he left the station that morning. Annapolis rarely saw snow until December, but today the air seemed cold enough and the clouds looked right.

For the next hour and a half he read a Travis McGee mystery. He was stretched out on a reclining chair, a rare relic of his marriage, a black Naugahyde monstrosity that he had patched in spots with electrical tape. His head rested near the window, and at around three in the afternoon his reading was interrupted by a quiet ticking against the glass.

He raised the blinds and looked out again. The sky was

lower and darker, and tiny pellets of sleet were clicking against the window.

Where there was sleet, snow usually followed. It wouldn't be much, Warner thought. In any quantity, he would welcome it. Snow was hell on the traffic detail, maybe, but to almost every other cop it meant relief. For armed robbers, who relied on their cars, it was a nuisance. Muggers and rapists found few potential victims on the streets, and anyway seemed unwilling to suffer the discomfort of wet feet in slush. Burglars knew that it kept people at home.

The thought of snow brightened Warner, and he decided that he would go to work early. He could have a long lunch and still be in the office a good hour before his shift began at six. Give the captain something to chew on.

He put on a London Fog overcoat, wrapped his neck in a wool muffler, and folded a pair of rubber overshoes into a pocket. Outside, his breath billowed in the cold, and the sleet stung his cheeks. He drove away happy, cheered by the thought that crime, for at least a few hours, would be out of the hands of all but the maddest and the most desperate.

Sherk entered the grove, a shadowy figure moving among the trees, moving under the bare limbs and the low gray sky, moving silently among the faded tones of winter. He wore a dark blue watch cap and a black wool jacket, and he carried a brown gym bag.

Snow was falling thickly, large wet flakes. Sherk plunged into it, and in a moment the snow and the muted woods swallowed him up.

"Come *on*, Sarah, it'll be fun."

"I shouldn't," she said.

"Sarah, he's a senior. Almost eighteen. And big-time cute. Really, I've seen this guy. I hear he just broke up with his girlfriend. I'd go for him myself, except that I'm kinda hooked on his friend. Don't tell me you've got so many boys on hold that you can pass up a chance like this."

Actually, she had no boys at all. Since coming to Annapolis she had met none, and Nordbrook wasn't much help. Now Stephanie, from home room, wanted to introduce her to one. She had an older brother, and the brother had a Trans-Am and two friends, and after school the three boys and the Trans-Am were going to be waiting.

"I'd like to," Sarah said.

"Then do it. Call your mother, tell her you want to run around with some friends, and we'll get you home by four-thirty. Sarah, we just want to drive around and have a few giggles. The guy's not going to jump your bod or anything."

They were in the cafeteria, finishing lunch. Sarah thought that she would not have to call her mother; if she were back by four-thirty, Elise would never know.

If she found out, however, she would be furious.

"I'll think about it," Sarah said.

"Sarah, I have to know. If you can't come, I have to find somebody else. I promised I'd get two other girls, and my brother'll kill me if I don't."

The bell rang for fourth period. Sarah gathered up her books.

"Tell you what," she told the girl. "I'll meet you between periods, just before two o'clock. Right in front of the library, okay? And I'll let you know."

They left the cafeteria together.

"You're crazy if you don't come along," Stephanie said.

"Okay, okay."

"This guy is six feet tall. And built. You hear what I'm saying?"

"I hear you."

They reached a staircase. Sarah had a class on the second floor, and she began to climb the steps. "He's on the track team," Stephanie yelled. "Throws the javelin or something. Think about it, Stannard."

Elise knew they were in trouble when they left the restaurant on Connecticut Avenue and walked out into the sleet. In Vermont, she drove through ice and snow for at least five months of every year. But she knew the reputation of D.C. drivers for panicking at the sight of a few flakes, even a cold drizzle.

She told Joy that maybe they should think about starting back, cutting the day short.

"Nonsense," Joy said. She didn't seem to notice the sky. "We haven't done half of what we came to do. I'd feel cheated, wouldn't you, if we turned tail so soon. Besides, Harry would rib us without mercy if we let a little bad weather chase us home."

Elise didn't say so, but she thought that Harry had plenty to rib them about already. Under Joy's direction the trip had turned into a shopping expedition. Instead of touring the White House, they had explored Saks and Neiman-Marcus in Chevy Chase. Joy had carried an armload of purchases out of each store. There had been time for pedicures and facials at Elizabeth Arden before they hurried downtown for lunch at a place downtown that Joy called a "power restaurant," where a light lunch for two had cost them $60 with the tip. Except for the hat check girl, they had been the only two women in a packed room. And the only two diners, Elise thought, who would not use the lunch as a tax deduction.

They waited under an awning while a parking valet brought the BMW. Elise took a city map out of her purse.

"The National Gallery isn't far," she said. "We need to get down to Constitution."

"Hmm. And what's going on down there?"

"The Sunday paper said that the El Greco exhibition is showing until December."

Joy looked thoughtful.

"El Greco. He's the one with all the saints, I think. Yes, that's him, I'm sure of it. Don't you think he sort of overdoes it?" She left a brief pause which Elise was unable to fill. "It would be a crime to come all this way without showing our faces in Georgetown. And El Greco, really, I can take him or leave him."

Elise looked at the map and saw with dismay that Georgetown was across the city, far from any highway that would return them to Annapolis.

The BMW arrived.

"Yes. Georgetown," Joy was saying. "Down Connecticut, take a right on Pennsylvania, we can zip right over to M Street, no trouble at all."

"I'll do it," Sarah said.

"You will? Stannard, you're okay."

"Where do I meet you?"

"Make it the cafeteria—that'll give you a chance to call your mother."

"Why bother?" Sarah said. "I'm no kid. I can go fool around for a couple of hours after school if I want."

"Any way you want it. Right at the front door, then. Leslie, too, that's the three of us. All *right!*"

"I'm sorry," Joy Stannard said.

"It's all right," said Elise.

"It was such a dumb idea. Georgetown, of all places, on a snowy afternoon. Stupid."

Elise didn't bother to argue. She was concentrating on the two lanes of traffic ahead of her, outbound from Washington on Route 50, near Annapolis. The clouds had cleared after dropping about three soggy inches of snow, and the road was clogged with cars grinding through brown slush at fifteen miles an hour; it was an improvement over Wisconsin Avenue, where they had spent two hours covering ten miles to the Beltway.

At the top of a slight hill she lifted her eyes to glance in the rearview mirror. Behind her, closely bunched headlights were strung out in a long double strand. She could also see an obscenely large pile of packages that buried the back seat. Almost all of them belonged to Joy, who showed an apparently limitless vigor for shopping. Elise had never seen her mother-in-law apply half so much enthusiasm to any other endeavor.

For Elise the day had been a waste. No White House, no museum, and much tedium behind the wheel of the BMW. Now she wanted nothing more than to be home, to hug her daughter and then melt in a hot bath.

Outside Annapolis she took the exit that curled down to

meet the northbound lane of Ritchie Highway. About fifty yards ahead on the turn was a green Fiat. Going too fast, she thought. Elise let off the gas. She saw the Fiat's tail slowly, inevitably, slide out. The car spun out of control, performed one complete revolution and half of another, and stalled broadside in the sweeping exit. Elise could clearly see the driver, wide-eyed in her headlights. She remembered: pump the brakes, don't mash them. She felt the tires at the edge of traction, and made a small movement of the wheel to catch the rear end as it slewed.

They stopped within ten feet of the driver's side door on the Fiat. After a couple of tries, the driver got it running again, and the Fiat crept, chastened, down the road.

"I'm really sorry," Joy said, breathing again.

When she turned down Whittier Lane, Elise relaxed for the first time in hours. They had left Georgetown around three. The digital clock in the dash said 6:22. Sarah would be worried, Elise thought. At least, she hoped that Sarah would be worried.

Out on the highway the snow had been churned and cindered and plowed, but it still lay white on the lane, disturbed only by two or three sets of tire tracks. The snow was slippery on packed gravel; Elise sensed the car sliding momentarily when she slowed for a curve.

Home. And about time, she thought. It looked dark, not a light burning. That was strange. Sarah was terrible about turning off lights; every room she visited, she usually left ablaze.

Elise parked beside the main house and they both carried an armload of packages through a side entrance. Elise dropped hers on a settee and hurried over to the new wing. She threw open the hallway door, hit a bank of switches that threw on half a dozen lights, and she loudly called her daughter's name.

She crossed the living room.

"Sarah!" she shouted, even louder.

Come on, kid, answer your mother.

She heard only silence, then the sound of her own feet as she checked the kitchen. The table was empty except for a bowl of fruit. That was wrong, she thought; when she came home from school, Sarah always threw her books on the table, and there they sat until she was told to move them. It had become a daily joke.

Elise bolted out of the kitchen and ran upstairs, again shouting, nearly frantic now. It struck her that the house had an empty feel, an undisturbed look.

"Sarah!"

She tried to contain her alarm. Into the studio.

"Sarah, honey?"

Her own bedroom. Down the hall to Sarah's room. The bed was rumpled, but exactly as it had been left that morning. Not a trace of the skirt and blouse and blazer that festooned chairs after she had changed clothes.

Elise ran downstairs and into the main wing. She found Joy bringing in a second armload.

"Have you seen Sarah?" Elise said breathlessly.

"No. She wouldn't be here."

"She'd better be."

This part of the home was larger, and it took her longer to run through the rooms. When she had covered the entire house, she found Joy in the dining room, heaping the bright bags from Saks, Lord and Taylor, Bloomingdale's on the table.

"Sarah's not here," Elise said.

"It's not that late, really. Six-thirty? That's not so bad."

"She should have been here three hours ago."

After a few moments' thought, Joy said, "The snow. Maybe the school bus had trouble."

"The snow wasn't that bad."

"It's a simple matter to call the school and find out."

Elise did. She was back to Joy quickly, her voice quavering.

"They said the buses were late, but that the last one finished its run before five. Joy, something has happened to my girl."

"Nothing serious, I'm sure."

"She's three hours late."

"Tonight a lot of people will be three hours late getting where they're supposed to be."

"We have to do something."

"Let's not panic. I don't know what to do, exactly. But Harry will. It can't be long before he's home. And until then, we're going to keep ourselves together."

Harry Stannard's second car was a Ford Escort. He considered it a dinky little thing, suitable mainly for infrequent errands, and he had been slightly peeved when Joy appropriated the BMW for the trip to Washington. But his annoyance had decreased with every snowflake that fell during the afternoon. The Escort had front-wheel drive, and it sliced through the snow with miraculous ease.

He had spent the day in southern Maryland, Charles County, a place called Hughesville where he was in a partnership to build two hundred semi-detached townhouses. Harry realized that the term "townhouse" might not precisely apply to a residence built in the middle of an alfalfa field, but the term had a cosmopolitan ring, and it led buyers to expect no more than the tiny swatch of property that his planners had grudgingly allotted to each home.

Now he was returning to Annapolis. The Escort tracked unerringly through the snow that remained on the highway. Other cars were not so steady. In front of him, a Mercedes fishtailed slightly over a slick patch, and Harry cheerfully cursed it through the windshield.

Seven o'clock, and there was no sign of Sarah. Elise kept going to the window, looking out back at the lane where the grove swallowed it up.

She put on an overcoat and walked up the lane. She had to do something. The snow was already melting, sloppy under foot, pattering down from where it had collected in the trees. She shouted Sarah's name, walked farther into the woods, and shouted again, feeling foolish. It wasn't like calling a dog, after all. If Sarah were close enough to hear, she would be home.

She was walking back when a moving splotch of white light overtook her from behind. She turned and saw headlights. Harry's Ford stopped where she stood, and she got in. Elise felt a surge of gratitude. The old dinosaur. His stubborn strength was exactly what she needed at this moment.

"Sarah's missing," she said. "Didn't come home, didn't call . . . Harry, I'm so worried."

"Not a word from her?"

"Nothing."

"Did she make it back home?"

"Harry, I don't know anything, except she's gone and I'm about sick with worry."

He put an arm around her.

"First thing is, let's stay calm. Let's go home, sit down, and figure out what we're going to do."

He drove slowly through the snow, and she could tell that he was figuring already. By the time they reached the house he was decided.

"She'd be home by now if she could get home," he said. "She'd have called, at least. That's how I see it. So we're going to get some help. I think it's time to start calling in some chits."

Warner passed Whittier Lane twice before he found the unlit sign. He had never been down the lane before, but even in the dark he knew that this was an enclave of real money. He had been wondering where the juice came from. Where there was money, there was often juice.

And juice was involved here, no question.

Start with the phone call from the captain of detectives, personally assigning him the case, telling him that people up high would be watching this one, and let's do it just right, shall we? Nor was it routine for the department to react so quickly to the disappearance of a fifteen-year-old, especially one who lived outside the city, in an unincorporated area of Anne Arundel County. The name Stannard was unknown to Warner, but he told himself that it must mean a great deal to someone who mattered.

With any luck, he thought, he would be off the case before morning. Best of all, the girl would appear. Next best, he would be able to leave it to the county. He was here because the girl was last known to be in Annapolis, at school. But let him find a witness to place her outside the city limits, and he could walk away, leave someone else to worry about the juice and where it came from.

Warner reached the end of the drive. Sitting outside the house were a county patrol cruiser and an unmarked county detectives' car that Warner spotted right away: a blue Plymouth, no chrome, VHF antenna on the roof. Warner was impressed. This was some turnout for a fifteen-year-old girl gone just a few hours.

A man in his late sixties met Warner at the door.

"Harry Stannard," he said. "Sarah's my granddaughter." He looked directly into Warner's eyes, and he had a powerhouse handshake. *The juice,* Warner thought.

They walked together into the living room, where Warner found two women talking to a county detective and a couple of county uniformed officers.

Harry Stannard began introductions, but Warner took a second to look around the room. It struck him as something you might find one day as a Smithsonian exhibit. How The Rich Lived, Late Twentieth-Century America. The room was at least three times the size of his apartment. Warner didn't know Oriental rugs, but he guessed that the one which nearly covered the entire floor was worth as much as *Amaranth*. And it was probably paid for. The sofa was gold brocade, and there was a love seat to match, framed oil painting, a pastoral. He supposed that it was not something you would find for $79.95 at a Starving Artists clearance.

"My wife, Joy." Warner nodded to a blue-haired woman with a slightly bewildered expression.

"And Sarah's mother, Elise."

She was sitting on the couch, and extended a slim, frail hand to Warner. He stepped forward to take it. His first thought was that on another day she would be a very good-looking woman. Tonight she was showing the strain, looking generally frayed, face pale. But she had dark, searching eyes, full lips, cheekbones that were high and balanced, a nose that was long and slender and perfectly straight. Her hand was soft and warm in his before he let it go.

He knew that he must have stared too long, because

after a couple of seconds she averted her eyes. As she did, she brushed aside some strands of hair that had fallen across her face, and the unconscious gesture struck Warner as delicate and feminine, endearingly vulnerable. He looked away, reluctantly.

"You know your colleagues," Harry Stannard said, motioning to the three cops. Warner knew one of them, the detective named Tarver, a puffy-faced man who was wearing a porkpie hat. He looked at Warner and gave the slightest possible tip of the head in greeting.

Elise turned back to the`two uniforms. She was telling them how punctual Sarah was, how she caught the same school bus every afternoon. The cops exchanged bored glances as they listened; Warner guessed that they had already heard this more than once from her already.

Tarver motioned Warner out of the room. They stood together in the foyer.

"First thing we need to do is find the bus driver," Warner said. "See if she caught that bus, start there."

"Want to get her out of the city, huh? Wriggle off the hook. I don't blame you. We've got his name, the driver, some address in Glen Burnie. We'll talk to him. But it don't mean diddly anyway, whether she came home first or not. The kid up and split, no two ways about it."

"A good guess," Warner said.

"Hey, my friend, you haven't heard the half of it. Three months ago, mom and the girl move here from out of state. The father died a year ago. Kid took it hard. Starting to sound familiar? Mom tries a job, can't hack it, they move in with the grandparents. The kid's not too happy with that, either. She starts at a new school, her grades are just so-so."

They were standing with their backs to the living room. Warner realized that the mother had stopped talking. He put up a hand to quiet Tarver, but the detective ground on, loudly.

"So what are we talking here? A big emotional upset. A new home, which she didn't want. New city, new school, new friends, things are rough all around. A runaway, pure and simple. Kid's headed to New York by now, got to be."

Elise had come up behind him. She raised her fists to pummel the detective, and shouted, "She's not! Not my girl, not Sarah. My baby didn't run away."

Warner caught her arms at the wrists and turned her away. They didn't need this. Dumb stunt, he thought, a cop mouthing off that way.

"Hey, no more of that," he said soothingly. "Let's not make it hard on ourselves, okay?"

Warner released her wrists but lightly touched her on one arm. Time for some damage control, he thought. Somebody who cared about this child was very well connected, and might be able to ruin a career or two.

She looked angrily over her shoulder at the county detective as Warner turned her aside.

"Maybe you'd show me her room, huh? Would you mind? It might help. Who knows? You never can tell." Anything to make her happy.

She took him through the house to the new wing, up the stairs to Sarah's bedroom. To Warner, it was standard issue: posters of Rick Springfield, Christopher Atkins, and E.T., jeans and a sweater hanging over the back of a chair, stuffed animals in a corner, ruffles and a flowery print spread on the bed.

He looked at the top of the dresser. A small bottle of cologne, nearly full. A small wooden jewelry box that held a tiger's eye agate ring and a couple of silver necklaces. A sketch pad. He opened it and thumbed the pages down, stopping for a couple of seconds at each one.

"This hers?"

"She has taken lessons for several years."

"A quiet girl, I bet. Likes to stay home. Probably doesn't mind being alone."

She looked closely at him. "How did you know that?"

"A lot of time went into this." He held up the sketch pad. "Drawing's a solitary pastime, and you don't get it done if you're the type that has to be out all the time, running around."

"My daughter *is* quiet. She's a very sensitive child."

He thumbed past a couple more pages. "I could see that, too."

"Now you're going to tell me that she sounds just like the type who'd get upset over something and run away. A big emotional trauma, a new home. She fits the profile, is that it?"

"Most kids do, at one time or another. What we're talking about here happens hundreds of thousands of times every year. And it almost always comes out okay in the end. That doesn't stop you from going crazy when it happens to yours. I know. I had one run out on me."

She looked at him with real interest. Warner pulled a chair into the middle of the room and sat on it. She faced him from the edge of the bed.

"It's bad, I know that, Mrs. Stannard," he began.

"Elise," she said.

"Okay, good. Elise. And I'm Howard." He felt her softening up, the inner tension losing its grip.

"Like I say, I've been through it. I know it hurts. At the time, my daughter was just a few months older than yours is now. My wife and I were having a hard time of it. The marriage was coming apart. And one day Sharon—that's my little girl—is gone. Bam, just like that. Probably decided that what she found out there couldn't be any worse than what she had at home.

"They think they're so tough at that age. They have to prove it. But inside, they're just kids, children. They know nothing about the world and how it can be. They're growing up, they want you to treat them like adults, but all you can see when you look at 'em is the babies you know they are."

She nodded eagerly. Warner thought she looked grateful.

"And did you find her?" she said.

"She came back on her own, three weeks later. She'd found some semi-organized crash pad down at Virginia Beach. When she got tired of sand and sun and peanut butter sandwiches for dinner, she came home."

"Was she all right?"

"They make out, you know. She came back in one piece. And glad to be home, you can bet." He shrugged. "Now she's twenty-six, lives in Seattle. It's a couple years since I saw her last. Got her nursing degree last year, found a real good job. She's doing okay. Probably can't even remember Virginia Beach or why she ran away.''

Warner leaned forward in his chair.

''I'm not saying you shouldn't worry. Your daughter's gone, you worry. That's how it is, right? But while you're worrying, remember how often this happens. And most always, it turns out fine. It's the very few exceptions you hear about.''

''You're telling me that most runaways make their way home, sooner or later.''

''Exactly.''

''But my daughter didn't run away.''

''Maybe we should hope that she did,'' Warner said.

''Because if she didn't run away, then somebody or something is preventing her from coming home. Isn't that it? And that's a lot more serious. That kind of thing doesn't usually turn out so right, does it?''

''There are a lot of possibilities,'' was all he would say.

Roland T. Simms lived in a trailer court outside Glen Burnie. One of the two county officers found the mobile home in a maze of alleys and cul-de-sacs; the glow from a TV danced across a drawn shade in the front window.

A man about fifty answered the door in a sleeveless undershirt. He looked warily at the cop.

''Roland Simms? You work for Nordbrook School, driving a bus?''

''What's the matter? Something wrong?''

The patrolman held up a snapshot of Sarah that he had gotten from Elise.

''Do you know this girl?''

Simms squinted at the picture, took it and held it in the light from inside.

''She takes my bus. Afternoons only. Gets off along the Ritchie, a little ways up from Route 50.''

''Her name is Sarah Stannard.''

''You could tell me her name's Greta Garbo, it'd be all the same to me. I only know 'em to look at. She's one of the nice ones. Not like some of the hyenas that sit back there. Is this kid in some trouble?''

"Did she take your bus home today?"

"Sure. Like I say, every day, afternoons only."

Then he hesitated.

"Wait a minute. Not today. I remember thinking it was funny, 'cause the kid is always there."

"You're positive it was today she missed."

"Uh-huh. And I'll tell you how I know. Driving the bus, you get like an old horse pulling a milk wagon. You know your route, you make all the stops without even thinking. I pull over as usual at her stop, forgetting she never got on. And she's the only one who gets off at that stop, so when I pull over and open the door, nobody stands up. And it turns into a big fuckin' joke, you know? All these spoiled brats back there, laughing like hell. And I remember thinking, the snow's falling, the roads are a mess, I'm worried about keeping this vehicle right side up so all the little misses get home in one piece. And all they can do is laugh at me. I'm asking myself, do I need this aggravation? So I remember, okay? This girl, whatever her name is, was not on my bus today."

Tarver took Warner aside and relayed the news with undisguised glee.

"We've got a history teacher says the girl was definitely in her two o'clock class this afternoon. And we've got the bus driver, says no way did she get on the bus. You want my opinion, she walked out of school and started to thumb. I still say she's a runaway, and she'll come back when she's ready. But I don't have to wait until then to bow out. Uh-uh. This one is definitely all yours."

Monsignor Herrity occupied a simple bedroom on the second floor of the rectory at St. Bartholomew's. Except for the crucifix on one wall, the room could have belonged in a clean, inexpensive boardinghouse. In one corner opposite the bed, a portable black-and-white TV sat on a metal stand. But it was rarely used. The monsignor craved quiet when he was alone: quiet for reading, for prayer, for thought.

He happened to be reading when he heard the scream.

The scream, or whatever it was. He only heard it once, so he couldn't say what it was, or where it had come from. But his first impression was that it had been a woman screaming from somewhere near the church.

At first he didn't move. The book was by Teilhard de Chardin, dense and difficult, requiring all his attention. The scream didn't penetrate immediately. He needed a few seconds to disengage from the words on the page, to shift from the abstract to the immediate. When he realized what he had heard—or, more exactly, what he seemed to have heard—he put the book down and went to his window and pushed aside the curtains.

His bedroom, like his office, looked out across the parking lot to the church and the hall. Since it was on the second floor, it gave a somewhat better view than the office window. But even from here he could see nothing amiss, no disturbance in the total composure of the night.

He let down the blinds, went back to bed, and tried Teilhard again. But this time the effort was too great, and the ideas were too slippery to hold. It was late for him, anyway; he was saying a 7 a.m. Mass in the morning. So he put the book down and turned out the light. For a few minutes he lay awake, listening for another sound like the one that had jolted him out of his book. But he heard nothing more, and after a few minutes, sleep overcame him.

—NINETEEN—

SATURDAY
NOVEMBER 10
1:30 A.M.

"WHAT I'd do if I were you, I'd crawl into bed and get a little sleep," Warner said.

"I couldn't sleep," Elise told him.

"Sooner or later you have to. Everybody does."

"I'll sleep when I'm sleepy."

Elise had wanted to be near her own phone, so she had gone to the new wing, and Warner had followed her. They had sat together for about an hour, talking, Elise on the couch and Warner in a chair across from her.

He was staying at the house through the end of his shift. Captain's orders. There was little else to do that had not been done already. Sarah's description had been broadcast to patrol cars. In a few hours her photo would be distributed by the hundreds to policemen in Annapolis and Anne Arundel and surrounding jurisdictions. The county was sending a patrolman soon, just to stand by. A technician was coming to wire the telephones with recorders in case the Stannards should receive a ransom demand.

When you knew the right people, Warner thought, you could get a lot done. And quickly. He told himself that Harry Stannard must know a lot of the right people.

"The waiting is awful," she said. "Not knowing . . . imagining . . ."

"Don't let your imagination run away."

"But I keep asking myself what could have happened. Something that happened right in school, something that must have kept her from getting on the bus. Right there at the front door of the school. She walks thirty seconds and she gets on the bus. She does it every day. I keep wondering what it could have been."

"It's a mistake to take wondering too far, is what I'm saying. Things are usually not so complicated. You want to figure out the truth, you look for the simplest explanation. Any cop'll tell you that. Otherwise you run down too many blind paths, chasing phantoms."

"So you go by what your good sense tells you."

"Exactly," he said.

"Then what am I supposed to think? Because everything I know about my daughter tells me that she isn't a girl who'd go to school one day and then run away."

"You don't give up," he said.

"I've done it too often. It's a bad habit to get into." A shy smile passed over her face. Warner realized that it was the first he had seen from her, and he was sorry when it left.

"I've got another piece of cop wisdom, such as it is," he said. "Don't torture yourself with speculation. It does no good." He got up from the chair. "Coffee's still on, right? No, sit. I can take care of myself."

He went into the kitchen, filled his cup from the percolator, lightened it with some milk. Standing at the kitchen window, he looked out into the night and thought about the girl, wondering where she was at this moment and why she had not returned.

All the statistics and all good sense insisted that she was a runaway. Fifteen-year-old girls did it all the time, thousands every week. Most had a story that sounded very much like Sarah's. Elise had said it: *She fits the profile*.

A perfect fit, if you stayed at a distance. But get closer, and there were angles that didn't mesh, bothersome details.

There was the school uniform. It wasn't an outfit a kid would wear to run away in. And her savings account. Elise had dug through drawers to find the passbook. The balance was $210, no withdrawals in the past three weeks. Yet a kid planning to run away would want to put together all the money she could.

A county patrol car was emerging from the grove, rolling slowly down the lane as it neared the house. Warner decided that he could leave now. His shift was nearly finished. He poured the coffee down the sink, washed out the cup, put it in the dishwasher.

Elise had stretched out on the couch. He got closer and saw that she was asleep. Her face was untroubled; the lines of worry had disappeared from the corners of her mouth and her eyes.

Draped over an arm of the couch was a crocheted afghan. Warner unfolded it and let it fall lightly over her body. She didn't move. He turned out all the lights but one table lamp, and he took a business card out of his wallet and left it on the coffee table in front of the couch.

At the door in the hall he turned and went back to the couch. He fished in a coat pocket for a pen, and wrote his home number on the front of the card. Then he left the room and went to find the grandparents.

Joy Stannard was slumped in a living room chair, also asleep. Harry was in the foyer, talking to the patrolman, still wearing the white shirt and the pinstriped trousers of his business suit. The shirt was open at the neck and his sleeves were rolled up, and on his feet he wore only socks. His face was grim. A tough old bird, Warner thought.

"You leaving?" he said to Warner.

"She's sleeping. Nothing's going to happen for a while."

"I'll see you in the morning."

"If they send me," Warner said.

"They'll send you, I wouldn't worry about that."

Warner went out to his car. Late night was warmer than the afternoon had been. On the front lawn, the snow cover had melted down to a scattered white archipelago. Warner drove up the lane, feeling his way through a thin fog that hung down to about waist height. It was crazy weather, he thought, gone from summer straight into winter and back again.

He was about a hundred yards into the grove when a

speck beside the road gleamed hotly in his headlights. As he drove past he told himself that he had nothing better to do, so he stopped and backed up until he found the gleam again. It was in a bare patch where the snow had melted.

He got out to look. As he got close he saw that it was a small gold charm with an enameled emblem. He read it where it lay. MONT TREMBLANT, it said.

Friday was payday. The pay envelope was in his jacket. He removed the check, put it in his pocket, and with the envelope held open, he picked up the charm by its edges and dropped it in. A long shot, he thought, but you never know.

He was going back to his car when he heard a noise in the woods, a rustling of brush. Then silence. He got a flashlight out of the glove compartment, turned it on, and walked a few feet into the brambles and the weeds along the side of the lane. He pointed the flashlight into the woods.

The beam touched brush, grass, and trees. Nothing out of the ordinary. He walked in a little farther and found a small clear spot among the trees, a place that the weeds hadn't overgrown. The grass there looked trampled. But he told himself that the weight of the wet snow could have done it. He was no Natty Bumppo, able to read volumes in a broken twig. To him it was just trampled grass.

His head jerked up. Off to his left was the rustling again. He turned his head and the light in time to see a lump of wet snow slide off the branch where it had collected, slide off and rattle the brush as it fell.

Suddenly Warner felt silly, standing in an empty forest, playing woodsman while the rest of the world slept. He walked back to the car and drove straight home.

—TWENTY—

SATURDAY
NOVEMBER 10
8:40 A.M.

THE tape recorder was a compact reel-to-reel machine in a black metal case that fit neatly into the Stannards' phone hutch downstairs. The technician installed one there and one on Elise's phone in the new wing.

They were ring-activated, he told Harry. Just like an answering machine, except that this gave no message. It recorded any sound on the line until the connection was broken.

Harry had not slept. He stubbed out a Lucky Strike in an ash tray that was already brimming with butts, and he stared with bleary eyes at the recorder. At first the idea of a kidnapping for money had struck him as ridiculous. He didn't consider himself wealthy, not by his own standards. Not when he personally knew a dozen men who could write a single check to buy his company and all he owned.

Now he hoped it was as simple as a ransom. When the banks opened on Monday he could put together a quarter of a million. Maybe three or four times that in a week.

He would pay it, he thought. He would pay it gladly, if it meant getting her back again.

"Howard, are you all right?" said the captain's voice in the telephone earpiece.

"Fine, fine. I'm fine."

"Tell you what. I'll call back in five, give you a chance to clear your head."

"No, no, I'm wide awake. Fire away."

Some distant part of Warner's head was talking to the captain, but the rest of him was asking, Where am I? *Who* am I? The clock said quarter of ten, and to Warner it felt like the middle of the night.

"We need to talk about the Stannard girl."

That brought Warner back into the here and now.

"I want to know how we handle it," the captain said.

"You're asking me?"

"It's your case, Howard. You tell me. Is this something serious, or do we treat it like a runaway? I mean, I've got three men who're going to spend all weekend running down the kid's classmates. That's a helluva commitment, and I don't want them wasting their time on a flier. It's not as if we have nothing else to do."

"I had the feeling that there was some pull involved," Warner said, digesting this.

"The old man has plenty of pull with the county. Not so much with us. Somebody asks for a favor, I don't mind. But we've done all right by these people and there's a question of how far we want to go. Understand? Starting now the case gets what it deserves. Nothing more. So you tell me where we go with it."

Warner forced his mind back a few hours. He remembered the passbook. He remembered the unstylish uniform that a girl would never wear to run away.

"I want to run up to the house," he said. "Give me an hour, that's all."

"An hour won't break my back," the captain said.

"Hey, I've got one for you," Warner said. "You ever heard of a place called Mont Tremblant?"

He said the name as if it were English, but the captain repeated it with a French pronunciation.

"Mont Tremblant," said the captain. "A very popular resort area in the Laurentian mountains, not far from Montreal, province of Quebec."

"That would make it close to Vermont."

"Maybe a hundred miles from the border, maybe less. But if you're considering it for a vacation, I'd advise you to brush up on your accent."

"Uh-huh," Warner said. "One hour, right?"

He dressed quickly. He put on a clean shirt, and made sure to brush his teeth and comb his hair before hurrying out.

Sherk didn't answer his door. He wasn't in the church, and wasn't in the school, or anywhere else the monsignor had looked in twenty minutes of searching.

Yvonne was right, he thought. Sherk was a queer one—the adjective was perfect, at least in the old-fashioned sense. Materializing suddenly where you least expected him, or disappearing just when you wanted him. The monsignor had seen very little of Sherk in the last week, and nothing at all of him in the past twenty hours.

Now there was a clogged toilet upstairs in the church hall, where already the caterers had begun to set up a wedding reception for a party of two hundred.

He had done it before, he thought. He could do it again, if he had to. If he remembered, the plunger was here in the closet. Yes. And he might need the plumber's snake, as well. He brought both upstairs with him, and after he had rolled up the sleeves of his cassock he went to work.

Elise had changed into jeans and a Mexican-style blouse. Her face was scrubbed and her hair was pulled back behind the neck.

Warner watched her reaction as he walked into her living room, and it seemed to him that she was not unhappy to see him once more.

"Good morning," she said. Warner thought he saw a stirring of that smile. "I don't suppose you've brought good news."

"Brought something for you to look at."

Warner took the chair opposite the couch, and Elise sat across from him once more. Harry had followed him by a few seconds, then Joy had followed her husband, and they looked curiously over Warner's shoulder as he removed the pay envelope from his jacket. He slid the charm out on the coffee table.

Elise reached for it, and he caught her hand.

"Don't touch," he said. "There might be prints, you can't be sure."

"Where did you get this?" she demanded.

"You know it?"

"Sarah wears it on a bracelet."

"Was it lost?"

"I don't know. No . . . she'd have said something if it was gone. She'd be heartbroken."

"She wear it yesterday?"

"Every day. Her father gave it to her. He bought it in Canada—she never takes the bracelet off. I said, where did you find it?"

"Not far up the road that goes through the woods."

She looked at Warner, up to Harry and Joy, back to Warner.

"Then she was here," she said, hopeful.

"Maybe," said Warner. "But she could have lost it Thursday. Then it wouldn't mean anything."

"No. No. She'd have told me, I know she would've. Don't you see? She was here. Harry, Joy, she was here." At first she was triumphant. Then it hit her. "She was here. But she never got home."

"It's all conjecture," Warner said, but she wasn't listening. Her eyes filled. She stood, turned. Warner had to watch her walk away.

He found a telephone and called the captain, told him about the gold charm and the uniform and the savings account. He said that it might mean nothing. Maybe she liked the uniform. Maybe she had money from someplace else. The charm could have been missing for a month; daughters don't mention everything to mothers.

"Fine," the captain said. "So tell me what you think."

Warner tried to find the right words.

"I can't get away from it," he said. "I get the feeling something hinky is going down here," and between good cops that said it best; they all knew the flutter of instinct which told them that some line was bent which should be straight, some door ajar which should be shut, some element misplaced in the correct order of life. Just a feeling that good cops get. Warner hoped that the captain was still a good one. He heard a silence of a few seconds on the other end.

"Then we won't let it go," the captain said. That was half of what Warner wanted to hear. "You're on top of it, you stay with it." And that was the other half.

The black Trans-Am was stopped in the lane, just at the edge of the woods where the Stannard home is first visible. Inside sat two seventeen-year-old boys.

"Is this the place?" one of them said.

"She said at the end of the road. This looks like the end."

"The girl must be loaded, Spoon."

"At Nordbrook they're all loaded."

"Like this? I doubt it, pal. I sincerely doubt it."

Harry Stannard spotted the Trans-Am rolling toward the house. He decided that he was going to give them hell, whoever they were. It was a shame when twenty acres wasn't enough to keep them away: peddlers of raffle tickets, magazine hucksters, religious nuts with their pamphlets, political nuts with their petitions. Harry thought that they had some nerve, whoever they were. Driving up his road in a damn black hot rod. And today of all days.

He was tired and wound about as tight as he could be. When he saw a teenage boy get out of the car, he blew up. Kids. Trouble, guaranteed. He stomped down to the front door, hoping to get first crack at the trespassers.

Warner was finished with the captain, hanging up, when Elise appeared. She seemed distraught. Her mouth was tight, and there was concern on her face.

"Please come," she said, and Warner knew that it was important. He followed her to the foyer.

In the front door stood a boy—a boy in years, Warner thought, though taller than anyone in the room. He was holding a couple of textbooks and a loose-leaf binder, and he had a startled look. Harry and Joy were standing in front of him, Harry glaring.

"Look," the boy said, "I didn't want any trouble, I just wanted to bring back her books. I thought she'd need them."

Warner saw a name penned on the cover of the binder. A precise script: Sarah Stannard. Warner took out his badge and showed it to the boy.

"Oh, God. I didn't do anything. Really."

"First tell me your name."

"Timothy Witherspoon," the kid said.

"And tell me how you got the books."

"This girl I met, Sarah, left them in the car yesterday. My friend's car, I mean. There were three of us guys, and we met three girls at Nordbrook, and we went bumming around for a while. My buddy out there, Larry, he'll tell you it's the truth. We didn't do anything."

Over the kid's shoulder, Warner could see a black Trans-Am with the second boy at the wheel.

"Look. We drove out to Sandy Point Park."

"In the snow?" Warner said.

"It wasn't snowing bad at first. We just wanted to, you know, goof around a little. Nothing heavy. The girls were all sophomores, they acted kinda young, and anyway one of 'em was Larry's sister." He fidgeted, avoiding Harry's stare. He appealed to Warner: "Six of us in a Trans-Am, the middle of the afternoon, what can happen? We stayed about an hour, and then we left."

"After you left the park," Warner said. "Then what?"

"We took the girls home. This one girl named Leslie, she lives over by Whitehall, we dropped her off first. Then Sarah. She was next."

"You brought her here?"

"Sure. Well, almost. By then the snow was pretty bad, and the sun was going down. This little road right here wasn't plowed, and it was too slick for the Trans-Am. Sarah told us her house was at the end of the road, and Larry was worried he'd slide off—he's kind of a dork—so she said not to worry, she walks home all the time. So we let her out."

"Where, exactly?"

"About halfway down the road," the kid said. He looked at all of them, and his eyes got wide as he saw Elise. She threw her head back, and she leaned against Harry for support, and a low moan passed over her lips.

Terry Dean was among the first patrolmen on the force to see Sarah's photo. He stopped by the station house before his lunch break and found a clerk stuffing the five-by-seven glossies into the bank of pigeonhole mailboxes near the squad room. He pulled one off the top of the stack and snapped it into his clipboard without a look.

Outside, as he returned to the car, he glanced at it for the first time. The glance became a stare as he stopped on the sidewalk.

He told himself that he had met this girl. Where, or how, he couldn't say. But the long blond hair, the pale skin, the deep eyes: he had seen them all somewhere before.

As a cop he encountered at least a thousand people every year, names and faces that came and went. He was sometimes shaky with names, but the faces never got away from him.

He read the label on the reverse of the photo. SARAH STANNARD. It meant nothing.

But he was sure that he had seen this girl.

—TWENTY-ONE—

SATURDAY
NOVEMBER 10
3:30 P.M.

AT least an hour of fair light remained when the county police search team gathered at the south end of the grove, on Harry Stannard's lawn. There were nearly forty of them, mostly volunteers, and they were subdued as they waited in the shadow of the big house. A sense of duty had brought them to a job that none of them relished; the odds were high that they would find the dead body of Sarah Stannard as they tramped through the dark woods.

Timothy Witherspoon's story had been corroborated by his friend and by the other two girls who had been in the car. It meant that Sarah had entered the grove at about 4:45 the previous afternoon, and apparently had not left it—at least, not of her will.

Warner, standing nearby, knew that death was too often the outcome of a young girl's abduction in a setting like this, quiet and private, a madman's playground. He looked back at the house and thought about the grief that might descend upon it tonight.

His eyes caught a figure in an upstairs window: Elise, her hands flat against the pane, staring out with a sorrowful look.

He walked over to the county detective, Tarver. It was

now a county case, since the girl had disappeared here, outside city limits.

"Go on home," Tarver said. "The turd's outa your pocket now, for sure."

"I'm in," Warner said. "I can use the walk."

"Up to you. It'll be cold and wet. But they're your feet."

Tarver looked up at the sun, and he clapped his hands twice.

"Okay, people," he yelled. "Let's do it while we got some light. Spread out, get your intervals even, keep the line straight whatever you do."

The gray, silent woods faced them as they began to advance.

There was nobody in the corridor when Frank Herrity walked briskly from the sacristy to the church hall. Five minutes later he returned and found Sherk painting the baseboards, sitting in the middle of a dropcloth, as thoroughly occupied as if he had been there all day.

He looked up only when the monsignor stood over him.

"Joseph, I was looking for you this morning," the monsignor said.

"Don't know why you didn't find me."

The monsignor saw a taunt in Sherk's eyes, and it irritated him.

"I didn't find you because you weren't around."

"Oh, I was around," Sherk said. He dipped a brush in a can of paint and went back to his job.

"I don't think so," the monsignor said. He tried to keep his voice from rising. "I looked everywhere, and I couldn't find you."

"You just didn't look in the right places," Sherk said without looking up. The monsignor thought he heard a smirk behind the words.

"Please try to keep yourself available during the day," the monsignor said.

Still bent over his work, Sherk nodded. He turned it into an insolent gesture, and the monsignor wanted to kick the brush out of Sherk's hand, fracture his coolness.

The impulse shamed him. He swallowed his anger and stalked away. He didn't look back, and so missed Sherk finally raising his head, showing a broad contemptuous grin.

The searchers strung out like a skirmish line, about ten feet apart, indistinct forms moving among the trees in the colorless twilight.

It was slow work. They were supposed to examine every inch of ground, turn over every fallen branch. They had been at it for about half an hour, and had reached the spot where Warner found the gold charm, when one of them came upon a patch of electric blue among the grove's muted greens and grays and browns.

He ran forward to get it, and held it up: a small bag of flimsy nylon, about large enough to hold a loaf of bread.

"What the hell?" he said.

Some of the others had joined him. One of them was a young reserve officer who had done some backpacking. She recognized it at once.

"It's a stuff sack," she said. "For a sleeping bag."

"Put a sleeping bag in this? No way."

"Sure, if it's a down bag. You can cram one in there easy."

They moved on. The light was dimming when they reached the north end of the grove. They had found no body, and the blue stuff sack was the only object in the grove that seemed to have even the thinnest possible connection to Sarah's disappearance. Nothing else even remotely suggested where she had gone, or how she had been taken.

Elise sat in a rocking chair in her room. The shades were drawn, the lights turned off. Outside she heard car doors slamming, engines turning over. The searchers had come to look for Sarah, and now they were leaving.

Sarah was gone. Really gone. She knew it now, but she had gotten no further in coping with it. Accepting as fact this ridiculous, fantastic absurdity was all she could manage for the present.

A form, a bulky shadow, moved across the low light in the open bedroom door.

"Elise? It's me. It's Howard Warner."

"Hello, Howard," she said dully.

"I wanted to tell you goodbye." Warner's thick fingers nibbled at the hem of his jacket. "Wanted you to know I'll be thinking of you, hoping all this comes out right."

"You won't be back?"

"It's not my case anymore. A matter of jurisdiction."

There was a long pause before she answered in a flat voice: "That's too bad."

"You shouldn't get discouraged. Be thankful that she wasn't out there. It's the best you could hope for at the moment, it really is."

She gave no sign that she had heard. After a few seconds he left the room, and she was alone. Her chair pitched forward and back in slow, tiny arcs. Elise folded her arms across her chest, in the manner of someone cold, painfully cold.

—TWENTY-TWO—

SUNDAY
NOVEMBER 11

By now the newspapers had the story. It got eight inches, double-column, on the front page of the Metro section of the *Washington Post*. In Baltimore, the *Sun* ran nearly twelve inches of copy on page two. Both stories quoted a county police spokesman to the effect that all possible leads were being developed.

At 3 p.m., the number of those leads increased from none to one, when the state crime lab completed its analysis of the blue stuff sack. The material was common 1.5-ounce ripstop nylon. It was of unidentifiable manufacture, probably an import from the Far East. Microscopic examination disclosed fragments of the spines and barbs from goose down feathers; apparently these particles had escaped from a garment or sleeping bag that the sack had held.

Though any connection between the sack and Sarah's disappearance was a triumph of imagination, the police had nothing else. They immediately compiled a list of sporting goods outlets in Anne Arundel and the surrounding counties, and soon they had begun to visit each of those stores, hoping to discover where the sack had been bought, and by whom.

The enamel face of the gold charm yielded no fingerprints.

And in Washington, the case was computer-logged at the FBI National Crime Information Center, and Sarah's name and description joined thousands of others in the files of the National Center for Missing and Exploited Children.

Half a dozen freighters lay at anchor off the west shore of Kent Island, waiting for open berths in Baltimore. Otherwise Warner had the bay to himself for as far as he could see. He also had a twenty-knot wind out of the north, and when he set the headsail *Amaranth* lunged through the whitecaps. A cold arm of spray leaped over the side, splashing his face, drumming against his sou'wester.

He imagined a girl he had never met, but whom he knew from her reflection in the old man and the grandmother and Elise. It was a sharper and truer picture than the image he got from the photographs. And he saw her in the woods, saw her alone in the lane, making tracks in the snow as she walked to meet a horror. Little girl lost. And gone, he thought. Some people are going to miss you, kid.

Sarah couldn't move. Bound at hands and feet, trussed and strung and gagged, she could do no more than breathe. There were voices and footsteps but they seemed to belong to a distant reality, nothing to do with her. She was hidden and alone and beyond the reach of the world. But she was alive.

—TWENTY-THREE—

FRIDAY
NOVEMBER 9
3:30 P.M.

"Don't be bashful—drink it," said the boy named Tim, whose friends kept calling him Spoon. "You've had beer before, haven't you?"

"Sure," Sarah said. "Plenty of times."

"Okay, then. Drink up."

Sarah tilted the can up to her lips. She got a mouthful of the stuff and nearly gagged. That would have blown it for sure, she thought. They would have seen her for the hopelessly backward child that she knew she was. Somehow she got the sour liquid down her throat, and she passed the can to her friend Stephanie.

The Trans-Am sat alone in a parking overlook in Sandy Point Park, beside the Chesapeake near the west end of the Bay Bridge. Outside its fogged windows, dime-sized snowflakes fell in a sudden flurry, melting on the warm black hood but collecting everywhere else. Stephanie's brother, Larry, and the girl called Leslie sat up front, in the bucket seats, and the other four were on the back bench, which had room to seat two in some comfort and three with much rubbing of shoulders and hips. Sarah was perched not so much on the seat itself as on Tim Witherspoon's knee.

"You smell good," Tim said. He nuzzled her behind an ear, and his lips softly grazed the back of her neck. "Is that perfume?"

Sarah tried to find a breath.

"I don't think so," she said. "I don't wear any to school."

"Whatever it is, it smells good, it sure does."

His voice was a murmur. Up in front, Larry had leaned across to kiss Leslie. Stephanie, in the back, was curled up against the third boy. The car seemed small and intimate; the windows were fogged. Sarah smelled a tang of sweat, felt the nearness of the boy Tim, his face so close, her thighs pressing against him where she sat: all thrilling, and most thrilling of all, knowing that they were letting down barriers and crossing boundaries, exploring. Her cheeks were hot and pink.

"Mmm, yes, smells real good," Tim said. He touched the tip of his tongue to her earlobe, and she shivered with surprise and pleasure.

When the beer came around again she took a big gulp, and it didn't seem so foul this time. There was a splash left in the bottom of the can, and she finished it with another gulp. One of Tim's hands was stroking her back, moving between her jacket and her blouse. She subtly shifted so that the hand could move more freely. A part of her remained detached, and she was both bemused and astonished to see such recklessness in herself.

There was a hiss and a burst of foam as Tim opened another beer. He drank deeply from it, and when he gave her the can she tried to match him. Her head was light. She thought of what her mother would say if she knew. But Sarah didn't feel guilty; it was as if she were breaking rules without truly doing wrong.

"You're really pretty," he was saying in a low voice. "The prettiest of all—I'm glad I ended up with you."

She closed her eyes and let him take her weight. Even through the fabric his hand was warm, moving against her back. He was kissing her neck, then the side of her face. And then her lips. He was kissing her lips, and it felt good, and with that part of her mind that was still making decisions Sarah decided that she wasn't going to stop him for a while.

• • •

Sherk hunkered down at his spot beside the lane. The snow was heavy, blanketing the road, the forest, his brows. He was as still as a stump.

The cold made his toes numb. Sherk closed his eyes. When he opened them again he was on the top of a ridge that overshadowed the hollow and his cabin. He was waiting for Margaret some summer afternoon. His knife peeled a long curl from a stick. When he looked down he saw no stick, no knife. His hands were red and blue from the cold. Snowflakes melting and refreezing had formed tiny pellets of ice in the hairs at the back of his hands. Below him a coal truck bellowed away from the mines, shaking the hollow. The forest was silent. He was sitting in the snow, waiting for Margaret, and he was sitting in the summer sun. Waiting for Margaret. It was as if the waiting was a bridge that let him pass without effort between the two realities, each image as real as the other.

She was late. Margaret had gone to the swimming pool and she was late. She was supposed to walk past in a gray skirt and a burgundy jacket, and she was late. A small flame of irritation began to lick inside Sherk. He didn't move. The snow fell around him, and collected on his shoulders and his woolen cap. While his breath plumed in the cold air, and the summer heat baked his face, he waited.

The snow lay pristine and trackless in Whittier Lane when the black Trans-Am turned in off the highway, its rear end waggling before Larry straightened it.

Sarah thought he was going too fast. The car's exhaust had a low, churning sound that reverberated among the trees when they entered the forest. Two hundred yards into the grove, the lane turned left. The Trans-Am didn't. Larry tugged at the wheel but the car plowed straight ahead. It clipped an evergreen sapling and stopped in the brush beyond the edge of the road.

Tim spoke first after the car stopped: "Nice move, Larry."

"Shut up, Spoon." Larry's face was drained. He put the car in reverse. For a few seconds the wheels spun, throwing up snow and clods of dirt before they caught traction and the car backed out of the brush.

"It's awful slippery," he said. "Maybe I shouldn't go any farther."

"Larry, you're such a nerd," Stephanie said from the back seat.

Sarah interrupted: "It's okay. I don't mind. It's not far, and I walk it all the time."

"You sure?" Tim said.

"Positive." Sarah would be glad to get out of the car. Larry's driving scared her, and she wanted to be alone so that she could run through what had happened in the last hour and a half, pick it apart and understand it.

She saw that the others didn't need much convincing— they would all be glad to get back out on the plowed roads.

"I'll be home in ten minutes," she said.

"Faster than driving, at the rate we're going," Stephanie said.

Tim stood outside to let her through. Her mind was busy, wondering whether she should wait for a kiss, how she ought to say goodbye, whether she ought to volunteer her phone number; he hadn't asked for it yet.

"See you around," he said as she stood in front of him.

"Uh-huh. See you around."

He leaned down to kiss her cheek, a gesture that was strangely reserved, she thought. Considering that half an hour earlier they had been grappling in a breathless lip-lock.

He got in and closed the door. Sarah stood to the side and watched the Trans-Am turn in the lane and then leave, the back tires spewing chunks of snow. The trees quickly muffled the burbling of the engine, and she was alone with the snow still falling in big flakes all around her. It was late afternoon. About four-thirty, she thought, quarter of five. The light was low and flat, giving way to evening gloom.

The walk wouldn't be so bad, she thought. She was dressed for it. She wore a glossy vinyl jacket the color of a green apple, and on her feet were low-cut L.L. Bean rubber pacs—winter equivalent of the Topsider deck shoes that were an inviolable standard at Nordbrook. But she still felt incomplete. Then she remembered. Her books. She had been so worried about the goodbye kiss that she had forgotten them in the back seat.

She looked back to where the car had disappeared. Long gone. She turned toward home, and put aside her worries about the books. Stephanie would bring them on Monday. For a few moments she thought about that awkward parting beside the door, the boy's impersonal goodbye. But as she began to walk, she put it out of her mind. She refused to let the afternoon be spoiled.

Instead she recalled clinging to the boy, wanting him and feeling wanted. She lingered with the memory. It was a far more pleasurable sensation than his kisses, which had been too rough to enjoy. But that wasn't important. Even *he* wasn't truly important. What mattered was that he had not treated her like a child. He had looked at her and found her desirable. He had kissed her the way men kiss women.

She walked through the forest. The wet snow caked between the lugs of her soles. She saw why the car had skidded: beneath the fresh snow was a thin layer of frozen sleet. She would slip if she wasn't careful.

The stranger appeared from nowhere.

Or so it seemed to her. She was looking down at her feet scuffing the snow, and when she looked up again he was standing in the lane, about twenty paces away. She got the oddest feeling that he had stepped out of the brush just as she came upon him.

She was frightened. She always had the lane to herself, so the emergence of this interloper—and in a snowstorm—was startling. And he was looking at her so strangely. As if he saw nothing else. His mouth was bent in the most chilling perversion of a smile she had ever seen, the leering grin of a death's head.

He stood directly in her path. She didn't falter, but as she approached him her mind sought an escape. Dense woods to the right and left. The slick and empty lane behind her. Home was where she wanted to be, and he stood between it and her.

She veered slightly to avoid him. Ten steps away. She looked down and pretended that he wasn't there. Closer. She glanced up; his eyes were following her, intent. As she passed him she looked down. At the edge of her vision she noticed a strip of wide, gray duct tape dangling from his right hand.

Tape, she thought. Now why . . .

His move was smooth, fast, sure. One arm whipped around her neck before she could react. The right hand went up to her face. Tape over her mouth. A squeal died in her throat, and she tasted adhesive.

With one arm locked around her neck and the other grasping a wrist, he pulled her out of the lane. She kicked backward and tried to jab him with her free elbow, but he was unstoppable.

"You was late," he muttered.

He dragged her into deep brush that hid them from the lane. Sarah tried to force up a scream, but the tape smothered it. With a sudden, deft movement he jerked her right arm backward and forced her to her knees. She felt him grab her left arm and bring it back, pinning both wrists together with his one hand—his fingers like iron—pinning her wrists while the other hand pulled a length of rope from the side pocket of his coat. He worked with a controlled intensity.

Twisting her head, she saw him wrap the rope around her wrists and draw it tight.

The stranger threw her to the ground. He pulled out another length of rope and bent over her feet, and in a few seconds he had tied her ankles. She was trussed and supine, limp from struggle. He stood over her and she told herself that whatever he wanted to do with her, he would do. His strength was overwhelming.

"You was late," he said. "You been swimming."

She shook her head, saying no, and she tried to tell him with her eyes and with plaintive grunts in her throat. The crazy man, he had it all wrong.

"Yes," he said. "Don't argue with your father. I know. You been swimming. With boys. You been a bad girl."

His voice was a rumbling threat. She shook her head violently.

"Yes!" he shouted, and he picked her up by the jacket, no effort at all, picked her up and tossed her backward into the brush.

"You been a *bad* girl," he said.

"You was swimming," he told Margaret.

"At the pool." She sat in an armchair in the front room of the cabin, her head bowed, biting her lower lip.

"There was boys."

"A couple."

"You been a *bad* girl."

She shook her head in desperate denial. A guttural noise came from her throat, and Sherk saw that she had a piece of duct tape across her mouth. Margaret in a chair, in the cabin, wearing duct tape across her mouth. He blinked and looked again. She was not in the cabin, but lying in the snow, snow still coming down around them. Lying in the snow with horrified eyes and tape across her mouth.

He tried to anchor himself in the moment. Annapolis. The forest. And Margaret, his daughter lost and now found, who did not know him but who was his precious Margaret all the same.

"Margaret," he said in wonderment, and he felt the flame gutter, the anger seep away.

Sarah, sprawled in the brush, thought his face showed the passing of a storm. It contorted and fought itself, and then a question replaced fury in his eyes, and an answer replaced the question. He relaxed, and it was over. A squall, come and gone.

"Margaret, sweetness, you all right?" he said.

She writhed against the rope and the tape, trying to speak, trying to tell him what a mistake he was making.

I'm not her, she thought, and tried to say it. Her mouth worked against the tape.

"Come on, don't fight it. There's nothing you can do. Believe me."

He walked away a few steps and returned with a gym bag. He sat at her side. Exhausted from squirming, she quieted under his gaze.

"Now that's it," he said. "Nice and easy, that's the way. Don't make this any harder on us than it has to be. Your daddy doesn't want you hurting yourself."

You're not my daddy!

He showed a knowing smile. He understood.

"I am. Yes I am." His confidence was insane and unnerving.

He dug in the gym bag and produced two belts of webbed nylon. Her eyes followed the movements of his hands. The belts had loops at each end, adjustable with toothed clamps. He replaced the rope at her legs with one set of the belts. When he untied her arms, he brought them around in front of her and tightened the second set around her wrists. They were as tight as the rope had been. Then he swiftly replaced the tape at her mouth with a handkerchief gag. His actions were deliberate and sure, not at all haphazard. He had thought this out. He knew what he was doing, what he was going to do.

For the first time she realized that she was cold. The woods were in shadow. There was snow on her bare legs, and some of it had slid down the back of her shirt when he flung her into the brush. It was chill and wet against her spine, and she began to shiver. Her arms and legs shook.

It sent him to the bag once again. This time he came up with a bulging blue cloth sack, tied at the top with a drawstring. He peeled away the blue cloth and revealed a sleeping bag that he shook out to full length.

"This'll do you," he said. "Goose down. It wasn't cheap, but I didn't want you getting cold."

He laid her out in it and zipped it around her.

"Not so bad, huh? Better?"

It was warm. She nodded sullenly, and for some reason that made the stranger grin.

"You'll come around," he said. "I guarantee you will."

A few feet away was a large elm. He cleared snow from a spot at the base of the trunk and sat, settling in. She saw that he meant to wait for some time; he had purposes that she could not guess. It was all confusion to her, but he seemed to find order in the confusion, perfect logic in the nonsense.

So they waited. His eyes didn't leave her. Once he opened a tin of snuff, and without looking away he tucked a pinch behind his bottom lip. He was like a hawk watch-

ing dinner, patient and vigilant, hunched beside her as
night closed in and the falling snow dwindled to nothing.

How much time passed, she didn't know—it was impossible to judge—but the last light had bled out of the sky
when she heard a car in the lane, rolling away from the
highway and toward the Stannard house. As it rounded the
bend, the beams from its headlights flitted through the
trees and fled. The car was gone and she heard it no more.

A few minutes later she heard Elise shouting her name
from somewhere along the lane.

"Sarah! Sarah!"

The call pulled at Sarah from out of her childhood, out
of her innocence: Elise at the back window, with a summons that was rarely obeyed until it had been issued at
least four or five times.

Sarah fought the gag. *Just one scream,* she thought, but
when the stranger saw her jaws working, he went over to
her and checked the gag, inserting a finger between the
rolled cloth and her jaw. It was still tight.

Again: "Sarah! *Sa-a-r*-ah!"

Sarah felt her eyes get wet. The gag choked all sound in
her throat, but there was nothing to check the tears. They
poured out, and the stranger had to dry her cheeks with his
coatsleeve.

"Now don't you pay no 'tention to that. Don't get all
upset over nothing."

A second car ground up the lane; the stranger picked up
his head and followed the sound until it was gone. They
heard no more cars, and no more of Elise, but he was
restive now, shifting his weight as he sat, his eyes scan-
ning the trees.

Finally he stood.

"Dark enough," he said. "Time we was gone."

—TWENTY-FOUR—

FRIDAY
NOVEMBER 9
10:55 P.M.

"KEEP still," Sherk said. "Don't move, you'll just get yourself in trouble. I mean it."

She had retreated to the far end of the pickup's seat, trying to get as far away from him as possible, her eyes huge and scared—scared by everything he did or said.

"Be a good girl for your daddy, I'll be back in a shake."

They were beside the church hall at St. Bartholomew's, in a parking space that was hemmed in on three sides by the hall, a high hedge, and a stockade fence along the sidewalk.

Sherk got out and looked around. He felt like a moon-walker, light and floating and unburdened. There was a wonderful joy in having Margaret with him again—scared and balky though she was—and he still tasted some residue of excitement from the moment when he had grasped her and swept her out of the lane and into his life again.

So far all had gone exactly as planned. The forest had been a haven for a couple of hours, and under darkness he had been able to bring the truck into the lane, carry her out of the woods and drive away. Then he had driven to an overlook above the bay, a deserted spot where he had parked for more than three hours, letting the streets empty before he came into the city. Again, unnoticed. Sherk was certain that nobody had seen her beside him. She was his alone.

He walked around the side of the hall and saw nobody. A single light shone behind an upstairs curtain in the rectory, but the hall was dark. The only movement he could discern was the sluggish stirring of ground fog under the street lamp. Otherwise the world was still.

Sherk went down the concrete steps that led to the basement of the hall. He unsnapped the padlock on the metal door at the bottom of the stairs and left the door open a crack. When he returned to the truck, he reached for her. She tried to wriggle away from him, but movement was impossible. She fell over on her side. Sherk smiled at her feeble effort.

"Come on, none of that. You know you ain't going nowhere." His arms lifted her, pulled her out. He carried her down the steps into the basement, to his apartment.

He sat her down in a chair beside a small round kitchen table.

She knew that they were in a building near a large church. But this room, quiet and out of the way, didn't have the feel of a church. It was more like an animal's den.

He stood over her, looming. She wondered numbly whether now he was going to do his worst. Never had she been more frightened than in the past few hours, but terror can't be sustained forever. By now she was just waiting to see what happened next. He reached down. She flinched. But his fingers only went to the cord that cinched the sleeping bag tight against her face. He loosened it, and pulled the bag off her head.

"Don't try shouting," he said. "Won't nobody hear you. You know that's true, or I wouldn't be doing this."

He loosened the knot of the gag, and pulled it loose. She swallowed some air. That was better; it was hard, breathing only through the nose. Then he stood her up, unzipped the bag, peeled it off.

"Go on, sit down," he said. "You must be hungry. I know I am. I fixed a little something. A surprise."

She spoke for the first time.

"Please don't hurt me," she said.

"Aw, sweetness, you know I wouldn't do that."

"I'll be good, only please don't hurt me."

"That's what I want to hear. You be good, you got nothing to worry about."

"I have to use the bathroom," she said.

"Guess you do. It has been a while."

"My legs." She nodded down to where her ankles were still fastened with the nylon belts. He removed them from her hands and feet.

"Bathroom's there," he said, pointing to a closed door across the room.

His voice stopped her as she went toward it on unsteady legs.

"There's nothing you can do," he said. "Don't get any ideas. You'll just make your daddy unhappy with you, is all that'll happen. Be a good girl, it'll all be okay."

She closed the door and looked around. There was a small, narrow window, up the wall at ground level. She tried it: locked and painted shut. The door had no lock. He would be there in seconds if she broke the window and tried to climb out.

She was powerless; he was so strong and smart. Obviously he had worked all this out some time ago, and it occurred to her that she could do nothing to surprise him, that he had planned for anything she might conceive now. It was a disheartening thought.

When she came out he was heating a casserole dish on a hot plate. Water boiled on the other coil. He poured the water into a cup with a packet of instant cocoa, gave it to her when she sat down. She watched him without a word, still frightened, but encouraged a little by his gentleness.

He spooned out the casserole onto two dishes that he put on the table. It was macaroni and cheese, ground beef, some slivers of onion.

"Your favorite," he said. "Even when you was little, and your appetite was so bad, you always ate this up. Always cleaned your plate when I put this on it. Go on, eat. That's what I fixed it for."

She took a few bites. He ate eagerly.

"I'm not her," she said quietly. She had to tell him. "I'm not who you think I am."

"Hush, child, eat your supper."

"You think I'm your daughter, but you're wrong. My name is Sarah Stannard, I grew up in Johnson, Vermont, I never saw you before tonight, I live on—"

His hands made hard fists on the table.

"I said *eat*."

He took a few more bites, not so noisily this time, staring down at the table.

"I knew it would be this way," he said. He looked up at her again. Most of the harshness was gone from him, as quickly as it had appeared. "I knew it'd be hard, and I told myself I wouldn't let it get to me."

The fork made a vague motion over his plate and he put it down.

"I want you to listen. It'll come to you, I know it will. My name is Joseph Sherk. Your name is Margaret. You're my little girl. We live together, you and me, in a cabin in a holler about six miles from Harben, Virginia."

He caught himself.

"We *lived* in a cabin near Harben. But something happened . . ." His voice trailed off momentarily, and he appeared to be searching his memory. "Anyway, we're going back there one of these days. It won't be like this for long. Pretty soon, before you know it, we'll be back to the way we was."

He seemed so sure, his conviction so unshakable. She was discouraged, and it showed.

"You really don't remember, do you, sweetheart?"

Sarah shook her head slowly.

"I wish I could figure what happened," he said. "I wish I could. Something we did that must have gone wrong." He sounded forlorn. "It's a trial, is what it is. We're being tested. That's the only sense I can make of it."

No use arguing. Sarah turned to her food and discovered that she was hungry. She devoured the food on her plate, and gobbled up the seconds that Sherk brought her.

He laughed. "Yes, you always did like it. I knew I could count on that." He wasn't nearly so frightening when she was doing what he wanted, what he expected.

After she had finished, he brought her jeans and a shirt in a paper bag.

"You can put these on," he said. "Get rid of that—" gesturing toward her uniform "—into something more like you."

She put on the clothes in the bathroom. They fit perfectly and Sherk grinned when he saw her.

"That's it, that's my girl," he said. "Now sit."

She did. Sherk replaced the belts at her ankles and hands, binding the hands in front of her.

"Good," he said. "Stay. I won't be long."

He went into the bathroom and closed the door behind him. Sarah thought of the cellar door, and beyond that the parking lot, the city streets.

If you've got the nerve, kiddo.

She tested the belts at her ankles. The loops were tight around each ankle, and she couldn't loosen the clamps. But he had left a few inches of slack between the loops, maybe enough for some short, shuffling steps.

She stood and got free of the chair, tried a few wobbly steps that brought her to the front door of the room. Over her shoulder she could see the bathroom door still shut. There was water running. She put both hands on the knob, turned it, pulled it toward her. It swung open, and she went through into the basement.

To the right was the lighted bottom of a stairwell that seemed to go up to the main floor. To the left was the metal door where he had carried her in. She shuffled over to it. The door didn't budge when she yanked on the handle. Outside there had been a padlock, she remembered, but he couldn't have replaced it already. She felt in the darkness, around the edges of the door. Down at the bottom was a sliding bolt that recessed into a hole in the floor. It stayed up when she pulled it.

Still the door wouldn't move. Had to be another catch somewhere. Her hands, like a blind girl's, pawed the door frame. There. At the top of the door, almost higher than she could reach, a second bolt. She slid it back, and pulled the door.

It came back at her suddenly. With her hobbled legs, she couldn't get out of the way, and it knocked her down, sat her hard on the concrete floor.

The blessed cold air of freedom poured in.

She struggled up, her movements nightmare-slow, and she went out. The bindings tripped her when she tried to climb the stairs. So she crawled, pulling herself up the cold wet concrete, hauling herself up, fighting gravity and the sharp angles of the steps that dug into her arms and her shins.

Finally, the top step. Up on her feet again, leaning against the rail for support. Between her and the street was a stockade fence, higher than the top of her head. It met a hedge nearly as tall, that ran beside a church driveway. To get away she had to get around the hedge.

In her imagination she could feel Sherk behind her, closing in on her. The hedge seemed endless as she stumbled along it. Near the ground it grew thinner, and she found an opening, maybe big enough to sneak through.

She fell flat and began to crawl through mud and melting snow. The branches' sharp ends were like thorns, tearing at her face, her hands. As her head emerged on the other side, a branch snagged her shirt. It dug into her back, a knife-point of pain, as she tried to pull against it. She pulled harder. There was more pain and then she was free of it, dragging herself out, crawling out of the hedge and into the driveway. She stumbled to its entrance, out into the empty street. A gray rat in the gutter saw her, turned, scurried into a sewer drain.

She shouted: "Help me, please. Somebody. He's going to get me." Screamed into the night, toward the darkened homes across the road.

In their upstairs bedroom at 270 Bellflower, the Corwins were watching the last segment of "Nightline" when the shouts reached through their window.

"You hear that?" said Marie Corwin.

"Punks," said her husband. The neighborhood had a

problem with teenagers, especially on Friday and Saturday nights. There would be car horns, blaring music, yelling in the middle of the night. And of course it did no good to call the cops; they always seemed to arrive about three minutes after the last of the troublemakers had peeled off to wake up another part of town.

Koppel was talking about Andrei Sakharov. Marie couldn't concentrate on the story. She sat up in bed when she heard the shouts again.

"Somebody's screaming," she said.

"Punks," her husband said again.

Marie listened for another sound outside. She heard nothing. When Koppel began to read a story about Michael Jackson, she got up and went to the window, and pushed up a slat of the blinds.

The night was undisturbed. Marie studied the familiar setting of church and hall, hedge and fence and parking lot, but she could see nothing amiss. Her feet were chilly, and she wasted no time in returning to the warmth of the bed.

Sherk was brushing his teeth when he heard the first shout. At first it didn't register. Margaret was in his room, a few feet away on the other side of the bathroom door. This came from outside.

Then he understood. He burst out of the bathroom and found her chair empty, the apartment door open. His stork's lope carried him into the basement. He could feel the frigid air flowing in from outside. The fire was suddenly huge in him, filling him up! Bad girl, she'll be sorry!

He vaulted the steps outside and looked around. There was the truck, the hedge, the fence. No Margaret. Then she helped him. She screamed again. Beyond the hedge, other side of the fence.

Sherk ran around into the driveway. Margaret was out in the middle of Bellflower, brittle white under a street light, looking over her shoulder at him and stumbling as she did. She fell.

He hurried out to her, looking up and down the street as

he approached. Nobody around. No cars, no spectators at the windows. Another yell was starting in her chest. He reached for her, slapped a hand over her mouth, muffled the sound.

Then all the fight seemed to leave her. She gave a helpless groan and went limp, dead weight in his arms as he carried her back around the hedge, hurrying toward the stairwell. Still there were no cars, no passersby, no protesting shouts from a front porch. As he leaped down the steps with her, Sherk could see a figure backlit behind a curtain in the rectory. The curtain parted and the monsignor peered out. Sherk kept a hand clamped over her mouth. He knew that they couldn't be seen.

The curtains fell closed as the monsignor left the window, and with that, Sherk pulled her through the cellar door and dropped her to the concrete floor. As he reached back to shut the door, she scrambled away. He lunged and caught her by one foot, but she shook free, lurched, stumbled, and fell into some rakes and shovels that stood in a corner. They toppled like big jackstraws and clattered to the floor. Sherk reached across them, grabbed her by the collar, and dragged her to an open spot on the floor. He knelt over her in the dark basement among the boiler and the racks of tools and the smell of fuel oil. One hand found her mouth. The second was reaching for her neck when she raised her arms, feebly, to push him off. Sherk swatted them away.

He felt the fire. In his mind a picture played out for him, indistinct at first. It was an image of what was going to happen next. Or maybe something that had happened already—he couldn't bring it into focus. One hand pressed harder on her mouth, contorting her face. The other caressed her throat. Yes. He could see it more clearly now, a furious, purgative act.

His right hand was spread over her throat. It was a thin throat, and his long fingers nearly circled it.

Under his thumb he could feel her jugular fluttering. Her body bucked beneath him, shoulders pinned to the floor by his weight. She kicked the air, and exhaled in rapid, gasping snorts.

His fingers tensed on her throat. He squeezed.

The stranger was incredibly strong. She could feel his calloused fingers contracting on her neck, his right hand a vise with the V between thumb and forefinger fitting snugly over her larynx, pressing down. She managed to draw in one lungful, and breathe out with great effort. His grip was tightening, tightening. He took his left hand off her mouth, but the scream that she tried to force up became a hoarse honk.

Now the left hand joined the right at her throat. She was writhing, trying to pitch him off, trying to slide away, but he was immovable and he had her shoulders pinned. She was getting dizzy. In her chest she felt an enormous pressure, as if her lungs were ready to burst.

She realized that she was going. He was killing her. Her arms and legs were too heavy to move anymore. The edges of her vision were tinged in red, a deepening red that went to purple and then to black, and the blackness spread over all that she saw, until she could see no more, think no more.

Margaret stopped struggling. He was choking the fight out of her. Choking the badness and the evil out of her, remembering her contrary ways. The fire fed on his pent-up misery. It would burn his insides clean.

He looked at her face. Her eyes bulged and rolled. He had seen that somewhere before. The dream. Terror on Margaret's face, and the faceless man's hands on her throat.

Hands on her throat.

No.

His hands on her throat.

No!

Memory and fantasy and intuition and the present all became one, and Sherk could see it clearly, a single brilliant illuminating flash.

He pulled his hands away, as if scalded. He released her. He stood and swayed over where she lay with her mouth agape. A thermostat clicked across the basement, and the oil jets flamed, roared, under the boiler.

• • •

She breathed in. Her vision cleared, and she breathed again.

I could be dead right now.

Sarah knew it had been that close. The concrete floor was cold and clammy through her shirt, and she realized that it might have been the last thing she ever felt. Damp concrete and the killing hands of a stranger. It was all so fast, she thought, so easy. Not this act alone, but death itself. No great struggle of soul torn from body, no drum rolls, no portentous shadows over the land. Just life one moment and death the next, the end of life as quick and casual as the crumpling of a paper cup.

"Get up," he said. She was slow to move. He said it louder. Somehow she staggered to her feet and stumbled ahead of him into his room.

"Sit down." He bit it off. She sat in the chair where he had left her before.

He slammed the door and turned back to her.

"What do you think, you can spit in my face, nothing happens?" His shouting made her cringe. He was circling her chair, gesticulating fiercely.

"You don't know what you're doing," he said. "What you're playing with here. Things . . . things . . ." His voice was softer, tortured. He stood in front of her, the hands dropping to his sides and then going up to his head. He looked up at the ceiling. "I don't know . . . things. Not quite right. Not the way they were."

His gaze was fixed on the ceiling. For a moment he seemed to have forgotten her; he was completely engrossed. Then his eyes found hers again.

"Get up we're going," he said abruptly.

"Where?" Her throat was sore and the word came out raspy.

"Don't worry about it."

She got up. He checked the belts, took some of the slack out of the ankles, and still looked at her with some doubt. As if this was not enough. Then he went to a cabinet and came out with a pillowcase. He shook it out, and she saw that he intended to put it over her head.

"Please don't," she said.

"It won't hurt." His voice was still cold.

"I want to see."

"You should have thought of that before you run off. Now I got to make sure."

He raised it over her head, and she closed her eyes. When she opened them again she saw only white cotton, faintly suffusing the room light.

"At least tell me," she said. "Please tell me where I'm going."

She thought she sensed him smiling.

"Home," he said. "We're going home."

She heard a silken noise that she tried to place. She knew that sound—the sleeping bag. He was putting it over his shoulder.

Then he surprised her completely. One arm around her back, another around her bottom. He picked her up and cradled her as if she were a bundle, a sack of grain.

She thought of his hands around her neck, thought of how he had brushed aside her resistance, how her struggles had seemed to infuriate him. This time she would not resist.

He carried her into the basement; she could hear the oil burner. Across the basement, up some steps. That would be the lighted staircase she had seen. Beyond this she was lost. Past the top of the stairs they seemed to travel down a long corridor with a low ceiling; she could tell by the resonance of his footsteps on a hard floor that sounded like linoleum.

Then one step up and they were on carpet. A small room that he crossed in a few strides. Two steps down, off the carpet. His feet were slapping on some hard surface again. For some reason stone came to mind. This room was much larger—he took longer to cross it. And there was a faint smell that she could not name, an elusive scent that was fragrant and smoky, like pipe tobacco but not so sweet.

Another set of stairs. This one doubled back on itself. Then a few steps on stone or concrete. Then wood, a sturdy wooden floor. He stopped and stood her up. She heard a door swinging, opening, followed by a sound like coat-hangers scraping on a pipe.

He came around behind her, grasped her shoulders and pushed her forward a few feet, halted her and turned her to the right.

"Down on your knees," he commanded.

She did as he said.

"Now go. Crawl." She hesitated, and he gave her a push from behind. She crawled.

She was in a passage hardly wider than her shoulders. If she leaned to one side or another, her elbows rubbed against a wall. Wood on the left, stone on the right, floor and ceiling both wood. She imagined a tunnel about two feet wide, not much higher.

"Go on, keep going, not much farther." He was behind her.

She continued forward into the unknown, the unimagined. Even without the hood, she thought, she must be in darkness. With each foot that she advanced, the passage seemed to constrict. The walls were closing in on her, trapping her, smothering her.

She stopped.

"I can't," she said.

"Crawl!" He shoved her from behind. Sarah forced herself forward. Moving one hand. Then the next. The legs following, her knees scraping on the rough wooden floor.

"Now stop. Off to your left is a space—feel it?"

She put out her left hand; there was a gap in the wall.

"Go through there. Uh-huh. There you go."

She crawled through the opening. When she stretched her arms, she touched nothing but air. The walls had retreated.

He came in behind her. A flaring match gave a saffron glow to the inside of the pillowcase. The glow brightened, and remained steady even after he blew out the match. A lamp, she thought. The cloth lifted off her face. She could see.

They were in an attic that was about the size of her bedroom at her grandparents' house. The floor was unfin-

ished wood planking. Rough-hewn beams angled upward
from two sides of the floor and peaked about five feet
high. At no place was there room to stand straight under
the sloping roof.

The attic was far from empty. Her eyes took in a
folding camp cot, blankets, a collapsible canvas chair.
Cardboard crates were stored along one side. A string
hammock hung across the far end of the room, suspended
from screw hooks in a set of beams.

Going home, he had said. From the looks of the place,
he had been making ready for someone. For her.

Her heart sank. He meant to keep her here. It seemed as
distant and obscure a hole as she could imagine. Nobody
would ever find her here.

Sherk made her stretch out on the floor, and he tested
the restraints around her arms and legs. He pulled the
sleeping bag over her again. Sarah barely noticed. She was
still taking in the room, realizing what it must mean.

He dragged out a shapeless pile of canvas. The fabric
rustled as he shook it out. There were straps and buckles
sewn on. It looked like a shroud, stitched together at the
feet. Or a full-length straitjacket.. Sherk was laying it out
on the floor, open, unbuckled. Then she saw. She knew.

"No," she said. "Not this, you can't."

With arms and legs tied, the sleeping bag zipped around
her, she had no way to stop Sherk from picking her up and
placing her in the middle of the canvas.

"Have to do this," he was saying. "Can't take chances."

The shroud enclosed her. He pulled it tight, closed the
buckles, tugged the canvas to find loose spots. There were
none. She was encased in a cocoon of nylon and goose
down and canvas. She wiggled her fingers and toes, and
canted her head to one side. Nothing else would move.

"Good. One last thing, we'll be about set."

He was holding what looked like a leather version of a
surgeon's mask, except that this one had a row of small
holes at the mouth, and straps both at the back of the head
and at the top of the skull.

"Deerskin," he said. "Nice and soft. Leather can be
rough on the face."

He put it on her. It pulled upward on her jaw as he tightened the straps.

"Can you breathe?" he asked. She nodded. "Through the mouth, I mean." There was just enough room for her to slightly part her lips. She nodded again.

"Now say goodnight."

She tried to form the words, but with the mask covering her mouth, restricting her jaw, all that came out was a throaty mumble.

"Just right," he said.

She realized that he had planned this, too. The mask let in air, but she couldn't scream, couldn't even whisper.

He picked her up, carried her to the hammock, and put her in it. There were two more belts yet, both passing through loops in the shroud, one tying her into the hammock at the feet, the other holding her in at the shoulders. When he was finished, she was completely enfolded, absolutely immobile.

He stood over her, somber, looking into her eyes.

"You know who you are?" he said.

She nodded. Yes.

"Are you Margaret?"

Maybe it was foolish, but she couldn't lie. She shook her head, No. And waited for him to explode.

Sherk didn't change expression. His eyes looked tired.

"It'll come," he said. "In its time."

He left her side and turned down the wick of the lamp. The flame died and night surrounded them. She heard him stretch out on the cot, pull up the blankets.

She thought of home, and school, and of her mother, all so far from this dark prison. Thought of a boy named Tim, whose friends called him Spoon, holding her close on a snowy afternoon that seemed years removed.

She could not imagine anyone finding her here. Wherever she was. If she was to survive, to see the light again, she could count on nobody else. It might be up to her.

Oh, God, why me?

So he had Margaret. Sherk should have been happy, but his pleasure was spoiled. He kept thinking of what he had seen as he knelt on the basement floor.

Already the episode was blurring in his memory. He remembered his anger, and remembered straddling her chest as she lay on the concrete. The rest was indistinct. But he knew that he had stopped at the brink of something bad. He had been ready to hurt Margaret. The thought made him ill.

And that was not the worst. All the rest might fade from mind—and would, very soon—but one instant he could never forget. It had to do with the dream, that crazy dream. With the shadowy, evil figure who stalked through it. The faceless one.

Only tonight he had seen the face. And it was his own.

—TWENTY-FIVE—

SATURDAY
NOVEMBER 10

SARAH woke in total blackness, arms and legs encased, immobile.

The darkness was almost palpable, surrounding her. She had the sensation of being buried in a deep, narrow cave, far from the light and far from the world, layered over by the stifling, impenetrable unknown.

Her heart raced in panic. She tried to call Sherk, gulping in all the air that her chest would hold, then shoving it up into her throat. It came out as the cry of one without a tongue: a formless grunt, inarticulate.

She waited. Except for her own pulse, loud in her ears, there was no sound.

So she was alone. He had left her while she slept. To return—who knew when?

Make him come back. I need him. Dear God I need him.

After bolting the apartment door, Sherk reached under his bed and retrieved the purse that he had brought in from the truck. He took it to the table and dumped it upside down in front of him.

He sorted through the contents. A couple of Tampax in their wrappers; he shoved them back into the purse. Half a roll of peppermint Lifesavers, several pens and pencils, two hair clips, a strip of four postage stamps, a plastic comb, a hair brush: all this he collected in one hand and returned to the purse. That left a red leather wallet.

He began to go through it. In a side pocket he found photographs. Margaret standing in a front door he did not know. Posing with strangers, a man and a woman about his age. Then a small portrait of this same man. He removed each of the photos and tossed them onto the table, making a small pile, as he continued through the wallet. An Anne Arundel library card in the name of Sarah Stannard, and an ID card from Nordbrook School in the same name. He flipped them both onto the pile. A folded newspaper clipping, the obituary of a man named John Stannard. That went on the pile, too.

When he had removed every trace of that name he replaced the wallet in the purse. Then he made a pile of the photos and paper in the kitchen sink. He touched a match to them and watched them burn, stirring them until they were completely consumed. The photos curled up brown at the edges before they blackened. The ashes crumbled under the heel of his hands, and they swirled down the basin as he rinsed it clean.

By now, he thought, she would be awake and hungry. He tucked her purse in the gym bag, put in a flashlight and a quart of orange juice and a box of graham crackers as well, and he went to rejoin his daughter.

She was whimpering softly when Sherk returned, the beam from a flashlight preceding him. By the time he lit the glass lamp she had nearly controlled her ragged breathing.

He came over to her in the yellow light and removed the mask.

"You been crying," he said.

"Hardly at all. I don't suppose you could let me out of this thing?" Meaning the cocoon.

"That's why I'm here."

"That would be good."

As he unbuckled the straps she filled her lungs with air and tried twisting her neck. A band of pain embraced her throat and marked exactly where his hands had gripped her. She could still feel his fingers.

"What was it, exactly, that bothered you?" He was distant, but not unfriendly. Sarah guessed that he had chosen to ignore the night before.

"I woke up," she said. "And it was dark. That's all."

"I never knowed you to be afraid of the dark."

"I'm not. But this was different." The words were out before she remembered that they were talking about two different girls.

"You left me," she said. "I woke up and I was all alone."

"I can't stay up here all the time, sweetheart."

"I didn't know," she said. "You should have told me. I woke up, and I didn't know where you were, or what happened to you. I didn't know if you'd ever come back. I'd be up here forever if you went away."

"I'm not going nowhere. I'm sorry you got scared." He sounded as if he meant it.

"It wasn't bad."

"Maybe next time I'll leave the lamp burning. Wouldn't that be better?"

She nodded, grudgingly. If this was going to be a contest of wills, she didn't want to concede anything.

"Then I'll do it," he said. He was removing the straps from her wrists and her ankles.

"Hungry?" he asked.

"Yes. But first I'd like you to bring me to the bathroom." She assumed that he would take her down into his room; there was no plumbing up here. "I'll be glad to get out of here for a while."

"Is that so?" he said. The crinkling corners of his eyes showed amusement. For some reason this was funny. "Suppose I bring the bathroom to you instead."

She watched him go to a corner and wrestle a large cardboard crate into the middle of the floor. He tore open the top flaps and lifted out what looked like a green toilet bowl without the tank.

"Camper's john," he said. "People pack 'em in the car. Put it in their tents, I guess. Can you believe it?"

"I couldn't possibly use that," she said.

"I think you better." He was back in the corner again, this time coming out with a gallon-sized plastic bottle of a blue fluid. "It's this or a tin pot. I don't think you'll like that any better."

He was pouring the liquid down into the bowl, releasing a smell that reminded Sarah of decaying flowers.

"You're not letting me out?" she said.

"Sweetheart, I wish I could. You don't know how much." Sherk's tone was wistful. "But it ain't such a good idea. Not now."

Nails protruded from a couple of the beams. Sherk had a blanket and he was hanging it from one of the nails, draping it across the attic. This was supposed to give her some privacy.

"I have to stay up here all the time?"

"Not forever. You'll get out one of these days."

"When?" she said. He was shaking the folds out of the blanket so that it would hang down to the floor.

"When I can trust you," he said. It was the voice of an unrelenting father. "When you're back the way you should be."

"But how long?"

The blanket went up between them, and his voice was disembodied.

"Long as it takes, Margaret."

She stared at the blanket. Her first reaction was to argue, but she stopped herself. He wouldn't be badgered.

"At least leave me alone for this," she said. "A couple of minutes, you can do that."

She waited a moment before she peeked around one side of the blanket. Sherk was crawling into the passage outside the entryway. But his presence persisted, and when she exposed herself she felt as if he were staring directly at her. She kept thinking that he would rush in at any moment, tear down the blanket, reveal her nakedness. She had never felt more vulnerable, more humiliated.

Sherk's first victory came when she ate all her graham crackers. For breakfast? Margaret had asked him. Graham crackers and orange juice for breakfast?

But she had eaten eagerly all the same, and it was a triumph, proof that the daughter he knew was not far out of reach. Many times he had seen her make a meal of grahams and orange juice.

Now she was brushing her hair, long slow strokes that pulled the yellow strands halfway down her back. She was ignoring him. Her way of showing that she was miserable. Punishing him. Sherk felt a great gulf between them, and he knew that his sternness so far was part of the reason. He didn't want it that way. His instinct was to say, yes, let's leave this prison, I'll give you exactly what you want.

But it couldn't be, not yet, not the way she was now.

"You used to go out on the front porch to do that," he said.

She looked at him without understanding.

"Don't you remember? I'd help you wash it in the sink, scrub it real good, and rub it with a towel 'til it was only damp. Then, if it was a sunny day, you'd go out on the porch and brush it out until it was dry. You used to say that the sun made everything smell sweet, clothes on the line and your hair, both."

She shook her head slowly.

"You really don't remember?"

"There's nothing to remember," she said. "Don't get angry. But I have to tell you the truth. I'm not her. You're all wrong, you're making a big mistake. I'm not your daughter."

He put out a hand to caress her cheek, thinking, Poor girl, she needs kindness.

She flinched at his touch. That riled him.

"Okay, let's get up," he said brusquely. Maybe she didn't know what she was doing, but he was insulted all the same. He didn't have to put up with this. "I been gone long enough, and it's time you got back in the bag."

Her expression was morose as he zipped and buckled the cocoon. To Sherk it looked as if she was trying mightily to hold back a flood of tears.

The deerskin mask was in his hands when he looked down at her.

"What's your name?" he said.

She looked away. "My name is Sarah."

"You ain't even *tryin'*," he said.

He was gone. And Sarah, who had prayed for his return, was now grateful that she would not have to see him for a while.

She told herself that claustrophobia didn't kill, but Sherk might. She had nearly set him off again, by instinctively drawing away from his scaly touch.

He could almost be nice, she thought, as long as he wasn't challenged. As long as she didn't argue with him, or contradict him. She couldn't afford petulance or even pride. Had to keep him happy.

Kid, we're talking survival here.

The hardest part would be swallowing the truth. Looking into his eyes as he stood over her and asked, What's your name?

What does he expect? she wondered. What does he want?

But she already knew the answer to that.

—TWENTY-SIX—

SUNDAY
NOVEMBER 11
8:55 A.M.

THE tower bell at St. Bartholomew's pealed with a deep, sonorous clap, and when she heard it the first time Sarah thought it sounded like divine thunder. The vibrant clanging shook the attic and seemed to penetrate down to her marrow.

It struck ten times, and when it was finished it left an imprint on the silence. Gradually the stillness restored itself.

Obviously the attic was somewhere very close to the bell. She had glimpsed the church when Sherk brought her in the truck; this warren couldn't possibly belong to the stone edifice that she had seen. But it was close, she thought. The bell could not have been louder, even if she had been in the steeple.

She hoped that she would hear it again. Anything to break the boredom. Anything to remind her that there was a reality beyond the room's slanting rafters.

Sherk was gone. Again he had slept in the cot, before rousing himself in what Sarah assumed was early morning. This time his stirring had awakened her, but she didn't let him know. Through half-open lids she watched as he crawled out, while she wondered where he was going

177

and—more important—where he was leaving. The attic existed somewhere.

Somewhere close to the bell.

She was waiting for it to ring again when she heard indecipherable voices seeping into the room, a muddy humming that was suspended in the quiet, like dust made visible as it drifts through a shaft of light. Voices, and footsteps, seemed to waft up into the attic. There were people below.

Suddenly she recalled the smoky fragrance, not as sweet as pipe tobacco. They had been walking in a huge room with a stone floor. She knew the smell now. It was incense. The floor was probably marble, and the room was not really a room, but a church. Sherk had carried her through the church.

She was telling herself this when the organ bellowed a chord that blasted through the back wall of the attic, even louder in its way than the bell had been, assaulting her with sound. It was the opening of a hymn. The bass rumbled and the high notes soared. And then voices—clear, reaching voices that lifted and chased the melody line. She was surrounded by song.

In the midst of the din, Sarah tried to sort through the evidence. And it was clear, she thought. Sherk had carried her through the church, but he had never taken her out. He had found a place in God's house that was as far from light and life as she could imagine.

The organ played several hymns, not continuously, but one every few minutes. Sometimes it accompanied the choir and at other times there was no singing. Then she heard the low babble and the footsteps, and then again the bell, but no more choir, no more organ.

The bell rang twice more, four times in all, at intervals, she guessed, of about an hour. All the while Sherk was absent. By twisting her sore neck, Sarah could see the level of kerosene in the glass bowl of the lamp, so she was not surprised when the light in the room trembled and dimmed and died. Out of fuel.

This time the darkness wasn't so bad. There were fewer unknowns to weigh on her. She was hidden away, maybe, but not buried. And she knew that Sherk would return. He loved his daughter—crazy as he was, he was capable of love—and he would not desert her.

At that moment she realized consciously what she had probably known from the first hour of her captivity: Sherk's delusion could keep her alive. But she had to nurture it. He had nearly killed her on Friday night, when she had reacted like a frightened stranger. Daughters don't flee from their fathers. And fathers don't kill their daughters.

It was something to think about. She had nothing but time.

Sherk's gym bag had become her pantry and her lifeline. This time it contained sandwiches: single slices of bologna on white bread with mayonnaise. And lemonade. Canned imitation lemonade.

A real gourmet, she thought, but she kept it to herself.

They sat cross-legged on the floor, with paper towels spread in front of them. She hadn't eaten in hours, and the first sandwich went down in half a dozen bites. She was nearly through the second when she put it down, chewed and swallowed, and without preface said to Sherk, "I want to know where we are."

His grin was at once coy and sinister.

"All the racket on Sunday mornings, ain't you got it figured out yet?"

"In a church."

"More or less," he said. Still grinning.

"But not really in church."

"You'd be surprised."

"Some place in the church that nobody knows about," she said.

"I know about it."

It was hopeless, she thought. He could dance around it all day if he wanted. She chewed on the remains of the sandwich and decided to try the back door.

"What do you do here? Am I supposed to know that already?"

"No reason why you should. I'm the one that keeps the

place together." He was serious now. "Without me this church would fall down around 'em."

"Who?"

"Priests." The word curdled in his mouth.

She was about to say, *I was baptized Catholic,* but she swallowed it with the food she was eating.

"One of 'em called me a church rat," Sherk continued. His back straightened visibly. "Maybe he was right. Rats know buildings better'n any architect. Rats and cockroaches. I seen places in this church that the priests never dreamed of."

"Like this," she said.

"Honeypie, you got that exactly right. We might as well be on the back side of the moon for all they know."

She tried once more: "You get here through the back of the church, is that right?"

"Questions, full of questions," he said in the light way that fathers will use with insistent children. "You'll find out soon enough."

"When?"

"When you're ready."

She knew better than to press him. She finished her meal without another word. Sherk watched her constantly, and for the first time she tried not to shrink from his eyes. Instead she met his gaze, and smiled what she hoped he would recognize as a shy, daughter-like smile. He caught it and studied her for two or three seconds, and she thought she saw his face soften as he looked away.

When they had both eaten, she thanked him for the meal and gathered up the empty cans and paper towels. She could see that this pleased him. A daughter would do housekeeping.

"How you doing?" he said. "You do all right, alone up here?"

"I get bored," she said.

"Well. Bored is better than scared, huh? Anything else?"

"I get lonely."

"Do you? Is that right?" He was prodding, testing. "Who you get lonely for?"

"People." Her voice small.

"You get lonely for your daddy?"

She nodded once. They were still seated about an arm's length apart. Sherk suddenly reached out and grabbed one of her wrists. His face was taut, intense.

"What's your name?" he said.

He was glaring at her. What could it hurt? she thought. But not all at once.

"I don't know . . . I have trouble remembering."

He let go of her wrist. The tightness dissolved around his jaw, and his face split into a wide smile. He was beaming.

"That's a start," he said.

He put her back in the cocoon anyway; she had known it wouldn't be that easy. But he had left happy, and Sarah felt more secure than at any time since the moment she encountered him on the snowy lane.

Not so hard to do, she thought. Be a child to the father. She knew that one by heart.

—TWENTY-SEVEN—

MONDAY
NOVEMBER 12
9:30 P.M.

DINNER was late. For two hours they had sat with the county detective named Tarver, listening to him say that everything possible was being done to find Sarah. And that no progress had been made.

Now the three of them were at the kitchen table in the main wing. They all looked worn and weary, eroded by anxiety.

"The tomatoes are terrible," Joy Stannard said, trying to make conversation. Anything to lighten the pall. "This time of year, they're so hard and tasteless."

"Not so bad," Harry said. "Probably got shipped two thousand miles to get here, it's a miracle we have them at all."

Elise sat rigidly, looking down at her plate, pushing her food around with a fork.

"Is the stroganoff all right?" Joy said.

"Delicious," Harry declared. His cheer sounded forced and brittle.

Elise looked down, mute.

"Elise, you ought to eat," Joy said. "You must keep your strength up."

"Is that written down somewhere?" Elise said. Her voice was harsh. "Let me get this straight. Your daughter

182

gets kidnapped, you have to eat so you can keep up your strength?''

Joy sounded hurt: "We're concerned about you, that's all.''

"I'll survive, I'm afraid.''

Harry struggled for words. "Time goes on,'' he said. He was trying to say that falling apart and starving won't bring her back. But the idea didn't come out quite right. "We have to live,'' he said.

She glared at him, put down her fork, and stood.

"I'll start to live again,'' she said, "when I get my daughter back.''

The monsignor, hidden in shadow, watched Sherk walk through the dimness of the church: a silent, fleeting figure, barely visible among the gray stone and the ranked dark pews, moving not so much with stealth as with total confidence, so sure in his passage that he made hardly a ripple in time and space.

The monsignor had been praying. To the left of the altar, opposite the sacristy, was a tiny chapel that seated no more than ten or twelve. Tonight was the anniversary of his parents' marriage—it would have been their fifty-fifth— and he had come there to remember them.

The chapel was dark; prayer required no lights. To his right as he knelt was a door, half-open, that faced the side of the altar. Behind him was a second door, open all the way, that looked down the left side aisle. At the end of the aisle, near the back of the church, was the staircase up to the choirloft.

At night the main altar sat under a couple of weak spotlights that cast uneven splotches from overhead. As he left the sacristy Sherk passed momentarily through one of these pools of low light, and the monsignor caught that movement through the half-open side door. It made him turn his head. Then he saw Sherk, already out of the light, unaware that he had been noticed.

At another time the monsignor would have called out; he had been meaning to tell Sherk about a clogged drain in the rectory. But he wanted to be alone for a while longer, so he stayed silent. Still, he turned his head and watched Sherk pass through the gate in the altar rail, down the main aisle.

The monsignor got up and went to the back door of the chapel to watch Sherk glide through the church, in and out of the shadows, soundless in his progress, making his way to the back of the church and up the stairs to the choir loft.

The monsignor found himself inexplicably disturbed as he knelt again. He tried once more to pray, but instead he caught himself wondering what Sherk could want in the choir loft at this hour.

He crossed himself, got up, and left the chapel by the rear door. The stairs to the choir loft were immediately in his path. When he reached them he hesitated. He knew somehow that Sherk would not want to be surprised.

Then he dismissed the thought. A drain needed fixing, and it was Sherk's job.

He climbed the stairs. Halfway up was a landing where the steps reversed direction and carried up into the loft. His footfalls sounded loud, and the monsignor was sure that Sherk would hear him coming. He reached the top step, came through the short passage and out into the loft.

It was empty. The monsignor looked around and saw nobody. He went to the front of the loft to be sure. Softly he spoke Sherk's name into the shadows. No reply.

Two minutes ago, he thought, he had seen Sherk come up here. Maybe three. He had watched Sherk climb the steps, then had turned his back and tried to pray again. Three minutes at most.

There was only one way up into the loft, he thought. And one way down. Sherk would have had to come back down the stairs almost immediately. Must have come back down and slipped away. Must have. Or he would be here. It stood to reason.

The monsignor walked across the loft to the closet door in the far corner. He had looked everywhere else. His hand rested on the doorknob for a few seconds before he pulled it open. It was dark. His hand felt along the wall until he found the light switch.

Choir robes, a few boxes. Of course, he thought. Why should he expect to find Sherk hiding in the closet?

He closed the door and crossed the loft to the passageway at the top of the stairs. There he paused and looked around once again. It was as quiet as he had ever known it. As quiet and as empty.

Even with the mask across her face, even with the gym bag zippered shut, she caught the aroma. Sherk loosened the straps of the mask. When it was off she sniffed again.

"McDonald's!"

"I needed to get away from home cookin'," he said. "I thought maybe you did, too."

With his help she shed herself of the cocoon, and they sat as before, with the gym bag between them. It was his third trip to the attic today, and each time he had seemed satisfied. Seemed calm.

"You can serve," Sherk said. He pushed the gym bag toward her.

She opened it. On top was a folded tablecloth, checked blue and white, that she spread out on the floor. Then she began to pull out a treasure trove, a wonderment of junk food.

"Big Macs," she said. "Fries. Shakes—is the chocolate for me? McNuggets. I don't *believe* all this."

As Sherk watched, she arranged the feast on the tablecloth. He seemed pleased with himself, pleased with her, and Sarah told herself that if she could only preserve that, keep him just that happy, she would survive until the time came for escape or rescue.

There was one last package in the gym bag, oblong and wrapped in brown paper, a little smaller than a shoebox. She took it out and held it.

"Give me that," Sherk said abruptly, and he snatched it away from her, laid it carefully to the side.

He was unpredictable, she thought. And frightening because of it. He might feed her burgers and treat her decently one moment, then humiliate her the next.

The package seemed sinister to her, and the food suddenly lost its savor. She wondered what indignity he planned for her now. She had to know.

"C'mon, what've you got over there?" Trying to sound playful.

"Just eat. You'll find out soon enough."

"Is it a secret? You can tell me, I'm good at keeping secrets."

"If I wanted you to know, I'd have told you already. You want to see, is that it?"

She thought she heard some impatience in his voice.

"Just kidding," she said. "Honest."

But he was reaching back for it, saying, "Maybe I better give it to you now."

"Really," she said, "I can wait. I never should have said a thing."

He held it out to her, thrusting it into her hands.

"Go on, you're so anxious to find out. Go on and open it. Right now."

He was leaning in close to her, his eyes laughing. Or mocking, she thought. He was enjoying her discomfort as she reluctantly plucked open one taped end of the wrapper.

She turned the package and opened the other end, then pulled off the wrapping. The box that it covered said SONY on the outside. She tore away one flap and slid out the contents. Inside, nestled in a styrofoam cradle, was a Walkman radio, smaller than a pack of cigarettes, with earphones.

She heard herself release the breath that she had been holding.

"For me?" she said.

"I don't see anybody else in this room that needs a radio." He was hugely pleased with himself. "Something to keep you company, make the time pass. You said you was getting bored."

She was speechless.

"I put the battery in already," he said. "A long-life. See, you can tune it to whatever station you want, put on the earphones, listen to music. Not so bad, huh?"

"It's really nice." She felt a rush of gratitude that was all out of proportion to the gift itself. It had to do with being rewarded, when she had expected punishment. The sense of relief was overwhelming.

"Thank you, Mister Sherk," she said. "Thank you so much."

She saw some of the smile leave his face.

"What's wrong?" she said. "Did I do something wrong?"

"Nothing," he said. "You don't have to call me mister, that's all."

She thought for a moment.

"Thank you, Joseph," she said. But that didn't seem to help. He was impassive, but she saw a touch of sadness in his look.

"Better eat," he said. "Food's getting cold."

She was reluctant to turn away.

"Come on, *eat*. I didn't buy it to see it wasted."

—TWENTY-EIGHT—

TUESDAY
NOVEMBER 13

TWELVE hours after he had left, the county detective was back in the Stannards' living room. Harry had called for him, and Tarver was there, standing in the middle of the Oriental carpet that, viewed obliquely, appeared to writhe under foot. It made him jumpy.

Harry's face was in peppery stubble, his eyes red-veined. He wore baggy trousers and a blue pajama top.

"You people talk to the papers, the radio and TV, is that right?" he asked.

"No more than necessary," Tarver said. "I mean, they tend to get in the way. Most times, they need us more than we need them."

"We can use them now," Harry said. To Tarver, he sounded like a man trying to hang on. Still fighting, but battered and close to beaten. Harry held out a sheet of lined yellow paper, folded in thirds. "Read it," he said.

Tarver took it, and read three lines handwritten in heavy block letters.

"Will that help?" Harry said.

"It'll bring the crazies out of the woodwork. That I can guarantee. Beyond that, who knows? If it comes up with anything useful, it'll be worth the trouble."

"I didn't know what else to do. Look, I'm sitting here, I'm helpless, going crazy." He raised his right hand in a plaintive gesture that fell incomplete. "You understand? I thought, the best I can do is to keep her picture in the papers for a couple more days, keep people talking about her. In case somebody out there saw something. Anything. Does that make sense?"

Tarver creased the paper tightly along the folds and poked it into the front pocket of his jacket.

"So long as you realize it's a long shot."

"At this point, that's really all I've got left."

Sarah, bound up in the cocoon, heard her own name spoken on the radio. It was a moment as unreal as anything else she had experienced in the last four days.

Before he left, Sherk had adjusted the earphones to her head—the mask didn't interfere—and he had put the tiny radio receiver in her hands before he fastened the canvas again. She could adjust the volume and change the tuning by moving thumbs and fingers.

She had worked across the dial before settling on an FM station in Baltimore that was playing a Stray Cats album. A set of commercials followed the last song in the sequence. Then news, with the disc jockey reading wire copy with the recorded clatter of a teletype machine in the background.

She listened. The D.J. read a story about the Ayatollah, another about the prison riot in Virginia. Then he was talking about a reward of $100,000 offered this morning for information leading to the safe return of Sarah Stannard, a teenage girl apparently abducted Friday afternoon near her home in Anne Arundel County.

"As of this hour," the D.J. was saying, "the young woman remains missing."

But I'm not, Sarah thought. I'm here.

Warner spent most of the day in a large garage at the north end of town, an automotive chop shop that had been raided the night before. Inside the garage were the chassis of two Porsches and a Corvette, in various stages of dismemberment. There were also bins full of starters and alternators, a stack of Blaupunkt stereos, and a back room where at least twenty used engines lay on wooden pallets.

He was supposed to take inventory; a patrolman was detailed to help. Together they pawed through the parts bins, counting pieces and noting serial numbers. In a shelf along one wall was a transistor radio, and the patrolmen tuned it to a country-and-western station in Upper Marlboro. That was how Warner found out about the reward.

It was late afternoon before they finished, when Warner washed his hands and went to a pay phone outside. He called Tarver at county headquarters.

"Anything come of it?" he asked.

"Hell yes," Tarver said. "So far we've found the girl eighteen, nineteen times. Hard to keep track. We got a guy in Severna Park, he's absolutely sure the kid's been living next door for the past six months. Another one up in Baltimore swears he saw her walking down Pratt Street at nine o'clock last night. I think my favorite is the lady down in North Beach who says she watched strange lights flying over the bay Friday night. You can fill in the rest.

"Thing is, it's all diddling anyway. He could put up a million—it won't bring that kid back alive."

"You don't know that," Warner said, but as he heard the words he realized he was talking like a rookie. Thinking with his heart.

"Man, give me a break," said Tarver. "She's been gone five days. We know she didn't just walk away. Some asshole caught her in those woods and carried her out. And it ain't taking him five days to figure out what to do with her, understand? Now if the old man wants to put up the money for an arrest and conviction, maybe he'll get somewhere. But at this point, to think about getting the kid back, that's dreaming. And somebody ought to tell him so."

"Maybe you," Warner said.

"Are you kidding me? Uh-uh. Some other brave fool, maybe. Not this good soldier."

—TWENTY-NINE—

WEDNESDAY
NOVEMBER 14

SARAH Stannard's photo—the same face that had perplexed him all weekend—greeted Terry Dean when he opened his evening paper. Just when he had managed to put it out of mind, having convinced himself that he was either mistaken or that the answer to the puzzle was so remote as to be untouchable.

Now she was looking out at him again. Those deep-set, searching eyes.

The photo accompanied a story about Harry's reward; one hundred thousand dollars was news. Dean tried to read the piece, but the photo kept distracting him. He knew that it would be that way all day, nagging at him, prodding his mind, until he managed once again to shove it aside.

Elise, alone in her bedroom, buried in sheets and blankets, heard her name spoken on the other side of the door. Joy wanted to come in. Elise didn't bother to answer, and after a few moments Joy opened the door and tentatively entered the darkened room.

"Elise, honey, I think we ought to talk."

Joy moved closer to the bed, cautiously reducing the distance between them. Elise raised her head.

"Are you okay?" Joy said. "Is there something wrong?"

Elise gave her a hard look.

"Dumb question, I guess," Joy said. "Look, this has hit us all hard. We love that girl. But Harry and I, we're as worried about you as we are about Sarah. The way we look at it, we can't stand to lose either one of you."

"Save your concern for Sarah."

"We can't do anything about Sarah. But you, that's different. We won't let you shrivel up on us."

Elise turned away.

"Please go," she said. She put an arm across her face. "You left the door open. The light, it hurts my eyes. Please, I'll be all right, I just want you to leave."

Alone again, Elise thought about tragedy, and about how people were always so anxious to flee from it. When disaster hit, the first thing you heard was, Got to get on with your life. Got to put it behind you.

That was fine, if it was death you were trying to deal with. Death was a huge maw that no amount of mourning could fill. Those on the other side were forever beyond reach; thus sorrow was squandered on the dead. Sorrow consumed life, and life was for the living.

But this was different. Elise believed that Sarah was alive. She would continue to believe it until proved wrong. If Sarah lived, then the pain that Elise felt was not without purpose. For pain came from keeping love fresh.

Time, unresisted, would blunt the hurt. Elise told herself she couldn't let that happen. She had to go on hurting, face the pain and feel it all and not shrink from it. No other way could she keep open the place in her heart that Sarah had always occupied.

Keep it open, to be filled again when the girl returned.

Joy Stannard, returning from Elise's room, found her husband sitting at the kitchen table, chin cupped in his hands, staring at the empty wall. She had always considered him to be as nearly impervious to age as a mortal could be. But tonight he seemed an old man. He had been talking to the detective, Tarver, and now he showed the strain, the frustration, of pushing against an obstacle that all his will and means would not budge. The sight of Harry Stannard helpless made his wife want to cry. But she resisted.

She took a seat beside him, put her arms around him, and kissed him warmly on the side of his head, where his coarse fringe met the smooth pink of his scalp.

"Harry, you tried," she said.

"The last time I got a medal for trying was in second grade. And even then I threw it away. Trying won't cut it."

"You can't give up."

"Give up or not, it doesn't matter. That's the hell of it. Don't you see? Whatever happens to Sarah has nothing to do with us. And we better get used to the feeling, because that's how it is. Hard as it is to swallow."

He rubbed his eyes and wheezed heavily in his chest.

"All we can do," he said, "is sit and worry about her. I know it's true. And I hate it."

—THIRTY—

WEDNESDAY
NOVEMBER 14
11 P.M.

"WHAT'S your name?"

Up in the attic. A languid yellow splash from the kerosene lamp playing across the beams and the wooden sheathing of the roof. The canvas cocoon was tight around her.

A little coyly, she answered: "I'm not sure."

All day, Sherk had been in a light mood. He leaned over her with a grin in his eyes.

"What kind of a girl don't know her own name?"

"A forgetful one, I guess."

"Maybe I can help," he said, the voice still playful. "Is your name . . . Amy?"

"I don't think so."

"Is your name . . . Ernestine?"

He mugged outlandishly as he said it; she hadn't seen him do that before.

"Definitely not Ernestine," she said.

"You kind of look like an Ernestine to me."

"No!" She giggled. This exchange had a familiar feel, and in a second she realized what it was. This was a father-and-daughter game. Daddy and little girl. She knew how to play that.

"If you're not Ernestine, you must be Delilah."

"I'm not. Not Delilah and not Ernestine."

"You got to have a name. Every little girl does. Let's see. You're not Amy, not Ernestine, not Delilah. Maybe your name is Sarah."

He was looking sidelong at her, watching her reaction.

"I don't think so," she said after a moment. "That doesn't sound familiar."

"Well, now. You ain't her either." He burlesqued a thoughtful look. "How about . . . Margaret?"

"I've heard that name before," she said.

"So have I. Could that be you?"

"It might be," she said. "I think you're right. That could be it."

His embrace was real and fervent. She didn't try to avoid him; there was safety in his arms around her. She had already decided that if playing by his rules would keep him happy, keep her alive, then she would do it. From now on she would be Margaret, only Margaret. She could do that for a while.

He turned down the wick on the lamp. The flame died and night surrounded them. She heard him unfold the blankets, stretch out on the cot, pull the blankets over him again.

His voice began, low and satisfied.

"Your room was painted pink 'til you was six years old," he was saying. "Then I painted it white 'cause you told me you didn't care for pink. Out back was a sunny garden patch where we grew squash, pole beans, spinach, and tomatoes. You always hated pole beans and I never knew why, 'til I figured out it was all the work of snappin' the beans that you couldn't stand.

"Your best friend was a little girl named Susie that lived about a mile down the road. The two of you was the same age, then one day her daddy died when the roof fell in at the mine, and her mother took her away. You was about eight then. Your favorite shoes was some red tennies that said 'P.F. Flyers' on the heel, and I always told you the P.F. stood for 'Purty Fancy.' "

The sentences were strung out aimlessly, but Sarah understood. He was talking about home and about the girl named Margaret, about things that she was supposed to have known. He realized that Margaret had forgotten, so he was trying to help her out. She closed her eyes and tried to form images from his words.

"You had a tabby cat named Banana that run away one day when you was nine years old. Broke your heart. I always thought the coyotes must have got it. In fourth grade you fell off a jungle gym and busted your right arm in three pieces. You wore a cast for more than two months, and you just hated it. The first song you ever sung was 'You Are My Sunshine.' You heard it on the radio, learned it, and ever after, when you saw that I was blue, you'd sing that song and pick me right up."

He went on for a while, about owls that perched on fenceposts and coal trucks that shook the house when they rumbled by in a hurry, about skinned knees and dolls and a maiden aunt named Beatrice. Sarah thought about the girl named Margaret, wondered where she could be, what could have happened to her. Sherk's words became soothing, and she heard only the tone, no longer the meaning.

Margaret. Whoever she is, he must really love her.

It was the last thought in her mind before she fell asleep.

—THIRTY-ONE—

THURSDAY
NOVEMBER 15

HE could still turn around, Warner reminded himself. He was in the car, stopped on Ritchie Highway and waiting for a break in the oncoming traffic. Could turn around and avoid the complications that would be waiting. He had done his duty here, all that had been asked of him. All that he could do.

The line of traffic cleared, and Warner turned left into Whittier Lane. Loose gravel rattled under the tires as he followed the twin set of shallow ruts to where they cleaved the grove.

The part of him that weighed and calculated didn't want to be here. In his mind the house was under a pall, touched by tragedy. Better for him if he avoided it. Yet the place and the people who lived here—and the girl who once had—would not leave his mind. He couldn't say exactly what had brought him back. A sense of unfinished business was part of it. And the mother, Elise. Even in her grief he wanted to see her again.

He could see dark pink brick through the latticework of empty branches. He followed the driveway as far as it would take him. The car had hardly stopped before Harry was standing at the front door. Almost as if he had been waiting for him, Warner told himself. Then he thought: No. Just waiting.

Warner got out of the car, and Harry came down the steps to meet him.

"I was in the neighborhood," Warner said. "Thought I might look in on you, see how you're all doing."

"Glad you came," Harry said. "We've been better. It's a very very rough time." His handshake had lost its power, and there was a slightly muddled element in his voice that Warner hadn't noticed before.

Joy appeared as they walked into the foyer.

"The detective came by to visit us," Harry said. Joy had a slightly puzzled look. There was an awkward moment as the three of them stood in the foyer, unsure what to do next, and Warner told himself this was a mistake, he didn't belong here, never should have come.

"I hope you can stay for at least a few minutes," she said, and the awkwardness passed. "I know my daughter-in-law will want to talk to you. You don't have to rush off?"

"Not right away," Warner said.

"Then why don't I bring you up? I'm sure she'll be glad."

Harry took his coat and Joy led him through the house, into the living room of the new wing. There she stopped him with a hand at his elbow.

"This has been hard on Elise," she said. "You'll see. I'm just asking, be good to her. Treat her right, and we won't forget it, Harry and I."

They went up the stairs. Elise was in Sarah's room. A mess. The bed was heaped with clothes from the closets. Dresser drawers had been opened, contents strewn about the floor. Elise was on hands and knees, picking through a pile of socks, her movements manic, almost wild, her face desperate in that first unguarded moment.

She glanced up. Warner saw her collect herself. In the span of two heartbeats her expression softened from frantic to just flustered. She was wearing jeans and a red V-neck sweater over a blouse. As she stood she straightened the sweater, smoothing it over her stomach in a nervous, unconscious motion.

"Elise, you remember the detective from Annapolis," Joy said.

"Howard," she said. "I didn't know you were coming."

Her long arms hung rigidly, slim fingers crumbling the air.

"Should've called, I guess. But I was nearby," he said, "and I thought about you. I thought maybe you'd want some company for a while."

"That would be good. I'd like that, I really would."

Her right hand went up to her face and swept away some invisible wisps of hair. Warner knew that gesture, and he found it no less endearing the second time.

"The last I saw you was . . . when?" she said.

"Sunday evening."

"No. Really? Last Sunday? It feels so long ago. Weeks."

Joy left, and said that she would be back in a while. Warner felt suddenly stranded. He looked around at the disarray.

"Everything all right here?" he said. "Trying to find something, is that it?"

"I remembered what you told me the other night. Any little thing might help, you said. I thought, I don't know, maybe I'd find something that might tell us what happened."

"Yeah, well. Could be. You come across anything?"

She shook her head.

"Look," he said, "why don't we just put this stuff away? I'll help you, we'll get it done in no time."

They worked without a word for a while. Elise replaced clothes on hangers, and Warner carried them over to the closets. Then he sat with her on the floor, filling the drawers that she had dumped out.

There was a scattering of tests and composition papers from school, all in a neat, compact script. He gathered them. About a dozen shoes; he matched each pair and put them on the floor of the closet. Warner found greeting cards from Christmases and birthdays past, a small round tin of lemon drops, a box of artist's pastels that leaked red and blue chalk on his hands when he picked it up.

It was all such ordinary stuff, little fragments of daily existence, personal and telling. Of course she had never expected to be revealed this way, the fingers of a stranger touching these bits of her life. He found himself thinking that the person who cared most about these things would never see them again. It was flotsam now. He was in a dead girl's room, touching a dead girl's possessions. She had walked out of here last Friday, alive and secure, had walked out into the day and had met a beast. Warner remembered the dark eyes in the pictures of her, and he wondered again what they had seen in the woods, what face she had looked upon.

He caught himself. Thoughts like that wouldn't help—not him, not the girl.

They had nearly finished when Elise left the room without a word. She returned carrying two shoeboxes. Warner sat beside her on the edge of the bed.

He looked sideways at her as she opened the first box and began to pick through what appeared to be an incomprehensible pile of trash. Warner watched as the lines around her mouth lifted and showed delight. He saw that she wore no makeup, but her skin was luminous in the diffuse glow of sunlight from a curtained window nearby.

He thought: If I had met you any other way.

Obviously she knew the junk. She plucked out a printed card, marked with ink strokes.

"Her first report card," Elise said. "See? 'Satisfactory' in every subject. She was always a very good student. It's just the first few weeks in this new school that she's had some problems. She'll come out of it, I'm sure. She's a hard worker, and very intelligent."

She replaced the card and pulled out a piece of lavender paper. Warner recognized a slightly larger and less certain version of Sarah's hand.

"A note she wrote us on her thirteenth birthday." Elise looked down and read it, and a smile formed on her face. She urged it on Warner. He didn't know how to refuse.

"Dear Mom and Dad," she had written, "I can't think of a better day to tell you how much I love you, and how lucky I am to have you as my parents."

Elise was digging through the second box now. More exhibits. She explained each one. Warner tried not to listen. This, she said, was the sequined tiara Sarah had worn at a school pageant. A blue ribbon for pen-and-ink drawing from the Lamoille County Fair, 1982. A plastic ID bracelet from the time she went into the hospital to have her tonsils removed.

"She didn't want to go in," Elise said. "She was just seven, but she knew that her grandfather, my dad, had gone into the hospital and never came out. She was so scared, poor thing. She kept saying 'I don't want to die, mommy. If I die I'll never see you and daddy again.' "

Her mouth was tight and strained. She turned to Warner.

"Every morning," she said, "I wake up, and for a second I don't remember what's happened. It's like everything is the way it was—she's here in this room next to mine, and if I walk a few steps I can look in on her. I mean, I don't *think* that—I know without thinking. It's the only speck of my life that isn't dark and spoiled and ugly. If I could only live in that moment I'd be fine. But it always comes back to me that something's wrong, and then I remember what it is. Each time it's like the whole world falls apart."

It was all too much, Warner thought. None of this had anything to do with him, it wasn't his concern. She was slumped over, head bowed, and Warner could see that she was biting her bottom lip. She was crying. Oh hell. She was crying, her delicate hands clasped and held to her mouth, her shoulders shaking.

"Don't," he said. "Please don't."

He got up and bent in front of her, crouching to be down at her level. From here the natural thing was to put his arms around her. He patted her awkwardly on the back; it had no effect. He pulled her closer, and then they were holding each other, her arms tight around him, her face pressed against his collar and dampening the bare skin of his neck.

"Don't," he said. "Don't cry. Everything's going to be all right."

"Will it?" she said. He could hear the hope.

"You'll see."

"They have to find her, Howard."

"They will. Everything's going to be okay," he said. Despising himself and every word he spoke.

• • •

The gold charm was gone. Sarah hadn't noticed until now.

She was out of the cocoon. Sherk had come to visit, as
he often did around mid-afternoon just to be with her.
Today he sat a few feet away, whittling a piece of dark
wood that was about a foot long and several inches around.
As always the hammock had knotted her muscles, so she
was trying to stretch the stiffness out of her arms and legs.

She was doing sit-ups when she realized that the bracelet wasn't ringing as it always did. Usually the single
charm that she wore on it would chime when she moved.

She sat up and examined the bracelet. Gone. The gift
that her father had brought from Quebec. Gone like everything else in that faraway existence.

Sherk had stopped whittling.

"What's the matter?" he said.

"Nothing. I'm okay."

He saw that she was looking at the bracelet. He put
down the knife and the piece of wood, and came over to
her. He held her wrist.

"I don't think that's yours anyway," he said. "Is it?"

She sensed a challenge in his words.

"No," she said. "I don't know how it got there."

He opened the clasp and took the bracelet off, and put it
in his pocket.

"Now don't be upset," he said. "No reason for it." He
reached across the floor for the wood that he had been
working. "Here, look. Almost finished."

She took it from him. It was a carved figure of a girl,
primitive but not crude. The work was smooth. She wore a
dress and an apron, there was a braid etched down her
back.

"Remember?" he said. "Your first doll. I made you
one when you was just a little thing. You kept it for a long
time. I know you don't play with dolls anymore. But I
thought it might be a reminder. You recall it?"

She fingered the smooth, burnished wood.

"Sure I remember," she said.

"Remember what you named it?"

She shook her head.

"It was Daisy. On account of the flower I put on her apron there."

"Daisy. I remember now," she said.

"I knew you would. Here, better give it back. I need a couple more minutes on it, then you can have it. Now let me see a big smile. That's it, that's what I want."

"It would be good to see you again," Elise said. "If you could drop by for a few minutes tomorrow . . ."

They were standing in the foyer, Warner with his coat over one arm, wishing he was gone. Wishing she had not asked.

"Oh sure," he said. "I was a big help. Fifteen minutes and I've got you blubbering."

"Next time I won't."

"Friday is a bad day. Even if I don't leave the desk I've got a ton of paperwork."

"Do you work Saturdays?"

He knew that he ought to say, Saturdays and Sundays both—honestly I don't know when I'll be able to come around again.

"As a rule I get weekends," he said. "I guess I could drop by on Saturday, not too early."

She squeezed his hand.

—THIRTY-TWO—

FRIDAY
NOVEMBER 16

ONE week after Sarah's disappearance, one week to the hour after the girl had been pulled into the forest, Elise stood in her daughter's room and looked with dismay at its untidiness. It was still unacceptably disheveled, even though she had straightened the disarray of the previous day.

She attacked the room. Dusted and vacuumed and arranged; changed the sheets and pillowcases. In the meantime she ran loads of Sarah's clothes through the washer and dryer. When she was finished in the bedroom she got out the iron and the ironing board, and she pressed all the clothing that she had laundered.

The job took her well into the evening. She worked without pause, forgetting dinner, taking her pleasure in the immaculate floors and the taut bedspread and the neat stacks of clothes that she tucked away in the drawers. She had never been fanatical about her housekeeping, but this was different.

Because when she was finished she could stand in the doorway, look around, and know that all was ready. Ready for the day—it must be soon—when Sarah returned.

Once Sherk and Margaret had seen a mama bear and her cub playing in the summer-high grass of a meadow near the cabin.

"We was downwind of her," Sherk said, "so she didn't smell us, and it must have been a couple minutes we got to watch her 'fore she noticed us and scrammed."

"Is that the meadow where we used to go for picnics?" Sarah said.

"No, no. That one's down the road some, not far from the highway."

"The one where I used to pick daisies."

"Right. But the one where we saw the bear was over on the other side of Drolsom's Ridge, where I used to take you for walks sometimes."

"Where you carved our initials on a popple tree, just like I was your sweetheart."

"That's the one," Sherk said.

She could see the cabin, the rooms, the furniture. She could see the hills, too, so high and steep, keeping the hollow in shadow for most of the day. She could even see some of the people, the few who came and went in their lives, Sherk's and Margaret's.

He liked to go on this way. It seemed important. She knew what was happening. Sherk was telling his daughter what she was supposed to know, but had forgotten. Filling her in. A crazy idea, but it kept him happy.

It was also mental recreation when she was alone. She was turning his words into a mural, starting with a broad sketch and now filling in the particulars, adding colors and definition, refining. At first vague, it was now sharp and concrete in her imagination, a place for the mind to roam. The more often she visited, the more swiftly and surely she could recall it.

She saw it as a happy life, father and daughter alone in the hills. Sherk and Margaret had lived just as a girl and her dad ought to live. She tapped into her own memories to give it the warmth that it deserved.

"There was the day Uncle George bought you that big roly-poly doll, do you remember?"

"Uncle George wasn't my real uncle."

"No. My cousin on my mother's side."

"But he was a really funny guy."

"The funniest," Sherk said. "A real card."

It went on that way past midnight, until Sherk was yawning as he spoke. He wrapped her up and put her in the hammock.

He blew out the lamp, and Sarah shifted in the sleeping bag until she had worked out the lumps. The straps weren't as tight as usual. Her mind still roamed, and she tried to put herself to sleep with a soothing image.

The first that came to her was Sherk and Margaret in their cabin, a small cabin out of the world's way, shelter for a loving father and a loving daughter. Only she put herself in Margaret's bed, and the father was both Sherk and her own father. It was nonsense the mind might accept in those minutes when consciousness and logic gave way to sleep and dream.

So the hammock became a real bed, and the attic was a cabin in the hills, small and snug the way she imagined the cabin must be. And she had a father nearby, someone to watch over her with loving concern, someone to keep harm from the door. She didn't question the image, just nestled herself in it, let it envelop her, and before too long it had put her to sleep.

—THIRTY-THREE—

SATURDAY
NOVEMBER 17

FIFTEEN minutes after he arrived, Warner knew he had to get out of the big house. It had the leaden soul of a mortuary chapel. Too many empty rooms, too many long silences, and everywhere the pervasive taint of tragedy, which was like a bad odor. Something dead behind a wall.

There was a path from the front of the house down to the river. Elise put on a heavy red woolen coat and wrapped her neck in a scarf, and they walked down the path together. She seemed to have turned her suffering inward, and Warner believed that someone meeting her for the first time would never suspect what pain was reflected in the stiffness of her back, the pale thinness of her lips, and the minute restless wandering of her eyes.

Outside the day was overcast again, with scudding clouds and a wind that clawed at bare skin. Warner walked with his hands stuck in the pockets of his coat. Elise lengthened her steps to match his. They took the path away from the house to the edge of the river's high bank, then down to a pier that stood about six feet above the water.

They went out to the end of the pier. The Severn was green and choppy. He could see nobody else, and Warner thought that under other circumstances he would be enjoying this, the river empty and so wild. Elise stood to his left, slightly behind, and he could feel a slight pressure at his elbow where the wind bent her toward him.

"This morning they took out the tape recorders," she said. "The ones on the telephones. They said if we were going to get a ransom call, it would have come by now."

In the corners of her eyes Warner saw a wetness that might have been from the bite of the wind.

"That's not good, is it?" she said.

"I wouldn't feel let down. The chances were against it anyway."

"I thought it might mean that they were losing hope." He saw that she struggled to get these words out. "That they had decided, you know, something must have happened to her by now."

He spoke toward the far shore: "I'd say it's way too early to talk like that. There are a lot of good people out there, doing all they can to find your girl."

The wind buffeted them.

"Sarah is her name," she said.

"I know. Sarah."

"When you talk about her," she said, "you never use her name. You always say, 'your girl,' or 'your daughter.' "

"I never met her," he said. "I don't feel as if I know her."

Another damn lie, he thought.

"All the people out there looking for her," she said. "I guess they couldn't search any harder or care any more. But it's too bad, really. I wish they could all meet her, get to know her, find out what a wonderful girl they're looking for."

A gust rocked them. Warner felt her hands come to his arm, holding it for support. He refused to look at her as she spoke; he just couldn't.

"Sarah is a special child," she said. "I know, that's what all mothers say about their children. But it really is true. Ask anybody who knows her."

He felt her hands shake on his arm, and he knew that she was crying. He stood rigidly and watched as the winds fretted the river's surface. It was a few seconds before she spoke again, her voice choked.

"I need her, Howard. She's the best part of me. She's all I've got. I have nothing left without her."

He turned to face her.

"You can't talk that way," he said. There was feeling in the words. "What if the worst happens? You don't stop breathing."

"I wouldn't want to live anymore."

"That's a stupid way to talk."

"Are they going to find Sarah?"

The question surprised him, and his answer was lame: "People are doing everything possible."

"Tell me."

"There are so many uncertainties—nobody knows." Trying to wriggle away. But she wouldn't let go.

"Then tell me what you think," she said. "You know these things. Tell me you think they're going to find my daughter. And I'll believe you. That's all you have to do."

He looked at her. His lips were pursed, as if withholding the answer. He moved imperceptibly on the balls of his feet. He had done his best, he thought. But he could not force another lie through his teeth.

"I wish I could tell you so," he said. Softly, as if in hope that the wind would carry the words from his lips. "I wish I could. But I don't believe it's true."

Elise was leaning toward him, intent. For a moment she seemed to question what she had heard. Then that quizzical look gave way to an expression of crushing pain. He thought that he had never before seen such open agony.

It was too hard to watch. He turned and looked across the water.

Her feet scraped on the wood as she took a couple of steps back.

"You bastard," she said behind him.

Warner looked back. She was standing at the edge of the pier, facing downriver, toward the city.

"You bastard, you son of a bitch. It's not true. I hate you."

But there was no enmity in her face. Only hurt, Warner thought. She was hunched over, huddled in the manner of

someone caught out in a hailstorm. A gust nudged her, and
for a second she wobbled on her feet, off balance.

Warner was about to tell her, Hey, you'll fall in if you
don't watch out. Then he saw her collapse, just fold up,
the shoulders sagging as if she were suddenly lifeless.

He turned to her and lunged as she toppled stiffly off the
edge of the pier. She fell and hit the water and kicked up a
splash that was freezing cold where it touched his face.

The river swallowed her. Warner looked down and waited
for her to surface. Finally she did, facing him, blankly
resigned. Only her nose and the top of her head showed
above the water. He realized that the soggy weight of her
coat must be dragging her down. She wasn't struggling.

He was already pulling off his coat and his jacket,
down to his shirtsleeves, kicking off his shoes. He tore off
his shoulder holster and dropped it on the pier. A wave
lapped over her face, and she was submerged for a couple
of seconds before her head slowly rose up again, pale skin
in the green chop.

He jumped. The water engulfed him, and he plunged
toward the bottom. He pumped his arms and legs, as-
cended, and his head bobbed out. He thought that the
water wasn't so cold, but then the shock hit him and he
knew that he had never felt anything like it. There was an
excruciating ache in his fingers.

He couldn't see her. She had to be close, and he
thrashed to keep his head above the surface. Water was
dripping down his forehead into his eyes. He kicked and
groped; one of his hands touched wet wool. She slipped
away, but he paddled to her and got an arm around her
neck.

Elise lay limply in the water, stunned, and he knew she
wasn't going to help. Warner had never been much of a
swimmer, even when he was young and in shape. He
could get to the pilings, no problem, but the pier itself was
higher than his arm could reach. He would never get her
up there, wasn't sure he could even pull himself out. A
swell washed over him, and he shook his head to clear his
vision. He looked over at the bank. Fifty, sixty feet away.
His thighs were spent.

Meanwhile the current was carrying them away from the pier. Warner tried to remember how lifeguards swam. Kicking their feet, backstroking with one arm. He moved Elise to his left side. She had begun to paddle, a feeble reflex. Warner hooked an arm around her neck and shifted so that he was floating on his back. He began to kick toward shore.

His mouth was open, gasping. Water would spill in, and it gagged him sometimes, and he would have to spit. So he was gulping and gasping and spitting. His arms and legs ached. He couldn't feel fingers or toes anymore. His back was to the shore, so he couldn't see his progress, but he expected to touch bottom at any moment, had to. Elise was flailing with more strength now—blindly—splashing water in his face and kicking his shins and thumping his chest with an elbow.

He had to stop. He was exhausted and breathless, and wasn't sure that he could keep his own head above water any longer. He kicked around to clamp Elise in his right arm and that gave him a view of the shore. He looked, and saw that if anything he was farther away than when he had started; the current was carrying him not just downstream but toward the middle of the channel.

Her weight in his arm seemed enormous. A swell surged over their heads and caught Warner with his mouth open, sucking in air. He swallowed water and gagged. His head went under for a few seconds before he found the strength to struggle up again, and the thought came to him that she was not the only one in trouble. He wondered how long they had been in the water. Three, maybe four minutes. Much longer and hypothermia might kill them before the river did.

She was grunting, spitting out water, trying to speak. Warner had seen corpses pulled out after a few hours in the water, and he got the image of Elise, lifeless, lips and skin ashen as she washed up somewhere in her damn soggy overcoat.

The overcoat, he thought. He pulled her around until she faced him, and he opened the top two buttons and tried to shuck it off her. When he pulled the coat down it pinned her arms and she resisted. Then she understood. Her eyes were lucid again, scared but no longer confused, and she pulled her arms out of the sleeves. She shook her shoulders and the coat slowly dropped away from her.

Elise held him by the neck.

"Don't let me die," she said.

"Swim."

"I can't swim."

"Then hold on." He was shouting. "Hold on and don't choke me."

He knew that he would never make it with a backstroke. But maybe a crawl, if he could use both arms. They had drifted nearly a hundred feet from the shore, and the pier by now was nearly as distant. So it was the shore or nothing. He twisted and kicked so that he was chest down, facing the shore. Elise held his shoulders. Warner willed one arm out, and he kicked, and he pulled himself forward. A sharp ache had spread from his chest out through his limbs, but he shoved it into a small corner of his mind and tried to contain it there. One arm. The other. He was kicking and so was she.

He looked up when he breathed. They were closer, he was sure of it. The sight gave him strength. One arm. The other. Pulling through the water. Pulling. Elise holding him, his life on his shoulders. Pulling.

His fingers, finishing a stroke, touched mushy bottom. He tried to stand, and sank in mud halfway up his thighs. He slogged through. Closer in the bottom was gravel, and together they stumbled onto the bank.

They collapsed in sand and dirt. The wind blew. Elise was gasping and coughing up water, and it was a few seconds before she could speak.

"I'm sorry," she said. She sounded miserable. "I don't know what happened. My legs wouldn't hold me, and something told me, just give it up, just let go, and I did."

"You fell," he said vehemently.

"I'm so ashamed."

"You *fell*. Anybody wants to know what happened, that's it. You fell, and you couldn't swim, and I had to help you. Nothing else. It was an accident, that's all."

Before she could speak again he got up and went out on the pier. The wind flayed his wet skin, and it was like being sliced by a dull knife, an awkward butcher laying him open. After he had picked up his pistol he got his sport jacket and his overcoat, brought them back, and wrapped Elise in them. She tried to walk but stumbled twice. He thought the wind and the wet and the cold would get them both at this rate, so he picked her up in his arms and carried her up the bank.

She held him.

"I'm sorry," she said. Her teeth were chattering violently but she still tried to talk. "I'm sorry, I'm so sorry."

He trudged with her along the path, across the rolling lawn, up to the house.

Elise felt the pricking of a thousand needles in her hands and feet. It was the return of sensation to her numb extremities. Joy had immersed her in a hot bath, and the warmth soaked through her skin as if rushing into a vacuum.

She kept seeing green water beyond the edge of the pier. Dark choppy water that promised the comfort of oblivion. Her legs were folding, her head an impossible mass. She was toppling. She might have fallen in any direction, but the river pulled strongest. She was collapsing, tumbling off the edge of the pier, the water rushing up to greet her. To claim her.

Joy came in with a mug of black coffee; Elise wrapped her fingers around it and held it tight before she tipped it up to her mouth. She looked into the cup and saw the Severn again, deep and inviting.

"Are you better?" Joy asked. "No more chills?"

"I'm fine," Elise said absently. She was thinking about standing at the end of the pier, talking to Warner.

She told herself that if he was right, then she was alone. Since her marriage both her parents had died. Sarah was her last tie with Harry and Joy, and even if she remained in their orbit there would be only memory and habit to bind her to them, no genuine force of emotion because there never had been that, not really. She would be truly alone at a time when more than ever she needed strength from outside herself.

Warner was wrapped in a quilt, standing in front of the living room fireplace, when she came downstairs. Harry had started the fire with pine logs, so there was the smell of burned pitch to go with plenty of flame and heat. He was basking in it, watching the fire. His hair was tousled from rubbing it with a towel. Hanging below the edge of the quilt was the hem of one of Harry's robes, and below that she could see his stocky calves, sturdy and muscular.

She too wore a blanket over her shoulders, and beneath that a gray sweatsuit. He didn't notice her until she stood beside him.

"Hey," he said. "You're looking better. Got a little color back."

"I wanted to apologize."

"Forget it." He gave a curt, dismissive shake of the head.

"I'm so ashamed."

"Forget that, too. And all the rest. You slipped, and Howard Warner showed off his lousy backstroke. That's all. I lose one worn-out pair of Thom McAn wingtips and I get to feel like a hero for a few days. I'd call it a deal."

He had the way about him of a beat cop swinging down his street, bouncing a nightstick on the sidewalk. Easy to like and impossible to get around. In command at least of his own sliver of the world.

"No," she said. "I need to say this. I'm not stupid. I realized what the worst could be, the worst outcome of this. But I talked myself into ignoring it and I didn't want to hear it."

"Understood," he said, and she knew that he meant it. The fire roasted her cheeks and forehead.

"I'm not the kind of person who goes throwing herself into the river every chance."

"I believe that. Listen, you have much more to worry about right now than what I happen to think of you."

"I need help," she said. It came out without a trace of self-pity, a statement of fact. "I've never been through anything like this, not even when Jack died. At least that had an ending. But this is burying me. It's more than I can handle, and I need help.''

His gaze raked her up and down, not cruelly, but not missing much either, calmly taking her apart and looking at what was inside. A stare that appraised but was not judgmental. She hoped that she would never have to get something past this man.

"I'm not asking you," she said quickly. "Just explaining, that's all. Just telling somebody."

His brows opened and lifted, and he broke his stare when he blinked. She guessed that he had found whatever he was looking for.

"I know what you mean," he said. "You think to yourself, If I could only turn this over to somebody else for a while. Even a few minutes. Get a load off."

"That's part of it."

"Your in-laws, I guess, are not exactly the answer."

"This hasn't been any easier on Harry and Joy than on me."

"Don't take this wrong," he said. "But there are psychiatrists. I'm told they know how to listen."

"I'm not ruling them out. But it seems a little early in the game for that."

He nodded and looked into the fire, and she sensed he had something else in mind that he was reluctant to mention. In an unlikely, diffident voice he asked, "You go to church?"

"Not for a long while. We had Sarah baptized, but Jack didn't really go in for it, and I got out of the habit."

"Some people find it helps."

"You?"

He shrugged his answer. "If I called myself religious, I'd be asking for trouble. I mean, I go months, sometimes, never get near a church and never even think about it. But I was brought up Catholic. The sisters had their hands on me for eight years in grade school. Then the Jebbies— that's Jesuits—for four years after that. Some of that is bound to stick."

"You're telling me," she said.

"You're a Catholic?"

"Used to be."

"Nope," he said. "Wrong. It's like being left-handed. Hard as you try, you don't just walk away from it. Once a Catholic, always a Catholic."

Each smiled; many times they had heard this from nuns.

"So you think I ought to go to church," she said.

"Shit, I don't know. I'm full of bright ideas for other people."

She remembered how it used to be. Kneeling in church, talking to God. The priests who taught catechism would say that was the best kind of prayer, talking to God. When you were a kid it was easy to believe that someone was actually listening.

"I've heard worse ideas," she said. "It would be cheaper than a shrink."

"Well, sure."

"Where could I go? I don't know this town."

"I know of one," he said. "I could show you if you wanted."

"You were planning to go to Mass tomorrow?"

"I make it a rule," he said, "to get holy once a year. Whether I need it or not."

—THIRTY-FOUR—

SUNDAY
NOVEMBER 18

HE came for her in his old Toyota. Came dressed in an ink-blue woolen suit that was tight across the shoulders and down in the seat.

It was eleven minutes before nine when they turned onto the highway, and Elise was sure they would be late. But Warner knew traffic and knew the streets. He got them over the river and across downtown and into the church lot without once hitting a light.

He gave her his arm as they walked to the front of the church. The bell in the tower was clanging when they walked up the front steps. They were hurrying and she barely had time to notice the brass plaque beside the door:

SAINT BARTHOLOMEW'S
ROMAN CATHOLIC CHURCH

When Sarah heard—and felt—the bell, she thought of Sherk. He had said when he left this morning that he would be back with breakfast. But she guessed that he wouldn't be coming for a while. Wherever she was, it was a place that he couldn't seem to reach when there were people around. The bells meant Mass, meant people.

217

She thought of how far she had come. This morning she was not fearful, only lonesome. The attic had first seemed a cramped and stifling place; now she found it monotonous, but cozy and almost homelike. And though she still feared Sherk, feared his quicksilver moods, she believed that she understood him. Understood him and pitied him in a way, because of the sadness that seemed to permeate him. She was unable to hate him, no matter how long she thought of what he had done to her, of the indignities she had endured.

Instead he made her feel . . . warm. She was ashamed to admit it. But he cared about her, in his crazy way. He was happy when she fulfilled his expectations. His pleasure, in turn, made her giddy with relief.

The bell's tolling ended. She clicked on the little handheld radio and awaited his return.

From his apartment Sherk could hear automobiles pulling into the parking lot, a steady drone behind the peal of the church bell. The noise irked him; he was in a dark mood, upset with himself.

He had gone down to get breakfast. But he knew he must have dawdled too long, because when he returned through the sacristy he met a couple of altar boys, dressing for the eight o'clock Mass. As he came down the aisle he ran into one of the priests, and Sherk knew that sneaking into the attic would be too great a risk.

He had been carrying Margaret's meal in the gym bag. Now she was alone up there, hungry, waiting for him. On Sundays the church was busy until late afternoon, and it would be hours before he could get up there again. He didn't like to let her down, but he had no choice.

Her first couple of days had been rocky, but now he could see evidence of the doting daughter she once had been. He had stopped trying to understand by what means she had changed so drastically. What mattered was that he had begun to reclaim her. Day by day she was closer to the Margaret he remembered.

Now he had hours to wait before he saw her again. In Harben at this hour, the congregation would be gathering for services. He had tried a couple of Baptist churches in

Annapolis, but he didn't like being an outsider. He had never returned.

He would pass the time in his room. In a storage closet he had found an old toaster that he wanted to rewire, and that would keep him occupied. He was at it all morning; the cars arriving and departing outside his window, the bell pealing, were background noise in his mind. His fingers were busy and his mind kept working, wondering how to bring his daughter all the way around to the girl that she had been.

—THIRTY-FIVE—

MONDAY
NOVEMBER 19

"Harry, she's gone," Joy said. "Elise is gone."

Harry had been searching the early papers for stories about Sarah. The time was just after seven in the morning.

"She's got to be around," Harry said.

"I looked all over," Joy said. "She's nowhere in the house."

Harry got up and looked outside, around the back where his three-car garage was. He noticed that one of the sliding doors was open, and the bay was empty. It was the space where Elise kept her station wagon.

"Oh hell," he said. He could imagine Elise doing all kinds of crazy things, the shape she was in. "Oh hell."

Joy was standing beside him, looking at the empty spot in the garage. "Maybe she had something to do," she said; it sounded preposterous even as she said it.

"Seven in the morning," Harry said. "What's she got to do?"

"I will go to the altar of God," the priest was saying.

Every morning, Monday through Friday, Saint Bartholomew's had a seven o'clock Mass. Generally the services were attended by about eighty or ninety, the genuinely faithful, who found time for worship between their first cup of coffee and punch-in at work. They were regulars, familiar enough with one another that at least some of them noticed the new face this morning, a woman who sat alone in a pew about halfway up the center aisle.

It was Elise. Her face had an alert, attentive look. She was actually listening to the priest. For ten days she had been desolate. But here, on Sunday, she had found some relief from her ordeal.

"To God who is the joy of my youth," the priest intoned.

It wasn't as if she expected a miracle, Sarah walking up the lane and into the kitchen as though she had never been missing. Elise didn't expect that prayer would return her daughter. She prayed simply for Sarah's well-being; to ask anything more seemed greedy, presumptuous.

She had come here mostly for her own sake, having discovered that the liturgy and the magnificent church building both helped her to feel that she was in the presence of some force much greater than herself. It diminished her and diminished her pain. She could see that her anguish was finite. As huge as it was to her, it had boundaries.

That wasn't a great spiritual revelation, she thought, but she was comforted. It was said that there are no atheists in foxholes, and she knew that this might be just another battlefield conversion. But she had come here yesterday and she would come tomorrow, too, and the day after. It was a respite. It felt right and for now that was all she needed.

Terry Dean was parked not thirty yards from the intersection when the silver Peugeot blew past the stop sign on Southgate Avenue where it crosses Franklin. Just rolled through without slowing. Dean never even saw a blink of the brake lights. Franklin feeds into the downtown several blocks away, and it can be a busy street. At another hour the Peugeot might never have gotten across. But this was just a few minutes before eleven on a Monday night, so it happened to be empty. The Peugeot kept on sailing up Southgate.

The cruiser was already running. He just put it into gear

and whipped a left and had the sedan pulled over within a block and a half. He parked behind it and called in the tag number before he got out and began to walk toward the driver's side.

The night was cold, and felt even colder here, within a quarter of a mile of Spa Creek; dampness seemed to let a chill penetrate to the bone. For his first few steps Dean was cast in a thin crimson from the rear lamps. Then the driver shut off the engine and killed the lights, and Dean made the rest of the walk in darkness. The window came down about halfway as he approached.

"Oh damn, this is awful, this is terrible," the driver said. It was a young woman's voice, he thought, maybe a teenager. The cars were parked in mid-block, away from streetlights. Dean was already holding the black flashlight that he normally carried at his belt. He flicked it on and shone it into the car, down toward the seat, where he could see hands. Always want to know what the hands are doing.

"Your license, please," Dean said. "And the registration." The driver got her purse and as she fumbled through it Dean pointed the flashlight into it. Not as a courtesy but to see what she brought out.

"I went through the stop sign, didn't I?" she said, talking into the purse. "I never saw it, but they told me I did." The interior of the car was dark. Dean couldn't see any faces, but from outlines and weakly lit profiles he could tell that there was one passenger in the front and two others in the back. All young women, girls.

"Here," the driver said. She came up with a driver's license, sandwiched in plastic. "This is *awful*. I just got my license last week, and my dad's going to *kill* me."

"And the registration," he repeated. She leaned to the glove compartment, and he angled the flashlight over there, and followed her hand as it returned with the registration slip. He took it from her through the window's opening.

The driver spoke from the dimness inside: "I'm really sorry. Do you give warning tickets? I guess there isn't any way, huh, that you could give me a break this once?"

"You got a break already," Dean said. "You're alive."

He took the license and registration back to the cruiser where he kept his citation pad. He turned on the overhead light, took a pen from his shirt pocket, balanced the pad on one knee, and flipped it open to the first blank page.

He wrote in the date and time and the location, and added the code number of the offense. The next line of the summons form was for the name of the accused. Then he looked for the first time at the license and at the thumbnail-sized color ID photo that was laminated into it.

The girls in the back seat watched him walk to the cruiser. They saw the light come on.

"What's going to happen?" one of them said. "Are we going to jail?"

"You don't go to jail for running a stop sign," said a second.

"No, but your insurance goes up," said the girl in the passenger seat up front. "You're in deep shit now, Em."

"Thank you very much," said the girl behind the wheel. She was already wondering how she could square this one with her father.

"He's coming back already," said one in the back seat. "Maybe he's changed his mind."

The driver looked back and saw that he was in a hurry. He was holding a clipboard and her license, and he did not so much walk as jog up to her door.

"Please get out of the car," he said. He seemed excited, and she obeyed quickly. He shone the flashlight directly at her face. She blinked and squinted.

"Walk with me into the light," he said. She followed him about twenty yards up the street, into the indistinct circle of illumination cast by a street lamp near the corner. It gave her the first good look at his face.

"Hey. I know you," she said.

He was studying her features in the light, then looking down at the clipboard. When he tilted it slightly she saw that the clip held her license and a glossy photo, side by side.

"Tell me your name," he said.

"Right there. Emily Caldwell. You came to my house, remember?"

His attention bounced from her to the clipboard and back.

"You go to a private school," he said.

"Nordbrook."

"That's it. Nordbrook." He fixed on the photograph for a few seconds and then studied her one more time. The hand that held the clipboard dropped to his side.

"Good God Almighty," he said.

—THIRTY-SIX—

TUESDAY
NOVEMBER 20

ONE of the younger priests was sick with a virus, so the monsignor took Tuesday-night confessions. It was a quiet hour, and while he waited in the box he read his offices by the soft light of a bulb overhead, just bright enough that he could make out the type in his breviary.

He had read uninterrupted for nearly half an hour, and after closing the book he checked his watch: eight-twenty. He knew that the church must have been empty for some time, but still he was reluctant to move. No place he knew was as quiet as the box. He turned off the light overhead, hoping to steal a few quiet minutes.

Soon he heard footsteps, something distinctive about the pattern of the sound. In a few seconds he knew it. Sherk. Sherk walked that way, with those loping strides. The footfalls grew louder, passed the box without pausing, headed down the aisle toward the back of the church. The monsignor drew back the heavy curtain across the front window of the box.

He saw Sherk walk behind the back row of pews, turn up the stairs that led up to the loft. From where he sat the monsignor couldn't see Sherk come out upstairs, but he heard the footsteps on the wooden floor. He could tell from the sound that Sherk was crossing the loft, from one side to the other.

The footsteps ended, and there was a sound like a door closing. The monsignor thought of the closet door in the loft. Then he didn't hear any more. No more footsteps or doors, just the heavy silence of the church.

All along his eyes had stayed on the stairwell entrance that Sherk had used, the only way up or down. This time he wanted to be certain that Sherk hadn't slipped by him.

He left the confessional and crossed over to the bottom of the stairwell. There hadn't been a sound since the closing of the closet door. The monsignor climbed the stairs, trying to make plenty of noise so Sherk wouldn't be surprised. He came out on the landing and stepped out into the loft.

It was empty. He looked around, then went to the closet door and hesitated several seconds before he opened it.

No one.

The monsignor looked around the loft again, just to be sure that Sherk wasn't obscured in some shadows. But there were no shadows, just a low thin light from the fixtures that hung from the high ceiling.

He turned again to the closet. Inside were the same stacked boxes and hanging choir robes. Last time he hadn't bothered to check. But this time the monsignor went in, looked in the corners, moved the robes around to be sure that they concealed nothing. Of course the idea that Sherk would hide among the choir robes was ridiculous.

But not nearly as ridiculous, the monsignor thought, as the idea that he would come up here and disappear.

Once when he was a kid his father had taken him to see Blackstone. The monsignor could still remember one trick, when Blackstone produced a big glass globe at his fingertips, a ball of creamy white glass, and it had begun to glow. It had lifted right out of the magician's hands and floated out into the darkened auditorium, dancing and bobbing out over the audience. The boy had been old enough to know that such things don't happen, old enough to be astonished and incredulous as he watched the dancing globe of light.

Now he felt the same disbelief, as if he had seen it wrong, had somehow overlooked the easy and obvious explanation.

He walked down to the front of the loft, looked under chairs and in the footwell of the organ, slowly circled the loft and ended up at the closet again. He looked around there once more, and even checked the ceiling.

Sherk had come up, he told himself. Had come up, hadn't come down. But he wasn't here anymore. For some time the monsignor considered this, standing in front of the closet. Then he went to the stairs, and gave one more look over his shoulder before he went away.

"I've done this before," said Claire Johansen. "I know what I'm doing."

"We came up with a list of questions," Warner said. He took a folded piece of paper out of his coat pocket, and slid it to her across her desk. She promptly slid it back, without looking at it.

"You can keep your questions," she said. "I know what you want, and I know how to get it."

She was fifty years old, weighed nearly two hundred pounds without being fat, and she maintained at all times an air of command. The Annapolis P.D. didn't keep a psychologist on staff—not enough demand—but it sent plenty of business her way.

Now she faced three nervous men across her desk. There was Carl Caldwell, father of Emily and owner of a 1984 silver Peugeot sedan, who was concerned about his daughter's well-being. She had never before been in a psychologist's office. Flanking him were Warner and the county detective named Tarver, who was anxious because they believed that Emily Caldwell might have seen Sarah's abductor.

The two girls were almost identical in appearance—close enough for government work, was the way Tarver put it. In September Emily had been accosted by a man claiming to be her father. Nine weeks later Sarah had disappeared.

"You're sure this won't harm her," Carl Caldwell said.

"I promise," Claire said. "Look, there are lounge entertainers in Las Vegas who do this without ill effect. I've never played the Sands, but my training is better.''

Tarver said: "What we need . . .''

"What you need," she said, "is to sit back, find a magazine to read, and let me get on with it."

She stood up, her bearing almost regal.

"I believe I have business in the other room," she said.

Transcript
INTERROGATION UNDER HYPNOSIS
Conducted by Claire F. Johansen, Ph.D.
Subject: Emily Caldwell
Time: 7:38 p.m., 11/20/84

CFJ: How are you feeling? Comfortable?

EC: I'm fine.

CFJ: I want you to think about a day last September. The first day of school.

EC: I remember.

CFJ: You won a part in a play.

EC: Millie. In Picnic.

CFJ: That's right. You won the part. Now you're walking home. I want you to tell me what happens while you're walking home.

EC: I'm walking down Main. Looking in the windows. There's a green Benetton sweater I want daddy to buy for me. Lime-green.

CFJ: Okay. Then what?

EC: I've got to go into the Ralph Lauren store down by the dock. (Giggles.) Definitely have to go check out some blouses. Then I leave. I'm hungry and I'm ready to go home.

CFJ: And what happens after you leave the store? I want you to tell me what you see.

EC: There's a kid, this little twerp, almost runs me over with his skateboard. A little brat.

CFJ: You're on what street now?

EC: I'm crossing Randall, heading up Prince George.

CFJ: And then what happens?

EC: (with some distress) He's coming after me!

CFJ: Who is?

EC: Him. The guy who thinks I'm somebody else.

CFJ: Tell me about him. Tell me what he looks like.

EC: Can't see him very well. He's a block away. He's yelling for some girl named Margaret. I look over my shoulder at him, but I get scared, and I keep walking. (Pause.) I can hear him. He's coming after me. (Pause.) I don't like this. Can I stop?

CFJ: You're all right. Just tell me what you see.

EC: I'm hurrying. Not far from home. He says, Margaret, turn around, Margaret, it's your daddy. But I know it's me he wants. I can hear him breathing, he's so close. I try to get across the street. There's a car . . . oh! Almost hit me.

CFJ: The car?

EC: Yes. Then he puts his hand on me. He's got me. He's real strong. He needs to cut his fingernails—they're too long. And they've got dirt, grease, something, under them.

CFJ: You see his clothes?

EC: Farmer's overalls. Oshkosh. And a red-and-black flannel shirt. His sleeves are rolled up to his elbows. What a hayseed. He sounds just like it.

CFJ: What do you mean?

EC: He talks like a hillbilly. His accent.

CFJ: You see his face? Tell me what you see.

EC: Those eyes. Like he's real mad at me or something. Except he's not mad. He just doesn't understand. He's got a long face. Big bushy eyebrows. A long neck. He's a skinny guy. Tall. Maybe six-three. Whiskers on his face. He needs a shave.

CFJ: He has a beard? A moustache?

EC: No. He just needs a shave.

CFJ: How old, would you say?

EC: An old guy. About forty. (Pause.) I feel sorry for him.

CFJ: Why?

EC: He's looking for somebody. It's his daughter. But he can't find her.

CFJ: What happens next?

EC: I get away. He sort of lets go, he's so surprised. I start walking real fast. Got to get home.

CFJ: But something happens before you get there.

EC: Uh-huh. Oh, God, this is the pits.

CFJ: What do you see?

EC: I'm walking down the alley. There's this truck, this pickup truck, coming up toward me. Coming too fast. I'm scared it'll hit me. It's him. I can see him driving it.

CFJ: Tell me about the truck.

EC: It's a Ford. It says so on the hood. Blue. Kind of robin's-egg-blue. A little darker than that. (Pause.) It's been in a wreck. The fender is bent. Not too bad, though.

CFJ: Which fender? The front? Left side or right?

EC: Yeah, the front. My left . . . it's the right fender, I guess.

CFJ: This is important. Can you see the license plate?

EC: I think so. Yeah. The sun is shining on it, but I can see it.

CFJ: Tell me what you see.

EC: It's from Virginia. Z . . . F . . . B. Eight. Oh. One.

CFJ: You're doing great. What happens next?

EC: The truck rushes past me. I start to run. He stops the truck and grabs me, so fast I can't believe it.

CFJ: You see him up close again, right? Anything else you notice about him?

EC: He's got a knife in his overalls.

CFJ: A long knife?

EC: No. Like a big jack knife. It's in this black holder, with a snap over it, but I can tell there's a knife folded up in there. It's fastened to the pocket of his overalls.

CFJ: Anything else?

EC: His shoes. They're just the clunkiest you can imagine. Like these real plain work shoes.

CFJ: What else?

EC: Just that I feel sorry for him. He really loves her.

CFJ: The other girl?

EC: Uh-huh. Margaret. He feels bad that I'm not her. He doesn't really believe that I'm not her. You can tell he doesn't understand. 'Cause he really loves her. (Pause.) He's going to find her, too.

CFJ: The man in the overalls?

EC: Uh-huh. I can tell. He's going to keep lookin' 'til he finds her.

CFJ: How can you be so sure?

EC: (Agitated) I can *see* him. His eyes. He touched me. I can tell. (Pause.) And I know something else. He's crazy.

CFJ: How do you mean?

EC: I mean crazy. Whacked-out. Looney Tunes. From the way he acts. No doubt about it. The guy is totally crazy.

Warner phoned in the registration from the psychologist's office, and ten minutes later got a call-back. Virginia Motor Vehicles Division had reported that ZFB801 belonged to a blue 1978 Ford pickup, registered to Joseph Toller Sherk (6–3, 185, black hair, brown eyes, date of birth 7/27/41), last known address Colgan Road, Harben, Lee County, Virginia. No outstanding warrants.

Within thirty minutes a description of Sherk and the truck was broadcast to patrols throughout the county, with instructions to hold the suspect for questioning.

—THIRTY-SEVEN—

WEDNESDAY
NOVEMBER 21

"You heard?" Warner said. "You heard already?"

"We heard you have a name," Elise said on the other end of the line. "We heard you know who did it."

"This is way premature," Warner said. Incredible. Police business wasn't supposed to leak like this. "It was Tarver, wasn't it? The guy can not keep his mouth shut."

"We haven't seen him. Harry has friends; you know that. They take care of us."

"If it was up to me you wouldn't be told a thing. I think it's wrong."

"But we do know," she said. "And I want you to tell me what it means."

Warner, sitting at his desk, heard barely restrained elation, and he knew he couldn't let that go.

"A name is all we have," he said. "A name and an idea that maybe whoever took your daughter . . . Sarah . . . tried first with another girl. We don't know where this guy is. If we find him, I'm not sure that we'd learn what really happened. He's a suspect in an assault that's more than two months old, that's been inactive for at least six weeks. And that's all. The truth is you're no closer to getting Sarah back than you were yesterday. I'm sorry."

There was a silence in the earpiece and Warner tried not

to imagine her at this moment, what she looked like and how she was reacting to this.

"I had to ask," she said.

There were more than five hundred parking spaces in the church lot, and Sherk could have used any. Habitually, he used only one: the patch of asphalt that was closest to the basement entrance of the church hall, a paved rectangle that was hidden on three sides by the great hedge, by the six-foot stockade fence along Bellflower Street, and by the hall itself.

He had chosen it for convenience, but its seclusion suited him as well. Tucked away in such fashion, it could be seen only from the middle of the lot itself, or from the rear of the rectory across the lot. At least six times a day police cruisers drove down Bellflower on their regular patrols. On this day, as always, every one of them passed by without stopping.

Sarah stood naked behind the blanket, slouching under the beams that met at a point just above her head. Her feet were in about three inches of warm soapy water.

Sherk thought of everything. At dinner she had mentioned that she needed a bath—not complaining, because he didn't like her to whine—but mentioning that the sleeping bag made her sweat, and didn't he remember that she liked to smell nice? He had left, returning a few minutes later with a dishpan and a two-gallon insulated jug of hot water, a towel and a washcloth, and a bar of Ivory.

She scrubbed her legs hastily. The attic was cold, and goosebumps appeared where the washcloth dampened her skin. It was mainly the cold, not apprehension, that made her hurry; Sherk had retreated outside the narrow portal of the attic, where he always waited when she had to be alone.

She stepped out of the pan and dried herself quickly with the towel. Her jeans were still warm. She buttoned them and pulled on a cotton sweater.

"All done," she said. She took down the blanket and in a couple of seconds Sherk was folding his body through the low opening, emerging in sections until he was stooped under the low beams.

"Better?"

"Much better," she said, and Sherk smiled.

Story time now. In the last few days the routine had been unvarying. They arranged two cushions on the floor, sat on them facing one another, and Sherk put the lantern between them. When they huddled close to it, the flame provided some warmth.

Overhead the roof gave a secure, sheltered feeling.

"I was thinking about the time you went to the hospital in Abingdon to have your tonsils out," Sherk said. "You was ten years old. You remember?"

"I was scared," she said.

"That's right. Scared they wouldn't let you come home. I believe it must have been the first night you ever slept away from your own bed. I remember how quiet you was when we put your things in a bag and started down the hill."

"Did we have the hot rod Chevy then?"

"Right. The souped-up Impala that I traded in on the truck. You was up there in the front seat like always, looking out the window, but instead of leaning against the dash the way you usually did, you set back in the seat, and your eyes was big as the rising moon. . . . "

The monsignor came out the back door of the rectory and headed across the parking lot. His shoes and his slacks and windbreaker were all black, and except for his ruddy face he was nearly invisible as he crossed the expanse of pavement. His steps were purposeful but not hurried. At nine the Knights of Columbus were meeting in the church hall, and he was supposed to give the invocation. That was fifteen minutes away, and he had something to do.

He headed, not for the hall, but for the back entrance of the church. He used a key to let himself in. The door opened at the back of the sacristy; he went through and came out beside the altar. There he genuflected toward the tabernacle, quickly but fully, before he continued down the aisle to the back of the empty church.

As he crossed behind the back row of pews, he stopped. He was in the doorway between the vestibule and the main aisle of the church. During services these doors were usually closed, but they were open now, and he stood framed against the darkened vestibule.

He had heard a voice. An indistinct monotone so faint it could have been a muttering of the subconscious. He stepped into the vestibule and there it was a little louder. A little. But he could make out none of the words, and he knew that any other noise—a passing car, footsteps—would obliterate it. From the sound alone he would have said that it came from outside. But he believed otherwise.

Back in the church. He went to the stairs at the back corner and tried to turn on the stairway light.

Nothing happened when he threw the switch. Bulb must be out, he thought. The only light was from a small wall sconce inside the door. He had no trouble as far as the middle landing, where the stairs doubled back. But beyond that, where they climbed into the loft, the shadows were deep and he had to feel his way up, across the top landing, then through the doors that opened onto the loft.

Once he got there he could see by the light from the fixtures suspended from the church ceiling. He walked slowly along the back wall of the loft, obviously looking for something. Once he came across a loose board in the floor, and he stooped to examine it before he went on, following the back wall until it ended.

He opened the closet door and flipped the light switch. All was as he had found it before. Hymnals and boxes, and robes hanging from a pole across the width of the space. He craned his neck and looked at the ceiling, and saw that it was unmarked, unbroken. Same for the plaster wall above the wainscot. Seamless.

The robes were in his way when he tried to go farther; he shoved them aside and went to the back of the closet. There he found more boxes that he lifted and pushed, and when he had cleared a space he went down on one knee— the motion identical to his genuflection—and he began to tap his knuckles against the wainscotting. He worked his way to the front of the closet, his knuckles thudding,

thudding, on the vertical strips of dark-stained and varnished wood.

Sherk was telling about her trip back from Abingdon when he heard the tapping. He shut up and listened. The sound seemed to emanate from the far end of the passage that lay on the other side of the narrow entryway. It grew slightly louder, and Sarah watched Sherk's face become stony.

Without a word he got the mask and buckled it over her face. He put the straps on her wrists and ankles, and he hissed, *Stay!* At the entryway his hand went to his side and came up with the folding knife. She could hear a snick as the blade locked into place; the polished steel looked clean and wicked in the light of the lantern. He crawled into the passage, and out of sight.

When he had sounded his way along the wainscot, all the way back to the door, the monsignor stood. He brushed the dirty knee of his trousers, turned off the light, and left. He closed the door behind him and left the loft.

No longer than a heartbeat after the monsignor had started downstairs, the closet door opened and Sherk stepped out with the knife held low. Sherk looked around, saw nobody. He walked silently to the edge of the loft, in time to see a figure dressed completely in black going up the main aisle toward the altar. A pudgy figure that Sherk knew at once. Sherk stood at the railing in front of the loft and he watched with scorching eyes as the monsignor reached the altar, genuflected, and disappeared into the sacristy.

Not until the monsignor was in the sacristy did Sherk fold the blade into its handle and sheathe the knife. The priest had been close, he thought. Tapping on the walls. Sherk wondered how close.

He went into the closet and closed the door behind him. About halfway along the inside wall, about where the coat rack was, he went to one knee and pushed with visible effort against the wood stripping. There was a mechanical click, and a section of the wainscot swung inward.

The raccoon's scratching had brought him here, and he had found a hollow spot in the closet wall. When he tore out some of the wainscot he discovered the crawlspace that led behind the organ, into the attic of the vestibule. Remodeling had concealed the crawlspace.

That same day he had taken out some more of the strips and fitted a door over the opening with hinges and a snap lock. The wood strips, applied to the door, camouflaged it completely. The wainscot appeared to be unbroken.

Now he stooped, got down on all fours, and crawled through the opening. When he was in he reached back and pushed the door shut behind him. Then he started forward. To the left, near the end of the passage, he could see the oil lamp's glow through the attic entryway. Not once in the last two weeks had that rectangle of light failed to lift his heart. Because there, hidden from the world, waited Margaret.

—THIRTY-EIGHT—

THURSDAY
NOVEMBER 22

SOMEWHERE, the monsignor thought. He had seen it down here somewhere, years ago. Surely it hadn't been discarded.

He was rummaging through a crate in the basement of the rectory. Above, in the living room, three priests were watching the Bears and the Packers. The aroma of roasting turkey had made its way throughout the house. Thanksgiving afternoon.

The dust on the crate was heavy, and it was tough on the sinuses. His nose was running. Finally, at the bottom of the crate: a large album, bound in cracked red leather.

He took it over to a work table, where there was some light. Opened it carefully and paged through. The album contained a full set of building plans for the church: architects' drawings and engineers' drawings more than a century old. He looked for the detailed chart of the vestibule. Found it, studied it. Then the choir loft and what lay behind it. The diagrams showed everything. He looked at them for nearly twenty minutes before he replaced the album in the crate.

In the big house above the Severn they didn't even try. Thanksgiving dinner would have been a disaster. Their main meal of the day was chicken noodle soup and toasted

cheese sandwiches that Harry would not touch until Joy
badgered him.

Elise didn't like to see the way his face had lost its
ruddy tone, its animation. She finished eating as soon as
she could, and then went outside for a walk, following the
lane as far as the road and back. For the first time she felt
that she was ready for the worst, if it came. The strength
would be there. She was ready, but she still believed. She
believed.

It was, predictably, a quiet day in the detectives' squad
room. Warner had volunteered for the shift so that one of
the younger detectives could have the day with his family,
and had left the office only once, driving out to Spa
Boulevard to question the ex-wife of a convict who had
escaped from the D.C. jail at Lorton.

He hadn't showed his ugly face, the woman said. And
the motherfucker was in big trouble if he did. Warner was
convinced. A boyfriend was in the living room, watching
the football game. A shotgun sat propped up against the
sofa beside him.

Warner had returned to find on his desk a sepia-toned
flimsy from the PhotoFax machine. It was a copy of the
photo on Joseph Sherk's driver's license, transmitted by
wire from the Virginia MVD in Richmond.

Emily Caldwell had described his bushy brows, his
rough-edged look: both were there. She had talked about
crazy eyes, too. Warner did see a guardedness, almost a
hostility. He didn't want to stretch it, but he thought there
might be a little madness as well.

He wished the picture could reveal more. There was a
chance that this man might be a quarry, an adversary, and
Warner wanted to know him: how long he had gone to
school and what he watched on TV and whether he owned
a dog. Things you would want to know about someone if
you had to find him and put him away for a long time.

"Has anyone seen Joseph?" the monsignor said. At first
nobody spoke. There were five at the rectory dinner table,
the monsignor and the housekeeper and the other three

priests of the parish. The wreckage of Thanksgiving dinner lay before them. One plate was clean: Sherk's.

"I invited him to dinner a couple of days ago," said the youngest priest, Jim Davis. "But I couldn't get him to answer. And I haven't talked to him since."

"Not in the last two or three hours?"

They all shook their heads. He had to be somewhere, the monsignor thought.

He said, "The man doesn't know what he has missed. Yvonne, it was magnificent. You've outdone yourself." He patted his stomach and stood. "If eating were a sin, I'm afraid you'd have us all in peril of our souls."

She blushed with pleasure. For a moment the monsignor considered his chances of absconding with a third slice of lemon meringue pie. He would never get away with it. Maybe later.

He went upstairs to the end of the hall, where a window looked out across the parking lot, to the church and the hall. Sherk's truck was in its usual place beside the hall. The monsignor had hoped that it would be gone. He had a task in mind and Sherk could only complicate it. But not stop it, the monsignor thought. Something was happening behind the loft. It might be trivial and it might be vile, but whatever it was, tonight he was going to discover it.

In the hills they always had a wild bird for dinner. Usually it was pheasant, Sherk told her, but one year he had come back with a wild turkey. Whatever the bird, it always tasted better than store-bought.

This year it was turkey roll. Processed meat pressed into the shape of a cylinder, frozen in an aluminum container with a murky, unidentifiable brown gravy. It was the best he could do with a toaster oven and a hot plate.

So it was turkey roll on paper plates. Sherk sliced off a chunk for each of them, dripped some gravy on it, and doled out cranberry sauce from a can. There in the attic they ate, in the chill, under the angled roof that was like a low canopy draped overhead.

"I'd be glad to take it tonight," Father Keegan said. In his mid-forties, Martin Keegan was a genuinely handsome man whose resemblance to Robert Mitchum at that age was more than just casual. He also had a touch of the Mitchum swagger. A woman's priest, the monsignor had thought more than once. But a good priest, a good man. With eleven years at Saint Bart's, he was second only to the monsignor in service to the parish.

"Business will be slow," he said. Thursday night confessions usually were, and this was Thanksgiving.

"I'll have my regulars," the monsignor told him. "I look forward to it, most times. Anyway I have a small chore to take care of when I'm finished."

They were standing in the first-floor hall of the rectory as the monsignor put on his windbreaker.

He zipped up the jacket. He was about to leave, but a thought that he had been mulling over for several days returned to mind, and he wanted to share it.

"Did it ever occur to you," he said to Keegan, "what an unusual building a church is? It's a house. But unlike most houses it has no tenants except the Lord. Nobody who knows it totally, brick by brick. Priests come and leave, and none of us really knows the building. Even simple things like the wiring, for example. If we had to draw a wiring diagram to save the building, it would be lost."

"I'm not the fix-it type," Keegan said.

"But if you owned a house you would be—you'd learn. Pride of ownership if nothing else. Live with a house long enough and you'd know all its eccentricities, all the places where spiders make their webs, where the cold air seeps in at night. But our church has no one like that. Certainly not us. We look at it but we don't know it."

"That's why we have a custodian. That's Joseph's job."

"Our Mister Sherk." The monsignor laughed drily. "Yes, we're very fortunate to have found someone who learned his way around so quickly."

He told Keegan goodnight and went out to the kitchen. But he stopped before he got to the back door. Yvonne kept a utility drawer in the cabinets, and he opened it and dug through it, looking for tools that the job might require.

He knew that the choice would be easier if he knew exactly what the job was. He found a hammer, a screwdriver, a putty knife that seemed sturdy enough for light prying. If necessary he could get a crowbar in the hall basement. But he hoped he wouldn't have to go down there.

With the tools in his pocket he walked across the pavement to the church.

Usually at this hour Sherk would be up in the attic to stay until morning. They would talk for a couple of hours before sleep. But this evening Sherk surprised her as she was gathering trash after the meal.

He had to leave for a while, he said. Something important to do.

She didn't complain as he bound her up. Didn't ask for an explanation. There was no point; he told her what he wanted her to know. Fishing for more could only infuriate him.

"I'll be back," he said. "It might be two or three hours, but I'll be back. So don't you worry. Just lay there and think good thoughts, and I'll be back before you know it."

He kissed her on the cheek before he fastened the mask, then disappeared into the passage.

When he was sure that the last penitent had left, the monsignor rose from the confessional's padded seat. He removed his sacramental stole—a gold-bordered strip of silk about three inches wide, three feet long, worn over the back of his neck. He folded it over several times, held it in his right hand as he crossed himself, and brought it to his lips. He had performed the action thousands of times, and usually he tried to make it a devotional gesture. But tonight he was distracted. His mind was elsewhere. Up in the closet. Behind the choir loft.

His windbreaker lay on the seat. The stole, folded into a square, went beside it. He wouldn't need either one for a while. In one hand he held the tools he had kept under the seat. He opened the door and stepped out into the church.

It was quiet and dark. Peaceful. For a few seconds he was immobile, and he let himself enjoy the brooding splendor of the church. In any other building, this mystery with Sherk wouldn't have been nearly so nettlesome. But the church was special. Whatever Sherk was hiding, whatever he was doing, he was polluting a holy place.

He looked around again, this time out of caution. He peered in all the shadows, all the corners, for Sherk's lurking form. Certain that he was alone, he slipped along one row of pews, down the side aisle to the staircase at the back.

He tried the light. Out. He had forgotten. And he hadn't brought a flashlight.

He started up the stairs. He could see all right, as far as the first landing, where the steps reversed direction. Beyond that was deep darkness, almost a tangible presence. He tried to remember why he hadn't asked another priest for help. Didn't want to embarrass Sherk in front of someone else. Didn't want to embarrass himself by crying wolf. But that was stupid, he thought now. He *knew* there was something behind the back wall of the choir loft.

He reached the first landing and continued upward, feeling his way. As he reached the top step he was swimming in blackness. Ahead was a vertical stripe of gray, thin as a pencil line, that marked the middle in a set of swinging doors. He groped across the second landing and pushed open the doors.

Out into the loft. There was more light now, from the hanging fixtures. He went across to the closet.

The closet, he thought. It didn't appear in the original plans. Instead they showed a small open room. Also a square hatch in the wall, hardly more than knee high. SERVICE ACCESS was the notation on the diagrams. The hatch led into a cramped passage, a crawlspace, on the other side of the back wall. Follow the crawlspace to its end and you would reach the back of the organ, its innards. But turn left a few feet sooner and you would find yourself above the vestibule, under the centuries-old rafters of the old chapel.

He had seen no hatch in the closet wall, only unbroken

wainscot. But he knew that crawlspaces do not vanish, that
Sherk somehow had found a way into the passage. Tonight, even if it meant tearing out the wainscot, he too
would find the passage. And find what it was that kept
bringing Sherk up here.

He opened the door, turned on the light, and closed the
door behind him so that he wouldn't be noticed. He tried
to remember the plans—where the hatch had been, where
he should begin.

Farther toward the back, he thought. Behind the robes.
He pushed them aside, glanced down, and looked into
Sherk's leering, hateful eyes. Sherk was crouched behind
the robes, his features contorted by a fiendish grin.

The monsignor recoiled.

"Joseph," he bleated.

Sherk sprang, snarling. He slammed into the monsignor's chest, knocking him backward. The monsignor reeled
and the tools dropped from his hands. He was sprawled—
Lord God protect us Lord Jesus protect us preserve us—
with his right hand reaching back, feeling for the doorknob.
No question that Sherk would kill him—he was insane.
But if he could get out. Open the door and get out. He
might have a chance.

Lord God Lamb of God hear my prayer.

Sherk gathered himself up again and leaped. A mad
dog, slavering mad dog. The monsignor's hand fell on the
knob and he wrenched it. Sherk fell upon him and the door
flew open and they tumbled together into the loft.

Sarah, dozing lightly in the cocoon, heard a single loud
thump that came from down the crawlspace. Then a brief
scuffling noise. Then silence. Ten days earlier the noise
might have excited or alarmed or frightened her, but now
she gave it only idle attention. What happened outside the
attic had become increasingly unreal.

She listened with mild curiosity, but heard nothing more.
After a couple of minutes she was back asleep.

Sherk knew he would come skulking around again. Trying
to take Margaret away. The thought made him livid with

rage, and he had plenty of time to let it boil, let it roar. Crouching in the closet. Waiting for the priest who came to the church every Thursday evening.

Now they were grappling on the floor of the loft. The monsignor had both hands up and he was pushing frantically to keep Sherk away. Sherk's hands clutched at the monsignor's throat, yanked the stiff white insert out of his collar, strained for a grip.

The loft was banked downward, like a theater balcony. It had a solid facing topped by a rail. Somehow the monsignor pulled free but Sherk caught him by an ankle and tripped him and the monsignor crashed into the rail. Then Sherk was on him for sure. This time the monsignor's hands were slow coming up and Sherk got a good satisfying grip right on the throat. He held the monsignor in close, denying him leverage to push away.

The monsignor's mouth was moving, forming words, without breath to give them sound. He was struggling but Sherk took strength from the struggle, feeling invincible, the kicking feet and the pummeling arms harmless as raindrops. Fury kept building in him until he could stand it no more.

He lifted the monsignor. Without taking his hands off the throat, Sherk lifted him off the floor. Ten, twelve inches off the floor. Eighteen inches. They were against the edge of the railing. With all his strength Sherk lifted and heaved. He pushed the monsignor over the edge and let go of him.

For Sherk, time and movement ended. As if existence were suspended. As if, had he wished, he could have prolonged forever this moment of exquisite lightness and freedom, this moment when he released his burden.

From below there was a sound that was almost like a raw steak slapped down on a cutting board. Almost like a sack of grain thudding on a warehouse floor.

Sherk looked down. Against white marble the monsignor's form was dark and motionless. He was face down in the aisle with one arm beneath him and another outstretched. Sherk looked at him and felt nothing. It was over and there was nothing more to feel. Nothing more to think, except that he had work yet to do. Get rid of the body. There would be trouble if he didn't.

"It isn't right," said Yvonne Duranleau. She pushed aside the print curtain at the kitchen window to look again across the parking lot. "Past ten. He should have been back two hours ago."

Behind her, Father Martin and Father Jim were making sandwiches from the evening meal's leftovers.

"I told you," Keegan said. "He had something to do when he was finished with confessions."

"And I'm asking you, what does he have to do on Thanksgiving night that takes almost three hours?"

"His car's there," Davis said. "Can't be too far."

"You worry too much," Keegan said.

She left the room and came back with her coat.

"Such friends he has," she said. "It's quite touching, the concern they show for his welfare." She wrapped a scarf around her head. "At least leave him a piece of pie. He'll want it when he gets back."

After she had crossed the lot she tried the back door of the church. Locked. The side door. Locked. She walked the rest of the way around to Bellflower Street and tried the main door to the vestibule. Also locked. Fine. The doors were supposed to be locked after nine o'clock. But the monsignor would have kept them open if he was still inside.

Which meant that he was gone. He was gone but had not taken his car. And he was not one to walk even two blocks if he could avoid it. They could laugh, she thought, stuffing themselves in the kitchen. But something was wrong.

Sherk watched the old woman tug at the front door of the church and hesitate. He stood outside, looking around the front corner of the parish hall. Only his face was visible from the front steps of the church, and he could pull back quickly if she happened to turn that way.

Behind him, in the bed of his pickup truck, lay what appeared to be a long, bulky roll of painter's tarps. In the church, the smooth stone floor where the monsignor had fallen was perfectly clean. Not a taint of blood.

With evident reluctance the housekeeper left the front doors and shuffled across the parking lot, returning to the rectory. Sherk went around the hall and watched her. She went in the back door, and a few seconds later the kitchen lights went out.

He went to his truck.

Sherk was gone. Something was going on with him. He had come back to the attic to tell her that he would be busy, that he had work to do and she might have to be alone.

He'd have to stay in his room, he said. Early tomorrow somebody might come looking for him and he ought to be there. Just this one night.

When he left, Sarah felt cheated.

From the start she had depended on him for the daily essentials. In two weeks she hadn't once been hungry; he supplied all that she needed. He kept her in clean clothes and kept the lamp's glass bowl full of fuel. At first each meal, each small kindness, had been like a miracle. Now she knew that he cared about her, and would care for her.

But there were other hungers. For contact.. For a reassuring human voice. And for touch itself, a powerful craving.

She couldn't remember the last time she had been held. It was a distant memory, a father's arms around her, feeling security in his words and in his manner and in the arms themselves. His strength would surround her, cushion her, and for a little while she could collapse and know that she would be taken care of. She could be a little girl again.

She was, after all. She was a little girl, scared and alone and tired of living inside herself.

There was plenty of open country when you got out of the town. Plenty of farmland yet between Annapolis and the encroaching suburbs of Washington and Baltimore. Sherk had no trouble finding a county road and then a clay farm road that ran beside a cornfield, a spot where he couldn't see a single light but what was in the sky.

The ground was frozen no more than two or three inches deep. Past that he had no trouble spading over the loamy earth. It didn't have to be too deep, he thought. Couple of feet.

When the hole was finished he lugged the body out of the back of the pickup, wrapped in the canvas dropcloth. He laid it out in the hole, threw in a screwdriver and a hammer and a putty knife, and the stiff white insert from a Roman collar. Also a pair of his own overalls, which had soaked up blood when he knelt to scrub the floor.

The dirt made a slight mound when he was finished. Sherk packed it with the spade and threw on some corn stubble so that it wouldn't look so fresh. He wasn't worried. Rain would erase the scar on the earth.

He tossed the spade into the pickup and drove back to the church.

—THIRTY-NINE—

FRIDAY
NOVEMBER 23

A COUPLE of minutes before eight in the morning, Warner was walking down the hallway to the detectives' squad room, ready to start his shift, when he passed two uniforms headed in a hurry for the elevators.

One of them called back to him: "Hey, Warner, they been trying to raise you. Tried to get you at home."

"So here I am," Warner said. He'd had breakfast at a diner.

"The guy you and county were looking for? Farmer John type with a Ford pickup, wrinkled fender, Virginia tags?" The uniform spread his arms with palms uplifted, insouciant. "You want action, ask the boys in blue. We got 'im, detective."

The housekeeper, Warner learned, had reported the monsignor missing just before six in the morning.

The patrolman first ordered to the rectory had checked the confessional where the monsignor was supposed to have been. There he found the stole and the windbreaker, which now lay on a table in the rectory living room.

Warner looked them over. In school he had learned the names of ecclesiastical vestments, and their meaning. He didn't know the stole by name, but he remembered that

priests wore it when they gave the sacraments and that
they weren't careless with it.

"Folded up like that?" he asked the patrolman.

"Like he was coming right back to pick them up."

The patrolman didn't look old enough to buy beer. They
got younger every year, Warner thought. This one was
also tall and blond. Could have played on the UCLA
volleyball team.

"You haven't talked to the janitor?" Warner said.

"No, sir. See, after I found the articles in the church, I
questioned the priests. One of them mentioned a custodian
living in the basement of the hall. The name sounded
familiar. As I was walking over to question him I noticed a
truck parked beside the hall that fit the description on the
duty board. I checked my notes and ascertained that your
suspect and the custodian are the same individual."

The patrolman grinned smugly.

"I figured you would want first crack at the S.O.B."

"You're sure he's still here?" Warner said.

"One of the priests just looked. He's in the school
cafeteria—one of the ovens is on the blink."

Terrific, Warner thought. The school. Wonderful.

"You need a backup," he said.

"There's two officers on the way."

"Call in and tell them I said send two more. Start a
house-to-house three blocks in every direction." He jammed
his hands into the pockets of his overcoat. "I'll talk to
Mister Sherk."

"The priest said he was wearing a tan jacket."

"I'll know him," Warner said.

He walked down the street to the school building, thinking, This is too strange for words. The man who had
called Emily Caldwell his daughter, and tried to snatch
her—and maybe had done much worse to Sarah—is the
janitor of a church where the monsignor one night walks
away from the confessional and disappears.

Warner ransacked his mind for a connection and came
up with nothing. Maybe there was none, he thought. Maybe
the monsignor did just walk. These days a priest might do
such a thing. It was a changed world. No telling anymore.

As he walked in the front door he thought about what he would say to Sherk. Instinct told him to go easy. Ask a few questions, nothing tough. But watch his eyes. Look the guy over, see how he reacts, what he's made of.

Warner thought about Sherk, imagined him from the driver's license and from Emily Caldwell's words. He had heard the tape, heard the terror in her voice. As he walked down the corridor he told himself that in a few seconds he might be looking at the last face that Sarah Stannard had ever seen. Something made his fingers tingle. He flexed them in the pockets of his coat and turned left at the end of the hall.

"Thing's on the fritz, huh? Is it serious?"

Sherk took his head out of the oven to see who belonged to the voice. It was a man about his age, but heavier. A city man, city-dulled, made out of dough. His hands were stuck in the pockets of a black raincoat that only a city man would wear. He smiled with false city friendliness, and his eyes were vacant. Sherk felt contempt. Another simpering fool.

"Heating element slipped off the bracket, shorted out," Sherk said. He was sitting cross-legged on the floor.

"An old dinosaur like this, I bet you have trouble finding parts."

"Do I know you?" Sherk said.

"Howard Warner, Annapolis police." The right hand emerged with a small dark wallet, flipped it open to expose a gold badge, flipped it closed and retreated back into the pocket. The smile didn't waver. "And you're Joseph Sherk, right? Like to talk with you for a couple minutes."

Police. Sherk had known they would come, though not so soon and not in this form. But it didn't matter, he thought. All the same, didn't matter.

"Sure," he said. "What is it you want?"

"We can't find the monsignor. You wouldn't know where he went off to?"

Sherk snorted. "Don't know," he said, "and don't care."

"I hear he's not so bad for a Holy Joe."

"Priests. They're all the same. One's as bad as the next."

"Well, *damn,*" the cop said. He laughed sharply. "You sure got yourself a hell of a job if you don't like priests." Still smiling.

Sherk realized that he had said too much. This cop was no fool. The eyes were veiled, not empty.

"It's a good job," Sherk said. "They treat me okay. We get along. But they got their ways and I got mine."

Suddenly the cop seemed to be looming over him. Sherk felt uneasy on the floor. He stood, and found that he was two or three inches taller than the other man. It restored his sense of security.

"You know the last time you saw the monsignor?" The cop was chatting amiably, like one neighbor to another over a fence post.

"Day before yesterday. Saw him in the church." Sherk had rehearsed the answer.

"You live down in the church basement, don't you?"

"In the basement next door."

"He came in there around seven to hear confessions."

"Well, I didn't see him. I was in my room the whole time."

"Who was with you?"

"Wasn't nobody with me. I was by myself."

"All afternoon? All night? Sounds boring to me."

His expression was bland and unreadable as he waited for Sherk to answer. Sherk didn't like this cop one bit.

"I don't mind," Sherk said. "I keep busy."

The cop nodded. He took out a notebook and riffled through it as if looking for something in particular. He stopped at a page.

"You're from Virginia," he said. "Outside Harben, in Lee County." He leveled his eyes at Sherk over the top of the book. He hadn't put it as a question, but waited for an answer anyway.

"That's right," Sherk said after a pause. He wondered how the police knew that already.

"Let's see," the cop said. "Last time you saw the monsignor was day before yesterday. You were alone in

your room yesterday evening and all last night. You never
saw or heard anything, you don't know where he is or
where he might have gone. Is that about right?"

"That's right," Sherk said.

"Then I guess we can wrap this up." The cop put away
his notebook. "You think of anything, let me know, okay?"

"I'll do that."

The cop turned away and started to leave. Sherk returned to the work, getting down on his knees and leaning
into the oven. Then the cop spoke again.

"Hey," he said, "I forgot to ask. You got any family?"

Sherk withdrew his head from the oven slowly, buying
time to think. This was the last question he had expected.
He wondered what the cop knew and why he had asked
and what was the right answer among all the wrong ones.

"A daughter," he said after he had straightened. "But I
don't see her much."

The cop registered nothing.

"That's too bad," he said. Then he turned and walked
away. This time Sherk watched him until he was gone.

"That's him," Emily Caldwell said. "I can tell from
here." She was sitting with Warner in his car, parked on
Bellflower. Half a block away Sherk was assembling a
creche on the front lawn of the church hall.

"Take your time," Warner said. "Use these."

She took the binoculars from him and studied him for a
few seconds.

"That's him all right," she said.

As evidence it was much weaker than a lineup ID. This
was for himself. An idea was coming together in his mind
and he had to make sure the pieces fit.

"What a creep," she said. She put the glasses down.

"When I was a kid," Warner said, "there used to be
these booths in drugstores. You'd put a quarter in and you
could take three or four pictures of yourself. About a
minute later they'd roll out in a strip. Do they still have
those contraptions?"

"There's a Polaroid booth at Annapolis Mall," she
said. "But I think you only get one picture."

"One is all I need," he said. "What do you say we run up there?"

This day the sky over Harben was a flawless liquid blue that looked freshly poured out of a Sherwin-Williams can. Not a fleck, a feather, of cloud impeded the sun. From his desk in the sheriff's substation, Hap Ammen could see at least half the town's dwellings draped over the hillside, streets clinging to its undulations. The houses seemed to have burst from the rock and dirt, seeking light.

Ammen wore freshly pressed khakis. Fresh every day. He kept his shirt tucked in, and his Wellington boots were as spotless as the Colt Python revolver that he wore at his hip. He refused to play the rustic slob lawman. Four deputies worked under him in the substation; he was a manager and he wanted to look it.

He heard a car pull up outside. The engine coughed once before it quit. That would be the Blazer, he thought. Eddie Fitt in the Blazer, back from the wreck on the highway. Ammen didn't even bother to look at the door as it opened and let in a gust that chilled the back of his neck.

The door closed.

"Bad one, Eddie?" he said.

"I seen worse." Fitt came into view for the first time as he homed in on the coffee urn, a scrawny man of about thirty whose narrow head was nearly lost in the blue pile collar of his jacket. "Fella from Roanoke in the Caddy went through the windshield, got tore up pretty bad. But he'll make it. Lady in the Chevy wasn't hardly hurt a-tall."

He poured two cups of coffee, tapped a teaspoon of Cremora into each, and handed one across the desk. Ammen considered him his best deputy; not a mental marvel by any stretch, but respectful of the job, and reliable. To some it was just day work.

Ammen took the coffee and said, "Joseph Sherk has showed up in Maryland. Annapolis."

"No shit," the deputy said.

"No shit. I just got off the phone with a sergeant there. Wanted to know all about him. Asked if he had a daughter. Get this. Two months ago the son of a bitch stops a girl on the street, says he's her father, tries to get her into the truck with him." He stirred the coffee with a Bic pen. "Tell me *that* don't give you something to ponder."

Fitt wrinkled his lips in thought.

"Two months," he said. "Hell, two months, his girl was just buried."

"First week in September. The ashes hadn't even cooled over in the hollow."

The deputy looked at Ammen, seemed ready to speak but withdrew the thought, went over to the coat tree and hung up his jacket. Turning back he asked, "What'd you tell him?"

"Tried to tell 'im the whole thing. I said the sorry mess smelled bad to me. I thought so then and I always will." He put the cup down on his desk. "But I don't know that he cared to listen to some hick from the sticks. He heard what he wanted to hear, and I think maybe the rest went by 'im."

He thought about how the cabin had been ripped apart by the fire. It just didn't *look* right. Then Sherk leaving so soon afterward. The whole subject still rubbed him raw. He had wondered a thousand times what an autopsy of the girl's body would have showed. If there had been enough left to autopsy.

"I want you to get over to the high school," he said. "Pick up a copy of last year's yearbook. Then find out if they've got Express Mail in Abingdon. There's something I want to get out this afternoon."

The deputy retrieved his jacket and left. Ammen looked up at the houses on the hillside. Sherk. Up in Annapolis, he thought. It was probably a nice place and he wished the best for his brother officers there. He had nothing against them. But he hoped Sherk would stay where he was.

Better them than us, he thought.

The cops had been all over the neighborhood, rooting through trash cans and looking behind hedges, knocking on doors. It was as close as they could come to frisking sixteen city blocks. They had gone through the parish buildings with even more care; a squad of four had spent more than an hour in the church, the sacristy, the parish hall, and the basement. Sherk had cheerfully admitted them when they asked permission to go through his apartment.

Now it was evening and the teams of officers were gone. In the kitchen of the rectory, Yvonne Duranleau was setting the table for dinner. There were still three priests to care for and she had vowed that she would resist collapse. So far she had managed.

As she opened a kitchen cabinet, the knob came off in her hand. They were always coming off; repair was as simple as tightening the screw at the back of the door. She went automatically to the drawer where she kept a few common tools. Among them was a yellow-handled screwdriver that was perfect for the job.

But the screwdriver was gone. She hunted through the jumble, scrabbled furiously, couldn't find it. This, after everything else, was too much. She went to the nearest chair, sat down heavily, and wept.

Sarah's world had contracted, tightening around her until at last it extended no farther than the confines of the roof and floor. It was an arid existence that sapped strength, strangled will, deadened the mind.

"I'm cold," she said, sitting on the floor. She drew her legs up in front of her and wrapped her arms around them. "It's so cold in here."

Sherk got up and went to the hammock. He pulled the sleeping bag out of the canvas cover and hung it, unzipped, over her shoulders. She wrapped it around herself and thanked him morosely.

"What's the matter?" he said. "Feeling blue?"

That was one way to put it, she thought. She was empty and drained, stultified by the bleak, endless hours. Even the radio had become just another condition of her imprisonment.

"Kind of like that," she said.

"Want to hear a story?"

"Yeah," she said. "That would be nice." It was the only recreation her mind ever got. When she imagined life on the other side of the roof she saw bluff hills surrounding the cabin. Sherk's words made that picture more immediate than any memory.

"It's a good story," he said. "A special story. I was saving it for a time when you was ready to hear it." His voice was sonorous. "This one is different. You never knew this one before."

Before, she thought. She pulled the quilted nylon tight around herself. Sherk turned down the lamp until only a sprite of flame fluttered above its wick. Darkness collapsed around them and they both edged in as close as possible to the sooty glass chimney.

"You think you're ready for it?" he asked. His expression was grave.

"Yes. I want to hear it," she said, thinking that not even the real Margaret knew this.

"It's about somebody that tried to take you away from me," he said. "You don't remember your mother, I guess. She weren't a good woman. And you wouldn't remember that the first few months after you was born, we lived in Kentucky, about a hundred miles from Harben—that's right, you're Kentucky-born. It's hill country, too, at least the part where we lived."

"What was her name?" Sarah said.

"Evelyn. And a beauty she was. You got her looks. Her hair, too. Maybe you guessed that already. I fell hard for her. We got married, then along you came. She weren't much of a wife and sure not much of a mother. But you can't choose who you fall in love with. There's only so little you can do about it."

His voice was heavy, but not bitter. She had never seen him so solemn.

"When it was just me and her I ignored a lot. But where you was concerned I couldn't shut my eyes. We had it out plenty of times. She'd say she was going, leaving for good. And I'd say, go, get out, what's keeping you? One day she did leave. She left and took you with her. Dear Lord, I 'bout went crazy when I saw you was gone.

"It was so stupid. She didn't *want* you, not the way I

did. But she got it in her head that you was hers, and she was gonna have you no matter what.

"She had family there, so I knew how to find you. Keeping you was another thing. Her family would think you belonged to them, see? They'd come after you. So I bided my time. Let everybody think I didn't care. I looked for a place I could take you, where we could live and nobody'd find us. Once I found the cabin in the hollow I was ready."

As she watched him she could easily see the determined young father, unswerving in his love. It all made sense now, all that he had done. Even the attic, the cocoon. There was no end to his devotion. He wanted his daughter and he would do all that was needed to have her returned. Of course he had made one huge mistake. Except for that, there was a touching logic to all that he said and did. He loved his daughter the way every father should.

"She had a sister without any kids of her own. I would drive by the place and see your aunt out on the porch rocking a cradle, and I knew it had to be you. I made my move one afternoon. Had the car all loaded and ready to go. I drove past the house and there was your aunt, rocking the cradle. I waited a few minutes and drove past again. The cradle was still there, but wasn't nobody with it. I parked and left the motor running and I run up on the porch. I was scared and excited, hoping you'd be there."

As she listened, Sarah thought that the real Margaret must be out there, somewhere. Thought about all the love that was hers, brimming out of Sherk, ready to be claimed.

"I looked into the crib. There you was. You knew me, too, you put your hand out and grabbed my nose. That little hand, the tiny fingers. I picked you up and walked out with you to the car. Laid you down on the seat beside me and drove off, straight to the hollow. It was all ready. I'd made a new crib, and moved in what furniture I had. And that's where you grew up.

"They never found us. But I don't think they looked too hard. See, they didn't want you as much as I did. Nobody ever could. You was my little girl. I loved you with all that was in me, and I still do. I always will."

When he finished there was only silence and the utter dark of deep night surrounding them, held off only by the feeble, dancing flame.

"I'm sorry, Joseph," she said, and she touched him lightly on the sleeve.

"You used to call me daddy," he said. "You never do that anymore."

To Sarah he looked just sad now, no longer menacing. She couldn't believe that she had ever feared him. There was a wet light in his eyes, and she felt her own eyes moisten. It had been so long, she thought, so long.

"I'm sorry, daddy," she said. She moved the lamp aside so nothing would separate them, and she reached out. His arms enfolded her, a father's arms, strong and full of unquestioning love, and he began to weep, and so did she, saying daddy, daddy, I love you too.

Outside, parked along Bellflower Street, was a plain brown Chevy. Howard Warner sat at the wheel, watching the parish hall, the blue pickup that was vaguely visible through the hedge, and the lighted window at ground level that belonged to Sherk's apartment.

The car was cold. Warner could have run the heater, but he needed to stay alert, and the chill helped him stay awake. He guessed that some time this night Sherk would be leaving, and Warner intended to follow.

He blew into his cupped hands and waited.

Sherk's arms ached, and his legs were cramped. But he didn't want to move. Margaret had fallen asleep in his arms as he sat on the floor. She had burrowed into his jacket, up against his chest, and had fallen asleep.

He had craved this moment of peace and fulfillment, and he didn't want it to end. Not yet. After the torture of the past weeks he could happily endure aching limbs.

Before long they were both asleep.

—FORTY—

SATURDAY
NOVEMBER 24

As Elise Stannard walked up the front steps of the church for morning Mass, she thought about the monsignor. A story about his disappearance had been in the newspaper that she scanned before leaving the house.

She remembered him. He had said Mass on Sunday, and once again early in the week. His eyes were kind, and she had told herself that she should talk alone with him, ask his guidance.

Now he was gone. Awful, she thought. It was depressing, as if she were under a cloud that rained tragedy wherever she went.

"Warner, you look like hell," said Claire Johansen. "When's the last time you got some sleep?"

"About four this morning. And I didn't want it—it just happened. I'm glad you're here."

"I know when a class act like you offers to buy breakfast, it'll be something special."

They were in a trolley-car diner at the north end of town. A state road crew had beaten them to the last open booth, so they were at the counter, sitting on stools.

"In a couple of hours I'm going up against more brass

than I ever wanted to see in one place," Warner said. "I've got an idea that I want to sell them. But first I'd like to know it isn't totally off the wall."

"I'm afraid to ask."

"I went to the library yesterday afternoon to look some of this up . . ."

"Spare me! A cop with a subscription to *Psychology Today* is as dangerous as a drunk with a loaded forty-five. Look. Don't worry about sounding inane, because you probably can't help yourself. Blow up your balloon and we'll see if it holds air, okay?"

Warner told her, while around them the waitresses shouted orders into the kitchen and dishes clattered in the sink.

When he was finished, she nodded and said, "It could be. It's possible."

"That's what I wanted to hear," he said, exultant.

"I said it's possible. But almost anything is possible. It would be one for the journals, if you're right."

"That's still good enough."

She didn't say anything for a moment. There was coffee spilled on the smooth counter in front of her, and as she looked down she drew circles in it with the tip of a fork. Warner knew there must be something else, something she hadn't told him.

"You have some interest in this?" she said. It wasn't really a question. "Something more than putting away a bad guy?"

"You get caught up in it," Warner said. "Especially when there's a kid involved. You know how it goes."

"Then I'll tell you what I'd tell her family," she said. "So you won't be disappointed. If she is alive, and you do find her, she may not be grateful. She may not even want to leave him."

"You're kidding, right?" Warner said.

"No. No joke. He's had two weeks with her already, and that's enough time for him to have turned her into anything he wants. More than enough time."

"Two weeks?" Warner said.

"It can happen faster than that. In a hostage situation,

everything is compressed. The kidnapper and his captive immediately establish an intense relationship. At first it's based on extreme fear, the threat of death. When that doesn't happen, the hostage is relieved and full of gratitude.

"The kidnapper, even if he's not especially intelligent, typically realizes how easily he can shape the behavior of his captive. Threat, followed by submission. It's a power trip. Before long the captive is volunteering the submissive response, anticipating the intimidation. That may be just a ploy at first, but it's not unusual for genuine sympathy and affection to develop. Not just in a few cases; this is a consistent, predictable pattern.

"It's not so hard to understand. You've got a constant threat. You've also got sensory deprivation—most hostages are held in dark, confined places. In essence, it's accelerated brainwashing. And it works. Throw in the fact that fifteen-year-old girls are generally insecure, their identities undeveloped and still malleable to a certain extent, and anything can happen.

"So you should know," she said. "If you do get to her, she may not be the girl you expect to find."

"Maybe I'll just stick to finding her," Warner said. "Sort out the rest later."

"That's not a bad idea." She toyed with the fork for a few seconds more before she put it down and looked at him.

"Something else you should know," she said. "There's a reverse to all this. I mean, the relationship isn't usually one-sided. The sympathy can work both ways; the more time a kidnapper spends with his hostage, the less likely he is to do physical harm."

"That's good," Warner said.

"It's true," she said, "in most cases. Political kidnappings, kidnappings for ransom. But if you're right, this is something else entirely. The man could be seriously ill. In which case all bets are off. Understand? She may think that she's figured out the rules, how it goes down. And it may seem to work. But I'm telling you, Warner. You want to find her before she discovers that he isn't playing by any rules at all."

• • •

The captain's office was paneled in glass, so when Warner rushed into the squad room, already fifteen minutes late, he could see them all: the captain and the chief of police and their counterparts on the county force. All here to decide how to handle Sherk.

The captain looked out and noticed him, and waved him in. Warner stuck up an index finger, one minute. He hurried over to his desk, looking for a certain manila envelope.

Warner spotted the Express Mail label—it had arrived. He ripped the envelope open. Inside was a single page from a high school yearbook. One side showed a blurry action shot from a basketball game, but when he turned it over he found a dozen head-and-shoulder photos, arranged in four rows of three each.

Hap Ammen had circled the middle one in the second row, but Warner didn't need the help. He could have selected the picture from among thousands.

He tore the photo out of the page and had it in his pocket as he walked to the captain's office.

The captain gave Warner a looking-over as he came in. Stuck on one cheek was a small scrap of toilet paper that he had applied to a shaving nick. His clothes looked as if they had been plucked out of a laundry hamper.

Warner took the last open seat, directly in front of the desk, the brass arranged in a crescent around him.

"Howard," said the captain, "the thinking is, we should get Sherk off the street. With the Caldwell girl, we've got enough for assault. Bring him in, let him stew for a day and a half in lock-up. Who knows what he might decide to talk about?"

"No," Warner said. He shook his head with conviction. "That'd be a big mistake right now."

"We can be sold," the captain said.

Warner studied the knuckles of his right hand. He raised his eyes and looked directly at the other men, each in turn.

"Sarah Stannard may be alive," he said, "and our best chance of finding her is to keep Sherk out where he can get to her."

The captain thought the others looked as skeptical as he was.

"First," Warner said, "you're just dreaming if you think that a couple of days in custody will crack this guy. I've talked to him, and I'll tell you: he is one hard son of a bitch. He could cut your heart out this afternoon and have no trouble sleeping tonight. You couldn't shake him up with ten years of hard time, let alone a weekend in county detention."

"Sarah Stannard," said the captain.

"Right," Warner said. He got up and went to the bulletin board along a side wall. Four pairs of eyes followed him. He took out the five-by-seven glossy of Sarah.

"We all know this young lady," Warner said, and he tacked the photo to the board. "Sarah Stannard, at age fifteen years, four months." Beside it he tacked a second photo, a color head shot. "This one you've heard about. Emily Caldwell, at age sixteen and three months. It's a more recent photo and she's also several months older than Sarah. By the way, she normally wears her hair swept back. But for comparison I had her put it in a braid, and she remembered that's how it looked the day she was attacked."

"We know the connection," one of the chiefs said.

"Not this one, you don't." Warner had his back turned. When he moved aside, a third photo was tacked to the board.

"Margaret Anne Sherk, at about age fifteen. It's a yearbook photo, taken almost nine months ago."

The captain's first impression was that Warner must be playing a convoluted joke. He looked at the picture and knew he had to get nearer, so he joined the others crowding around the board. He was amazed. The girls were nearly identical, their features and coloring and hair interchangeable.

"A sheriff's deputy where she lived described her as

about five-seven, hundred and ten pounds. Within five pounds and an inch of the other two.''

They all peered at the photos. The first two together had been intriguing, a curiosity. With the third added, the effect was startling and powerful.

"This is his daughter?" said one of the chiefs.

"His late daughter. Died last August in a house fire. Sherk disappeared before her funeral. Two weeks later he accosts Emily Caldwell, apparently after spotting her near the harbor. He calls her by his daughter's name and is angry when she doesn't respond. He's ready to haul her away, but she manages to escape. Two months later Sarah— her schoolmate and nearly her double—is missing. I don't know how Sherk ended up here, but I think he came looking for his daughter. And he found her. Only, her name is Sarah Stannard.''

The captain listened with the others as Warner laid it out for them, telling them what he knew, what he had learned from Claire Johansen, and what he guessed. While Warner spoke, the captain kept looking at his bulletin board, where the three girls stared down, implacable, demanding to be reckoned with. There was an almost mystical quality about the three of them, arranged together on the board. The captain couldn't keep his eyes off the pictures and he noticed that none of the others could, either.

"We've been through the church property," Warner was saying. "Sherk even let us into his rooms. So I'd say he's rented an apartment, maybe a garage, to hold her. He'd want to see her as often as possible, so it's probably someplace nearby. But he has to visit her periodically.''

The two chiefs and the captains looked at one another, and one of them asked, "What do you need?"

"A couple of days;'' Warner said. "Keep two people at the church, rotating shifts. One county, one from us. I can double-shift, I don't care. County has this jazzy surveillance van with one-way glass. It would help. We ought to tell the priests that Sherk is a suspect in an investigation, that they should keep him away from the school, but otherwise leave him where he is. And I'd repeat the house-to-house, see if anybody in the neighborhood recognizes Sherk or the girl.''

The captain looked at his own chief and got a silent nod. For a few seconds the two county officers whispered between themselves before one turned and gave a yes.

The captain shot his cuffs and said to Warner, ''Thirty-six hours. That'll be early Monday morning—I don't want him anywhere near when the kids come to school. It's more time than you need. He'll have to go to her at least once between now and then. If that doesn't cut it, then we bring him in. And we use what we have to put him away as long as we can.''

''Good,'' Warner said. He was bobbing his head vigorously. ''Perfect. I'll get on it right now.''

He left the office and swept into the squad room. The captain couldn't remember the last time he had seen Warner move so fast.

It was a warm morning for November. Sarah knew it as soon as she woke. She was sweating inside the sleeping bag, and reached up for the zipper tab. Only when she had pulled it down and thrown open the bag did she realize what she had done: she had moved her hands. There was no cocoon. No belts around the bag, no straps around her arms and legs. And no mask. She touched her face. No mask.

''Mornin','' Sherk said from across the attic. He filled a glass with orange juice, and as he brought it to her, hunched under the low roof, she understood that he had gone for breakfast already. He had gone and left her unbound as she slept.

''Sleepyhead,'' he said as he craned over the hammock. ''I thought you'd never wake up.'' He bent closer and kissed her on the cheek. It didn't feel unnatural to her, didn't feel wrong. Then she remembered. The sadness in his eyes, holding him, being held. Falling asleep that way. And a dim recollection of Sherk carrying her to the hammock, pulling the bag around her, some time during the night.

She swung her feet down to the floor and took the orange juice. Her head skimmed under one of the sloping beams as she found by reflex the high spot where the two sides of the ceiling met, the one place where she could sit up with her back straight. The roof pinched in directly above her, its underside just inches from her face, and on her cheeks she could feel warmth radiating from the wood.

"It ain't too cold," he said. "A good day for a bath, if you want."

"I'd enjoy that," she said.

She followed him to the cushions where they always sat to eat. He reached into the gym bag. Without thinking, she knew that he was going to pull out graham crackers. She had always liked grahams and orange juice for breakfast.

They ate. Sherk wouldn't take his eyes away from her. She didn't mind. They weren't sad this morning, his eyes, but proud and happy. She basked in his pleasure.

When he was finished he brushed the crumbs off the bib of his overalls. He told her that he was leaving to bring hot water.

"Anything else you'll be wanting?" he said. "Anything I can bring, I will."

She considered this.

"I'll tell you what. I'd like some shampoo." Until now the attic had been too cold for wet hair, but today it would dry. "That would be nice." She looked at the backs of her fingers. "Maybe some nail clippers. They're getting long and I don't want to bite them."

"I'll have to go to the drug store for clippers."

"You don't have to bother."

"No bother. I want you to be pretty. I mean, you already are. I want you to feel as pretty as you look."

He was ready to go. The straps and the mask were on the floor, beneath the hammock, and she expected him to cross over and get them. Instead he went to the other end of the room and hunkered down in front of the passage opening.

"I'll be a while. Maybe an hour," he said. His eyes narrowed by the slightest increment. "You'll be a good girl? Won't do anything you shouldn't do?"

"No." Her voice was tentative. "I promise I'll be good."

"I know you will," he said. He raised a hand and crooked his fingers twice, a small goodbye, before he turned and crawled through the portal. A few seconds later she heard the door snap shut at the end of the passage.

Alone.

At first, for two or three minutes, she didn't budge from the spot where she sat. Instead she stared at the portal, telling herself that Sherk had left and she could do what she wanted—she was free.

The idea was slow to root. Finally something nudged her off the cushion. She crossed the floor and stopped at the threshold of the portal, sitting on her haunches. She summoned all her courage and leaned forward. When her head was clear of the wall, she looked to the right and sighted down the crawlspace.

Sherk sat curled at the end of the passage, invisible in absolute darkness, a patient man who knew how to wait. He had opened the door and shut it without going through.

Her head appeared at the entryway, poking out, testing. She looked down the passage, and Sherk held himself still.

The lantern light behind her cut the gloom slightly. She could make out narrow walls, and a ceiling that was appallingly low; the tunnel was as cramped as she had imagined. Only the first few feet of the passage were illuminated. The rest was completely dark, and she knew that somewhere in that blackness, at the indeterminable end of the passage, was a door to the world.

The thought made her shrink inside.

She continued peering down the crawlspace. To move beyond the portal, to push herself into that narrow tunnel, was unimaginable. She did not fear the constricted darkness so much as what she would find at the end of it. Beyond that black buffer was noise, confusion, the disordered unknown.

Outside, a dog barked. It frightened her. She had never

been afraid of dogs, but the barking frightened her. She knew that she should leave, that it was expected of her, almost a duty. But she didn't understand why. At first the attic had nearly suffocated her, and she tried to remember how that had felt, the desire to escape. Tried to remember why she had sought the jumble and the brightness and the noise. The reason was incomprehensible now.

She pulled her head back. Sherk spoke, and the surprise nearly lifted her off the floor.

"Where was you going?" he intoned. The sound was disembodied, eerie.

"No place," she said. Her voice cracked.

"Who are you?"

"I'm Margaret. Your little girl."

"A good girl or bad one?"

"A good girl. I'm your good little girl."

"A good girl don't run off."

"I won't. I wasn't. I wasn't. I just wanted to look."

"Don't even look. Nothing for you out here."

"I won't. I won't even look."

For several seconds she heard nothing. Then the door opened and shut again.

She scrambled back from the opening, retreated to the hammock, got on and crawled into the sleeping bag, zipped it up in spite of the warmth. Her eyes avoided the portal across the floor. She drew her arms into the bag, clutched the fabric around her shoulders, and gently rocked, rocked in the hammock.

Warner thought Elise ought to hear it from him. Since she was going to hear it anyway, she might as well hear it right. But he took the time to shower and change, so when he reached the Stannard house, they had already heard. Clearly the pipeline made few detours.

He sat with them in the big living room anyway and gave a shortened version of what he had told the brass. Elise listened and interrupted only once, to say, "He works at the church? At Saint Bartholomew's?"

She didn't speak again until Warner had finished.

"I only want to know one thing," she said then. "Can I hope now?"

Warner looked at her before he answered. There seemed to be a dignity about her, an inward solidness. He had always prized composure, admired it in others and tried to cultivate it in himself. He wasn't sure that, in her place, he could have kept himself together so completely at this moment.

"What the hell," he said. "Why not? I do."

—FORTY-ONE—

SATURDAY
NOVEMBER 24
3 P.M.

FROM the upstairs window in the rectory, Warner could see the black Dodge van wedge itself into the last open parking space on Bellflower Street, directly in front of a fire hydrant. It was the county's surveillance van, taking up position.

Warner and a young officer in plain clothes had been upstairs in the rectory for almost an hour. They needed this second post to cover the rear of the church and the parish hall. The housekeeper had given them an unused room with an excellent view out back: the monsignor's room.

In the field glasses that he held to his eyes, Warner could see the driver disappear into the back of the van, closing the curtain behind the seats. In a few seconds there was a squawk from the Motorola handset that lay on the monsignor's nightstand.

"Orchid One," said the voice, "this is Two in place."

Warner picked up the transmitter, keyed it and said, "Two, check. Our man went down the basement steps of the hall about fifteen minutes ago. Possibly gone to his room."

The schedule that Warner had devised called for one county officer and one from the city to be on post at all times. His own shift wasn't supposed to begin until midnight, but he had to be here. He would be here as long as it took.

The young plainclothes man, sitting at the window in the monsignor's straight-backed desk chair, fidgeted on the hard wooden seat and said, "Let's hope he decides he has to see her real soon. Otherwise it'll be a lo-o-ng eight hours."

Warner stood behind him and watched the back of the church, the hall, Sherk's truck. One more time, he tracked over his theory, the reasoning of it. From Margaret to Emily to Sarah; he had tramped this path countless times in the last two days. It made sense if you understood fathers and daughters, and Warner believed that he did.

He remembered a slip of a girl who had once gotten off the bus from Virginia Beach. A small, scared girl who had let her long hair get too dirty. Who stood on the top step of the bus in Baltimore and wouldn't move until she had spotted him in the crowd. Who came down the steps and approached him shyly at first, then ran to his arms.

Father and daughter, he thought: that was something special.

The clipper chirped as Sarah trimmed the last of her nails. It was a small device of chromed steel, with sharp curved jaws; Sarah looked around for a place to put it, and slipped it absently into a side pocket of her jeans.

"How's your hair?" Sherk said.

It lay straight, fanned out across her back. She reached behind to touch it and said, "It's about dry."

She sat cross-legged in the middle of the floor. Sherk was a few feet away. He came over to her and put an arm around her shoulders.

"I want you to do something for me," he said. "Braid it down the back. Will you do that?"

She thought of the wooden doll with braided hair, and remembered that Margaret wore her hair that way.

"Sure," she said. "I can do that."

The lines on his forehead lifted as he smiled.

"You've been a good girl," he said. "Made me real happy. I couldn't ask for more." He swept her up in both arms and embraced her in a hug so fervent she nearly lost her breath.

He was beaming when he let her go. Sarah returned his smile and had begun to pull a brush through her hair when she saw his face change, the smile disintegrating, the furrows reappearing above his brow.

"Blood," he said. "Blood on your face."

"I don't think so."

"I can see it," he said. "All over your face."

She reached up and felt around. There was nothing.

"I'm sorry," Sherk said. His voice was distressed, his breathing fast and shallow. "I didn't mean to."

"It's okay. You just made a mistake."

He didn't seem to hear her. Didn't even seem to notice her, she thought. He was looking at her but seeing someone else.

"It just happened, came over me, I couldn't stop it. So much blood. It just happened. It wasn't really me."

"It's okay," she said. She put her hands on his shoulders and shook him gently. "I'm all right."

He didn't respond at first. Then he began to come around, as if emerging from a long sleep. He touched her cheek.

"It was all over your face," he said.

"I don't think so. You just made a mistake."

His breathing evened out again. There was still the trace of a question on his face, but in a few seconds even that vanished. He was calm.

He squeezed her hand and took the brush from her.

"Let me," he said. "You have trouble getting it all the way to the end. Go on, turn around. Don't worry, I'll go easy on the tangles."

She shifted so that she was sitting in front of him. He began to stroke the hair, gently pulling the brush through, starting at her hairline and ending at her shoulders, soothing and almost hypnotic, and after a couple of minutes she had stopped wondering what he had seen, what had really happened.

There were six telephones in the main wing of the Stan-

nards' home, and since Warner's departure Harry had been
lurking near one or another of them. After dinner he
camped in an easy chair a few feet from the phone hutch in
the hall.

Joy sat nearby and watched him try to read a newspaper.
For a few minutes he would scan the page he held in front
of him. But soon she would notice the paper slowly dropping into his lap as his eyes fixed on some distant point
beyond the walls, beyond the power of sight. Then he
would catch himself and snap the paper straight again.

When the phone rang that evening, first time in hours,
he leaped out of the chair. Joy was watching, and for an
instant she saw again the husband she knew, vital and
strong, reborn not just in the way he moved, but in the
hope he showed. He tossed aside the newspaper, sprang
for the phone, and reached it before the second ring.

"Yes!" he said, his voice piping, his whole being alive.

Let it be, she thought. As much for his sake as anything
else.

In less time than it had taken him to get to the telephone, she saw him deflate, crumble.

"No," he said. "No." His voice was flat. "I'm sorry,
nobody here by that name. No, un-huh, you have the
wrong number."

The sound of the receiver clacking down was harsh and
brutal to her ears.

Harry shuffled back to the chair, bent stiffly to retrieve
the paper, arranged the pages, and folded them in front of
him. He raised them up, but a few seconds later lowered
them and looked at Joy.

"He said he was close. Didn't he?" Harry asked. "A
matter of a few hours. Didn't he say that?"

"Give him time," Joy said.

His lips were pressed together, thin and colorless.

"I'm trying to hold on," he said. "That's all, no more.
Just trying to hold on."

At around ten that night the patrolmen finished their house-
to-house in the neighborhood.

A few minutes before midnight, Warner stood at the

window, alone in the room, thinking of Sarah. He had given up trying to put her out of his mind.

He told himself that she was alone tonight. Alone, a prisoner, in what must be some dingy hole. He could only imagine.

At this hour, he thought, Sherk would be in his room. The lights were low in the church and the hall was dark, so he had to be down in the basement.

Some father, he thought. Go to her. Go. If she was my daughter I'd want to be with her all I could. I'd be with her right now.

The cabin was a mess. A chair was on its side in the front room, a lamp lay smashed in the corner, and an end table beside the sofa had been overturned. Margaret kept a spun-glass figure of a horse there, a gift he had found for her at a shop in Abingdon. He went over to the table and found a thousand gleaming splinters on the floor.

There were also droplets of blood on the unfinished pine planks. Sherk touched one of the larger drops and saw that it was almost dry. The dark drizzle made a trail from this spot toward the back of the cabin, Margaret's room. Margaret was there now.

If he tried hard, concentrated, he could see her sleeping in a rope hammock under the attic's roofbeams. But not really. He knew where she was. She was in her room, at the end of a bloody track, and something horrible beyond words was wrong with her.

He could feel himself drawn to the room, the pull inexorable, and he knew that he would have to go in and look. It had to be. Maybe not now, not right away. But soon. Before long he would have to go into that room and see what he had done.

—FORTY-TWO—

SUNDAY
NOVEMBER 25

FOR more than six hours Warner had been peering through a night-vision scope that stripped away darkness and rendered life in a grainy green monochrome. Now he pulled back from the eyepiece and looked eastward. A flock of gulls scattered across a mother-of-pearl sky. A boy wearing a black Orioles jacket was delivering Sunday papers to the homes across Bellflower, and the old Caddy that trundled down the street was the third moving car he had seen in the past few minutes.

He keyed the radio and spoke: "Orchid Two, you still with me?"

"Oh sure, wide awake." It was Tarver in the county van. "A thrill a minute, this is. I'm not sure I can stand any more excitement."

Warner put the radio aside. The street lights went out along Bellflower.

Sherk was getting breakfast when morning arrived. He had left the attic early, so that he could return and spend the day with Margaret. He put two pieces of bread into the toaster, peeled some bacon into a frying pan, and stirred a pan of milk that he was heating for cocoa.

"Oh, no, daddy, not again," Margaret said behind him.

He spun around. There was nobody. Yet he had heard

her clearly. He went into the bathroom and looked around, thinking that she must have followed him down, somehow snuck in. When he didn't find her there he looked under his bed and in the closet.

"No daddy no, please don't."

A tortured plea, full of pain. This time it came from under the kitchen counter. He rushed around to the other side, but she wasn't there. He tore open the cabinet under the sink. Not there either.

She screamed. The sound seared inside his head. He clapped his hands over his ears but couldn't block it out. The shriek was excruciating. He had to stop it.

He reached out and she was there. His hands were on her throat, and he was choking off the scream. Only way to stop it—he couldn't take it anymore. He put all his weight and strength into the grip, wrenched himself downward with the force. The scream died to a moan and then to nothing. He was on his knees, soaked with sweat, hands still held out in front of him, clenching air.

Off to his left there was a hiss. He ignored it and tried to control his breathing. Tried to understand what he had heard, what he had seen and touched. There was another hiss, louder and longer than the first, and he turned around to see milk boiling up and out of the pan, frothing over the sides and splashing on the coils of the hot plate.

The watch changed at eight. Warner gave up his seat to the new man but didn't move far from the window. About half an hour later the housekeeper brought breakfast, and Warner ate standing up, holding a bowl of corn flakes in one hand as he watched the first worshippers arrive for the nine o'clock Mass. He was more alert now than ever. With all the activity around the church, they could easily miss one man leaving.

At about ten minutes before nine he put down the bowl and reached for his binoculars, brought them to his eyes and focused on a woman who was walking alone through the parking lot, toward the church. It was Elise. The wide brim of a hat hid her face, but he recognized her tall, slim figure, her straight back.

She approached the walkway that led around to the front

of the church. There she stopped and looked around. He knew: she had heard about this man, Sherk, and was trying to find him. Just to look at him, that would be enough now. She moved her head, and for a couple of seconds her face was visible, alert and curious and hard-set. "Got something?" said the cop in the chair.

Elise turned her back and started up the walk.

"An old friend," Warner said. He put the glasses down and resumed his scan. Rear of church, side door of church. Rear of hall, side door of hall. Basement steps, Sherk's truck. And then back again, again, again.

When he returned with breakfast, Sarah knew right away that something was wrong with Sherk. Something had happened while he was gone. He had put a distance between them, an almost palpable barrier that she sensed in his movements and in his voice as she took her place across from him on a cushion.

He pulled a foil-wrapped bundle out of the gym bag and tossed it on the floor between them. She opened it: six slices of buttered toast. It was cold. Another bundle: some black shards of bacon, also cold. He hadn't yet looked into her eyes. For the first time in days, she was scared.

He poured orange juice out of a carton into a plastic cup, and handed it to her.

"No cocoa," he said. "I burned the milk and there wasn't any more."

"I don't care," she said. She tried to catch his gaze, but he avoided her, and she thought that maybe she would be better off away from him. Maybe he wanted that. She brought the cup of juice with her as she went over to the hammock and sat cross-legged beside it.

He appeared not to notice. Instead he bit the corner off a piece of toast and stared out morosely. For a while they sat in perfect silence, Sherk with a wall around him, Sarah trying to be unobtrusive. Trying to be transparent, if that was what he wanted.

Some sounds below marred the silence. There were voices and footsteps, people coming to church. Sarah knew what was coming next, not long now. It arrived without warning, the first clap of the steeple bell, shaking the attic and shattering the quiet. Sherk's head jumped and he looked up toward the source of the din. At first he was riveted. Then he gradually relaxed, and his shoulders dropped. He lowered his gaze. Before the bell pealed nine he had withdrawn into himself again.

The organ piped alive a couple of minutes later. After one stanza, the choir joined. Their voices climbed; music surged through the room. Sarah ignored it. She kept looking at Sherk, hunched over and sullen.

After a couple of minutes he got to his feet and came over to her. He was stooped under the peak of the roof. To Sarah, on the floor, he seemed gigantic. The voices soared and the attic trembled, and Sherk looked directly at Sarah.

"I think I done something bad," he said. He had to raise his voice to be heard; even so his voice was mournful. "Tell me what I done to you. Something bad."

Sarah didn't know how to answer. By unspoken pact they both had put aside what happened that first night. But he couldn't have forgotten, she thought.

"Tell me. Tell me what I done. Something bad."

She knew he didn't want the truth. No matter how hard he asked. He didn't want to hear it.

"I can almos' *see* it," he said. "I have to know. Just tell me what I done."

The last bars of the hymn dropped away, and the attic was silent. He crouched beside her.

"Tell me," he whispered.

"You've always been good to me," she said.

"But I hurt you. Did something bad."

"You didn't."

"I never hurt you?"

"Never."

Sherk rubbed his temples. He looked doubtful, still distraught.

"My head hurts. Got to get rid of this headache," he said. He got up and went away to the farthest corner of the attic, where he retreated into the angle formed by the floor, the back wall, the pitched roof. His face was dismal in the lamplight.

Outside, beyond the back wall, there was a low murmur like distant thunder. Sarah didn't know the words, couldn't make them out, but she knew it was people praying out loud, praying together.

Sherk looked at her, almost accusatory this time, then buried his face in his hands. He remained that way a long while. Songs came and went. The Mass ended and the church emptied, and more people trooped in below. Sarah sat on the floor, forlorn, looking at Sherk and at the portal a few feet away, trying to find a grip on the slippery truth of who she was and how she had gotten here.

When the ten-fifteen Mass was underway, and the view was uncluttered again, Warner told the relief officer that he was going to try for a nap while he had the chance.

He took off his wingtips and stretched out on the white coverlet of the monsignor's bed. Threw an arm across his face, over his eyes, to block out the daylight. Within a couple of minutes he was dozing. But it was a shallow sleep, because he expected to be awakened at any moment. Sherk would leave, would go to Sarah. It was overdue, had to happen any time now—and he wanted to be ready when it did.

So he dozed without really immersing himself, skimming sleep. Sound or movement would lift him to the edge of consciousness. He was aware of the housekeeper bringing sandwiches for lunch. Periodically the radio would buzz, the county van checking in.

He intended to sleep through one Mass only. When he finally roused himself and trundled over to the window, the parking lot was emptying after the fourth and last service of the day.

"Nothing?" he said.

—FORTY-THREE—

SUNDAY
NOVEMBER 25
4 P.M.

For hours Sarah had sat at one end of the attic, away from Sherk, watching him where he crouched. Sometimes he would mumble down at the floor, ignoring her, but she knew she hadn't been forgotten. Every few minutes he would look up and glare at her—not a hostile look, really, but a sharp one, a piercing one.

She had listened all morning to the music and the chanted prayers, the bell and the organ and the sound of people periodically passing below. The pattern was familiar. There were four Masses on Sunday. A couple of hours earlier she had heard the end of the fourth cycle, people filing out, none replacing them. The church must be empty.

As the hours passed and Sherk unraveled, the attic seemed to shrink. Now it was oppressively close, and she didn't understand how she had managed to grow comfortable here.

Across the attic Sherk was fevered, talking out loud, the words garbled and incoherent to her. Then he stopped and stared at her, and this time spoke clearly.

"You're not here" he said. "You're in the room. I know it. You can't be here."

Sherk could feel the wall coming down, the wall he had

built in his mind without even knowing. Now images and feelings and memories that he had hidden away were escaping, bombarding him randomly, utter hatred seeping out of the cracks in his brickwork. It all had a meaning that he couldn't make out yet. But it was coming together.

There in the room. Her bedroom in the cabin.

He looked up and saw Margaret. Who was not Margaret. Because Margaret was in the room, waiting for him.

"You're not here," he said. "You're in the room. I know it. You can't be here."

She came over and knelt beside him.

"Look, I'm real," she said. "You can touch me. Look."

She squeezed his right hand, her fingers thin and delicate against his own.

"See?" She carried his hand up to her face, her shoulders. "I'm real. I'm me."

Like a blind man he ran his hand over her perfect skin, caressed her cheek, fingered the braid down her back. Verifying her existence.

But one thing he knew above all else. Memory and imagination might buffer him, but one truth he could hold on to. Margaret was in the room.

He looked closely at her.

"Who *are* you?" he said.

His words stunned her. She tried not to let it show because that would ruin her. That would end it all.

Get it together, Champ, don't lose it now.

"I'm me. I'm Margaret." This was her life.

He shook his head wistfully, as if he wished it were so.

"I am," she said. "I'm Margaret and you're my daddy. We lived in a little cabin in a holler near Harben, in Virginia. Just the two of us. I ever knew my mama—she ran off when I was just a baby and took me with her, and you had to steal me back. Remember?"

"I'll never forget." His tone was bittersweet, and he closed his eyes, bringing it back.

"I had a tabby cat named Banana that got lost one day, and we never found it. For three years you worked as a
  anic at a mine up the road, the summertimes I would
    work with you. You made a little playhouse for me

beside the mine office.'' She rummaged through her mind
for details, and when she dredged them up they had the
quaint feel of artifacts, arcane contrivances. ''We saw a
mother bear and her cubs once in a meadow on the other
side of Drolsom's Ridge, where we used to go for walks.
A beautiful meadow. Remember how warm and sunny the
days used to be, the grass so tall and thick and green? You
used to say I'd disappear if I lay down in it.''

His eyes were still closed and his head was thrown
back, and on his face was an emotion she had never seen
before, bliss somehow co-existing with misery. She was
disarming him.

''Yes,'' he said. ''Yes.''

''When I got up on cold mornings, and the windows
were iced over, do you remember what I used to do?''

''You used to scratch our names on the frost,'' Sherk
said fervently. ''You'd write 'Daddy and M.' ''

''A special way.''

''Backwards. You taught yourself how. You'd write it
that way so people going by could read it, and they'd
know who lived there.'' Sherk's eyes were closed, but a
tiny wet gleam had appeared at each folded corner.

''And why did I always write the two together?'' she
asked.

''Because you said that's how we'd always be. Together.'' A sob caught in his throat. ''You made me
promise that whatever happened, we'd always be together.''

With his eyes closed Sherk could see it all, daddy and
Margaret in the cabin in the holler, all the love that was
between them. Oh yes. He could see it, and it was good.

''And we are together, aren't we?'' she said at his side.

''Yes.''

''We always will be, right?''

''Yes. Always.''

''And aren't I your little girl?''

''My little girl,'' he whispered. Still with his head
thrown back, eyes closed, suddenly limp and wrung out.

''Then give me a kiss and tell me everything's the way
it was. Tell me everything's okay.''

" 's okay," he mumbled. She was holding his neck. Leaning forward to kiss her, he opened his eyes.

A leering corpse's head looked back at him. Blood-smeared, it lolled on a broken neck. One eye swollen and purple, one cheek sliced so deep that white bone showed through.

Margaret.

"Daddy?" the corpse said through distended lips. "What's the matter, daddy?"

Sherk roared fright and outrage. He roared grief, and threw up his arms to break the grip of her ghastly dead fingers. She bayed a mocking laugh, and he shoved her as hard as he could, flipping her backward, knocking her halfway across the floor.

When she picked herself up she was just a girl again, wide-eyed and ready to flinch.

"What did I do wrong?" she said in a tremulous voice. "Tell me what I did."

His head hurt something awful. He had to think, but he couldn't get things straight, not around her. She was part of his problem.

Sherk looked at her once more to make sure she hadn't changed again, and then he ducked his head and went through the opening, into the passage.

God was he strong. She had forgotten how strong. Her shoulders were sore where the explosive blow had fallen.

She listened to his boots scraping along the passage, behind the back wall. The sound diminished. He was really leaving, she thought. When the noise ceased she knew he was out of the passage, out and gone.

She stood and hit her head on a beam. Too low, she thought. The place was suffocating, the lamp's light woefully dim.

On hands and knees she made her way to the opening. She wanted to get away. Now. Only the thought of Sherk, out there somewhere, held her back; for about a minute she hesitated at the threshold. Then she imagined being here when he returned, and that was enough to send her through the opening and into the blackness.

The passage was even darker than it looked. After she had crawled about ten feet—beyond the opening, beyond the feeble reach of the lantern—she could see nothing. Her hands were invisible as she advanced them inches at a time, sliding them across the floor in front of her, blindly feeling her way along.

Her right hand touched something solid. She slid herself forward a few inches so that she was closer. The barrier was flat and wooden, standing directly in her path. She felt around her. Wall, ceiling, wall, floor. And then this obstacle, boxing her in darkness.

Boxed in. Her heart accelerated.

Keep it together. Keep it together. Think!

Okay. Sherk was through here all the time. There had to be an entry. The first thing she heard when he came in, and the last when he left, was a hard click and what sounded like a dresser drawer being firmly closed.

Or like a door. A kitchen cabinet maybe.

She remembered the first night. Sherk had put her down and told her to crawl, and she had crawled straight ahead into the tunnel. So there were no turns. The door opened directly at the end of the tunnel, and now she was at the end.

She moved her palms along the flat upright surface in front of her, and the fingers of her left hand fell across a metal handle. She pulled. The snap clicked and the door came back to her. It opened and she swung it through, then pushed herself through the space it made.

She came out behind the rack of choir robes, shoved past them, stumbled over a box and came out of the closet door.

The light burned her eyes. It was only indirect evening light through the stained glass windows, but it was more than she had seen in weeks, and it hurt, made her blink and turn aside until her irises had adjusted.

Then she looked around.

The church seemed huge. Its walls and arched ceiling overhead seemed to go on forever, the scale overwhelming after the confines of the attic. She looked upward to take it all in. Instantly she was dizzy. Her legs were weak anyway, and they began to wobble under her. She reached back and steadied herself against the closet doorpost.

Deep breath. Deep breath. Her equilibrium returned. She released her hold, and for the first time she straightened out of the constant stoop that the attic demanded.

The air tasted fresh, she thought. She could move. Breathe. Stand. Walk.

She went out into the loft, looked around, and saw the set of doors at the far end of the back wall. The doors were the only exit that she could see, so she crossed over and opened one. The light was meager, but she could make out a wide landing and a set of stairs that led down. She held the rail and made her way down to the bottom, through another set of doors, and out into the side aisle of the church.

When he left the closet, Sherk went to the first dark and quiet place he could find. Had to think. His head buzzed. Something was battering at the wall
Margaret in her room
trying to get through. He didn't want to see, but he knew
in her room
there was no more running from it, no more holding it back.

He sat and looked out dumbly, and he saw.

The fire burns inside as he scuttles down the hillside. He knows what's going to happen and he knows it's wrong, but he can't stop it. Doesn't know how. Doesn't want to.

Margaret's in the kitchen. He stands in the doorway until she notices.

Oh no, daddy, not again.

She thinks she knows what's coming. But she has no idea.

You was swimming. There was boys. The first blow, sharp and unexpected, cracks against her face. Just a hard slap but it feels so good. He does it again. A bad, bad girl.

For a while she just sits there, taking it, blood coursing ____, her head jerking back and forth. She takes that with ____ast down.

He stops. She won't meet his eyes. You bitch, you evil bitch. His hands go to her throat.

She wriggles upward, almost out of his grasp, but she's off balance and the chair tips back and she falls with it, slamming against the end table by the sofa, turning over the table and with it the spun-glass horse that he once brought her.

She gets up, dazed. He could grab her but he doesn't. No matter, no hurry, all over now but the shouting. She leaves blood droplets in a trail behind her as she stumbles off to her room, locks the door.

Margaret, Margaret, he thinks. That won't do the trick and you know it. Cheap little door lock.

He follows the deep red dots to her door. Decides he'll play a little game. Better open up and let me in. No I can't. I'm your father, let me in right now. No daddy I'm scared. Just makes the fire burn hotter, and when he's good and ready he steps back and raises his foot and kicks the door right beside the knob. The lock rips out of the mortise. She screams.

And now it really starts.

Next he knows he's sitting at the kitchen table. The holler is in shadow. He's done wrong. Isn't sure what it is, but he knows it's bad. Inside is that emptied-out feeling the fire leaves him with.

Margaret's in her room. He knows that. Already he's got it in his mind, how it'll go. She'll be cowering in the corner, naturally she'll be afraid. But he'll show her it's over, hold out a hand to her, pull her up. Then they'll kneel, talk to Jesus, pray about how life makes it hard for us to be good.

He gets up and goes to her room.

She's propped up in the corner.

He gets sick when he sees her.

Blood and bruises all over her face. Lips puffed and one eye swollen shut and her left cheek split open so deep, white bone shows through. It's all wrong, the crooked way her head sits on the neck.

Margaret, he says in a small voice. Margaret sweetness.

Wake up honey, time to get cleaned up. Come on, wake up, don't pretend.

When he prods her the only thing that moves is her head, which drops and finds another crazy angle.

Somebody's screaming, howling. He wishes it would stop, and realizes it's him, he's the one screaming.

Then he does stop.

Inside his head is a tiny hard-shelled kernel, unperturbed and unmoved. He surrenders himself to it, lets it take over.

It sends him out to the shed for a bit-and-brace. He picks a spot in the front room, and with the widest bit he has, a three-quarter incher, he drills a hole through the pine board floor, at a spot near the wall.

He goes through the house, shutting windows, drawing curtains, stuffing towels into the cracks under doors. He leaves Margaret's room for last, and when he's finished there he picks up her body, carries her into the kitchen, sits her in a chair in front of the stove.

Now the stove. It's an old-fashioned one with pilot lights that are always going out. He blows them out, two on the range and one in the oven. Then he turns up the oven's control; the propane gas makes a throaty sound coming out of the jets. He makes sure to get the box of safety matches off a shelf before he goes out and shuts the front door tight behind him.

Part of him knows this is wrong, knows he has sinned unforgivably, that he ought to be prostrate with grief and contrition now. But the hard kernel of self isn't moved. It sends him mechanically to the shed again; he comes out with a smudge pot.

It is about the size and shape and color of a cannonball— made of tin, slightly flattened at the bottom, with a wick at the top. Highway crews use them as long-burning flares to mark road work at night. Sherk once bought half a dozen at auction, to burn in his garden on spring nights when the temperature drops near freezing.

Now he needs only one. He shakes it near his head and hears the fuel slosh inside. Plenty.

The cabin has no basement, and no foundation except for concrete blocks that sit at the corners and at six-foot intervals along the base of the walls. There's a space of several inches between the ground and the floorboards. He gets on his back, finds the hole he has drilled, positions the smudge pot directly beneath it.

He lights it with a match.

It's already hazy in his mind, why he is doing this, what has happened. His drive down to the truck stop will be three-quarters of an hour, and by then he'll have forgotten completely. About the time he goes to work the house will be filling up with gas, and when it gets thick enough some of it will get pushed out through the hole, down into the burning smudge pot.

"Propane . . . the stove. She never got out," the deputy will say, and Sherk's mournful moan will be full, real, unrehearsed.

Sherk was sweat-drenched as he sat in the darkness. What these hands have done, he thought. What these eyes have seen.

He knew now that the fire was inside him every moment. Always had been, always would be. His to live with. He knew it was there because he had seen what it did. And because he could feel it even now. It was rising.

He couldn't stop it. Didn't want to.

There were footsteps, coming his way.

Sarah came through the doors at the bottom of the staircase, out into the side aisle. She had never seen the church before, so to find the fastest way out she had to stop and look around.

The front door, beyond the vestibule, was to her right and behind her. Not far away, but she had to pass through a section of pews to get there. Farther up this aisle was a side exit that the pews didn't block. She looked from one door to the other, and started up the aisle.

She could see nobody else around. To her right was the section of pews. To her left was the side wall of the church, and as she hurried up the aisle she passed two purple-curtained confessional boxes, and several bas-relief carvings that illustrated the Stations of the Cross.

The side door was close now. She passed a pillar on her

right and came up on a third confessional. She was almost running, and didn't notice the tremor in the last purple curtain.

Sherk stepped out from behind it, blocking her way. She tried to stop, slipped on the smooth marble floor, and fell into him.

He grabbed her by one arm.

"Well now, girlie," he said. His voice could have chiseled stone. "Well now. What are we doing down here?"

—FORTY-FOUR—

SUNDAY
NOVEMBER 25
7:15 P.M.

For more than a day Warner had been a presence in the rectory mostly unseen, an object of curiosity. Only Yvonne, bringing in meals, had had a chance to observe him.

Martin Keegan had spoken to him for a few minutes on Saturday, when Warner was arranging the surveillance. This evening Warner's relief had left around five; after supper, Keegan went upstairs. The door to the monsignor's room was slightly open. Through the crack the priest saw that all the lights were turned off. Warner was standing at the window, his weight forward, leaning against the sill.

Keegan knocked. Warner looked around, said, "Come on in, Father. It's your house," and went back to the window. He was worn, Keegan thought.

"I hope you don't mind. I knew you were alone and I thought you could use company."

"Good. Glad you came." He remained fixed on the window.

"I have to admit that I wondered what a stakeout was like," Keegan said. "I've never seen one before."

"As you can tell, the drama is relentless." His tone was wearily dry. "Any questions, feel free."

"Why no lights?" Keegan said.

"Reflections." Warner flicked a finger against the pane. "And I don't want him to know he's being watched. At night it would be pretty obvious." Then, in a tone that showed strain, he said, "I don't suppose anybody down there has actually seen him since yesterday afternoon."

"I did," Keegan said. "This morning, quite early. I was changing the altar linen when he came in through the sacristy. I think I surprised him. When he saw me he mumbled something and then went back the way he came."

"Back to the hall," Warner said.

"Yes. He must have been coming to make a repair, because he had a gym bag, almost a satchel, that I've seen him with. I think he carries tools in it. But he turned around and disappeared."

"Then he really is there," Warner said. "I was beginning to wonder."

"We all know the feeling. You'll think that he can't be far. Yet if you go looking for him, an hour later you still haven't come across him. I'm not saying that he dodges work. But sometimes I think that we find him only when he wants to be found."

"Does he have a TV?" Warner asked without looking back. A strange question, Keegan thought.

"I don't believe so," he said. "About a month ago I happened to speak with him in his room. It seemed bare. I don't think he had a television."

"What about books?" Warner said. "Is he a reader?"

"I'd be surprised."

Warner said nothing more for a while. He gave the window complete attention.

"I need a favor," he said abruptly. "I need somebody to cover for me, a few minutes."

"Me?"

"Nothing to it. Just keep watching. I don't suppose you'll see him, but if you do, get on the radio here. Press this button to talk, and just say you've spotted him and which way he's headed. That's all. Then let go of the button. It's on already."

Keegan held the set for a few seconds and put it back on the nightstand.

"The moon's plenty bright tonight. If you see something and you're not sure, use the night scope. But it'll give you a headache if you look through it all the time."

"You think I can do this?" the priest said.

"Up 'til now Ray Charles could've done it."

Warner stepped aside and Keegan took his spot at the window. Radio, night scope, and keep watching, he thought. He looked out on a setting that he had seen countless times, but now it took on a vastly heightened significance. Now that the responsibility was his, he didn't want to so much as blink. He could understand Warner's stare.

"Hey," Warner said. "Keep holy the Sabbath, is the way I was taught."

"It still is. We try."

"But Sherk was working this morning."

"Emergencies come up," Keegan said.

In the periphery of his vision he watched Warner fold his arms, then unfold them and put his hands in the pockets of his overcoat, then fold them again.

"What was the emergency this morning?" Warner said.

The question hadn't occurred to Keegan. He thought and said, "I don't know. Nothing, as far as I'm aware. I have no idea what he was doing."

"Okay. Won't be long. Any questions, you just push the button and talk."

Keegan wondered where he was going. Call of nature, he thought. But about half a minute later Warner was out of the rectory and walking across the parking lot, his path leading him toward the parish hall. His steps were compact and direct, shoulders slightly hunched. A man who lives within himself, was how Martin Keegan saw him. A man with no loose ends.

Kill me if that's what you want, Sarah thought. Whatever you want to do, go ahead. Just do it. Stop waiting. Do it.

She would have said so, if she could have. But the mask was over her face, tighter than ever before. She was bound and trussed in the cocoon. The canvas shroud was a strait-jacket, constricting her chest. A set of three belts cinched shoulders and waist and ankles, holding her fast in the hammock.

Sherk had broken her jaw, she thought. It was swelling against the mask. He had hit her just once, but that was enough to subdue her. Then he had led her back here.

He had left briefly and returned. Since then, for more than two hours, he had sat on a box in the middle of the room. Not like this morning, when he had seemed to be coming apart. Now there was no fervid mumbling, no confusion. Instead he was concentrated, hard and cold, as if he had sloughed off an uncomfortable human skin to reveal a center of pure vileness. Just seeing him that way was enough to make her fear for her life. She felt he was on the brink of an unspeakable evil.

He was waiting, she thought. Waiting and watching in a world that existed for him alone. She wondered what he saw, sitting on the box, looking out past the roof with disturbing calmness. Sitting on the box, and slowly whit-tling down the wooden doll he had made for her, drawing his open knife the length of the wood, raising a paper-thin strip that curled up and fell at his feet.

After thirty hours of looking out from the rectory window, Warner had to get closer. He couldn't say why. But he believed that he had earned the right to fly blind, indulge a small inexplicable urge when all else had failed.

And all else had, he thought. If something didn't break soon you could count ten on this one, ten and out.

He crossed over and went up the walk beside the church. At about the spot where Elise had paused this morning, he too stopped and looked around. Beside him was the granite palisade of the church wall, notched at regular intervals by the inset stained glass windows, colorless and almost opaque now.

He went up the walk and around the corner, past the front steps of the church, toward the parish hall on the other side. Sherk's apartment was a corner room on the far end. It was completely blocked from view of the rectory: its main window faced out on Bellflower, and a bathroom window around the corner was in front of the stockade fence.

The main window sat just a couple of inches above ground level. There was a light in it. Warner didn't want Sherk to see him, so he passed it quickly on the sidewalk, turning his head to look. The second time he walked past slower, a few feet closer. He thought there was something strange about the evenness of the window light, so on the third pass he stopped and approached.

It was painted over. One window in the place and it had been whitewashed. Somebody likes privacy, he thought.

There was nothing else to see, and he didn't know what he had hoped to find, so he walked back to the church. He went up the stairs, tried the front doors, and found them locked. It seemed early for that.

He crossed Bellflower and went over to the black van, another impulse. When he got there the rear door popped back at him. Tarver was holding it open. Warner climbed in and pulled the door shut behind him.

The van had a carpeted floor, a small refrigerator, and two contoured swivel chairs in the back. Warner took the empty chair as Tarver got two cans of Coke from the refrigerator.

"I thought I had him figured," Warner said. "I really did."

"He's a head case," Tarver said. "You go goofy trying to figure a head case. If a guy don't have all the dots on his dice, you'll have a long time to wait before he throws boxcars."

He yanked the tab on one can, dropped it into the opening, and passed it to Warner.

"Maybe it's drugs, I don't know," Tarver said, "but you see more head cases these days than you used to. Am I right? You meet 'em on the street, they seem okay. They walk, they talk fine. But there's nothing there. Night of the Living Dead. Lights are on, nobody's home. You know what I mean?"

"I guess." Warner kept looking at the lighted window,

imagining Sherk behind it, behind painted glass. "I'd like to know how he spends his time. No TV—did you know that? No books. Anybody'd go batty. What the hell does he do with himself?"

"Pulls his pud," Tarver said around a burp. "That's easy. Bet that dude plays a *mean* game of pocket pool."

Holed up all weekend, Warner thought. Alone in a shitty little basement room for thirty hours. Except when he's walking around in the church on Sunday morning, carrying a gym bag.

"I think he must sleep in the daytime," Tarver said. He was tearing open a bag of potato chips.

At first Warner wasn't listening.

"Either that or he's afraid of the dark, he can't sleep with the light off."

"What do you mean?" Warner said.

"The light. That's his room, right? Corner window? I was here midnight to eight, and it was on the whole time. I get back about an hour ago, thing's still on."

Tarver tipped his head back with his mouth wide open, like a baby bird at feeding time, and inserted half a dozen potato chips. He chewed, chugged from the can of cola, swallowed.

"Maybe he sleeps with his head under the covers, I don't know," Tarver said. "But I guarantee the jag-off ain't worried about the electric bill."

He wiped his hands on his pants.

"So what do we do? You want to take him now, fold the tent?"

"No," Warner said. "I don't mind giving it a couple more hours. You?"

"Shit. Lap o' luxury here, pal. I don't live this good at home."

Warner got out and closed the door. He fished in his pocket for a key ring, twirling it on his index finger as he walked, a distracted, unconscious gesture. Head case, he thought. Find him only when he wants to be found. Came through the sacristy, saw me and turned around. Sleeps with his head under the covers.

And something else that Tarver had said. Warner tried to remember. Most times you had to tune out Tarver, the way he went on.

A head case. Night of the Living Dead. Lights are on, nobody's home.

Light's on. Nobody's home.

He stopped in the middle of the parking lot, grabbed the keys in mid-swing, turned on a heel and came back. Past the front of the church, to the painted-over window at the far corner of the parish hall. He dropped to one knee on the grass in front of the window, placed an ear against the pane. He couldn't hear anything. He tapped on the glass.

Knock on the door, he thought, that's one thing. Somebody might ignore that. But not this. He tapped again, harder.

Not this either. Half-buried in the turf was a stone about the size of a walnut. Warner pried it out, stepped back a few feet, and cocked his arm. He told himself that in about five seconds he was going to be one brilliant or very silly cop.

He flung the rock.

A fist-sized hole appeared in the middle of the window, and chunks of glass fell out of the frame. Warner could hear them shattering on the floor inside.

Nothing happened. No shouts from inside, no angry face at the shattered window. He went close, kicked out some of the hanging glass, and bent down to look. He could see almost the entire room, and there was nobody. Not now, probably not all weekend.

Tarver was coming out of the back door of the van. Warner waved him back.

"There's a priest on the radio," Warner said. "Tell him we need keys for every lock in these two buildings—to bring 'em down. The radio too. She's here. Son of a bitch, he's got her here."

Sarah found that she could move her hands in the cocoon. The middle strap outside the canvas pinned her arms tight against her sides, but her hands were free and she could move them at the wrist. It made no noise, no rustle, that

Sherk could hear. He was still rapt, enmeshed in his fantasy.

Under the thumb of her right hand, in her jeans, she could feel a flat metal object. It might work, she thought. If she could somehow get it out of the pocket. Maybe. If Sherk would leave. Maybe.

—FORTY-FIVE—

SUNDAY
NOVEMBER 25
7:35 P.M.

WARNER and Tarver stood beside the van, watching Father Keegan come toward them with a big hoop of keys and a flashlight in hand.

"I could call for backups," Warner said. "Get half a dozen others in here, really do a job on it."

"Bad idea," Tarver said. He believed Warner was still trying to out-think a head case. "Why hang yourself out to dry? If we spend an hour putzing around in here, we're the only ones have to know. But you call for the cavalry, and still find nothing, they'll still be laughing about it five years from now. You can only make yourself look bad."

"I don't mind," Warner said.

"I do. It's my ass, too. Look, extra bodies get the job done faster, that's all. Not better."

They watched Keegan cross the street and come over to them.

"I'd like to help," the priest said. "I know my way around in there."

"So much the better," Tarver said. He looked at Warner. "Now we got three. We get many more, we'll be tripping over each other."

Warner pursed his lips for a few seconds and said, "I guess we could do it with three. The father and I'll start in

299

the hall basement, work our way toward you. You stay back in the church. If we flush out Sherk he'll be coming your way.''

''Now you're talking,'' Tarver said. Less he had to do with this foolishness, he told himself, the happier he would be. Standing in the church for an hour, he could do that. Let the others chase around.

They went across the street, up to the front door of the church.

''It should be open,'' Keegan said. ''Nobody from the rectory closed it.''

''Then somebody inside did,'' Warner said.

The priest picked out a key, slid it into the tumbler in the front door, twisted it, and pushed the door open.

They walked into the darkened vestibule. There was a switch by the door, and when Keegan hit it a series of fluorescent lights popped on overhead. The church remained dark.

''We'll start next door,'' Warner said.

Tarver said, ''I'll stay right here. Stay here behind the door, I can see out, he won't see me. And if he comes my way I'll get him.''

Thinking, What a crock.

He watched Warner and the priest go up the main aisle, cross in front of the altar, and into the sacristy. A pure crock, he thought.

The hall was easy. Warner decided to get that out of the way. Easy part first. A few closets, two lavatories, a small kitchen in the back. They were done in ten minutes, and from there he went down to the basement.

She saw Sherk change again. He seemed to have seen something, something he had been waiting for. He was alert. If anything his demeanor turned even colder and more brittle.

Under his knife the carved doll had become a smooth wooden shaft. Now he suddenly lost all interest in it. His knife hacked at the wood and sliced off two thick chunks, and he let the piece of wood slide out of his hand, hitting the floor.

Sherk got up and came over to her, and looked directly

at her for the first time since he had tightened her mask.
He stood stooped over her, the arm with his knife hanging
loosely at his side.

Tarver heard the thump, something hard hitting the ceiling
immediately overhead. Then silence.

He looked up. Fluorescent fixtures and acoustic tile in a
low ceiling. But he had heard something.

"Sarah?" he said out loud.

And again, louder: "Sar-ah!"

The noise arrested Sherk. First low voices—he had ignored that—then somebody down below calling her name.

He lifted his eyes away from her. When he heard the
name a second time he looked down at the floor where it
had come from, glanced at her, back to the floor. He was
torn, she thought. The knife twitched at his side, flicking
small slices out of the air. The lamp was at his feet, and he
cast a monstrous shadow on the back wall.

He stared at her and then turned away. Silently he went
across the floor, folded himself into the entryway, and
slithered out of sight down the passage.

The door closed; the catch clicked.

Sarah realized what she had heard, what it meant. Somebody calling her name. It was weeks since she had heard it
spoken.

She gulped in air. Somebody looking for her. But how
hard it would be for anyone to find her, anyone except
Sherk. She would have to help herself, couldn't count on
anybody else.

In the pocket. The outside straps were binding, but she
managed to lever her right shoulder up, crook the arm
slightly, and slide her hand up on her hip until her fingertips touched the open slit of her pocket. She slid her
fingers in and they touched smooth metal. The nail clippers.

She withdrew her hand and brought the clippers out.
They slipped from her fingers and she had to feel for them
against her hip. There. Got them.

The clippers were folded flat, useless this way. They
had a small lever that had to be swung around, pulled up,

before they would work. She tried to manipulate it, tried to find room for it between her thigh and the close-fitting sleeping bag. She wiggled in the bag, momentarily created about an inch of space, and managed to twist the lever into place. There.

All this was happening at her right hip. The cocoon was tight, and the three outside straps constricted her even more at shoulders, stomach, ankles. But now the clippers would work. She held them against the fabric of the sleeping bag and closed the jaws.

There was an audible snap as the clippers nipped a tiny hole in the nylon. She was elated, and shoved the edge of the crescent jaw against the fabric again. Again it grabbed nylon, and bit. She repeated the action a dozen times more, then felt with her fingers where she had been working. It was ragged, chewed, but not yet completely ripped.

Her wrist was aching. She told herself to ignore the discomfort, and she set to work again with the clippers, nipping, tearing, biting at the fabric, a small chrome terrier at her fingers.

There had been a sound, Tarver thought. A thump overhead. He waited about half a minute, wondering what he had heard, what he ought to do. He was waiting when he heard the second noise—this not so loud—like the quiet shutting of a door.

Some noises in an old building were insignificant, almost random. But Tarver didn't hear these that way. Instead they seemed to be a part of something else. A thump, the quiet shutting of a door. The kind of noises you might hear in a house with people, not an empty church.

Part of his mind was still saying, ah, it's a crock, but the rest of him was alarmed enough that he didn't want to leave and find Warner. If the noises meant something he shouldn't leave.

Wouldn't hurt to look around some, he thought. He went into the church, let the vestibule door swing closed behind him, and looked around. He saw only one way up, set of doors to his left that had to go a staircase. He walked behind the last row of pews and went through the doors.

He found stairs. There was a weak hooded light set into the wall, no other light. He tried the switch but nothing happened.

Shit, man, you don't need this aggravation.

But he started to climb the stairs. When he got to the first landing he saw that he faced thick darkness. He drew his pistol, nickle-plated snubnosed .38, and held it with his arm crooked, the stubby barrel pointing up, as he climbed the stairs.

Dark as the devil's asshole up here.

He stumbled at the top of the stairs and had to catch himself at the rail. He steadied himself, found his balance, and took two short steps across the landing and into the soupy blackness, thinking that he had to run into a door.

He felt around and found a handle.

Behind him a voice said, "Dead meat if I get him."

This time when she stopped, Sarah could feel a tattered patch where she had been working. There was at least one hole big enough for the tip of her finger. She put it in and pulled at the fabric. It tore raggedly.

Now she could feel feathers, the down stuffing. She pawed at it and tried to clear it away, best she could manage with her arm pinned. After about a minute she could feel nylon again. The outside covering of the bag, she thought. After that the canvas of the shroud.

Her arm ached from the tips of her fingers up to the elbow, muscles that had never worked so hard. But she could feel the rough canvas through the second layer of nylon, and that gave her strength. She took up the clippers and went back to work.

When Warner got down to the basement the jets were flaming in the furnace, a hellish racket, and it made him think that this would be the place. Dark and full of nooks. From the way the priest groped around down here Warner could tell that he didn't come here often. Who would, if he could avoid it?

With the burner going, he thought, Sherk wouldn't have heard the rock through the window. The noise had been in his room, behind a closed door. He wouldn't have heard it out here. So he could be here and wouldn't have known.

They started at the corner farthest from the outside entrance. There was a big gray locker and Warner went to it, jerked the handle down, and threw the door open. It held at least fifty one-gallon cans of paint, room for nothing more.

Next a closet. He went in and found a floor polisher and an assortment of brooms and dust mops.

No good, he thought. People were through here two days ago. They'd have checked closets and lockers. Had to be someplace else, kind of place nobody would think to look.

Think!

There was more than one, Sherk thought. His mind was mostly a void now, but he could reason, the thoughts pinging and echoing through his head. He had heard at least two voices below the floor. So there was more than one, and one would come looking for the other. He could wait. What was in the attic for him would be there when he got back.

Sarah got through the second layer of nylon. But the canvas was tougher. She could nip it, but it wouldn't tear when she pulled it. It was too tough, and she knew she was losing strength in her arm. Will could do only so much.

She thought of Sherk coming back. This time there was no question, not the smallest excuse for hope.

She fit the clippers' jaws over the ragged edge of a hole in the canvas, and began to work them again.

Warner had cobwebs in his hair, and a smear of grease across his face, when he trudged up the stairs with Keegan. They came up into the hall and turned down the corridor, toward the church.

"I know the church," the priest told him as they walked. "The basement, no, it's not in my purview. But the church is where I work. If you added up all the hours I've spent there, you'd have years. I know the church, and I can't imagine where she would be.''

But the priest still didn't understand, Warner thought. With all their searching they hadn't come across Sherk. And yet they knew he was here someplace. Keegan himself had seen him here this morning. They had been watching, and knew he hadn't left. So he was here. Not in the hall; not in the basement. Had to be in the church, hidden someplace.

Unless Tarver had seen him. Warner wanted to start in the sacristy and work his way forward, but he thought he ought to check in with Tarver first.

The priest followed as Warner left the sacristy and walked down the main aisle. Warner couldn't see him at the door where he was supposed to be. Damn Tarver, he thought, lazy bastard.

He looked in the vestibule, just to make sure. There was nobody. Gone to the van, had to feed his face. Only other place he could be was the second set of doors, in the corner to the right.

He motioned to them and asked, "Where do they go?"

"The doors?" Keegan said. "Up to the choir loft."

Could be he was there, Warner thought. It was worth checking before he blew up at the guy. He slipped behind the back row of pews, the priest a few steps behind.

There was blood on the floor. A dark crimson puddle of it was leaking out from under the stairwell doors.

Warner reflexively stopped, put out his left hand to halt the priest, reached with his right to the holster that he wore at the small of his back. He brought the pistol out.

He went forward, stepped over the puddle, grasped the door handle. Paused. Then whipped the door open suddenly and swung around it. He looked. There was only blood. A pool of it lay in the stairwell. Warner went in and saw that it had come from upstairs, flowing down, filling the stair treads. More blood than Warner had ever seen before.

The light switch was across the puddle, and he didn't want to step in the blood. So he put a hand back and said, "flashlight"—impossible to look away—and the priest put it in his palm.

Father Keegan was crowding in behind him, trying to see. Warner heard a gasp and then a guttural, hurried, Hail Mary. He found his own lips miming the words.

"Stay," Warner said. He picked his way around the puddle, then upstairs, gun in his right hand and flashlight in his left. As he climbed, the blood was even thicker on the steps.

He got to the first landing and started up the next flight. Slowly. Poking the flashlight around. He knew he was stepping in blood. Bad practice, bad copwork. But there was no avoiding it. The blood was everywhere.

At the top of the last step the flashlight fell on a hand, fingers curled upward. He got closer and saw that the hand belonged to an arm and the arm was on Tarver's body. Tarver *My God* with his throat cut *Oh my God* with his throat cut straight across. A bloody grin cut straight across his throat.

Warner tried to contain himself, tried to keep his voice steady as he leaned over the rail and spoke to the priest.

"Are you there?" he said.

There was no answer.

"Father, are you there?" he said, louder.

"You mean me?" Keegan said.

"Yes. Listen. I want you to go to the rectory. Run. Dial Nine One One. Tell the dispatcher there's an officer needs assistance at this address. Understand?"

"I understand." He sounded shaky.

"Hurry," Warner said.

Warner listened until he could no longer hear the priest's footsteps behind the back pew. He was out, Warner thought. Help was coming, and there would be no disgrace in going downstairs, waiting for it.

But he knew he couldn't do that. Tarver had come here for a reason; something had brought him up these stairs. About half a minute passed before Warner's gun hand stopped shaking. When he could hold the pistol still he stepped over Tarver's body and put his left hand on one of the two swinging doors, ready to push through it.

Sarah stopped snipping and chopping at the canvas. There

was a hole in it now. She could get two fingers through it.
Three fingers. Her entire right hand.

A few inches above the hole was the strap at her mid-
riff, around the hammock and the cocoon. Sarah turned
her wrist and felt for the strap. She touched the webbing.
Good. Now usually Sherk fastened them right along the
top of the cocoon. There. Piece of metal. It had teeth of
some kind that gripped the belt, kept it from slipping when
there was tension put on it.

But he had a way of releasing it. A button, something
like that, she thought. She pressed it and prodded it, and
suddenly it let go. The pressure disappeared around her
midsection. And her arms weren't trapped any more. She
could move them. The left was still tucked inside the
cocoon, but she could poke the right one through the hole.
Unbuckle the cocoon halfway up her sternum.

Now she had some movement. There were still straps at
her shoulders and her feet, holding her to the hammock. She
released the top one, at her shoulders. Now she was free
from the hips up, only her legs still trapped and encased.

She was bending forward to release her ankles when she
heard the shot.

Warner put his left hand on the door and pushed it outward. He took one step into the loft and was turning to look
around when a thunderclap filled his head. He felt himself
lifted, picked up by an unseen force, thrown against the door.

He fell dazed at the foot of the door, his weight holding
it back, keeping it open. He knew that he had lost his gun.
His first thought was to search for it, but nothing happened
when he tried to feel around where he lay. His right arm
wouldn't work.

It burned terribly at the shoulder. He looked, and saw a
small neat hole in the upper front of his jacket. There was
blood coming from it. The sight was so fascinating that at
first he didn't notice Sherk coming toward him from where
he had been waiting, about thirty feet distant. When he
looked up Sherk was a couple of paces away, then standing over him with a nickle-plated snubnose revolver pointed
at his head.

"You," Sherk said, breaking into a grin. "You! This is great!"

Sarah heard the shot and hurried to free herself. Her upper body was out of the canvas, but the strap at her ankles still pinned her to the hammock.

She bent at her waist to touch the buckle. It was beyond her reach. She rocked forward to get closer, and the hammock swung to one side with her movement. Had to get out. She lunged again; the hammock kicked out and spilled her to the floor.

Sarah fell with her legs still strapped to the foot of the hammock. But her upper body pitched out, landed hard, and her left arm flew out as she tried to break her fall. It struck the glass-bowled lantern on the floor. She knocked it backwards, and heard the breaking of glass as it smashed in the corner, out of sight.

The light should go out, she thought. A lamp breaks, the light should go out. But it didn't. It grew brighter behind her. She was hamstrung, legs suspended above her head, tied into the hammock. By twisting she was able to get on her side and look back.

The attic was on fire. In one corner the wooden floor shimmered red and orange, and flames were licking up the roof, starting up the back wall, spilling across the floor in front of the entryway.

Her ankles were out of reach, but she could get to the mask on her face. She ripped it off and screamed.

"You!" Sherk exclaimed again, delighted.

"Talk to me," Warner said. In a couple of minutes there would be cops all over. If he could hold out that long. "Tell me what's bugging you, we can work things out."

"I don't think so," Sherk said. "I think it's time to die."

He thumbed the hammer back. Warner could hear it notch into place.

Sarah screamed.

Sherk swung his head toward the sound.

"What the hell did you do to her?" Warner said.

"Didn't do nothing."

A second scream, long and sustained. Sherk looked alarmed.

"Help her," Warner said. "She's in trouble. I know. You do too."

"No," Sherk said. He stared at Warner. The gun was waving, circling, and he used both hands to steady it.

"It's fire," Warner said. Almost softly. "Look. Just look. It's fire."

Smoke was streaming out around the edges of the organ, patterned waves that grew thicker, heavier, as Sherk watched.

She screamed a third time.

"Get her," Warner said.

"Shut up."

"She's your daughter. Go get your daughter." Warner's voice was louder.

"I'll kill you," Sherk said.

"Kill me, fucker, but don't wait," Warner shouted. "Kill me and get her. She's your girl. She's Margaret. You love her, go get her."

Margaret? Sherk thought. Maybe. His head hurt and he was very tired, and there were things he was supposed to remember but couldn't. Margaret, he thought. Margaret was someplace.

She screamed. A single long continuous scream. Sherk couldn't stand it. Had to make it stop.

He dropped the gun.

Sarah was on her side, legs twisted and tangled in the hammock, watching the fire advance. She could feel its heat and she could see it creeping across the floor toward her.

Overhead, it wasn't just creeping. The steep angle let it burn faster there, and one entire side of roof and beams was aflame.

She wasn't going to scream any more. The air that she sucked in was too hot. It singed her throat and her nostrils, so she was going to try not to breathe again.

A figure appeared in the flames at the entry, a gaunt stooped figure. He walked through the fire without even picking up his feet. When he got to her the bottoms of his overalls were burning.

For a second he stood above her, reeling. Then he bent over the foot of the hammock.

Her feet fell out on the floor, and she kicked free of the canvas. But there was fire all around, everywhere she looked, flames knee-high on the floor that she would have to cross.

He reached down and picked her up. So strong, she thought. He carried her in his arms, his feet dragging through the flames, and he put her down in the passageway, where the floor hadn't yet started to burn.

"Go," he shouted. The fire was deafening, and the smoke choked her. She looked across the flames at him, and he shouted, "Go!" again.

Warner watched Sherk throw the gun down and run for the closet. He dragged himself to the revolver, picked it up, and stood. By leaning against the wall he was able to make his way over to the closet.

The wainscot door was open, and there was smoke coming out. He could hear sirens. Not much longer, he thought. He looked in the opening and saw a girl coming out toward him. A beautiful girl. He could almost understand.

She clambered out, and when she was clear he planted himself in front of the opening. He held the pistol in his left hand and braced it with his right, the best he could. He pointed the gun at the opening and waited.

She was touching him on the sleeve, on the face.

"He's not coming," she said. "You don't have to worry. He's not coming out."

—FORTY-SIX—

SATURDAY
APRIL 27

Two county detectives were on elbows and knees in a freshly plowed farm field west of Annapolis. In front of them was a shallow pit that had been dug between two of the dark new furrows. The detectives had plastic sheets to protect their pants, but their hands were caked with dirt from sifting through the moist loam.

The coroner had left, and they were picking up the rest, putting each find in a bag that they closed with a tie-wrap and marked with a numbered tag. So far they had come up with a hammer, a screwdriver, and the curved white insert of a Roman collar.

"I've been doing okay," Sarah Stannard said. "Better. I guess this is sort of a ten-thousand-mile checkup, huh?"

"Something like that," said Claire Johansen. "It's been a month since we talked, and I didn't want to lose touch. Not yet. Are you sick of coming here?"

"No. I like it."

It was true. You could talk to this lady, Sarah thought. Tell her anything. Sarah had been here almost daily at first, then less often. Almost from the start, she had felt at ease with Claire's strength and calmness.

"I like it too," the psychologist said. "You want to tell me what's been happening in your life?"

"I guess the big thing is that my grandparents are moving. They're going to Arizona. Scottsdale. They said we can stay in the house, but I think we're going to get another place."

"Staying in Annapolis?"

"For a while. It's okay with me. I'd just as soon not go through the trouble." She smiled. "Look what happened to me the last time we moved."

"How are grades?"

"School is great. My marks are getting better. They hung my drawings in the halls for Parents' Day. It was just a school show, but what the heck. Better than a poke in the eye."

"What else have you been up to?"

"Not much. We went out on the boat last Sunday. Howard's trying to teach us to sail. He keeps saying that we have to learn before we sail to the Caribbean."

"Do you want to do that?"

"I think I'll let Mom do it. Anyway, it sounds like one of those things adults talk about and never get around to doing."

"How goes it with you and your mother?"

"Better. At first it was like before, only worse. I couldn't go anywhere, she always had to be there. I told you that. I thought, here we go again. But lately, it's been different. I can tell she's trying to make it different, without making a big deal over it. I can feel her letting go. A little bit."

She laughed.

"Not too much. But enough. I can tell the difference."

"What about all the rest? Do you think about it often?"

"You mean with Sherk and me."

"That's what I mean."

"I think about it sometimes. Maybe not every day, I don't know. It doesn't get to me the way it did at first. Mostly I'll look back on it and think, Wow, that actually happened to me. It's hard to believe. Really. I'm just an ordinary person."

"And your nightmare? Does that bother you anymore?"

"Once in a while. But like I said, it's not really a nightmare. It actually happened. I remember. I try not to think about it, but when I'm asleep I can't control what I think about, so it comes to me."

She crossed her legs, put her back flat against the chair, and let out a long, slow breath.

"It definitely happened. I can still see it. It's not something I'll ever forget."

She could still see it. The attic was full of fire. Sherk had carried her through the sea of flames and dropped her in front of the entryway of the passage, one of the last untouched spots on the wooden floor.

And he had backed away into the middle of the floor. "Go," he shouted at her. "Go."

She ducked into the passage. But before she crawled away, she turned back to see him.

Sherk was kneeling on the floor. His legs were aflame, and he was crying. When he saw her he reached out, extending his hand to her over the inferno. As if he wanted to touch her one last time. Their eyes met, and in his face was sorrow and pain, and a last look of perfect understanding that lingered until she turned and fled.